MPRE:

MPTION

SEMPRE: REDEMPTION

J.M. DARHOWER

Gallery Books
New York   London   Toronto   Sydney   New Delhi

G

Gallery Books
A Division of Simon & Schuster, Inc.
1230 Avenue of the Americas
New York, NY 10020
www.SimonandSchuster.com

First Gallery Books trade paperback edition April 2014

GALLERY BOOKS and colophon are registered trademarks of Simon & Schuster, Inc.

For information about special discounts for bulk purchases, please contact Simon & Schuster Special Sales at 1-866-506-1949 or business@simonandschuster.com.

The Simon & Schuster Speakers Bureau can bring authors to your live event. For more information or to book an event contact the Simon & Schuster Speakers Bureau at 1-866-248-3049 or visit our website at www.simonspeakers.com.

Manufactured in the United States of America

10 9 8 7 6 5 4 3 2 1

Library of Congress Cataloging-in-Publication Data has been applied for.

ISBN 978-1-4767-6077-3
ISBN 978-1-4767-3420-0 (ebook)

SEMPRE:
REDEMPTION

1

On October 12, at 11:56 in the evening, Corrado Alphonse Moretti died.

There had been a strong lurching in his stomach and a sudden wooziness as blood gushed from the bullet wounds in his chest. Pain swept from his body like a rolling wave, numbness swallowing him whole. Everything blurred, sights and sounds distorted, as reality twisted and the world around him faded away.

And then there was nothing.

No bright lights. No gentle voices. No angelic presence. Only blackness. He heard nothing, he saw nothing, and he felt nothing. After everything Corrado had done in his life, he had expected hellfire and brimstone.

He was a bit disappointed, to say the least.

A few minutes later, at exactly midnight, Corrado was violently shocked back to life. His heart beat once again as oxygen saturated his body, but his newfound peace was instantly destroyed: The moment they brought him back into the world, ripping him from the darkness of afterlife, he was transported to a time he had long ago wished to forget.

It was a decade earlier but only a few feet away from the small, dingy hospital room he now lay in, soiled with blood, sweat, and bitter tears. The room from ten years before had been filled with the same feeling—heartbreak and misery, the harsh stench of imminent death thick in the air.

Corrado stood quietly in the doorway that warm October day, his eyes fixed inside the sterile room. Carmine DeMarco had always been slightly small for his age, but he seemed so minuscule in the large hospital bed. Tubes and wires ran from his frail body to various machines surrounding him, their humming and beeping not enough to drown out the strangled voice in the corner.

Vincent DeMarco sat near his son, rocking and frantically muttering to himself. Corrado had never seen him so out of control before, agitated and deranged almost like a feral animal. His sanity was slipping, his hair a dirty mess and his shirt soiled with blood. Vincent's wife's blood, to be precise . . . blood that had been spilled less than twenty-four hours before.

The sight of it sickened Corrado. It wasn't the first time he'd seen Maura's blood, but it would certainly be the last. She was dead and never coming back, but Vincent was clearly struggling to accept the truth.

"She's can't be gone." The words caught in his throat. "This is my fault."

Corrado wanted to tell him to stop being absurd, but it would be a waste of breath. He couldn't comfort him. No words would take his pain away. And, truthfully, Corrado couldn't imagine the anguish his brother-in-law felt. He didn't fear death, didn't fear jail or eternal damnation, but one thing he couldn't fathom was losing Celia. He'd vowed to honor her, to cherish her, to *protect* her . . .

It was no wonder Vincent was so quick to take the blame. He had failed at that—he had failed to protect Maura.

"It's my fault," Vincent repeated. "She's gone, and it's my fault."

Sighing, Corrado glanced back at his nephew. Carmine had been found near death behind Tarullo's Pizzeria. They didn't know what had happened yet, but one thing was clear: whoever ambushed them intended for the boy to die, too.

That fact made Corrado feel even sicker. He had never been particularly fond of children, with their needy ways and grubby little hands, but one thing he treasured was innocence. He envied it. He had murdered many men during his years with *La Cosa Nostra*, but he prided himself on never killing anyone he felt didn't deserve his wrath.

And staring at his nephew, so helpless and vulnerable, Corrado couldn't imagine what would possess someone to harm him. It was unheard of. Some things even the wickedest of men didn't tolerate, and killing a kid in cold blood was one of those things.

Things were different now, though. As much as it infuriated him, times were changing, and he wondered what that meant for Carmine. At only eight years old, he had been thrown headfirst into the lifestyle. When he woke up—if he did—his world wouldn't be the same. Whether Carmine liked it or not, he couldn't escape the life. Not after this. He was now a part of it, and Corrado knew he would spend the rest of his life trying to make sense of the chaos.

Hatred brewed in Corrado's gut, hot like molten lava. The longer he stood there, listening to the babble of a devastated man, the angrier he grew. All he could think about was getting revenge on the people who had hurt them. Not only did his vow to the organization demand it—an eye for an eye—but so did his weary heart.

Corrado's heart, a decade later miraculously holding steady on the cardiac monitor, grew stronger every passing day. He would survive the shoot-out in the Chicago warehouse. The Kevlar Killer would live to see another day.

On December 1, after being comatose for six weeks, Corrado Alphonse Moretti opened his eyes.

2

The black Mazda RX-8 sped along the worn gravel road, twisting and turning as it penetrated deeper into the foothills of the Blue Ridge Mountains. Haven clutched the passenger seat as the car haphazardly weaved through the dense forest.

"Are we lost?" she asked hesitantly as she stared at her boyfriend. Carmine was slouched in the driver's seat, fiddling with the radio. Sunglasses shielded his eyes from her, so she couldn't tell if he was paying any attention to the road.

"No."

Haven glanced out the windshield, squinting from the early morning sunshine. Things looked the same in every direction—nothing but endless trees surrounding them. How could he know? "Are you sure?"

"Positive."

She shook her head. *Stubborn.* "Where are we going?"

"You'll see."

She started to grow frustrated when he jerked the wheel to the left, nearly skidding off the narrow road. Her seatbelt locked in place, tightly confining her in the seat, as she inhaled sharply. Before she could let out the scream that bubbled up in her chest, Carmine pulled beside a fence along the road and cut the engine, turning to her with a satisfied smile. "See, not lost."

Haven shook her head and surveyed the area. At first it appeared to be nothing unusual, a small gap in the trees with a cabin set a few yards away, until she spotted the faded white sign in the distance. LANDELL CHRISTMAS TREE FARM, it said in green hand-painted letters. Excitement stirred inside of her, but it was quickly crushed when she read on: OPEN NOVEMBER 22 TO DECEMBER 22.

Although it felt as if time had stopped for the two of them, the calendar told a different story. It was December 23 already, a month since they had returned to the small North Carolina town of Durante in an attempt to get back to their lives . . . in an attempt to regain a bit of normalcy and piece together their relationship. Dealing with the fallout of her kidnapping had been a struggle, but they took it day by day . . . minute by minute . . . second by second.

"They're closed, Carmine," she said, frowning as they got out of the car. She shivered and wrapped her coat tighter around her to ward off the cold. "Yesterday was the last day."

Carmine opened the trunk and pulled out an ax, slinging it over his shoulder. "I know."

She watched, mouth agape, as he climbed the wooden rail fence surrounding the property and leaped to the other side. "Isn't that breaking and entering?"

He held his free hand out to help her over. "More like trespassing."

"What's the difference?"

"One's a misdemeanor," he said. "The other's a felony."

Haven sighed and started to respond, but his look pleaded with her not to argue. Hesitantly, she conceded and took his hand. Carmine helped her across the fence, lacing their fingers together and squeezing gently.

"Are you sure about this?" she asked.

"Yes, I'm sure. It's Christmas, and this is what Christmas is all about."

"Trespassing?"

"No, picking out trees and decorating them with colored balls and other frilly shit. It's about mistletoe and presents and lights and stars and family and eggnog. A lot of fucking eggnog, but without the egg and the nog and the other shit they put in with the alcohol. It's disgusting."

"So the meaning of Christmas is . . . rum?"

He laughed. "Sure."

"And here I thought it had something to do with religion."

Carmine slid his eyes to her. "Technicalities, *tesoro*. Just technicalities."

Together, they walked through the tree farm. Haven would occasionally stop and point one out, but each time Carmine seemed to find some fault with it. Too short or too tall, too thick or too thin, too many branches or not enough needles. He disregarded them because of their color, refused trees because of their shape, and simply scoffed when she suggested they look at the pile of leftover precut evergreens.

"How about this one?" she asked after a while, stopping in front of a tree a few inches taller than her. "Do you like it?"

Carmine hardly even looked. "It's too bare."

Haven's brow furrowed, unsure as to what he was talking about. The branches appeared full to her. "So finicky."

"Whatever," he muttered. "Do you see any others?"

"Uh . . ." She glanced around, randomly motioning toward another tree a few feet away. "What about that one?"

Carmine scanned it. She awaited his complaint, sure he would find a flaw in it, but he smirked instead. "Perfect."

She was surprised. "Are you sure?"

"Yeah, why? Don't you like it?"

Haven shrugged. Every single one of them looked the same to her—just like the hundreds of others they had passed along the road on the way. "It's fine with me."

Letting go of her hand, Carmine studied the tree, deciding how to go about taking it down. Haven watched him for a moment, the scene surreal, and burst into laughter when he took his first swing. It barely even sliced the thick bark.

Carmine's groaned. "What's so funny?"

"This is going to take you all day," she said. "We should've just picked one that was already chopped down."

"That's cheating," he said. "Just because it's the easy way doesn't mean it's the best way. Sometimes it's better to put in the work."

Haven thought coming to a tree farm was cheating itself, considering they could have taken one of the small ones from the backyard, but she thought better of pointing that out. His frustration mounted with each swing of the ax, and she didn't want to make it any worse.

He whacked the trunk repeatedly, the blade eventually cutting through the wood. Despite the cold temperatures, by the time the tree tilted Carmine was huffing and drenched with sweat. It gathered along his forehead, ran down the side of his face, and dripped from his chiseled jaw. Haven watched him struggle in silence, a familiar pang of guilt deep down inside of her gut. It was always subtly there, lurking, violently striking when she least expected it to, like a startled viper fighting for its life. It viciously gnawed at her, poisoning her insides and conjuring up intense feelings of shame when she was reminded of what he had done.

This boy—this stubborn, selfless, stupid boy—had given himself to the Mafia. He had handed control of his future over to the men they hated most in exchange for her life. For her *safety*. And he had done it so easily, so quickly, like he didn't have to think about it at all . . . like sacrificing for her came just as naturally as breathing.

The act had left him fractured, and Haven was still trying to come to grips with the fact that it might be a long time before he was whole again. And as grateful as she was to be alive, as blessed as she felt to be standing there, picking out a Christmas tree with the boy she loved, she was also angry. Not at him—not anymore. That anger had been unfounded. She was mad at herself now, and at the universe, because no matter what she did, she couldn't help Carmine. She was helpless to his plight. There was no way for her to end his torment. No way for her to save him.

Once again in her life, Haven felt powerless.

So she stood by silently, continuing to watch, terrified of looking him in the eyes one day and seeing regret. Frightened that someday, he would turn to her and she would see her worst fear playing out in his face: that she hadn't been worth it.

Eventually, the evergreen toppled in Haven's direction. She jumped out of the way at the last second, the tree nearly hitting her.

"Sorry, *tesoro*." Carmine dropped the ax and pulled his black long-sleeved shirt up, exposing his toned stomach as he wiped the sweat from his brow. "That was *a lot* harder than I thought it would be."

He grinned proudly as he lugged the tree toward the car. She picked up his ax, surprised by how heavy it was, and followed behind. He threw the tree over the fence like it was no trouble at all and helped her to the other side.

"What are we going to do with it?" she asked.

"Tie it to the car and take it home," he replied, taking the ax from her. He tossed it in the trunk and pulled out a coil of rope, holding it up to show her.

"Are you sure?" she asked as Carmine grabbed the tree and shoved it on top of the car. The branches scraped against the shiny black paint. She couldn't imagine they would get it home without causing some damage.

He sighed exasperatedly. "Of course I'm sure, Haven. What is it with you and that damn question today? Don't you trust me anymore?"

She was taken aback by his question. She hadn't realized she had been repeating it. "Of course I trust you! I was just . . . double checking."

"Well, I guess questioning me is always better than saying *okay*," he replied, positioning the tree and tying it down. It hung over all sides of the small vehicle, blocking half of the front windshield and most of the back. "I still mean everything I say."

"I know," she said. "I believe you."

Carmine tugged on the evergreen, making sure it was secure. Satisfied with the job he had done, he motioned for Haven to get in the car, but she didn't budge.

"So, what's theft?" she asked. "A misdemeanor or a felony?"

Carmine stared at her for a moment before the question sunk in. Instead of answering, he pulled out his wallet and counted out some money. He hopped the fence and jogged over to the building, slipping the cash under the door for the tree they had cut down.

"Theft?" he asked when he returned, smiling sheepishly. "What made you think we were stealing something today?"

Haven had been right.

Tiny scratches sprinkled the roof of the car, a more noticeable jagged gash down the center. Carmine ran his pointer finger along it. "Fucking tree."

"Is it easily fixed?" Haven asked.

"Yeah," he said, "I just hate seeing my baby abused. We should've taken my dad's Mercedes. The scratches would match the mark you put on his side mirror."

Haven smiled at the memory of her first driving lesson. "I prefer riding in yours."

"Do you?" Carmine asked, looking at her with genuine curiosity. "You like the Mazda?"

"Yeah," she said. "It's nice. Feels warm and familiar. Besides, I've never been thrown in the trunk of yours."

Carmine blinked rapidly, gaping at her, before turning without a word to where the tree lay in the front yard. He grabbed it by the trunk and dragged it toward the house, leaving a trail of fresh pine needles behind him.

The next few hours were a flurry of activity. Vincent joined them in the family room with a tree stand and a box of decorations, and the rest of the family started showing up later in the day. They had just gotten the tree up straight and the lights strung on it when Carmine's brother, Dominic, burst through the front door, home for winter break from Notre Dame. He threw his bags down in the foyer and rushed right for them, tackling Carmine to the hard wood floor. He playfully ruffled his hair before scooping Haven up in a hug. "Twinkle Toes!" He swung her around in a circle. "I've missed you, girl."

"You just saw her a month ago," Carmine grumbled, standing back up. Pain shot down his spine as he stretched, and he cringed. "And hello to you too, motherfucker."

Dominic laughed, setting Haven on her feet before shoving his brother. Carmine stumbled again, falling into the tree and knocking it crooked. "I missed you, too, bro. Glad to see you."

Carmine rolled his eyes, feigning annoyance at his brother's antics, but a small involuntary smile tugged at his lips. He couldn't deny he missed the lightheartedness that usually accompanied Dominic's presence. Carmine always envied that—his brother's ability to ease any situation. They could have certainly used it the past month as everyone tiptoed around, walking on eggshells and ignoring reality, in fear of accidently hitting the red button that set off a nuclear disaster.

Carmine's future, Haven's past, Vincent's charges, Corrado's health . . . the words Carmine longed to say were always there, on the tip of his tongue, but they never made it through the meaningless chatter. They were always talking, but no one ever fucking *said* anything.

It wouldn't stay that way, though, and Carmine knew it. As long as the rest of the family was around, their bubble invaded, the issues wouldn't be ignored. They were about to be thrust front and center, whether they liked it or not.

Half filled with relief, the other half of Carmine was terrified.

Rocking the boat opened up the risk of it capsizing, and if that happened, he couldn't guarantee that someone wouldn't drown the second they hit the water.

He just hoped it wouldn't be him and Haven.

————

Celia and Corrado weren't long behind Dominic. Carmine had placed the last ornament on the tree when there was a light tap on the front door. Before anyone could react, it opened and Celia's voice rang through the house. "Knock, knock!"

They, too, dropped their bags right inside the foyer. Celia swiftly made her way into the family room, hugging the boys and Haven before focusing on her brother. Her voice was loud and cheerful, love pouring from her words as she greeted each one of them. Corrado, on the other hand, only made it as far as the doorway, where he watched them interact in stone cold silence.

Carmine eyed him warily. He hadn't seen Corrado since the warehouse, when he watched him collapse in a pool of blood. He had never felt particularly close to his uncle, fearing him more than genuinely caring for him, but something else existed now. Something bigger. Something stronger. There was a deeper respect, almost an admiration.

For the first time in his life, Carmine felt like he could relate to the man.

Corrado, however, showed no sign of it being mutual. His continued muteness, even after being greeted by Vincent, relayed a deeper message than any words could say. He remained motionless and aloof, as if he had nothing to say to any of them. His skin was paler than usual, his body frail to the point he was almost skeletal, but there was still darkness in his features that seemed to have grown harsher during the weeks.

If anything, he was more terrifying.

Corrado's eyes found Carmine's after a moment, so dark they were nearly black, with not a single flicker of emotion registering.

It sent an uncomfortable chill down Carmine's spine, the affection he had started to feel quickly replaced once more with apprehension. Carmine wondered if Corrado could sense it too, because he turned away. He limped slightly as he grabbed their bags again and disappeared upstairs without having uttered a single word.

Carmine had no idea what to say, and Vincent and Haven appeared just as speechless, but as expected, Dominic let nothing slip by. "Damn, we can't even get a hello?"

Celia smiled sadly. "Don't take it personally. He's still getting his bearings. Give him some time and he'll come around."

From the look on Vincent's face, Carmine suspected his father didn't believe that.

3

The sun had started to set when they settled into the family room that evening to watch a movie. Long shadows stretched across the floor, accented by the colored lights twinkling from the tree. Dominic ordered Chinese food before calling his girlfriend, Tess, to come over. She, too, was in town from Notre Dame and arrived within a matter of minutes, squeezing beside Dominic in a chair with a bowl of popcorn in her lap. Haven and Carmine lounged on the couch, sitting so close their arms touched. Celia had excused herself to join her husband, while Vincent claimed to have some work to do upstairs.

"What's Dr. DeMarco doing?" Haven asked quietly, leaning closer to Carmine. "He's never around anymore."

"Yeah, I think he's up to something."

"Like what?"

"I wish I knew," he said. "But desperate times call for desperate measures, so whatever it is has gotta be drastic."

"You think there's trouble?" she asked, a tinge of panic in her voice.

He laughed dryly. "When isn't there?"

A string of loud knocks vibrated the front door. They all glanced around at one another, nobody making a move to answer it. Carmine stood, shaking his head. "Don't everyone get up at the same time."

"I would've gotten it," Haven said, "but I don't have any money."

"I know," he said. "Don't worry about it. I'll pay."

"Thanks, DeMarco," Tess said, tossing a piece of popcorn across the room at him. "At least you're good for something."

He flashed his middle finger at her.

Tess scrunched up her nose. "You can shove that finger up your ass."

"Fuck you."

Carmine headed for the foyer and pulled out his wallet to sort through his cash. The person at the door banged impatiently, loud and forceful. "Christ, I'm coming. Who do you think you are, pounding like the fucking—?"

He froze abruptly when he opened the door, his gaze falling on a shiny gold badge held up at eye level. "Police," the officer said stoically.

Carmine's response was immediate. "I have nothing to say."

"You don't even know what I want," the officer said with a sharp laugh, amused by Carmine's reaction. "I'm Detective Jack Baranski. Is there a girl named Haven here?"

"Why?" Carmine asked.

"I'd like to talk to her about a boy named Nicholas Barlow."

Carmine's muscles immediately seized up, his heart pounding aggressively as a brutal vision of his former friend forced its way to the front of his mind.

The loud bang of a gunshot ringing out in the distance. A piercing scream cutting through the air. Nicholas dropping to his knees and clutching his chest as he opened his mouth to speak, but no sound came out. There was nothing but strangled silence. He was gone within a matter of seconds.

Dead.

Fucking dead.

"It'll only take a few minutes," the detective said when Carmine didn't respond. "May I come in?"

Carmine shook his head, barely able to get out the words. "Go away."

Before he could slam the door in the man's face, Vincent's voice rang out behind him. "Let him in, son."

Carmine turned to see his father standing on the stairs. He had to have heard wrong. Vincent DeMarco would *never* willingly invite law enforcement into his home. "Excuse me?"

"You heard me." Vincent descended the last few steps into the foyer. "Let him ask his questions."

"No way," Carmine spat. He was about to ask his father if he had lost his mind when his brother interrupted.

"Where the hell's the food? I'm starving here," Dominic hollered, stepping out of the great room and glancing toward the front door. His eyes went wide when he saw the police officer. "Whoa, definitely not the delivery guy! What did you do now, bro?"

Carmine groaned. Why did he have to assume it was *him*?

"He isn't here for Carmine," Vincent said. "He just has a few questions for Haven, and then he'll be on his way."

Begrudgingly, Carmine moved aside so Vincent could lead the detective into the family room. Dominic excused himself, bolting upstairs and dragging Tess along with him. Carmine went to close the door when a car pulled up, the Chinese delivery guy parking behind the unmarked police cruiser. Carmine shoved some money at the guy, then snatched the food and slammed the door, dropping their dinner off in the kitchen before hurrying to the family room.

Carmine sat on the arm of the couch beside Haven, not wanting to be far from her, as the man cleared his throat. "I'd prefer to speak to her *alone*, if you don't mind."

"Unfortunately for you, I do mind," Vincent said. "I invited you in, but I won't be put out by you."

"Fine." Detective Baranski pulled a small notebook from his pocket and flipped it open. "Haven, do you know Nicholas Barlow?"

Haven picked at her fingernails as she started stammering. "Yes. Well, I know who he *is*, but I didn't really know him that well. Or, I mean, I don't . . . not didn't."

Her panicked eyes darted toward Carmine briefly before settling on the floor.

"When's the last time you saw him?" Detective Baranski asked.

"The end of September," she said. "Carmine had a football game that night."

"And did anything out of the ordinary happen at the game?"

"I kicked his ass," Carmine chimed in, wanting to spare her from having to recount it. "That's not really out of the ordinary, though. We fought all the time."

"Huh. Well, what happened after the fight?"

"He ran off," Carmine said, "just like every other time we fought."

The officer eyed Carmine suspiciously. "Was that the last time you saw him?"

"No, I saw him a week after that," Carmine admitted. "I was taking the SAT at the high school when he showed up."

"Why?"

"For shits and giggles. Why does anyone take the SATs?"

"I'm not asking you why you took the test," Detective Baranski said impatiently. "I'm asking why *he* was there."

Carmine shrugged, knowing what he meant the first time but not wanting to answer that question.

"Did anything happen then?"

"Exactly what happened every other time the two of us got together."

"Another fight." The officer nodded as if it were no surprise. "And the last time you saw him, Haven, was at the football game?"

"Yes." She hesitated before shaking her head. "Well, no. I saw him later that night at Aurora Lake. We talked and then I went home."

"And *that* was the last time you saw him?"

Her eyes quickly scanned the room as Vincent nodded, the movement so slight Carmine barely caught it. "Yes," she whispered. *Lying.*

"Do you have any idea what might've happened to him?"

She didn't hesitate this time. "Yes."

Tensing, Carmine looked at her incredulously. *What the fuck?*

"The night at the lake, he said there was nothing left here for him," she said. "He talked about leaving, just disappearing, to start over somewhere where nobody knew him. I thought he was venting, but I wonder if that's what he did."

"It's possible." The officer closed his notebook and returned it to his pocket.

"I can't help but think it's my fault," she continued. "Maybe I could've stopped him, or helped him. Maybe then he wouldn't be . . . gone."

Carmine's chest tightened with guilt at her words.

"You can't blame yourself for decisions other people make, miss," Officer Baranski said, standing to leave. "I appreciate your time. If you think of anything else that might help us find Nicholas, give me a call."

He pulled out a business card and Haven gingerly took it from him. Vincent showed the officer out and Haven sat still for a moment before crumpling the officer's card up in a tight fist.

The tension in the room mounted. Carmine couldn't stand the silence and turned to her as soon as the front door closed. "You really think this is your fault?"

"Of course," she said quietly. "If I hadn't—"

"That's ridiculous," he interrupted, not giving her a chance to explain. "You didn't cause any of this."

"But I did," she said. "Don't you see? All of it was *me*, Carmine, all because I'm some *Princi*—whatever! A stinking princess! Your mother and Nicholas died, Corrado got hurt, and you gave your life away like it didn't even matter! What's next? How much more is going to happen because of me?"

Carmine knew it then, seeing the tears flooding her sorrowful eyes, tears she had been holding back for weeks. The button had been pushed. The nuclear bomb had been ignited. Their fragile bubble of contentment was about to fucking explode.

"I won't let you take that burden," he said. "And don't you dare feel guilty for what I did. If you wanna blame anyone for it, blame *me*. I did it because I wanted to, not because I *had* to. I did it because I love you, Haven, and you didn't force me to fucking love you. I did that shit all on my own. And I don't regret any of it."

"Why not?"

"Why would I? You're finally safe. You're finally free."

"Am I?" Haven shook her head with frustration. "Am I safe? Am I *free*?"

"Of course you are." His brow furrowed. "Why wouldn't you be?"

"I don't know," she said, tears running down her cheeks. "I don't even know what that means."

"We've talked about this," he said, throwing up his hands in exasperation. "It means you can do anything you want—go where you wanna go, be what you wanna be, do what you wanna do. Fuck, be who you wanna be."

"Can *you*?"

The question caught Carmine off guard. "Uh . . ."

Her voice cracked from distress. "Don't you see, Carmine? How can I ever be free if you aren't? How can I do those things if you can't?"

"I think . . ." A ringing cell phone in Carmine's pocket shattered his train of thought. He trailed off, pulling it out, and didn't have to look at the screen to know it was Salvatore. Haven stood up without a word and started out of the room, but he called after her. "Wait, Haven. We need to talk about this so just . . . wait, okay? This will only take a minute."

She stopped near the foyer and turned to him, tears still falling from her eyes. She said nothing.

His phone continued to ring in his hand and he groaned, knowing he needed to answer it. Taking a few steps over to the couch, Carmine sat down, his back to her. "Yes, sir?"

"I wondered if you were going to take my call," Salvatore said.

"Of course I was," he muttered, dropping his head and running his hand through his hair. He spotted the cop's business card in a ball on the floor and snatched it up, frowning. "It's just hectic here. I didn't hear my phone."

"Ah, well, I'm just calling to see how your holiday's going. I assume Corrado has arrived, but I can't get him to answer a phone, either."

Carmine's brow furrowed. *A social call?* "Yeah, he's here. I think he's asleep."

"Makes sense," Sal said. "He's still recuperating, so I'm sure he needs his rest. It hasn't been the same without him. It'll be wonderful to have both of you on the job after Christmas."

The color drained from Carmine's face. "Excuse me?"

"Corrado didn't tell you yet?" Sal asked. "I've requested he bring you back with him. I've been more than accommodating with your, uh, *situation,* but it's time you build your life here. Chicago's your home now. It was always supposed to be."

"But it's only been—"

"It's been a month," he said pointedly. "There's nothing left there for you."

Carmine knew there was no arguing with Salvatore. He had made his decision and nothing would change his mind. "Yeah, okay. Fine."

"I'm glad that's settled," Sal said. "I look forward to having you close by, *Principe.* Tell Corrado to call me when he wakes up. *Buon Natale.*"

Carmine hung up and glanced out of the room, wondering how much Haven had heard, and frowned when he saw the deserted foyer.

She hadn't waited for him, after all.

———

"Is he okay?"

Vincent looked up from the papers on his desk, peering through his reading glasses at his son. Carmine strolled into the office, throwing himself down in the leather chair across from him. He slouched, his body language one of nonchalance, but Vincent could see the genuine concern in his eyes. "Your uncle?"

"Yeah."

"He's, uh . . . he's still recovering," Vincent said. "He's only been conscious for a few weeks. He shouldn't even be traveling yet."

"But will he be okay?"

"You heard your aunt Celia. She said he'd—"

Carmine cut him off. "I know what she said, but I'm not asking her. I'm asking you."

Vincent set the files down and leaned back in his chair. He removed his glasses, rubbing his tired eyes while his son quietly awaited a response. Carmine rolled a small ball of paper in his palm, tossing it from hand to hand.

"Look, Corrado was clinically dead. The human body is resilient, but the brain is vulnerable. It's rare for someone to make a full recovery if they're down for more than three minutes."

"How long was Corrado down?"

"Four."

Carmine seemed speechless, his mouth open but no words coming out.

"I'm not saying he won't be fine," Vincent continued, not wanting to alarm his son, but he couldn't lie. He couldn't sugarcoat it. "I'm just saying it's too soon to tell. There's no way to say what type of long-term effects Corrado will endure."

"You mean like brain damage?"

"Yes, but not just that." Vincent absentmindedly fumbled with the case file on his desk again. "Death has a way of changing people, son. When faced with our own mortality, we tend to start seeing the world differently. What once mattered may not be a priority anymore, and that's not always easy for others to accept. We rejoice when people are saved, when lives are spared, but sometimes you have to stop and think, *At what cost?* Are we just prolonging the inevitable? Are we intervening when we have no right? Are we tampering with fate? We want them to live, but we have to consider that maybe they're better off . . . not."

It wasn't until Vincent looked over at his son that he realized he had said too much. Carmine's eyes were wide yet guarded, his mouth once again agape.

"I'm just rambling," Vincent said, backtracking. "I'm exhausted and stressed and don't know what I'm saying. Your uncle is going to be perfectly fine, Carmine. He defied medicine by even waking up, so there's no reason to believe he won't continue to do so. After all, according to the media, the man's made of Kevlar."

"I've heard," Carmine said. "Mom tried to keep us from it all, but Dom and I used to see the newspaper headlines in Chicago. Corrado Moretti, the Kevlar Killer . . . arrested dozens of times but never convicted for any of his crimes."

"Alleged crimes," Vincent said. "I lost count on how many times he's walked away from things that should've taken him down."

"That's a good thing," Carmine said. "Since he has a record of beating charges, the two of you will probably get off of this RICO shit. Problem solved."

"It's a nice thought, but there's a problem with that theory," Vincent said. "The prosecution filed to have our cases tried separately, so I think I'm on my own."

Carmine started to respond, but a voice stopped him before he could even get two words out. Vincent stiffened as he glanced past his son, seeing Corrado in the doorway to the office.

"You'll be perfectly fine," Corrado said, his voice flat.

"You think so?" Vincent asked.

Corrado nodded slightly. "We both will be."

Vincent would have said more had he not been alarmed by his

brother-in-law's sudden presence. He had showered, his slightly curly hair still damp, his face smooth from a fresh shave.

"I'm going to bed," Carmine muttered, standing up and bolting out of the room before Vincent could wish him a good night. Corrado stood in place for a moment before strolling into the office, sitting down in the chair Carmine had just vacated. He said nothing, but his eyes stared into Vincent intently.

"How much did you hear?" Vincent asked.

"Enough."

"And?"

"And I think you're right about people changing," Corrado replied, "but I don't think you were talking about me."

4

The shrill sound of a familiar ringing phone shattered Carmine's light slumber. He forced his eyes open, slapping beside the bed to find the offending object. He cursed as he accidentally knocked it off the stand, sending it crashing to the bedroom floor.

"Turn it off," Haven mumbled, not even opening her eyes.

"Fuck, I'm trying," he said, snatching his phone off the floor. He groaned as he answered it. *Salvatore. Again.* "Yes?"

"You don't like to answer promptly, do you?" Salvatore asked with a hard edge to his voice. Definitely not a social call this time.

He glanced at the clock, seeing it was a few minutes past four in the morning. Haven had been asleep when he made it upstairs . . . or pretending to be asleep, more likely. He could still feel the tension between them, the conversation she was obviously avoiding having with him.

"Sorry, sir," he said, covering his burning eyes with his forearm as he lay back down. "It's just kind of fucking early."

"You're full of excuses, aren't you?" Sal asked. "And you didn't have Corrado call me like I asked."

"He was asleep, and I, well . . ." He had forgotten. "I fell asleep, too."

"Well, it's a good thing you're awake now, because you need to pick up a package in Charlotte."

"Now?" Carmine asked incredulously. Charlotte was two hours

away, and it was Christmas Eve. The last thing he wanted to do was leave Haven alone all day.

He laughed bitterly and Carmine clenched his free hand into a fist. The sound grated on his nerves. "Yes, *now*."

Salvatore rattled off an address. Carmine jumped out of bed and rooted through his desk for something to write with, grabbing a cheap BIC pen with a chewed-up cap. He spotted one of Haven's notebooks and grabbed it, flipping it open to the back and scribbling down the address as Sal hung up.

"Just great," he muttered, staggering over to the closet. "Just what I need."

"Where are you going?" Haven asked.

He glanced at her, seeing her eyes were open now. She watched him with confusion, and he spouted off the first thing that came to his mind. "I need to finish Christmas shopping."

"Now?" she asked with disbelief. "Is anything even open?"

"They will be by the time I get there," he said, hoping she wouldn't press him about it. He dressed and kissed her quickly, running his hand across her cheek as he brushed some wayward hair out of her face. "I'll be back later, *tesoro*."

Haven mumbled incoherently, her eyes closing once again.

Carmine grabbed his things and the notebook, heading out of the house as quietly as he could, and climbed into the Mazda to start the trip to Charlotte. He had a hard time focusing on driving, his vision hazy from exhaustion, and ran off the road a few times. He cursed, agitated, and turned up the music while rolling down the windows, hoping the noise and cold air would keep him awake.

He arrived in Charlotte shortly after dawn and drove around for twenty minutes to find the address. It turned out to be a dingy hole-in-the-wall barbershop, the bricks crumbling and the barber pole barely hanging on to the ancient building.

Carmine grabbed the gun he kept tucked under the seat and stuck it in his waistband before getting out of the car. He headed toward the building and grabbed the door but it wouldn't budge, so he pressed the square black doorbell underneath the mailbox. A loud buzzer went off and he cringed at the obnoxious noise, hearing commotion inside before the door opened.

A light-skinned black man stood before him, a tattoo on his neck and his hair halfway braided. Carmine could see the gleam of gold teeth in his mouth, his neck and ears framed with diamonds. He didn't look to be someone Salvatore would ever do business with. He briefly wondered if he had the wrong address.

The man stepped to the side before Carmine could consider fleeing, motioning for him to come in.

The interior was just as raggedy as the outside, everything covered in wretched-smelling filth. Carmine surveyed it with disgust as the guy slammed the door behind them and staggered across the room. He reached into his pocket for a pack of cigarettes, sticking one in his mouth and another behind his ear before crumpling the empty pack and tossing it on the floor.

"DeMarco's kid, right?" the man asked. "You don't look like your daddy, though. You sure you're his? I think your mama might've fucked around."

Narrowing his eyes, Carmine's hands violently shook as he reached for his gun.

The guy caught on and put his hands up defensively. "Damn, you might be his boy, after all. Neither of you can take a joke."

"Don't talk about my mother," Carmine spat as the man turned his back to him and opened a cabinet.

"Whatever you say," he muttered. "Tell me something . . . do you have a girlfriend?"

"Excuse me?"

"You fucking deaf?" he asked, turning back around. Carmine tensed when he saw him grab a Glock 22 from the cabinet and point it without hesitating. Carmine aimed his gun quickly, his heart racing wildly in fear as they locked in a showdown. The amusement had faded from the guy's expression, his eyes sparking with anger. "I asked if you had a girlfriend."

"Yes," Carmine said, trying to keep his composure, but the guy was clearly unstable. The thought that it could be a setup ran through Carmine's mind but he pushed it back, not wanting to consider that Salvatore would do that to him. Not now. Not like this. He hadn't done a damn thing to deserve any punishment.

"What's her name?" the guy asked. "And don't lie to me. I can find out on my own, but I don't *think* you want me to."

"Haven," he said. "Her name's Haven."

"Good." The guy lowered his gun and grabbed a duffel bag from the cabinet. Carmine took it from him hesitantly, keeping his gun aimed just in case. "You have twelve hours to bring me my money. If it isn't here by seven tonight, at a minute after seven I'm gonna be in my car and on the way to visit Haven to make *her* pay me for it. Understand?"

"If you ever fucking touch—"

"I said do you understand?" he snapped, raising his gun again.

Carmine took a step back on instinct. "Yes."

"Good. Now get out of my fucking shop before I shoot you for the hell of it."

Shoving open the door, Carmine bolted outside in haste, the duffel bag feeling like it weighed more than him. He tucked the gun back away as he sprinted to his car, fumbling with his keys and cursing as he got the door unlocked.

He heaved the duffel bag over to the passenger seat and sped off, wanting to get away from there. A few miles away, he glanced in the bag curiously and saw it was full of guns and ammunition. Slamming the breaks, stunned, he whipped the car into the parking lot of a nearby restaurant. He stared at the bag, wondering what he was supposed to do. He wasn't sure if Salvatore had told him, considering he hadn't paid attention, and he suddenly worried he was missing something.

Carmine grabbed his phone and scanned through the list of contacts, stopping at his father's name. He hit the call button and waited as it rang.

"Carmine?" Vincent answered, sounding concerned. "Where are you? I saw your car was gone this morning."

"I, uh . . . I think I need some help."

"With what?"

"I'm in Charlotte," he said. "I got a call this morning to pick up something from some guy. He gave me this bag and said he wanted his money by tonight, but I don't know what the fuck I'm supposed to do about any of it. What money?"

"You must've met Jay," Vincent said, sighing. "Just pull some cash out of your account and pay him for it. We have a set arrangement, fifty grand each visit."

"And what about the damn bag?"

"There's a storage unit here in town, at the place beside the grocery store. I'll leave the key for it at the desk. Unit nineteen-B."

Carmine stood in front of the storage unit, the duffel bag the only thing inside. He stared at it for a moment, shaking his head, before slamming the metal door and putting the lock back on it.

He pocketed the key and strolled next door to the grocery store for something to drink, the place empty except for the lone cashier. She barely looked at him, her nose stuck in a cheap gossip magazine as he tossed her some cash for a bottle of Cherry Coke and a Toblerone.

On the way back out, Carmine's footsteps faltered when his eyes fell upon the crinkled paper taped to the glass near the exit. He snatched it off, studying it as he strolled through the parking lot in the dark. The word MISSING was written along the top, ominously black and bold, while a familiar picture of Nicholas Barlow covered most of the page. He was wearing his favorite camouflage cargo pants in the shot, his baseball cap pulled down low.

Carmine could remember the day the photo had been taken. Straining his eyes, he could even faintly make himself out in the background. They had been out at Aurora Lake a mere few days before their friendship had fallen apart . . . before their lives took a dramatic turn. They had both ended up in the emergency room later that day after roughhousing—Nicholas with a sprained ankle and Carmine with a gash in his eyebrow. It was the day Carmine had dared his best friend to sleep with the nurse at the hospital, Jen.

The only dare the boys had made that they never saw through, since Nicholas was dead now, and the nurse was, too.

The subtle glow from the streetlight illuminated Carmine's car in the back of the lot. Sunset had come and gone, the entire day fading away. He had missed Christmas Eve with his family.

Climbing into his car, Carmine turned on the interior light to get a better look at the flyer. Guilt nagged him when he saw they were offering a reward, Haven's earlier words running through his mind. *How much more is going to happen because of me?* she had asked, but Carmine wondered exactly how much more hurt *he* would cause. How many more families would he ruin, how many more lives would he fuck up? He felt like a curse, devastating anyone who dared to get close to him.

He had gotten his best friend killed. Who would be next?

Sighing, he tossed the paper onto the passenger seat and grabbed Haven's notebook, hoping to put those thoughts out of his mind. After the day he had had, he just wanted to forget for a while. He glanced through the scribble, looking for a distraction, but the sinking feeling in the pit of his stomach only grew as he took in Haven's frenzied words. She wrote a lot about the pain she had been through, the writing growing more frantic the further he got. There were dozens of sketches accompanying her words, some so vague he couldn't tell what they were, while others were so in depth it was like seeing it with his own eyes.

Turning to a page about halfway through, Carmine's name jumped out at him, and his eyes cautiously scanned the surrounding paragraph. Haven mused about what kind of future they would have together, disheartened by their situation. He read it all with anxious eyes, tensing when he came upon the very last sentence: *What do you do when the thing you want most suddenly feels like it's beyond your fingertips?*

As much as Carmine didn't want to let that get to him, her question stung. After giving her freedom, he had yanked it back away. He hadn't meant to, but she was right . . . as long as she was with him, she would never be in control of her life.

He flipped through a few more pages, barely able to pay attention to them, and was about to toss it aside when a drawing caught his eye. It was startlingly in depth, the man's features perfectly detailed. One side of his face was pristine, while the other half was severely disfigured. His skin appeared to be made of melting candle wax, drooping and dripping from his grotesque face. The word *monster* was scribbled along the page, the handwriting frantic and barely legible.

It may not have been as horrifying had Carmine not recognized the man.

———

The house was silent when Carmine made it home, the notebook tucked in the crook of his arm. He headed upstairs, mentally exhausted from the day, and hesitated on the second floor when he saw the door to his father's office open. Carmine strolled over to it, curiously pausing in the doorway.

Vincent sat at his desk with his phone to his ear, unaware he was no longer alone. He impatiently drummed his fingers on the arm of his chair, periodically huffing as he listened to whomever was on the line.

"That's not acceptable," he said, his expression severe. "I understand your situation, but you need to understand *mine*. I have a family to consider, and you may not care about them, but I do. This is my *life* we're talking about so don't patronize me! I don't need you to make this out to be something it isn't, and I don't appreciate being lied to. Find another way."

Another brief pause ensued, followed by a sharp, angry laugh from Vincent. "Then count me out."

Carmine shifted position, caught off guard by the serious conversation. The movement drew his father's attention. Panic sparked in Vincent's eyes. He hung up without giving the person a chance to respond and eyed Carmine carefully, but he offered no explanation.

"Who was that?" Carmine asked.

"Lawyer."

Carmine narrowed his eyes. "What were you doing, bribing your way out of trouble?"

"More like settling things before they tie the knot on my noose."

"That bad?" They may not have been close over the years, but Carmine didn't like the thought of losing his father.

"Yes, it's that bad, son," Vincent said. "We used to be able to talk our way out of anything, but our power has even less influence than our money these days."

Curious about his father's bitterness, Carmine took a seat without waiting to be invited. "Can I ask you something?"

Vincent leaned back in his chair. "Sure."

"Do you regret getting involved?"

"Yes . . . and no. I've made plenty of mistakes, and those I do regret, but taking the oath for your mother . . . I can't regret that. I wish I wouldn't have had to, but I did. And I'd do it again." Vincent paused. "You know, I was furious when I found out what you'd done, and as much as I still hate it, I get it, son. It's genetic, I guess—ingrained in your DNA. You would've sacrificed for her eventually, someway, somehow. You *are* your mother's child, after all."

"I'm apparently yours, too."

Vincent smiled sympathetically. "Is there a reason you asked? Are you regretting—?"

"No way," Carmine said. "It's just, Christ . . . I know it was necessary, but I feel like I fucked everything up by doing it."

"I felt that way, too," Vincent said. "I initiated to free your mother, and all I did was take her from one dangerous world to another. It was dressed up pretty and called another name, but it wasn't much different. Your mother never got a chance to live a life where no one knew her . . . where no one knew what she'd been. She never got to invent herself."

Carmine nodded. "That's what I thought."

Vincent drummed his fingers again. "Don't get me wrong, I wouldn't trade the years I had with your mother for anything, and I surely wouldn't give up you boys. You're the only thing I ever did right in life. But I'll never forgive myself for not giving her a chance. I know she loved me, and having a family made her happy, but I don't think she even realized she had another option. I did it all to give her choices, and then I never told her she had them. I can't help but wonder, all these years later, how different things would be had I let her go."

"Mom wouldn't have left you," Carmine said.

"She didn't know any better," he said. "And that's the point, really. She never got to *choose* to be with me."

"That's why I feel like I fucked up," Carmine said. "I figured I could keep those parts of my life separate, do what I had to while still giving her everything she wanted, but I don't know if that's possible anymore. I don't know what I'm supposed to do about it and I'm running out of time, considering I'm expected in Chicago after Christmas."

"I'm not surprised," Vincent said, reaching into a drawer and pulling out a gold key. He fiddled with it for a moment before pushing it across the desk to Carmine. "The key to the house in Chicago."

Carmine carefully picked it up. "Why are you giving it to me?"

"You'll need somewhere to stay, won't you?"

He wanted to argue, to give the key back, but he couldn't. It was true. He hadn't thought about what he would do once he got there. "Uh, yeah. Thanks."

"You're welcome," he replied. "Are you going to be okay?"

"Oh, I'll be fine. It's Haven I'm worried about. I grabbed this notebook of hers today, and I can tell you after reading it that she's a fucking mess." He flipped through pages haphazardly, shaking his head when he reached the drawing titled *monster*. Laughing bitterly, he held up the sketch for his father to see. "Look at this shit."

The drumming of Vincent's fingers ceased instantly, his posture rigid as his expression went blank. Carmine's hair bristled at his father's posture. Vincent stared at the notebook intently, like he was memorizing the mangled face.

"She'll be okay," Vincent said after a moment. "She has nothing to fear from him."

"Maybe not, but she calls him a monster, like he's the fucking Chupacabra. She's terrified, and that's the kind of people I'll have her around. Monsters."

"Carlo's a friend of ours."

Carmine scoffed. "He's no friend of mine."

"On the contrary, son . . . he is. He's been in the organization for years. Salvatore initiated him right after your grandfather passed away."

It struck Carmine then why he recognized the guy. He remembered exactly where he had seen him. "We have to tell Sal."

"Tell him what?"

"That one of his men is dirty," he spat. "He was involved in the kidnapping. He was in that warehouse!"

"What makes you think he was there?"

Carmine stared at his father incredulously. "Haven saw him. He *had* to be there!"

"No, he didn't." Vincent shook his head. "He wasn't even in Chicago."

"Yes, he was. I saw him! They were arguing in Sal's office, but when I showed up, he left."

Vincent hesitated. "That doesn't mean he was in on anything."

"Then how the fuck did she draw him?"

Sighing, Vincent flipped the page in the notebook and paused, holding it up. The color drained from Carmine's face as he stared at another drawing, this one just as in depth as the other—except, instead of a monster, he was staring at an angel.

The drawing of his mother struck something deep inside him, seizing his heart in a vice grip and constricting his chest.

"The same way she drew Maura," Vincent said quietly. "From memory. She's already told me she hallucinated in the warehouse, and Carlo has a face no one would forget—clearly, considering you remember him and you rarely notice anyone except for yourself. It's not a far stretch to say she saw him as a child."

Carmine rolled his eyes, not buying that explanation. "What if you're wrong?"

"I'm not," Vincent said.

"But what if you are?" Carmine asked again. "What if he was in on it all?"

"He wouldn't be. His loyalty to Sal is unwavering. He'd do anything for the Boss, would never betray him, and Sal feels the same way about him. It's just not plausible. You can ask Corrado if you don't believe me."

"And you can ask Haven," Carmine said, his father's unwillingness to even consider the idea annoying him. It was certainly nothing new, but it grated on his nerves now more than ever. "I'll leave you alone now so you can call back whoever it was you were *really* talking to. I have my own shit to figure out."

He stood to leave when his father cleared his throat. "*Ascoltare il tuo cuore*, Carmine. Just remember that, and I'm sure you'll do the right thing . . . whatever that may be. Like I said, you are your mother's child."

Ascoltare il tuo cuore. Listen to your heart.

If it weren't so distressing, Carmine might have seen the irony of what his mother had always said. A person couldn't escape fate, because what was meant to be would always be. No matter how hard Carmine tried to avoid the Mafia, he came back to it in the end.

And Haven had been destined for freedom . . . his mother made sure of that.

Carmine stepped out of his father's office and pulled his cell phone from his pocket, scrolling through his contacts until he came upon his friend, Dia. He dialed her number, listening as it rang and rang, and let out a deep breath when her voicemail picked up. "Call me when you get this."

5

Merry Christmas!"

Haven jumped at the unexpected voice and spun around from the kitchen window. Celia stood just inside the doorway, smiling warmly, her eyes bright and awake with enthusiasm, even though the sun had barely started to rise outside.

"Uh, Merry Christmas," Haven said. "Good morning."

Strolling over to the pantry, Celia rooted around, pulling out what she would need to make Christmas dinner. She was dressed in a gray long-sleeved dress and a pair of matching heels, her shiny dark hair cascading down her back and her makeup freshly applied. It was the complete opposite of how she had appeared when Haven last saw her in Chicago a mere month ago. Her glow was back, compassion and love radiating from her like warm sunlight.

Longing struck Haven's chest. It made her think of her mother. Oh, how she missed her, especially on days like this, days when she needed someone to talk to, someone who truly knew her and would know what to say.

"Isn't it awfully early for you to be awake?" Celia asked.

"I guess so." Haven turned back to the window. The darkness gradually faded with every second that passed, making Carmine's car more visible in the front yard. "I couldn't sleep. I had a lot on my mind last night."

"Like?"

"Like everything."

Celia laughed. "Well, that certainly clears it up."

Haven managed a smile as she peeked at Celia, her good mood infectious. "It's just that Carmine got back really late last night. He was gone all day, told me he had shopping to do, but he didn't bring any bags home."

"Ah, shopping." Celia sighed knowingly. "Corrado used that one. Of course, he knew enough to stop by a store and buy something before coming home—usually throwing in some flowers to butter me up. I kind of miss those days, believe it or not. He doesn't bother anymore."

"With flowers?"

Celia laughed again. "With excuses, kiddo . . . although, flowers again would be nice. It's been ages."

Haven toyed with the hem of her shirt, mulling over Celia's words. "Doesn't it bother you to be lied to, though?"

"At first it did. I would get so angry with him, thinking it meant he didn't trust me. I told him I wanted us to have the kind of relationship where we told each other *everything*."

"What changed?"

"He told me everything one day. I never asked him again." She closed her eyes at the memory, pausing to shake her head. "I think it's easier for them to not bring that stuff home. It helps to know they have a sanctuary, that one place they can go and not have to be *Mafiosi* for a while. I'll never be able to forget the things he said that day, the look on his face as he talked, as much as I wish I could. I don't like my husband killing, and while I selfishly prefer it to him being killed, I learned that day that I don't want to hear about it, either."

Haven wasn't sure what to say. "I can't even think about Carmine being that way. That's *not* him. That's not the boy I know. He doesn't . . . kill."

"You're right," she said. "It wasn't Vincent, either, believe it or not. Maura was afraid the man she loved would disappear, but they won't if they have a reason not to. Carmine will always be the same person deep down inside. He'll see things he'll wish he could forget, and he'll have a lot of guilt over things he can't control, but don't we all? Your love will still save him at the end of the day."

Haven frowned. "It doesn't feel like it anymore."

"That's because you're scared," she said, wrapping her arms around Haven in a hug. She stroked Haven's hair with her hand, just like her mother had when she was younger. The ache in her chest intensified. "Neither of you seem to realize fear can be a good thing. It's healthy and keeps us safe, warns us of danger. When you stop fearing things, you stop fighting. You lose motivation. You lose perspective, and you never want to do that."

A throat cleared behind them. Celia let go of Haven and turned to look, tensing. Corrado leaned against the door frame, his arms crossed over his chest. "Am I interrupting?"

Haven dropped her gaze to the floor. She hadn't seen him since they had shown up. He had remained upstairs, secluded from the family. "No, sir."

"Of course you are," Celia said. "We were having girl talk."

"So I heard," he said. "I thought we agreed you would stay out of it."

"And I thought you knew me better than that," Celia replied. "You really can't be that dense, Corrado."

Haven gaped at Celia, stunned anyone would speak to him that way.

"Pardon me for hoping you'd listen to common sense for once," he countered. "Meddling in other people's affairs—"

"Only gets people hurt," she said, cutting him off. "I know. I've heard you say it a million times, but they're just kids, for heaven's sake."

"They're adults," Corrado said. "What they choose to do in their private lives is none of our concern."

Celia laughed dryly. "None of our concern? Have you forgotten you *vouched* for her?"

"That doesn't mean I own her!" Corrado snapped, shooting

Haven a quick glance that sent a chill down her spine. She had never heard him raise his voice before.

Celia narrowed her eyes. "No, but it's your job to help her."

"I know what my duties are," he responded coldly. "I'll watch her."

"Like Maura was watched?" Celia raised her eyebrows. "You told me to stay out of it, to mind my own business. A lot of good it did then, huh?"

"Maura was *not* my responsibility. She was Vincent's."

"You're right," Celia responded, "but Haven is yours."

Corrado stood silently and stared at her, his expression blank. Celia stared right back, her gaze unwavering. The tension in the room mounted with each passing second. Uncomfortable, Haven fidgeted, feeling dizzy as the blood rushed furiously through her.

"I, uh . . . I probably shouldn't be here," she whispered, turning for the door. She made it as far as the foyer before Corrado's firm voice rang out, the sound of it halting Haven in her tracks.

"Stop."

She turned around as Corrado stepped into the foyer, glancing at her briefly and nodding before heading for the great room. She watched him for a second, unsure of what to do, before following slowly behind.

The sun started to peek over the trees outside, but the room remained eerily dim. Haven was as quiet as a corpse as she took a seat on the couch and picked at her brittle fingernails, purposely avoiding Corrado's powerful gaze.

"Do you know what it means to vouch for someone, Haven?" he asked, breaking the tense silence that quickly enveloped the room like a thick, toxic cloud.

Without looking at him, Haven nodded stiffly. "Carmine said it meant if I ever told about where I came from, you'd get in trouble, but I swear I never will."

He held his hand up to silence her before she could really start pleading her case. "It's more than that. It's not just what you say and who you say it to . . . it's what you do, too. People like me—we vouch for others every day. Associates, friends, family. We swear they're good people, that they'll never bring us any harm. We swear they're trustworthy. If we're wrong, it means we lied. It means they don't benefit us by being out there in the world, by being alive, and frankly, maybe we shouldn't be either. Your life may be your own now, but I can't have that doubt lingering over my head, so there are some limitations because of the circumstances."

Haven tensed. "Limitations?"

"Yes, limitations," Corrado said. "It's better than the alternative."

"What's that?"

"Going to stay with Salvatore," he said. "Or death. I'm not sure which you'd find worse, but neither would be pleasant. So limitations it is. Besides, everyone has them. Most people are ruled by petty laws—wear your seat belt, don't take what's not yours. Catholics follow the Commandments—don't covet thy neighbor's wife or take the Lord's name in vain. Nuns commit themselves to celibacy, lawyers and priests rely on confidentiality, and we, Haven, take a vow of silence and loyalty. We all live through the same Hell, just with different devils."

Pausing, Corrado tinkered with his wedding ring. Haven wasn't sure what she was supposed to say, so she said nothing. He continued after a moment. "Our devil doesn't give the benefit of the doubt. Our devil shoots first and asks questions later, if at all. One look, one wrong move, and you're guilty. They'll carry out your punishment before you even know you were accused. Our devil shows no mercy. He can't. You got that?"

She nodded. "Yes, sir."

"If you want to stay safe, stay out of the limelight," he said. "Mind your own business, lay low, and never associate with the police. If a cop ever tries to question you, ask for your lawyer and call me. I don't care what it's about. And never invite one inside your home. *Never.*"

The color drained from her face, coldness running through her as she immediately thought of Officer Baranski. "I, uh . . . I didn't know . . ."

"Didn't know what?"

"An officer came by to ask about Nicholas. I didn't know I wasn't supposed to talk to him. Dr. DeMarco said I should answer his questions so he'd go away."

Corrado stared at her. "Vincent told you to talk to the police?"

She nodded hesitantly. "He invited him inside."

Corrado's mask slipped, his brow furrowing briefly before he straightened it back out. "When was this?"

"Two days ago," she said. "You were upstairs. It was right after you arrived."

Silence permeated the room for a few minutes. Haven did nothing, terrified of what his reaction would be. He just stared straight ahead, unmoving, and if it weren't for the fact that he was blinking she might have wondered if he were even still alive.

"You didn't know any better," he said finally. "No one explained it to you, but now you know."

"Yes, sir."

Corrado stood and without a word started to walk away. He made it as far as the doorway before his footsteps faltered. He lingered there for a moment as Celia approached from the foyer, smiling proudly. She had clearly been eavesdropping.

"Stay out of it," he warned her again. "I don't want you meddling anymore."

———

Christmas morning passed in a blur. Carmine seemed distracted, distant, his eyes watching everyone as if he were waiting for something to happen, lost somewhere in his mind instead of being there at home.

Haven would occasionally catch him casting angry glares and hear heated whispered conversations when she was out of earshot.

Confused, she asked a few times what was going on, but he merely smiled and told her not to worry.

Don't worry. She had heard it so many times the past week that the phrase alone was starting to worry her.

They watched holiday movies and exchanged gifts in the evening. Haven got some books and art supplies, clothes, and a new pair of pink-and-white Nike's. The festivities were quiet, almost gloomy in a sense. Something lingered in the room with them, infecting the air they all had to share. She wouldn't call it misery, but it was certainly close—guilt mixed with sadness, confusion, and morose thoughts.

They sat down at the dining room table when dinner was ready, Carmine pulling out the chair beside him for Haven as Celia and Corrado took seats across from them. Dr. DeMarco cleared his throat and Carmine immediately grabbed Haven's right hand as Corrado reached across the table, holding his out to her. She blanched as she stared at it, studying his extended hand. Other than a long jagged scar diagonally on his palm, nearly camouflaged by the natural creases and lines, it appeared unscathed. His nails were freshly manicured, the skin smooth with not a single cut or callus. She wasn't sure what she had expected, but it surprised her—his hands appeared awfully clean for a man with a lot of blood on them.

Taking it carefully, so not to cause a scene, Haven bowed her head.

"Lord, thank you for the blessings on the table today, and for all the people gathered around it," Dr. DeMarco said. "We ask that you help us to remain mindful of the needs of others and continue to bless us with love and forgiveness, happiness and peace, and most of all we ask that you help the innocent among us find the freedom they deserve. In Jesus's name, we pray."

"Amen," they all murmured, letting go and raising their heads. Haven glanced at Dr. DeMarco curiously, surprised by his words, and he smiled softly when they made eye contact.

"Dai nemici mi guardo io dagli amici mi guardi iddio," Corrado muttered under his breath as he picked up his fork.

Carmine laughed dryly. "Amen to *that*."

They started eating but Haven merely pushed the food around on her plate as a tense silence once again overcame the room. Everyone cast glances at one another while avoiding her gaze. It was as if they all shared a common secret, one Haven was certainly not aware of. She fidgeted nervously as she listened to the forks clanking against plates, her appetite dissipating as her stomach churned from anxiety.

Haven was so uncomfortable with the stillness she briefly considered leaving the room. Before she could act, Dominic cleared his throat. It seemed to be magnified, echoing off the barren walls. "It's hard to believe it's been ten years."

Carmine went rigid, his fork stopping midair. Realizing Dominic was referring to their mother's death, Haven looked around cautiously, waiting for the imminent explosion of rage.

Dr. DeMarco's head dropped, his eyes drifting closed as he set his fork down. "Seems like just yesterday we lost her."

"We didn't *lose* her," Carmine spat, the edge of anger stabbing his words. "That makes it sound like we were negligent. It's not our fault that shit happened. She was *taken* from us . . . from all of us."

"You're right," Dr. DeMarco conceded. "She was unfairly taken from us."

The atmosphere was suddenly lighter after he said those words, as if that one simple phrase had lifted a heavy weight from their shoulders. Everyone chatted casually, laughing as they shared stories of the past. They spoke about Maura, and instead of clamming up, Dr. DeMarco chose to chime in.

"She loved Christmas," he said, smiling. "She'd get the boys dozens of presents, so many we'd hardly be able to fit in the den Christmas morning."

"I remember that," Dominic said. "She spoiled the shit out of Carmine."

Rolling his eyes, Carmine picked up a green bean with his fork

and flung it down the table at his brother. "You were just as fucking spoiled."

"You were," Dr. DeMarco confirmed. "Anything either of you
wanted, you got, and not just on Christmas."

"I never got that bike I wanted," Dominic said. "Remember it?
It was that little camouflage Mongoose with that wicked horn on
it and the wooden basket. I begged and begged for it."

Dr. DeMarco sighed. "You got it."

"No, I didn't."

"Yes, you did," he said quietly. "You just didn't know. It was
delivered to the house after . . . well, after she was taken from us.
She bought it for you because Carmine was getting the piano. She
wanted to be fair."

Solemn silence festered in the room until Dominic spoke up
again. "Do you still have it?"

Dr. DeMarco shook his head. "I gave it away."

"Damn," Dominic said. "I'd still ride it, you know."

Laughter escaped from Dr. DeMarco's lips. "I know you would,
son."

They went on to talk about trips they had taken, things she had
taught them, and books she had read, every memory accompanied
with smiles instead of tears. It was heartwarming to witness, the
love for Maura still just as strong even though she had been gone
for more than a decade.

After dinner, Haven offered to help Celia with the dishes. The
two of them worked silently, Celia's attention elsewhere as she
went about it in a daze. They were finishing when Celia let out a
resigned sigh, taking a plate from Haven's hands. "I'll finish here.
You should go enjoy the rest of your Christmas."

"Okay," she mumbled, drying her hands before quietly heading
for the family room. She made it halfway there when she heard
Dominic's boisterous voice, his words catching her off guard.

"You're making a mistake, Carmine," he said. "There's no way
you mean that. You're not thinking clearly."

"Leave him alone," Dr. DeMarco said. "You can't understand the situation unless you've been in it."

"You're wrong," Dominic said. "I do understand, and he's going to regret it! It's not too late to change your mind, and for all of our sakes, *please* change your mind. I'm begging you, bro."

"It *is* too late," Carmine said. "I get that you don't agree, but you don't have to. I'm the one who has to live with it."

"Can you?" Dominic asked incredulously. "Can you *seriously* live with this?"

"I have to."

"No, you *don't*," Dominic said, the passion in his voice startling. "I can't believe anyone would actually think this is a good idea!"

Haven finished the last few steps in their direction, pausing at the entrance to the family room. Dominic paced the floor, frenzied, as Carmine stood off to the side, clutching his hair in aggravation. Vincent and Corrado merely watched the boys, the atmosphere so tense she could feel it pressing on her skin.

"He's my son," Dr. DeMarco said. "I'll support him any way I can."

"This is bullshit!" Dominic spat.

The force of his words startled Haven. She flinched. Heads instantly turned her way, four sets of eyes now boring into her.

"Is everything okay?" she asked hesitantly.

"It's fine," Dr. DeMarco said. "We are just having a disagreement, but this isn't the time or the place for it."

She glanced around, dread running through her as she took in their expressions. Despite what he had said, something was definitely wrong. She turned to Carmine, raising her eyebrows, expecting him to offer some sort of real explanation, but he shook his head. "Don't worry about it."

Don't worry about it.

"I think I'm going to go lie down," she said, taking a step back.

"I'll come with you," Carmine said, shooting Dominic an angry glare as he stalked past. He took her hand and she mumbled good-bye to everyone as he pulled her toward the steps, not saying a word.

"Are they mad about what you did in Chicago?" she pressed when they reached the bedroom.

"Something like that," he muttered. "Look, I don't want to talk about it right now. I'd rather just . . . *be*. Just for a little while."

"Okay," she said, trying to push back the sick feeling in her stomach. He plopped down on the bed and she followed his lead, lying down beside him.

"*La mia bella ragazza,*" he murmured, pulling her into his arms. She tilted her head to the side as he leaned in and kissed her neck, humming against her skin. "I was hoping today would be perfect."

"We were together," she whispered. "That makes it perfect to me."

6

Haven hadn't intended to fall asleep, but her exhaustion was deeper than she anticipated. Emotionally drained, she drifted into unconsciousness within a matter of minutes.

Rolling over in the middle of the night, her arm dropped on the other side of the mattress. She felt around for Carmine in the darkness, sighing when she realized she was alone.

Climbing out of bed, she quietly made her way to the door, the faint sound of "Moonlight Sonata" meeting her ears. The disjointed notes washed through her, the familiar broken melody forcing a frown onto her lips.

Carmine sat in his usual chair in the library, casually strumming his guitar. A sliver of light filtered in from the large window, illuminating his somber expression in the darkness. She called his name but he remained still, continuing to pluck at the strings almost as if he hadn't heard her. She took a step toward him and was about to say his name again when he let out a long, deep sigh. "I had a dream."

"Another nightmare?" she asked, walking over to him. He glanced up at her as his fingers stilled, the music stopping, but Haven barely noticed. She couldn't focus on anything but the green eyes boring into her. Once so alive with passion, she saw nothing but deep sadness marring the bright color.

Carmine set the guitar aside and moved his legs to make room, motioning for her to join him. She climbed into his lap and he wrapped his arms around her.

"Not a nightmare this time," he said. "It was a good dream."

"What was it about?"

"You," he said quietly. "You made a painting—some abstract shit, I don't know—but it was so good they hung it in a museum and raved about how talented you were. It was like you were the next fucking Picasso, *tesoro*."

She laughed. "I don't even know how to paint, Carmine."

"You could learn," he said. "Would you want to?"

"Maybe, but I don't know how good I'd be."

"Oh, you'd be good," he said confidently. "You shouldn't doubt yourself. You can do anything you set your mind to."

"Except for play the piano," she said playfully. "Or the guitar."

He chuckled. "Yeah, for the sake of everyone's ears, we ought to leave music to me, but the rest is all you. You can probably do all of that, you know. Draw, paint, sculpt shit into weird shapes and tell people it's something it doesn't look anything like. *That* takes talent."

She smiled. "And you think I have that kind of talent?"

"Of course," he said. "There's gonna be no stopping you once you get started."

"Thank you," she whispered, a swell of emotion surging through her at his words. "It means a lot that you believe in me."

"I'd be an idiot not to," he said, kissing the top of her head. "You know, we never finished our conversation from the other day."

"Which one?"

"The one about your freedom."

Haven sighed, snuggling closer to him. "What else is there to say?"

"I wanna hear what it *really* means to you."

They spent the next hour sitting together in front of the window in the dark library, digging into each other's minds. They didn't talk about the torture they had endured or the hurt they still felt, instead focusing on the things that made them happy. He asked about her deepest desires, wanting to know what kind of things she would do if she woke up tomorrow with a clean slate. What would she do, if someday, she could start over, brand new?

She talked of friends and a family, a house full of books and half a dozen pets. The American Dream, complete with two-point-five kids and a freshly painted white picket fence, weekend barbecues with neighbors and summer vacations to Disneyland.

It felt like everything else faded away that long moment, the reality of their situation taking a back seat as they considered an alternate future, one Haven had always wanted but never believed she could have. A future away from it all. A future with no strings.

Freedom.

"I just want people to see me," she said. "I want to walk into a room and have them know I'm there. It doesn't matter where it is, really. I'm just don't want to be invisible anymore."

Carmine ran the back of his hand along her warm cheek. She hummed contently, leaning into his touch.

"I see you, hummingbird," he whispered, a twinkle in his eyes.

"I know you do."

"You wanna know what else I see?"

"What?" she asked.

He nodded toward the window. "Snow."

Haven glanced over, spotting the thick white flakes fluttering down from the sky. Before she could comment, Carmine jumped up and yanked her to her feet. "Come on."

She laughed as he pulled her into the bedroom. "What are we doing?"

"We're going outside."

"Now?" she asked with disbelief, glancing at the clock when he let go of her hand. The red numbers shone brightly in the darkness: one in the morning.

He shoved open the bedroom window. It groaned, but offered little resistance. Cold air entered the room in a whoosh, stirring the thick curtains and making Haven shiver. Wrapping her arms around herself, her brow furrowed in confusion. "Didn't Dr. DeMarco nail that down?"

"Yeah, but he did a shitty job," Carmine replied. "I pried it back open."

Haven wanted to ask when he had done it, or even why he bothered, but she didn't have a chance. Carmine had his shoes on and was already preparing to leave.

"Come on," he said again, tossing her coat to her. He was halfway out the window before she could think to object.

Haven quickly bundled up before joining him on the long balcony that wrapped around the house. It was the third time she had navigated it, but this time was more difficult than the other two. A light sheen of frost covered everything, making Haven slip a little as she walked along the narrow wooden path toward the massive tree on the corner. It was barren, the leaves long gone as winter settled in, but the thick branches were as sturdy as ever.

"Is this necessary?" Haven asked as she started climbing the tree. "Couldn't we have gone out the door?"

"We could've," Carmine said, jumping down to the ground, "but where's the fun in that?"

Haven managed to scale the first few obstacles easily, but her foot slipped when she neared the bottom of the tree. She lost her grip on the branch and screeched, closing her eyes when she started to fall. She braced herself for sudden impact, but Carmine reacted quickly. He grabbed her, attempting to gracefully catch her, but the blow knocked them both down.

Carmine groaned as the air was brutally forced from his lungs. Haven pulled away from him, rolling over. The frozen earth felt like solid concrete against her back. "That was sure . . . *fun*."

"Yeah, I didn't think that shit through," Carmine said, standing up. He brushed at his clothes before grabbing Haven's hand and pulling her to her feet. "Maybe we should've just used the damn door."

The cold night air felt like pins and needles, stabbing against Haven's flushed face, but she smiled regardless as she took in her surroundings. The flakes were starting to settle on the ground, dotting the lifeless grass with small patches of white. Thick clouds covered the sky, blocking the stars from view, but the vibrant moon continued to shine through. There were no animals or birds out at that hour, no fireflies flickering in the night—no sign of life except for the two of them.

It was as if they were alone in the world, and as terrifying as that was to Haven—the thought of nothing else existing anymore—she felt secure knowing at least he was still out there.

She took a few steps out into the yard, glancing up into the sky as snow rained down on her. Wetness hit her skin, coldness seeping through her clothes. A chill ran through her body as she closed her eyes and opened her mouth, capturing some of the bland flakes on her tongue.

Despite the fact that it was bitterly cold, warmth spread through her.

Haven opened her eyes and peeked over at Carmine to find him staring at her. Flakes stuck to his thick, dark locks, and she reached up, running her fingers through his hair to wipe them away.

"You're beautiful, *tesoro*," he said quietly.

Heat rose to her cheeks at his words. "Such a charmer."

"Run away with me," he continued, leaning down to softly kiss her lips. "We can disappear before the sun comes up."

Pressing her hand against his chest, she pushed away from Carmine with a laugh. "We can't run away."

He sighed. "It's a nice dream, though, isn't it?"

"I don't know how nice it would be," she replied. "How would we ever feel safe if we constantly had to watch our backs? I don't want to run from anything anymore. I'm tired of running. I want to be able to walk away, just stroll away somewhere together, hand in hand, nothing else mattering. I want to stand at an intersection and choose which way to go without having to worry about what happens if it leads us somewhere someone else doesn't want us to be. Now *that's* a nice dream."

"Yeah, you're right," he said, still staring at her. "Beautiful *and* smart."

She timidly ducked her head, peering at the ground as her blush deepened. She started kicking around at the small accumulation, her toe digging into the frozen dirt. "Does it snow a lot in Chicago?"

Carmine was quiet for a moment. She glanced back at him, seeing he wasn't watching her anymore. He stared off into the distance, a dazed look on his face. "Too much," he said eventually. "I like snow and all, but they get blizzards. I'm not looking forward to it."

"But think of all the snowmen and snow angels and the snowball fights."

His lips curved into a smile, but she could see the sadness back in his eyes. She felt guilty for bringing up Chicago, not wanting to ruin his mood. It wasn't often they had carefree moments anymore.

"It snows in New York, too," he said. "Just as much as it snows in Chicago."

"I bet Central Park is beautiful when it's all white," she said. "Actually, I bet it's beautiful all year round. I'd love to see it someday."

"You will," he said, turning back to her. His smile faded. "You look cold."

Her fingers were numb already, the tips of her ears stinging, but she just shrugged, not wanting the moment to be over yet.

Carmine pulled her into his arms, his body heat instantly warming her. Snuggling into his chest, she wrapped her arms around him as she hugged him tightly. He leaned his head on top

of hers, a soft hum vibrating Carmine's chest as the snow continued to fall, covering them.

The melody was sweet and vaguely familiar. It took a minute
for it to register with Haven. "Blue October," she whispered, recalling the song they had made love to on Valentine's Day.

"You remember," he said.

"How could I not?" she whispered as he continued humming,
the sound slowly turning into words as he began to sing. A chill
ran down her spine, her heart aching when his voice cracked on
the words.

A strange feeling brewed in the pit of Haven's stomach, longing and desperation mixing with fear. *Fear's healthy,* she tried to
remind herself, but it didn't feel like it at the moment. It felt crippling, like the fortress walls she had built that kept her safe and at
home were on the verge of collapsing.

"Are you okay?" he asked, pulling back as her body shuddered.
Haven nodded, her eyes starting to well up with tears as she
avoided his gaze, once again terrified of seeing that look in his
eyes, the look of regret.

"Do you want to go inside?" he asked when she didn't speak.

She nodded again.

He grabbed her hand, leading her to the back door instead
of the tree. He pressed the code in the keypad, unlocking it, and
ushered her inside.

Haven took her coat off as soon as she made it upstairs to the
bedroom, kicking her shoes off right inside the door. Her pants
were damp and she stripped them off, pulling her shirt off next
and tossing all of her clothes on the floor in a pile. She turned to
Carmine, watching as he took his coat off and carefully hung it on
the back of his desk chair.

"Carmine," she said, her voice shaking. He turned his head and
froze when he saw her standing there in her bra and underwear,
his eyes scanning the length of her like it was pure instinct.

His gaze reached her face and their eyes connected, goose

bumps dancing across her skin at the intensity of the green shining back at her. He stared at her curiously, the sadness still there, but more than anything she could see the love he had for her.

Thank God, she silently pleaded in relief.

"Make love to me, Carmine."

It came out a strangled whisper, the words catching in her throat. She needed him in that moment. She wasn't entirely sure why, but she could feel it deep down to the bone. She didn't want to just see his love—she wanted to *feel* it. It had been months since they had been intimate, since before the devastation had taken hold, and she desperately needed to be consumed by Carmine DeMarco once again.

He appeared torn as he stared at her, but the agonized expression on his face faded away. He slowly took a few steps toward her but didn't say anything, no words necessary. They both knew they would give in to the need, unable to resist the pull between them that had been there since the moment they first touched.

He paused in front of her, his hand running the length of her arm as he leaned down to kiss her. Reaching around and unclasping her bra, he pulled it off slowly and allowed it to drop to the floor. A moan escaped Haven's throat as he gently caressed her breasts, her nipples pebbling under his gentle touch.

His hands drifted down to her hips as he slowly backed her up to the bed. She scooted back onto it and he hovered over her, not once breaking their kiss.

Haven closed her eyes as his mouth moved to her neck, his shaky breath hitting the wet spots left behind. Shivers ripped down her spine as he trailed kisses down her stomach, and she inhaled deeply as his tongue dipped inside her belly button. It tickled, her body tingling from head to toe.

Carmine took his time, kissing and caressing every inch of exposed skin, before slowly pulling off her panties. She clutched the sheets tightly as he kissed along her inner thighs, gripping her hips, holding her in place as his tongue gently caressed her flesh.

Haven's noises grew louder and her legs trembled as the pressure built inside her. Writhing, she let go of the sheets, reaching out for him. She ran her hands through his hair and moaned his name, a groan vibrating in his chest at the sound of it. He pulled away from Haven quickly and she opened her eyes as he sat up, watching as he grabbed the bottom of his shirt to pull it off.

Reaching out, Haven ran her fingers over the ridges of his stomach, tracing the lines of the tattoo on his chest as he unbuckled his pants. He pulled them off and Haven's breath hitched at the sight of him already erect. She ran her fingers down the light trail of hair on his stomach before grasping him and stroking a few times.

"Are you sure?" he asked, placing his hand on top of hers.

"Now who's second guessing?" she asked. "Don't you trust me?"

He smiled, amused she would turn his words around on him, and pulled her hand away. She held her breath as he pushed inside of her, filling her completely with one deep stroke.

"Of course I trust you," he whispered. "I'm just giving you a chance to change your mind."

"I'll never change my mind," she said. "Not when it comes to you."

His thrusts were slow and gentle at first as he kissed her softly, whimpers escaping her throat. She wrapped her arms around him, clinging to him as her hands roamed the sculpted muscles of his back.

The pleasure was intense as it swept through her, and it didn't take long before the pressure built again, her body quivering.

Carmine's movements grew more frantic after a while, his thrusts harder and deeper. His breathing grew labored, his body trembling in her arms as he slid in and out of her body with fervor. She could feel the desire seeping from his pores as he gave himself to her. The love, the need, the yearning . . . the raw passion between them was enough to take her breath away.

Skin soaked with sweat, Haven felt as if she were on fire, every inch of her aching for all of him. She could hear his pants and gasps, his hands gripping her firmly as he challenged logic by pulling her closer than she had ever been before. It was as if they had melted into one, where he ended and she began nothing but a blur.

Bodies pressed together, she could feel his pulse, blood furiously rushing through his veins. "Your heart," she whispered. "It's racing."

"You feel it?" he asked. "You hear it?"

"Yes."

"What's it saying?"

She smiled, her eyes fluttering closed. "It's saying you love me."

"I do," he said. "No matter what. *Sempre.*"

That word washed through her. "*Sempre.*"

Carmine's body shook as his climax hit. He smashed his lips to hers as he thrust a few more times, holding Haven so tightly it was as if his life depended on it.

He stilled his movements, nuzzling into her neck, and let out a shaky breath as a shudder ran through his body.

"Good night, my hummingbird," Carmine whispered. "I'll keep you in my dreams."

7

Sitting at the bottom of the stairs, Carmine dropped his head low as his hand gripped his unruly hair, his eyes fixed on the black duffel bag full of clothes near his feet. His old acoustic guitar was carefully balanced against it—half teetering on the bag, half on the foyer floor.

A chime echoed through the downstairs from a clock in the family room, an eternity seeming to pass with each tick of its hand. Time was a merciless bitch, taunting him as it slipped away. One second; two seconds; twenty minutes; an hour. A century could have gone by, or no time at all.

Carmine's chest ached. He wished it would just fucking stop.

Footsteps on the stairs behind him made him feel like he was going to be sick. He was afraid Haven would wake up and catch him sitting there alone—part of him treacherously hoping she would find him and stop him, even though he knew it was too late.

"I'm surprised you're still here," Vincent said, stepping past. "I thought you'd be gone by now."

"So did I," he said, his voice shaking as he continued to stare at the bag on the floor. "She's gonna hate me. She's gonna regret ever letting me into her life."

"She'll understand someday."

Carmine clenched his hands into fists as his eyes burned with unshed tears. "This is gonna fucking devastate her."

"Yeah, it probably will."

"Great," he spat, glaring at his father. "Thanks for making me feel better."

"Do you want me to *lie* to you?" Vincent asked, raising his eyebrows. "Of course it's going to hurt her, Carmine. There's no getting around that."

"This is fucked up," he said, shaking his head. "This isn't how it's supposed to be. It wasn't supposed to end up like this. We're supposed to be together, get away from all of this bullshit and just *be*. For once in our fucking lives, we were going to just *be,* and now look at everything."

"Are you rethinking this?" he asked. "It isn't too late."

"It *is* too late," he said. "The moment I went to Sal, it became too late. She's better than the life I can offer her."

"Then what do you want me to say, son?"

"I want you to say she's better off without me, that we're better off apart."

"Fine," Vincent said, "but who's going to convince *you* of that?"

His question caught Carmine off guard. He stared at his father pointedly, awaiting some answer to ease his concern, but the mere thought of stepping out of that front door without Haven hurt worse than Carmine ever imagined it would.

Before he could come up with something to say, the front door opened and Dominic stepped inside. He froze when he caught sight of Carmine and narrowed his eyes as he slammed the door. Dominic rarely lost his temper, but when he did another side of him came out that was unpredictable, his words often hurting just as much as Carmine vaguely recalled his fists did.

"I see you haven't walked out on her yet," he said, his words cutting deep.

"Leave him alone, Dom," Vincent said. "You're just making it worse."

"I'm making it worse?" he asked with disbelief. "*Someone* has to try to talk him out of this before he makes the biggest mistake of his life. She's the best thing that ever happened to him!"

"You think I don't know that?" Carmine snapped. "She deserves to be free to do what she wants!"

"Then why are you taking that from her?" Dominic asked. "You're doing this so she'll be free to do what she wants, but you're making the choice for her!"

"I can't let her first decision be whether she follows her dreams or me. What kinda bullshit is that to ask of her? She always worries about everyone else because assholes have beat her down, and I'd be no better than them if I asked her to put me first! She deserves to find out what's out there for her, whether she realizes it or not."

"That's the stupidest thing I've ever heard," Dominic said. "Do you even hear yourself? What gives you the right to decide for her—because you know better than she does? Could you be more condescending?"

"Fuck you! I may be what she *wants*, but I'm not what she *needs*!"

"According to you," Dominic spat, stalking forward and getting in Carmine's face. "But like I said, you didn't even ask her. You just assumed. Who cares what Haven *wants*, right? We'll all just claim to know better than her and make her decisions and pretend it's what she needs when only *she* knows."

"She wants a future, Dominic. She wants to be *free*."

"But she *isn't*," he said. "Not as long as people like you are making decisions for her. I thought you were better than that, Carmine, but maybe I was wrong. Maybe you don't love her, after all."

The moment the words came from his mouth, rage ran through Carmine. He jumped up, drawing his arm back, and hit his brother with as much force as he could. Carmine's fist connected with Dominic's jaw, which made him stagger a few steps, but he lunged for Carmine the moment he gained his balance. Carmine tripped over the duffel bag, his foot tramping on the guitar and smashing through it as Dominic shoved him into the nearest wall. Vincent tried to come between them, but Dominic was too strong. He pinned Carmine there with his left hand as he drew his fist back. Carmine waited for the blow, blindly striking back at his brother, but before Dominic could follow through, a firm voice echoed through the downstairs.

"Enough!"

Corrado started toward them from the kitchen. He shoved Dominic away, physically coming between the two brothers.

"He doesn't know what he's saying," Carmine spat.

"Me? You're the one fucking up!"

"I said *enough*! Neither of you know what you're talking about! Are you boys so dumb that you can't grasp the concept of cause and effect?"

Dominic scoffed. "This isn't just some unfortunate side effect."

"Yes, it is," Corrado said. "It doesn't matter what Carmine does—Haven will always have choices taken from her. *I've* taken choices from her! It can't be helped! Certain things were determined the moment she was conceived and there's *nothing* anyone can do to change that. You can't rewrite history!"

The commotion drew Celia's attention. She slowly descended the stairs to the foyer, carrying her luggage. Her eyes scanned the room, frowning when she saw Carmine's things on the floor.

"*All* of us are forced to sacrifice," Corrado continued, turning to Dominic, staring at him pointedly. "And isn't this how most breakups go? One walks away while the other has no say. Or are you insinuating Carmine has no right to end the relationship? Isn't that hypocritical, given your rant? The fact is, Carmine isn't deciding Haven's future. Carmine's deciding his *own*."

He turned to Carmine, the anger in his expression staggering. "And you need to grow a backbone. You've been sitting here all morning feeling sorry for yourself, and it's wearing on my nerves. You either go back up those stairs or you walk out that front door, but there will be no more wavering in between. You belong in Chicago now, so be a man and do what's expected of you. Either take her along or don't, Carmine. She's going to lose something regardless. The only question that remains is *what* she loses."

The foyer grew quiet as everyone stared at Carmine, whose stomach churned with nerves. "I can't bring her to Chicago. Those people fucked up her life enough."

Dominic threw his hands up in exasperation as Corrado nodded. "Then pull yourself together and meet me in the car in five minutes. If you aren't there, I *will* come back in here for you, and I assure you—you don't want that to happen."

Corrado pulled his keys out of his pocket and headed for the door, motioning for Celia to follow him. She smiled sadly at her brother before giving Dominic a quick hug, merely casting Carmine a look as she followed her husband outside.

Carmine took a deep breath and glanced at his father as he reached into his pocket for his keys. He took the key for the house in Chicago off before holding the rest of them out. "Give my car to Haven. She's gonna need one. If she doesn't want to keep it she can sell it or trade it in or fucking burn it, whatever she wants to do. It doesn't matter anymore."

Carmine grabbed his bag, leaving the smashed guitar laying on the floor, and turned for the front door. He came face-to-face with his brother as he blocked his path. "Don't expect me to be there for you when you fall apart," Dominic said, nostrils flaring. "The only thing you'll ever hear from me is *I told you so.*"

———

Haven peeled her eyes open and glanced at the clock, surprised to see it read noon. A chill ran through her and her throat ached as she tried to clear it, an uncomfortable tickle deep inside her chest. She clung to the blanket for warmth, covering her nude body as she looked around.

No sign of Carmine anywhere.

Begrudgingly climbing out of bed, Haven took a hot shower before dressing in some comfortable clothes, feeling worse and worse as time trickled past. Her head started pounding, her eyes burning and body sore. Although she shivered, unable to get warm, her skin felt hot to the touch, like flames coursed through her bloodstream.

She spotted a piece of paper laying on Carmine's pillow and eyed it suspiciously, seeing her name written across the front. That feeling Haven had fought hard to push back the night before hit her again. Picking up the paper, her hands shook as she opened it, seeing it was a letter written in Carmine's messy scrawl.

Haven,

FDR said freedom couldn't be bestowed, it had to be achieved. I think I was in fifth grade when I heard about him, and I remember being pissed because I didn't see the point in learning history when it was over. I was an ignorant little shit, but I guess that's the point. I took a lot for granted in life and didn't appreciate the little things—things you missed out on. It's not okay what happened to you, and it's only from knowing you that I understand that. I wish more people could see it. More people need to see you. Maybe then the world wouldn't be such a fucked-up place.

I should've known telling you that you were free wouldn't make you so. Freedom has to be achieved, and that's exactly what you have to do, *tesoro*. You have to go out there and achieve that shit. You have the world at your fingertips, a life waiting for you full of opportunities you can't have if you stay with me. And I know they're dreams you want, dreams you've always had, and you shouldn't sacrifice them for me. You've sacrificed enough of your life because of selfish motherfuckers, and I'm not that selfish . . . not anymore. You made sure of that.

By the time you read this, I'll be gone. I can't stay here. It's not fair to you, and I'd never forgive myself for denying you a real life. A life away from all of this bullshit, where you can just be Haven. Go be you and not what people tried to make you. You have to go show those motherfuckers what they've been missing by not knowing you. Show them they can't hold my girl down.

And don't you be fucking scared. You're ready for the world, Haven, and it's been waiting eighteen years for you. Don't make that shit wait any longer.

Carmine

Haven jumped up, the letter falling to the bedroom floor as she bolted down the two flights of stairs, tripping over her feet along the way. Tears flowed from her eyes as she burst into the foyer, hesitating briefly when she accidently kicked Carmine's broken, discarded guitar.

After fumbling with the keypad, furiously pressing numbers until she got the code right, she opened the front door. Cold air blasted her and stole the breath from her lungs, her bare feet slapping against frozen wood as she ran out onto the icy porch.

The Mazda was still parked out front, the windows covered in a thin layer of frost. Last night's snow had already started to melt, but a few white patches remained on the car. It was untouched, unmoved, and the sight of it made hope sweep through her.

"Carmine?" she called, her shaky exhale a cloud of fog. "Where are you?"

"He left."

She swung around at the sound of the voice, her heart beating wildly. Dr. DeMarco stood in the doorway, sympathy shining from his eyes. Haven's stomach churned ruthlessly at the sight of it. *No. No way. Nuh-uh.*

"You're wrong," she said. "He didn't."

"He did."

"No!" she yelled. "He's still here!"

"He's not."

"I have to change his mind!"

"You can't."

His voice lacked all trace of emotion, the words coming out as if there was simply no room for argument, but she couldn't accept them. It *couldn't* be too late.

She waved frantically toward the Mazda. "His car's still here!"

"He didn't drive."

"He wouldn't leave it!"

"He left it for you."

"There's no way! He loves that car!"

"He loves you more."

Haven lost her composure at those words. Tears streamed down her cheeks as a loud sob ripped from her chest, echoing through the quiet yard. Her knees buckled and she collapsed on the porch, shaking her head.

"That's not right," she cried. "It can't be right. He wouldn't just leave!"

Dr. DeMarco continued to stand there, not moving from the spot in the doorway. "I'm sorry."

"Sorry?" she asked with disbelief. "You're *sorry*?"

Before he could respond, he was shoved out of the way as Dominic burst past him. He crouched down on the porch and pulled Haven into his arms, softly shushing her as he glared at his father.

"Dominic," Haven said. "Make him come back!"

"I can't," Dominic said. "I tried, Twinkle Toes, I really did, but he wouldn't listen."

Haven started sobbing harder, hiccupping as she tried to catch her breath. She was splintering, her heart ripping from her chest as she shattered into a million tiny jagged pieces.

"You need to calm down," Dominic said, stroking her hair softly. "Take a deep breath, will you? It's going to be okay."

"How can you say that?" she asked desperately. "I need him!"

Dominic squeezed her tighter. "No, you don't. I know it feels like it, but you don't. You're strong. You'll be just fine on your own."

Those words didn't have the impact Dominic seemed to think they would. Instead of comforting her, consoling her, she felt all remnants of lingering happiness fade away, like the last bit of water from a faucet swirling down a narrow drain.

On your own. The words seeped into her skin, inciting the same terrified feelings she once had in Blackburn when she ran through the desert, desperate for her life to be spared. Everything she knew disappeared into the night, leaving her alone with a cloudy future.

Alone.

"How can he be gone?" she whispered. "He didn't even give me a chance to say good-bye."

8

Carmine stood in a pile of slush along the street. His socks clung uncomfortably to his feet as wetness seeped through the soles of his old Nike's, but he couldn't move from that spot. He was as frozen as the ice that coated the sidewalk.

The house stood only a few feet away from the curb, the blue door illuminated by the glow of a nearby streetlight. It was just after sunset, but the cloud-covered Chicago sky made it feel much later.

They had been traveling all day since leaving Durante, two hours in the car before quite a few more on a plane. There hadn't been any arguing, no judgment or pity—in fact, no one said much of anything at all. He was left alone to his thoughts, and while he usually appreciated it, today was an entirely different case.

Because Carmine's thoughts were about as calm as a fucking hurricane.

When they had landed, Corrado had asked him where he wanted to go. Not thinking, Carmine muttered the lone word *home*. He had meant Durante, back where he yearned to be, but his uncle took him literally.

And an hour later, he stood in front of the house he grew up in, his soaked feet refusing to budge. A chill ran the length of him as a car sped by, hitting a small puddle and spraying his back with filthy frigid water. He immediately took a big step forward, out of the way, and shook his head as he moved onto the sidewalk.

"Quit being such a pussy," he muttered to himself, reaching into his pocket for the key his father had given him. "It's just a fucking house."

Clutching his duffle bag tightly, he made his way to the porch and unlocked the front door. The air was just as cold inside, his teeth chattering from the dampness. He reached for the light switch upon instinct and groaned when nothing happened.

No electricity.

He strolled through the downstairs in the darkness, coming upon empty room after empty room.

No furniture.

"Fuck." He dropped his bag in the middle of the living room and stood there for a moment, peering around at the barren walls, before closing his eyes.

There was nothing there anymore.

He could faintly remember the last time he stood in that spot. The room had been cluttered, lived in and loved, every bit of space filled except for the back corner. It had been bare; reserved for the one thing Carmine wanted most. He had been asking for months and finally . . . *fucking finally* . . . it was the day.

"How are they going to get it in the house, Mom?" he'd asked. "It's too big to fit through the door!"

"Oh, they'll find a way," Maura had replied, stepping into the room as she slipped on her jacket. "Even if it's piece by piece, they'll get the piano in here." She ruffled his messy hair, beaming at him. "Now come on, *sole*. We have things to do, and we don't want to be late for your recital! The new piano will be here when we get home tonight."

Carmine smiled fondly at the memory of his mom's sweet voice, but his expression fell once he reopened his eyes. His gaze drifted to the back corner of the living room. They never made it home that night.

Tears burned his tired eyes for the second time that day, but this time, he didn't fight it. There was no one to hold them back from, no reason to keep it in. No reason to be strong. Tomorrow he would pick himself up and move forward, walk out the door with his head held high, but not tonight. Tonight he was alone in a cold, dark house, surrounded by nothing but fuzzy painful memories.

———

Vincent DeMarco sat alone in his office, drumming his fingers against the wooden desk. The sun had set hours ago, the room enshrouded in total darkness. His eyes slowly adjusted so he could view his surroundings, but he didn't bother trying to look at anything. He'd seen all he needed to see.

Haven's notebook lay open in front of him to the page Carmine had shown him days before. He had studied the drawing of Carlo intently, taking in every line of his face, every distortion in his grotesque scar. His skin crawled at how chillingly accurate her rendering of his appearance was, every crack and ripple, down to the small oblong shaped mole under his left eye.

A mole, Vincent knew, that had only appeared in the past year.

He had run his finger over the spot on the page when he noticed it, wondering if it was just an ink smudge, trying to convince himself it was a crazy coincidence. There was no way she could have known it was there. She couldn't have seen it before.

Unless . . . she had.

His stomach was in tight knots as he considered that.

It didn't help that the house was deathly silent—no laughter, no chatter, no ruckus upstairs. No yelling, no fighting, no nothing at all. Dominic had stormed out after Carmine left, and soon both of his boys would be hundreds of miles away. Vincent felt like he was alone, although Haven was technically still there. She was above him on the third floor, passing the hours like a ghost as she lurked around in a trance.

He wanted to say something to her, but he couldn't find the words.

Soon she would be gone, too. She would step out the front

door within a matter of days and likely never look back. Vincent felt a sense of accomplishment deep in his chest, but pressing upon it was something heavier.

It was the knowledge that his work was still not done, and he was beginning to wonder if it ever would be.

Pulling out his cell phone, he squinted from the harsh bright light as he dialed the Chicago phone number. It rang twice before it was answered, the familiar voice on the line simply saying, "I'm listening."

Vincent took a deep breath as his gaze settled on the notebook, Carlo's menacing eyes staring back up at him.

"We need to talk."

———————

No one bothered Haven as she locked herself away on the third floor. The days passed quickly, one after another morphing into the next, as the winter clouds drifted away, the sun again making itself at home in the sky. She read the letter Carmine left countless times, the words stinging as much the twentieth time as they had the first. She sought out some hidden meaning, some little nugget of information that could explain how it was all a misunderstanding, bordering on delusional as she waited . . . and waited . . . for him to return.

But he didn't.

She heard people moving around the house and could hear their voices on the floor below, but it wasn't until the end of the week that someone finally came upstairs. Dia didn't bother to knock, just walked in and sat on the edge of the bed. Haven remained in her seat near the window, staring out at the barren back yard.

"How long?" Haven asked without even looking at her, her voice scratchy from not speaking in days. "How long ago did he tell you he was leaving?"

"Christmas Eve," Dia answered. "He called, asked if I'd watch out for you."

Haven blinked rapidly. *Christmas Eve?* "Why didn't he tell me?"

"You know why," Dia said. "He wouldn't have been able to leave if he did. Walking out the front door was probably the hardest thing he's ever done."

"And all of you knew it was going to happen?" she asked, finally turning to her. The quirky Dia looked uncharacteristically subdued in jeans and an oversize sweater. Her hair was nearly completely blonde, her natural shade, the ends tinged a faded light pink. "Everyone knew Carmine was leaving and *no one* told me?"

Dia sighed. "He only told me. He didn't want anyone to know because he didn't want it to ruin Christmas, but I let it slip to my sister and she told Dominic. I don't think anyone told the others. They just put the pieces together. His aunt Celia was the last to know."

"Besides me," Haven said bitterly, turning back away. "What am I supposed to do now?"

"You go on," Dia said. "You can come to Charlotte with me if you want, or we can find you a place around here. Whatever makes you happy."

"He makes me happy," she whispered.

"I know," Dia said, "but it'll get easier. In time it won't hurt as bad, and eventually, the day will come when you'll be ready to move on."

Haven shook her head, brushing away a few wayward tears. "It may not hurt as much, but I'll never move on."

She stood up and glanced around at the room, taking in all of Carmine's possessions. It all appeared to be exactly where it had been weeks, even months earlier when he'd still been there. "Did he take *anything*?"

"Clothes," she said. "Money. He left you an envelope of cash, you know, to get you through. He said you could have anything else you wanted, too. Whatever's left is going to be shipped to him in Chicago after . . ."

Dia trailed off as Haven walked over to the desk and started sorting through things, separating her belongings from Carmine's. "After I leave," she said, completing her friend's thought.

"You don't have to do that now," Dia said. "Take as much time as you need. They said you're welcome to stay here as a guest as long as you'd like."

"Guest." The word sounded so foreign on Haven's tongue. Once upon a time she had been a slave within these very same walls, trapped like a prisoner behind bulletproof windows and locked doors. After that, she had almost felt at home, like she had finally found somewhere she belonged, somewhere she was wanted. But now she was a guest, a visitor passing through on her way to God knows where.

It's strange how those things work. One minute you're the servant, the next you're Cinderella, and then . . . *then the story is over and you're forced to close the book.*

"How am I going to make it?" she asked. "I don't know what I'm doing."

"None of us really know what we're doing," Dia replied. "We just go out there and do it and have faith it'll turn out okay."

Haven thought over those words as she continued to separate their belongings, unsure of what to say. Dia got up when she realized Haven had no intention of stopping, leaving the room and returning with some empty boxes. She silently worked alongside Haven, helping her pack up her things.

It wasn't until then, as they filled box after box with belongings, that Haven realized exactly how much she had acquired while living there. A little more than a year before, she had walked through the front door for the first time barefoot and empty-handed, with nothing she could call her own except for her name. *Haven.* It was the only thing her mother had given her, the one thing, she thought, no one could ever take away. But now she was preparing to walk out the door for the last time, half a dozen boxes already packed full of material things.

Just thinking about it made her uneasy. She suddenly wanted to leave it *all* behind.

It took nearly two days for her to sort through everything—two days of wavering, two days of packing and unpacking and repacking again. She took some necessary clothes but left most of it hanging in the closet, hoping Dr. DeMarco would donate it to charity so someone who needed it would have something to wear. She packed some books and notebooks and all of the drawings she had done during the past year. She took the basket from their Valentine's Day picnic, but she left all of Carmine's things untouched.

Dominic and Tess appeared long enough to say good-bye before leaving for school again. Neither one mentioned Carmine, both of them feigning happiness about the future that lay ahead of her, but she wasn't naïve—she could tell they were concerned.

As the time slipped away, Haven's sadness gave way to anger, before guilt set in once again. It was because of her that Carmine had given himself to the organization; because of her he had had to go to Chicago. She obsessed about the unknowns, wondering how she could have missed the signs.

Looking back, it seemed so obvious he'd been saying good-bye.

Dia appeared around dawn on New Year's Eve, while Haven was already awake and waiting. She sat in the library with her knees pulled up to her chest, her arms wrapped around herself as she stared out the window. She wondered if it was what Carmine had been doing that last night, contemplating leaving just as she was.

Had he been frightened? She wasn't sure. He made leaving seem so easy.

"Are you ready?" Dia asked, having already placed Haven's things in Carmine's car the day before.

Haven nodded, unable to say the words. The truth was she felt like she would never be ready, but she got up and slipped on her coat anyway. Dia handed her Carmine's car key before heading for the stairs, and Haven hesitated in the library. "I'll meet you downstairs. I need a minute."

Stepping into the doorway of the bedroom, Haven's eyes scanned the room slowly, her chest aching. A tear slipped down her cheek.

"Good-bye," she said quietly.

9

Haven walked blindly down the long hallway, the boxes in her arms obstructing her view. She shifted them around, trying to catch a glimpse in front of her, and ran straight into Dia.

Haven smiled apologetically but Dia simply waved it off as she pulled out a set of keys and opened her door. Haven juggled the boxes once more, careful not to run into anything else as she walked into the small, quiet apartment. Her footsteps faltered when Dia flicked on the light, illuminating the room surrounding her. Photos covered every surface, blanketing the paint like wallpaper.

Haven had been here before, once, on her eighteenth birthday. She forgot Dia wanted to be a photographer.

Her eyes scanned the pictures instinctively, recognizing some of the faces, but they all felt foreign to her except one. Straight in front of her, on the wall above the couch, was an old photo of her and Carmine. His face was all over, infiltrating the sea of colorful memories, but this one was different. This one called to her, silently screaming her name above the others. Neither had even known the photo was being taken as they stared at each other that Christmas day more than a year before. Their love had been new, untainted and naïve. Blissful ignorance shone from their eyes, two souls completely unaware of the anguish on the horizon.

Dia kicked the door shut, the slam echoing through the room

and making Haven flinch. It suddenly felt as if the memory-clad walls were closing in on her. The boxes slipped from her arms, hitting the floor with a thud.

Stepping around them, Haven walked over to the couch and grabbed the photo, wordlessly yanking it off the wall.

"Sorry," Dia said, setting the other boxes down. "I should've reminded you . . . *warned* you."

Haven closed her eyes. Warning her they were there would have done nothing to dull the ache. It resided deep inside her, infecting her tissues and seeping into her bones, clenching her heart as it took over her chest. Her lungs felt stiff, like brand-new leather, stubbornly refusing to expand as she took a deep breath. She was suffocating from the pressure of what could have been.

"It's okay," she whispered, forcing the words out. "I'm okay."

Dia said something else, but Haven didn't wait to hear. She walked away, slipping into the spare bedroom and closing the door, pressing her back against it as she clutched the photo to her chest.

————

Sleep evaded Haven that night as she lay in bed, ringing in the New Year by staring out the foggy window. Fireworks went off in the distance, noise permeating the air as people in Charlotte celebrated, but Haven did nothing.

She hardly even moved.

When the early morning sun started to peek through, she gave up on finding sleep and quietly crept to the living room. The photos were all gone, the cream-colored walls vacant except for the subtle orange glow enveloping the apartment from the sunrise. Dia had taken them down sometime in the night, a few stray pieces of tape remaining. Haven pulled them off, rolling them together in a ball in her palm.

"Morning."

Haven turned, watching as her friend strolled out of a bedroom behind her. Dia wore a pair of orange polka-dotted pajamas, her hair knotted at the top of her head. She rubbed her eyes and yawned as she made her way toward the tiny kitchen.

"Good morning," Haven said quietly, glancing back at the empty walls. "Your pictures are gone."

"Yeah, I thought it would be easier if you didn't have to see them," Dia mumbled sleepily, opening the fridge and pulling out a jug of milk. She poured herself a glass and saturated it with a mountain of chocolate syrup. "Are you hungry? I think I have some cereal around here somewhere."

Haven shook her head as Dia started toward her again. "No, thank you."

"Well, if you get hungry, help yourself to anything in the kitchen," she said. "I don't have much right now, but I'll grab some groceries on my way home."

Haven eyed her curiously. "Way home from where?"

"School," she replied, sipping from her glass. "I have to register for my classes today and buy my books."

"Oh."

"I'd stay with you, but I technically already missed registration, so it's my last chance," she continued. "But if you don't want to be alone, I can—"

"It's fine," Haven said, cutting her off. She didn't want to be a burden. "I have things to do today anyway. You know, like unpacking and . . . things."

Haven forced a smile, but Dia didn't look convinced. "We can do something together when I get home. Maybe order a pizza and watch a movie? It'll be fun. We can have girl talk."

"Yeah, sure," Haven said. "Sounds great."

Dia smiled warmly, giving her a quick hug before going about her morning ritual. Haven lingered in the living room, absent-mindedly rolling the small ball of sticky tape between her fingers. Once Dia left, Haven headed back into the bedroom and shut the door, leaving her things in the boxes in the living room.

———

There was no pizza that night. No movie. No girl talk. There wasn't even sleep.

Days passed in a blur of insomnia and exhaustion, thrusting Haven deeper into depression. The nights were tortuous but the days weren't much better as Haven walked around in a stupor. She felt like she was drowning, slowly slipping away as she grasped desperately to the surface, just waiting for something to pull her back up.

Pain was something Haven knew well. She had always had a high tolerance for it, keeping her head held high as she faced unimaginable torture, but this feeling brewing inside of her now was different. The heart-clenching, suffocating dread was enough to knock her off her feet. She had been frightened before, certainly, but this was the first time she truly felt lost. Until then, her life had been an endless cycle of do-this-and-do-that; there was always a task, always a purpose, always a point. But not anymore. Her future was empty. A blank canvas. There was nowhere for her to escape from. There was nobody looking for her.

She was free, she realized, and freedom terrified her.

———

Luna Rossa sat back off the highway, partially shielded by rows of trees. The brick building, massive in size while subtle in style, blended into the surroundings of the quiet south Chicago neighborhood. The rustic tan sign above the door displayed the name in deep red cursive letters, the only indicator of its true nature the word *lounge* below it in gold. No flashing lights or neon signs attempted to lure passing visitors inside.

While it appeared welcoming, almost quaint at first glance, *Luna Rossa* catered to a certain crowd. The dark sedans spread throughout the parking lot hinted it was the type of place you didn't visit unless someone invited you to.

Carmine always found it strange that his uncle owned a social club, but standing in front of it for the first time, it made sense to him. The place was low-key, a lot like Corrado.

Taking a deep breath to steady himself, Carmine opened the door and stepped inside the building. The bouncer eyed him peculiarly, taking in the sight of his faded jeans and Nike's, but he didn't move or say a word as Carmine strolled through the crowd. It was a Thursday, and men in suits lingered around with a few younger women clinging to their sides. *Goomahs*, he realized. Mob mistresses. *Luna Rossa* was *La Cosa Nostra*'s hideaway, their home away from home. It wasn't a place where a man took his wife—it was a place he went when he had something to hide.

And it was easy to hide there. The dark wood with red trim, the lighting dim, concealed secrets and masked sins. Cigar smoke infused the air as Frank Sinatra crooned from tall speakers positioned along the side, blending with the sound of friendly chatter and laughter in the club.

Carmine felt completely out of place as he made his way to a large corner booth in the back. The noise coming from it was louder than the others, the table covered in an array of bottles of alcohol. Sal sat in the middle of the group, a young brunette woman snuggled up to his right. Beside her was another girl, a blonde no older than twenty, while half a dozen men surrounded them on both sides.

Carmine cleared his throat nervously as he approached. "Salvatore."

Sal looked at the sound of his name, his face lighting up. *"Principe!"*

"It's nice to see you."

"You, too, dear boy." Sal grinned widely as his hand swept across the table. "Join us. Have a drink."

Instead of squeezing in with the mass of bodies, Carmine grabbed a free chair and pulled it to the other side of their table. "You know I'm not old enough to—"

He didn't even finish before Sal's mocking laughter cut him off. "Nonsense!" He motioned for the waitress. "Get my godson whatever he wants. Put it on my tab."

The waitress paused beside him, smiling politely. "What can I get you?"

"Uh, vodka," he said. "Straight up."

"Bring him the whole bottle," Sal chimed in. "Something from the top shelf, sweetheart. Nothing but the best for young De-Marco."

Carmine forced a smile, but he got no satisfaction from Sal's words. The waitress returned after a moment with a bottle of Grey Goose and a thick glass, setting it in front of Carmine before walking away. He wordlessly poured himself a shot, feeling Sal's eyes on him as he swallowed it to ease his frayed nerves.

The burn was familiar. Warm. Numbing. He savored the sensation.

Sal's focus shifted back to the others, the conversation at the table flowing freely between the men. It made little sense to Carmine so he sat back quietly, sipping on the liquor as he tried to disappear into the background. His mind wandered, his eyes drifting toward the two girls. They giggled, hanging on to Sal's every word as if the bullshit he sprayed was made of pure gold. Carmine wondered what they saw in him, why they stuck around. Money? Presents? Did they get off on his power? Was it just for kicks? It sure as fuck couldn't have been attraction.

"So, *Principe*, are you settling in?" Sal asked, capturing Carmine's attention again. He tore his eyes from the girls and looked to his godfather, who stared at him with his eyebrows raised.

"Yeah." He poured another drink. "I'm moving into my parents' old house."

"And you have all of your things?"

"They arrived today."

"And the girl?" Sal asked. "Has she arrived?"

Carmine tensed, his glass to his lips. He set it down after a moment without taking a drink, afraid the liquor wouldn't make it past the lump in his throat. "Uh, no. She's not."

Sal's expression fell as concern clouded his face. Pulling his arm from around the brunette, he leaned closer to the table, his high-pitched voice uncharacteristically low. "What do you mean she's not?"

"She's not coming," Carmine clarified.

"Never?"

"No. She's, uh . . . not with me now."

Tension swept over the table. Sal remained strangely still, just staring at Carmine. Anger brewed in his dark eyes. The others sensed the shift in atmosphere and grew quiet, watching the two of them cautiously.

"You broke up?"

Carmine nodded.

"After what everyone risked for that girl, you're not even together anymore?"

Again, he nodded.

"She's off on her own? Free to do as she wishes?"

Another nod.

"And you're not."

Not a question that time, but Carmine nodded anyway.

After a bout of strained silence, Sal broke the tension by laughing once again, abruptly loud and genuinely amused. "Well, I believe there's a lesson to be learned in there somewhere."

"What's that?" someone else asked.

"No matter how beautiful you think a woman is," Sal said, "she's never worth the trouble."

The men erupted in cheers, toasting Sal's words, while Carmine remained silent. Picking up his glass, he sipped the hot liquor, absorbing the bitterness into his bloodstream. He watched as Sal turned back to the young brunette, putting his arm around her again. He pulled her to him, whispering, "Not you, baby."

She blushed and giggled, while Carmine grimaced. *Fucking sick.*

"There is an upside, though," Sal declared, glancing back at Carmine. "You can join in the fun around here. There's no reason for you to have to go home alone tonight. I'm sure Ashley's friend, Gabby, would be happy to show you a good time."

Carmine looked to the blonde when Sal motioned toward her. She smiled devilishly, her blue eyes scanning him slowly, surveying, and judging. "Absolutely."

Shaking his head, Carmine looked away from her. "No, thanks."

"Not your type?" Sal asked. "There are plenty more around here—redheads, blondes, brunettes, girls in all shapes and sizes. Just pick your poison."

"I'm just . . . not interested."

"My godson, not interested in a woman? Unheard of! Pick one. My gift to you."

Carmine tried to think of a way to explain it that didn't make him look susceptible. The last thing he wanted to do was expose his biggest weakness in front of so many. "I'm not in the mood right now."

"You don't have to be in the mood," Sal said. "These ladies know what they're doing. Ten minutes alone with one and you'll be begging for more."

"I don't beg."

"I seem to remember you begging me once, *Principe*. And correct me if I'm wrong, but wasn't it because of a girl? A girl you're no longer with, at that. Maybe you should've just left her where she was. Maybe we'd all be better off."

Anger swept through Carmine. He clenched his hands into fists in his lap but fought to keep it from showing on his face. Sal stared at him, challenging him to react.

"Come on now, Boss," Corrado's voice rang out directly behind Carmine, startling him. Heavy hands clamped down on his shoulders, keeping him locked in place so he couldn't turn around. "Cut the boy some slack. Even you know what it's like to make mistakes. He's just being cautious so he doesn't make another."

"I suppose that's admirable." Sal relaxed again as he took a sip of his drink. "The last thing I want is another careless man on my team."

"Especially one that's careless with a woman," Corrado said.

Sal laughed bitterly. "Like his father. Vincent's only flaw was his choice in females. Talk about a man who made mistakes . . ."

Carmine's calm mask slipped, his eyes narrowing. He shifted forward a fraction of an inch at the insinuation about his mother, preparing to pounce without a second thought, but Corrado's grip on Carmine tightened.

"You live and you learn," Corrado said. "Carmine here will do both, hopefully . . . as long as he remembers his place. And I think right now, his place is at home. He hasn't even unpacked and he's already partying."

"True, true." Sal waved his hand dismissively at Carmine. "Get out of here."

Corrado let go of Carmine, stepping to the side so he could stand up. He glanced around the table one last time before nodding his head. "Good night, sir."

He briskly walked away, relief soothing his nerves as he bolted for the exit. As he approached the bouncer, the man suddenly jumped from his seat and stood at attention. Carmine's brow furrowed at the reaction until he heard Corrado tell the man to relax. His uncle was right on his heels, walking out behind him.

"Thanks for that," Carmine said quietly once they were outside, taking a deep breath of the cold night air. A cloud surrounded him as he exhaled.

"You're welcome, but I won't always be around," Corrado replied. "You have to learn to control yourself, no matter what he says."

"I know, but I just didn't expect *that*. I mean, fuck, he flipped on me quick. It caught me off guard."

"He's testing you," Corrado said, "and based on the little bit I saw, I have to say you're going to fail."

10

After two weeks of fleeting hunger and fits of insomnia, Haven's grip started to slip. Every time there was a knock at Dia's door, a swell of hope ran through Haven that it was Carmine, but each time she would end up crushed all over again. She grew anxious, conjuring up wild scenarios of where he was and what he was doing. She couldn't understand how he tolerated being away from her. If he loved her as he claimed, he had to feel the same pain she did.

Didn't he?

She started imagining things that weren't there again, whispered voices in the night calling out to her as she struggled to find solace in sleep. She heard noises in the apartment, footsteps outside her door, and loud bangs that sent her heart wildly racing. It got to the point where it felt like someone was always there, lurking around the corner, watching, waiting. She could hear them moving around but they were always out of sight, never within her reach. *He* was haunting her, his memory lingering everywhere she looked, while his absence cruelly taunted her.

Until, suddenly, one day, she saw him there.

Haven stood in place, staring at the vision in front of her. Carmine sat in a dark room in nothing but a pair of gray sweatpants, hunched over his piano with his fingers ghosting across the ivory keys. He didn't press down on them. There was no music, no sound at all—nothing but strangled silence.

Nothing but him.

She reveled in the sight, the contours of his muscles and the rise and fall of his chest as he breathed deeply. His hair was a mess, overgrown and unkempt, sticking up in every direction and falling forward into his eyes. She could even make out the scar on his side, shining a shade lighter than his naturally tanned skin. She longed to touch it, to trace the old wound with her fingertips.

"Tesoro." He whispered the word in a shaky voice, as if saying it any louder would hurt too much. *"Ti amo."*

She opened her mouth to speak, but no words came out. She clutched her throat, startled, unable to find her voice. It was gone.

I love you, too, she thought. *I always will.*

"Only you," he whispered. *"Sempre."*

Sempre.

"You're my life," he said. "I'd die without you."

I'm yours. I always have been.

His shoulders slumped. "Forgive me."

For what?

"I destroy everything I touch."

She shook her head. *Not me.*

"Maybe not you, yet," he said. "But I will . . . if you let me."

You won't. She took a step closer. *You wouldn't hurt me.*

"I hurt you when I left," he whispered. "But I had to do it. I had to."

He slowly turned in her direction as he lifted his head, and Haven's heart pounded furiously as he looked straight at her. Instead of the bright vibrant green she had expected, there was nothing but darkness. There was no life, no light, no spark. His words were just as cold. "I would've destroyed you had I stayed."

A violent shiver tore down her spine as she frantically shook her head.

Over his heart, where the words *Il tempo guarisce tutti i mali* were inked on his skin, a small black circle appeared. She watched, horrified, as it expanded rapidly, his face twisting in anguish as the blackness took over his body.

A loud crack shook the walls as he vanished into the darkness.

Haven sat straight up in bed, her heart pounding erratically. It was pitch black, no streetlights shining through the window, not even the glow from the alarm clock nearby. She rubbed her burning eyes, disoriented, and colored splotches sprung up in her line of sight like splatters of translucent watercolor paint.

A severe storm waged outside, rain splattering against the building as the wind screeched. The noises echoed through the room as a prickly sensation danced across Haven's feverish skin, almost like there was an electrical charge in the air.

Glancing toward the bedroom door, her panic flared as a thump rang out in the living room. "Dia?" she called out, her voice gritty. She swallowed harshly, trying to get a grip, and pushed the comforter away. Her legs shook as she tiptoed toward the door, pressing her ear against the crack to listen.

A gust of wind whipped by, violently rattling the window, and Haven turned to look. Confusion rocked her as her eyes fell upon the glass, and in the blurry reflection she caught a glimpse of a pair of eyes. Not just any eyes . . . familiar eyes, ones that had beckoned to her since the first time she gazed into them.

"Carmine," she whispered, the pain in her chest intensifying at the sound of his name. Tears formed and she blinked, trying to force them back. When she reopened her eyes, the image was gone. "Carmine!"

Another strong gust of wind hit and the tears slipped past as she started to tremble. She hit the light switch, frantically flicking it up and down, but nothing happened. No electricity.

Flinging open the bedroom door, she gasped as shadows swept across the living room. She heard the click of the front door and panicked, looking up to see the chain lock dangling, swinging from having been disturbed.

"Dia," Haven yelled, running to her friend's bedroom. She pushed open the door without knocking and blinked to clear her vision, dread running through her when she saw the bed was empty. She quickly searched the house in the darkness, finding Dia nowhere.

"I can't do this anymore," Haven said, panicking. Running back into the bedroom, she slipped on some shoes and grabbed her things in a frenzy before heading out of the apartment. In too much of a rush to wait for the elevator, she descended the six flights of stairs as fast as she could. She nearly tripped when she reached the second floor, pausing when she heard footsteps in front of her. A moment later they stopped and the outside door opened, a crack of thunder echoing through the building as whoever it was disappeared into the storm.

Rain pelted Haven the moment she stepped outside, the water startlingly cold against her skin. Stepping off the curb, she started to dart across the street for the Mazda when a yellow taxicab pulled up in front of her. A man climbed out from the back seat and was about to shut the door when he saw her.

"You need the taxi, lady?" he asked. She stared at him, debating his question. She had no idea what she was doing, her confusion deepening as she took in his concerned expression. "Hello? Are you all right?"

"Uh, yes," she said, not sure if it were true or not. She brushed by him, mumbling thanks as she slid into the backseat. Her heart pounded rapidly and she fought back the sickness that built in her stomach as the guy slammed the door.

"Where you headed?" the driver asked, glancing in the rearview mirror.

"Chicago." The word rolled from her lips before she processed what she was saying.

The driver laughed. "Can't go that far, but I can drop you at the bus station."

She nodded in a daze. "Okay."

He pulled onto the road. The rain bombarded the car, wind gusting and thunder cracking, making Haven jump every so often. She zoned out and couldn't focus, slipping further and further into a trance. She was too exhausted to stop and think, acting on impulse out of desperation.

When the cab stopped, she handed some cash to the driver without counting it first. She got out, standing on the curb in the pouring rain as the vehicle pulled away. The brick building in front of her was shabby, the blue GREYHOUND sign barely visible through the storm. Buses idled in the side parking lot while a few people lingered inside the brightly lit lobby, waiting.

Haven didn't have the slightest clue where to start. Her body shook as she approached the thick glass window in the building, dripping water all over the grimy tile floor.

The lady sitting in front of a computer eyed her peculiarly. "Can I help you?"

"I, uh . . . I need to go to Chicago."

Reaching into her pocket, Haven pulled out a wad of cash—twenty, forty, sixty, eighty, a ball of fives and ones, and a handful of loose change. She laid it all out on the counter, everything she had left in her pocket.

The lady counted it out, carefully unfolding the damp bills. "There's a bus that leaves here in about four hours for Chicago."

"Do I have enough?"

The lady smiled, punching it into her computer and printing out a ticket. "With ten cents to spare."

Haven took the ticket, dropping the spare dime in an empty coffee cup that a homeless man held as he sat against the wall nearby. She quietly walked over to an empty metal bench, lying down on it as she waited. Four hours, she chanted in her head as she closed her tired eyes. Just four more hours.

––––––––––

Sleep viciously pulled her away, deep in the throes of another surreal dream. The lightning that crashed outside the bus station translated as gunfire, pulling her into the middle of the warehouse shootout again. On and on it went, a cycle of violence she couldn't escape. She thrashed around on the hard bench, whimpering in her sleep, until someone shook her awake.

She sat up abruptly and her eyes fell upon the familiar man beside her. She scanned him quietly for a moment, blinking a few times, thinking if she waited he would fade away with the dream. "Dr. DeMarco?"

He sat back against the hard bench with an exasperated sigh. He, too, was drenched from the storm, his wet hair slicked back on his head. His eyes, dark and expressive, avoided her for a long moment.

His proximity put her on edge, his presence alarming. Her heart pounded furiously as confusion set in. "How did you know . . . ?"

"Maura and I tried to run away once," he said quietly, shaking his head. "We made it as far as the bus station, too."

Haven eyed him warily. "I'm not running away."

He ignored her declaration. "What you're doing is dangerous. So many things could've gone wrong . . . could *still* go wrong. You have the right to go where you want to go, but this just isn't smart."

Haven moved over a bit, settling on the bench a few inches from him. Her eyes scanned the building for a clock, finding one above the ticket window. Three and a half hours had passed. Her bus was scheduled to leave in thirty minutes.

"Do you remember the day I took you to the hospital?" he asked. "We sat in my office. I told you Carmine was naïve and impulsive."

"Irrational and volatile," she whispered.

"Carmine's always done things without thinking, and I was worried he'd do the same with you. I honestly thought he'd take you and run, because he's my son. Because he's so much like me. But he didn't. For probably the first time in his life, he considered the consequences.

"I've lost a lot, you know. I lost my wife, but before that I lost my *life*. I gave it away by initiating. That's the world Carmine belongs to now. They tell him where to go and what to do, and if he doesn't . . . well, you know what happens when people disregard orders. He doesn't want you subjected to that, and I agree with him. I believe Chicago's the *last* place you should go, but if you decide you really want to, I'll do whatever I can to help."

Haven looked at him with surprise. "You'll help me?"

"Yes, but not today," he said, his expression serious. "Carmine needs time to figure things out, and quite frankly, so do you. Don't you agree?"

She stared at him, unsure of how to answer. "I guess so."

"After you've given life a chance, if you still want to go to Chicago, I'll make sure you get there, even if it's the last thing I do. But before you can choose to be with Carmine, you have to understand what you're giving up."

"But—"

Dr. DeMarco raised his hand to silence her. "If you can't do it for yourself, at least do it for Carmine. Show everyone he was right about you, that you're the person he believes you are. Prove everyone wrong who threw you aside, and prove Carmine right, because he needs it."

Tears welled in her eyes. "Okay."

"Good," he said, standing. "Now let's get you back to Dia's. She was terrified when she called me, thought you'd been kidnapped again."

Shivering, Haven wrapped her arms around herself, guilt running rampant. She was chasing a ghost through the city, risking everything out of desperation, and scaring the few people who truly cared for her.

She followed Dr. DeMarco outside and slipped into the passenger seat of his Mercedes, which was parked haphazardly along the curb. He started it, cranking the heat to get her warm. She laid her head against the foggy side window, frowning as she faintly heard the intercom announce boarding for the bus to Chicago.

11

Things change.

Sometimes it's abrupt, knocking you off your feet as life throws a curveball nobody expected, turning worlds upside down and leaving those left behind to pick up the pieces. But other times, it happens slowly, an hour, or a minute, or a second at a time, so immeasurable no one can pinpoint exactly when it happened. You find yourself somewhere you've never been, doing things you've never done, being a person you never imagined you would ever be.

Because Dia was busy and everyone else she knew lived hundreds of miles away, Haven was often left on her own in the small Charlotte apartment. She ventured outside on the days she was alone, the fresh air and change of scenery helpful in clearing her mind. She would walk across the street to a small park and sit on one of the swings, the place deserted in the mornings because the weather was still cold. Haven welcomed the temperature, the icy air stinging her cheeks and reminding her she was still alive— that no matter how much it hurt, or how much she felt like she was dying inside, she wasn't. She was still breathing, each exhale reaffirming that with a cloud of warm breath lingering in the air around her.

As long as she was still breathing, she was okay.

Dia helped guide Haven through the simple things, things Carmine had never gotten around to showing her, like how to mail letters and use a computer. Haven bought postcards at the store to send to Tess and Dominic across the country, and she set up an email account to keep in touch with them.

The sensation of seeing something in the mailbox addressed to her was indescribable. Most people took it for granted, communicating freely, but it was a big deal to her. It was proof she had an identity, that she was real.

The first time she received junk mail, a flyer from a local business about a sale, Haven was elated. She wasn't sure how they got her name and Dia shrugged it off, telling Haven to trash it, but she refused. She had been acknowledged as existing, like she was just another person in the world. She wasn't Haven Antonelli, former slave; she was Haven Antonelli, potential customer.

To her, that was *everything*.

Things went smoother after she decided to give life alone a chance, but she still had her moments. She missed Carmine immensely, her love never wavering. She often wrote him letters, too, but she never mailed them. Whether it was pride, or anger, or straight-up fear, something kept her from reaching out to him again.

Haven awoke one morning to sunlight pouring into the Charlotte apartment. Winter had faded away, January turning to February before March blossomed before her eyes. She climbed out of bed and opened the window, breathing in the fresh morning air as she looked out at the street below. The trees were full of lush green leaves, small flowers starting to bloom and freckle the landscape with color that hadn't been there the day before.

After getting ready for the day, Haven strolled out to the living room. It was quiet and still, Dia having already left. Where her books had been strewn out the night before lay a single pamphlet, a yellow sticky note attached to the front. Haven picked it up curiously before strolling into the small kitchen.

Thought you might be interested in this.—Dia

Pouring a glass of juice, Haven sipped some as she opened the brochure. *Charlotte Academy of Arts Spring Schedule* was written along the top, followed by a list of upcoming workshops. She scanned them, stopping at one halfway down.

Painting 101

This free workshop will help students loosen up and see the world in a different light. Participants will experience the joy of painting, learning to express themselves in a new creative way. No experience needed. All materials included.

Mon–Fri, March 12–23, noon–3 P.M.

March 12. Haven glanced at the calendar, realizing it was today.

She read the pamphlet three times before setting her glass on the counter. She debated for a moment, wondering if she could really do it, before shrugging away her doubts and grabbing her things. She headed out of the apartment, finding the Mazda parked in the lot across the street.

Hesitating, she ran her hand along the sleek hood before climbing into the driver's seat and starting it up.

She was nervous as she drove across town, chanting to herself the entire time: *If not for you, do it for Carmine.*

———

It took Haven a while to find the place and just as long to figure out where to park. By the time she stepped into the Charlotte Academy of Arts, it was already a quarter after twelve. Discouraged, she walked up to a lady sitting at a desk in the front lobby, clutching the pamphlet in her hand. "I know it's probably too late, but I was wondering about the art class that started today."

"Painting?" the lady asked.

Haven nodded. "Yes, ma'am."

"You're in luck," she said. "There's one opening left."

Haven filled out the paperwork, trying to keep her hand from shaking as she wrote her name. Once she registered, the lady showed her to the classroom. The lighting was dim, soft classical music playing from speakers in the ceiling. Art stations were set up in rows as a man stood in the front, sitting on top of a desk with his arms crossed over his chest as he scanned the class. His eyes settled on her and he smiled, walking over to the door.

"We have another student," the lady said, handing him the paperwork. "Haven Antonelli."

"Pleasure to meet you," he said, shaking her hand. "Let me show you to your place."

He situated her at the last empty station and instructed her to just explore today. She sat there for a moment, staring at the blank canvas when he walked away. A smile tugged her lips as she picked up a paintbrush, dipping it into a container of red paint.

She started off by drawing a simple heart in the center.

———

For the first time, Haven arrived home after Dia that night. She headed up the stairs to the sixth floor apartment close to dusk, her first painting tucked under her arm. Dia was sitting on the floor in the living room, stacks of freshly developed photos sprawled out around her. She looked up when Haven walked in, her eyes darting straight to the wrapped canvas.

"How was it?" she asked, her voice guarded.

"It was good," Haven said. "I liked it."

Dia took the painting from her, unwrapping it and holding it up, examining the streaks of color and distorted hearts. "It's amazing! Let's hang it up!"

Haven laughed. "It was just practice."

"So?" Dia waded through her sets of photographs on the way to the closet to find a hammer and nails. She jumped up on the couch with it and crookedly hung the canvas in the center of the wall above it. She leaped down when she was finished and surveyed her handiwork. "It's your first painting! You should be proud."

Haven stared at it for a moment, a smile tugging her lips. "I really am."

Every night that week, after Haven arrived home from her class, another painting joined the first one on the wall. Soon dozens of photographs surrounded them, new ones that Dia had taken over the few months Haven had been there. Their surroundings, once stripped bare to avoid facing pain, were again alive with vibrant color and happy memories.

La Cosa Nostra in Chicago runs differently than the factions in the east. In New York, the five families maintain separate entities within the city while still belonging to a bigger organization as a whole. The bosses, the commission, meet regularly to discuss business and hash out solutions, maximizing profit while lowering the infighting. It's a committee, a congress of elected Mafia officials, voting and drafting and governing with their guidelines.

It's a democracy, in other words. Bloody and violent and entirely illegal, but still a democracy, nonetheless.

Not in Chicago. For decades, Chicago has been a strict dictatorship. They often try to give the illusion of fairness within the ranks, and the men play along to feel important, but nobody is truly fooled. One man runs it all. One man makes all the rules. One man decides whether you live or die.

Because of this, New York and Chicago have had a rocky relationship from the beginning. Sometimes they love each other, sometimes they hate each other, but there is always a bit of lingering jealousy. For the bosses in the east crave the independence the Chicago Don holds, while the men in the Windy City yearn for more control.

Under Antonio DeMarco's reign, the cities maintained open communication, but that had since fallen apart. They had taken to calling on each other for favors whenever one needed something, strained allies in a bigger war, but the last time someone in New York called, Salvatore ignored their pleas.

And if you aren't friends, you may as well be enemies.

Bitter blood simmered and deals were kept off the record, money passing between the cities under the bosses' noses. No one knew if they were fully aware of what went on, if they got a taste when all was said and done, but one thing was undeniable: the respect was dead.

Because of that, everyone was fair game, and they wouldn't hesitate to turn against each other. They found themselves in tumultuous times . . . another source of contention Corrado didn't want to have to deal with.

"Where are we with this casino deal?" Sal asked, swirling scotch around in his glass as he casually lounged in a chair in his den. Men sat around quietly, some steadily drinking while others, like Corrado, were just biding time until they could go.

Silence strangled the room. Nobody answered.

"It's like that?" Sal asked, bitterness lacing his voice. "None of you have anything to say? You're supposed to be the best, but none of you can talk? None of you can make this happen?"

"It's impossible," a *Capo* muttered from the other side of the room. "It can't be done, Boss."

"Nonsense," Sal said. "Nothing's impossible."

With so much heat on the organization, the Fed's attention focused on their dealings close to home, Sal was shifting business elsewhere. But while they had been busy maintaining control of a chaotic Chicago, clashing with the Russians while dealing with a long-standing Irish feud, their New York counterparts had spread throughout the country. The problem with that, however, was those factions held a grudge, so all Sal faced were roadblocks and swift denials when trying to expand.

Nobody wanted to do business with the Salamander.

"The guy who owns the casino grew up in Manhattan," the

Capo explained. "He's under protection. We can't funnel money through there without approval, and they ain't giving it. Not to you."

"Make them," Sal said. "Don't let them say no."

"Start another war? Over a casino?"

Sal shook his head, taking a small swig from his glass. "It's principle."

"It's suicide."

A dry, unmistakable laugh cut through the room. Corrado turned his head to where Carlo stood, casually leaning against the wall. "Since when are we cowards? We don't back down or ask for permission. We take what we want."

Sal nodded. "I'm glad *someone* here gets it."

"Of course," Carlo said. "And don't worry about it, Boss. You need their cooperation? I'll get it. I have ways. You know these kind of deals are my specialty."

A sinister smile twisted Sal's mouth. "I know I can count on you."

Murmurs filtered through the room in waves, but Corrado remained silent, waiting until Sal dismissed them with a flippant wave of the hand. He stood up, nodding to the boss before heading out of the mansion.

Corrado drove straight home, finding his house dark and quiet. There was no sign of Celia anywhere, and for once, Corrado was grateful to return to an empty home. He packed a bag, not even bothering to turn on a light, and scribbled a quick note to his wife.

Don't wait up for me.

Celia wouldn't. She didn't anymore. She knew if he hadn't arrived by a certain hour, he likely wouldn't make it home that night, so she would go to bed with nothing but hope in her heart that she would see him the next day—alive and well and about as whole as a man like him could possibly be.

Corrado headed to the airport that night, buying a ticket on a red-eye flight to Washington, D.C. His plane landed close to dawn and he rented a car, driving to a small diner on the other side of Arlington, Virginia. He had been there twice before, years ago, in the company of the man he was looking for that morning.

The quaint diner was fairly empty at that early hour, all of the booths vacant, with a few customers scattered along the stools around the bar. A bell above the door chimed when Corrado walked inside, everyone casually turning to look at him except for the one he was there to see. Corrado slid onto the stool beside him, their elbows ever so slightly brushing. The man tensed, a cup of coffee halfway to his lips, as his eyes slid toward Corrado.

Corrado tipped his head slightly in greeting. "Senator Brolin."

"Uh, Mr. Moretti." He set his cup down before glancing behind him, cautiously surveying their surroundings. "What are you doing here?"

"I came to speak to you," Corrado said.

"How did you know where to find me?"

Corrado shook his head as he peered at the man. "You come here every morning for coffee, two creams but no sugar, and a wheat bagel with a bit of strawberry cream cheese before heading into the city for work."

Shock registered on the man's face. "How . . . ?"

"Oh, give me some credit, Senator. You think I don't do my homework?"

Senator Cain Brolin hailed straight from New York City, born and raised near Hell's Kitchen in Manhattan. He hung with the wrong crowd growing up, had befriended some unlikely men before running for office, and it was through those men that he had crossed Corrado's path. He, along with another senator from Illinois, had been involved in a labor scheme years before with the New York and Chicago families, rigging bids on government construction sites so Mafia-controlled companies got the jobs for a hefty profit.

They still did it, as far as Corrado knew, but Salvatore had been cut out of the scheme long before, deemed too much of a risk.

A waitress walked up before Senator Brolin had a chance to respond, interrupting their conversation. "What can I get you, dear? Coffee?"

Corrado shook his head. "Just water. I—"

"He doesn't drink coffee," Senator Brolin said. "It upsets his stomach."

Corrado stared at the man as the waitress walked away. "I see I'm not the only one who pays attention."

"Of course not, Mr. Moretti."

They were quiet until the waitress returned with Corrado's water. The two men moved to a booth in the back, away from nosy ears and prying eyes.

"So what do you want?" Senator Brolin asked, picking at his bagel but eating none. "You aren't a man who makes social visits."

"True," Corrado said. "And I don't want something . . . I *need* something."

"Look, if it's about your pending case, I'll tell you the same thing I told Dr. DeMarco. I can't really—"

"It's not about that," Corrado cut him off, his eyes narrowing. "DeMarco? You spoke to Vincent about the RICO case?"

"Yes, a few weeks ago. He contacted me."

"What did he want?"

"Uh, I don't know, really. We didn't get that far. He asked what kind of influence I had within the justice department, if any. I told him my hands were tied there and the conversation ended."

That made absolutely no sense to Corrado but he shook it off, making a mental note to come back to it later. He didn't have time to be concerned about what his brother-in-law was up to. There were more immediate things needing to be dealt with. "Well, like I said, this isn't about that."

"Then what's it about?"

"There's a new place in Connecticut Salvatore wants to do business with—Graves Resort & Casino. Guy named Samuel Graves owns it."

"I know of it," Senator Brolin said. "Graves grew up with the underboss of the Calabrese family. He's a friend of mine. They both are, actually."

"I figured that much. And the Calabrese family isn't our biggest fan these days. The Amaro family, the Geneva family, sure . . . I still have connections. But the Calabrese family?" Corrado shook his head. Sal had offended them one too many times. "Without their approval, no deal."

"What do you expect me to do?"

"I *need* you to get this partnership to go through."

"Why would I do that?"

"Why?" Corrado scoffed, leaning back against the booth. "Because they're going to push for this to happen one way or another, whether it is done amicably or otherwise. They're already making plans to escalate the matter. And I'm sure I don't have to tell you, Senator, what might happen if a war breaks out between New York and Chicago."

Senator Brolin continued to pick at his bagel, his eyes downcast as he quietly sat deep in thought. "Why this casino?" he asked finally. "You have men down in Vegas already. Why not focus there?"

"Too much attention in Vegas," Corrado replied. "The gaming commission is all over us. Half of us can't legally step foot inside a casino there, myself included. We have to look elsewhere."

"Fine." He shoved his plate aside, glancing at his watch before meeting Corrado's eyes. "I'll talk to some friends and see what I can do."

"Good."

"You'll owe me," Senator Brolin said, tossing some cash on the table before standing. "You know how it goes."

"Absolutely," Corrado said. He would expect no less. "A favor for a favor."

"Precisely." Senator Brolin put on his coat, shaking his head. "Although, to be honest, keeping the peace is a favor to all of us . . . and it seems to be getting harder and harder as the years go by. I don't know what's gotten into that boss of yours."

"Yeah," Corrado said to himself as the man walked away. "Me neither."

Corrado was back home by dusk that night. He walked into his house to find his wife fast asleep in their bed, her cell phone clutched tightly in her hand. He pried it out, setting it on the small wooden stand beside the bed, and kissed her warm forehead before leaving for his club to do some work. It was a Thursday— the busiest night of the week for his business. The weekends were usually reserved for family dealings for *Mafiosi,* celebrations and obligatory dates with wives, whereas Thursday night was when the men let loose.

He stepped into *Luna Rossa,* waving off the security guard when he jumped to attention, and strolled toward his office in the back. His footsteps faltered about halfway there when the Boss's high-pitched voice called his name.

"Corrado!" Sal gestured for him to join them at the booth. "Come, have a drink. Celebrate with us!"

"What are we celebrating?" Corrado asked, pulling a chair up as he motioned for his favorite waitress. "Bring me my usual."

"We're celebrating the casino deal," Sal said. "It's finally gone through."

Corrado raised his eyebrows. "Really?"

The waitress walked over, holding out a small glass full of clear liquid to Corrado. "Here you go, sir. Top shelf. Chilled, just as you like it."

"Thank you, sweetheart." Corrado reached into his pocket and pulled out some cash, holding it out to her as a tip. She took it and scampered away as Corrado took a sip from his glass. The cold liquid soothed his throat, going down smooth.

FIJI Natural Artesian Water. No one ever asked him what he drank. They all preferred dark liquor—scotch, brandy, sometimes even bourbon—so they didn't bother inquiring about what was in his glass.

"Carlo didn't even have to do, uh . . . whatever it is he does." Sal motioned toward Carlo sitting off to the side, his arm around a young blonde woman. "Seems they came to their senses on their own. Called about an hour ago and said the deal was on."

"That's great," Corrado said, taking another drink. "It's good to know who we can count on these days."

12

The black dress shoes, half a size too small, made it difficult for Carmine to wiggle his toes. The suit, crisp and brand new, was stifling, the material scratching his skin as he rode in the passenger seat of Corrado's Mercedes.

Uncomfortable, he tugged at his blue silk tie. It suffocated him, like a noose tied around his neck. He wanted nothing more than to loosen his collar and take off the coat, maybe even kick off the damn shoes, but he was pretty sure that would only irritate his uncle.

"What's wrong with you?" Corrado asked as if on cue, cutting his eyes to him from the driver's seat. "Stop fidgeting."

"I'm trying." Carmine shifted in the seat and pushed the small switch to lower the automatic window, but nothing happened. Corrado had them locked. "It's a furnace in this car. I'm sweating like I'm in a fucking sweat box here."

"Such a way with words," Corrado deadpanned. "I advise you to keep your day job."

Carmine rolled his eyes. Like he had a choice. "Do you have the heat on or something?"

Corrado shrugged him off. "It's just your nerves."

He wanted to argue, but he couldn't. They were heading to a party at Sal's house and Carmine was on edge. He hadn't wanted to go, making excuses to get out of it, but even the social gatherings were mandatory.

"Stay away from the alcohol tonight," Corrado warned him.

Carmine looked at him incredulously. *Not drink?*

"You'll be in a room with some of the most dangerous men in the country," Corrado said, noticing the question in his expression. "You'll want to be coherent."

"Why?" Carmine asked bitterly. "I thought we were all family."

"We are family," Corrado replied. "And you saw what I did to my only sister."

Carmine's stomach lurched at the memory.

———————

By the time they reached Sal's mansion, Carmine was pouring sweat. He took a deep breath, trying to relax as he followed his uncle to the door. A young girl swiftly opened it for them. She didn't speak, nor did her eyes move from the floor.

Once they were inside, she closed the door and positioned herself against the wall out of the way. She couldn't have been older than seventeen, a skinny girl with blonde hair and pale skin.

Carmine eyed her cautiously, knowing what she was right away. Her body language, the way she slinked into the background like a chameleon blending in with its surroundings, told him a story no words would ever say.

The pressure in his chest nearly bucked his knees as he thought of Haven.

"Carmine! Corrado!"

Sal's voice drew Carmine's attention away from the girl. His godfather approached, his arm around his wife's waist. She scowled, sipping a glass of champagne, refusing to lower herself by speaking to any of them.

"I'm glad you gentlemen could make it," Sal said, pulling away from her to hold his hand out. Carmine fought a grimace as he pressed his lips to the back of it, near the man's massive gold ring.

"Of course," Corrado said. "Wouldn't miss it for the world."

Sal raised his eyebrows, dramatically looking over Corrado's shoulder. "And your wife? Where is Celia this evening?"

"She's feeling under the weather tonight," Corrado replied.

"Ah, such a pity. Send her my well wishes, will you?"

Corrado nodded, and it took everything in Carmine not to roll his eyes. There was nothing wrong with Celia. She had just refused to spend her evening with them.

They delved into conversation and Carmine lingered there, knowing it was expected of him. People sought out Sal all evening long as they arrived, and he always made a point to introduce them to Carmine. He plastered a smile to his lips as he played along with the game—pretend to like them, pretend to have fun, pretend there's nowhere in the world he would rather be.

Pretend he didn't want to fucking punch somebody in the face.

Each minute felt like forever, the two hours that passed an entire lifetime in his mind. Sal constantly chattered, boasting and bragging as he showed off for Carmine. He was being groomed, he realized. Sal was already trying to mold him into one of them, a puppet, a soldier, by poisoning his mind with thoughts of money, power, and respect.

He waited until Sal was drunk before slipping away from the group, hoping he would be forgotten. The smile fizzled from his face as he strolled through the house, heading straight for the drink table. He grabbed a small glass and filled it from an open liquor bottle, disregarding Corrado's warning. The burn lessened the pressure in his chest, unwinding the knots and loosening his taut muscles.

He leaned against the table as he drank, his attention shifting to the front door. Hours had passed, yet the girl still stood there, as silent and still as ever. He studied her, wondering where she had come from and how long she had been trapped in Sal's home. He couldn't recall her ever being there before.

She snuck a peek after a moment, tipping her head up slightly so her blue eyes met his. Her brow furrowed when she saw him watching her, and she dropped her gaze again quickly.

"What's your name?" Carmine asked curiously.

She peeked up once more but didn't have a chance to respond before laughter sounded out behind him. Carmine turned at the noise of a clinking liquor bottle and froze, the glass nearly slipping from his hand as he stared at the badly scarred face. The familiarity took his breath away.

"Her name's Annie, I think," Carlo said, casually pouring a glass of scotch.

"Abby," the girl whispered, her voice shaking as she corrected him.

"Not that it matters," Carlo continued, shrugging. "You can call her anything you want."

Carmine couldn't tear his eyes away from him. Everything about the man screamed *vile*, from his callous words to his horrid face. "I prefer to call her by her name."

Carlo looked over at him, studying him carefully. "DeMarco's kid."

"Yes."

"Makes sense." Carlo brought his glass to his lips. "She's your type."

Anger swept through Carmine. He fought to control himself, forcing his feet to stay where they were. He wouldn't be provoked. Not here, not now. "Excuse me?"

"Ah, no reason to be ashamed," Carlo said. "If it's any consolation, I've always liked to sample the help, too. Little Annie over there is a sweet thing. Submissive. Didn't even put up a fight. Not that any of them do. Well, except yours. Feisty one, isn't she? Didn't get that from her mother."

Carmine's rage spiraled over. "You son of a—!"

Before he could leap over the liquor table and pound his fists into the man's grotesque face, the noise in the room grew louder as a slew of guests filtered in. They scattered through, some heading for the door while others made their way to the back den. Carlo took a step back, tipping his glass at Carmine with a menacing smile. "Nice to officially meet you, kid. I'll see you around."

He sauntered away as Corrado approached, grabbing the glass from Carmine's hand and slamming it on the table. "Your ability to listen is astounding."

"Do you know what that motherfucker just said to me?" Carmine asked, clenching his hands into fists. "He just—"

Corrado cut him off. "I don't care. He's made, Carmine. You don't disrespect a man who earned his button."

Those words did nothing to lessen his temper.

"It's time for you to leave," Corrado said. "Party's over."

Carmine remained in place, looking to his uncle as he started walking through the house. Corrado clearly planned to stay. "How am I going to get home?"

Corrado grabbed a guy as he strolled past, clutching the collar of his shirt to stop him from leaving. "Take DeMarco here home, will you?"

The guy nodded tersely. Corrado posed it as a question, but they all knew it wasn't open for negotiation. "Yes, sir."

"That's how," Corrado said before disappearing into the den.

Carmine followed the guy outside, finally loosening his tie and pushing his sleeves up as he went. The guy was fairly young, mid-twenties at most, with bushy eyebrows and short brown hair. He wore a pair of baggy jeans and a plain white t-shirt that made Carmine bitter. Why had *he* been forced to put on a suit?

He expected to be led to yet another Mercedes, but was surprised when the guy stopped beside an old gray Impala. Carmine eyed it peculiarly. "This is yours?"

"Yeah," the guy said, unlocking the doors so they could climb in. "Something wrong with it?"

"No, I just thought . . ."

"You thought I'd drive one of those?" he asked with a laugh, nodding toward the row of black cars. "I wish I could afford one. Maybe someday. But for now, this baby will do."

"It's nice," Carmine said, settling into the cracked leather passenger seat. The interior was stained and it smelled like a combination of oil and sweat, but he felt more at ease in it than he had in Corrado's car.

Laughter cut through the air, nearly drowned out by the engine roaring to life. It rumbled as the car shimmied, violently shaking as it almost cut off. "She's a piece of shit, man, but she's paid for."

Carmine didn't say much during the drive, but the guy's endless chatter filled the car the entire time. It was distracting and consuming—exactly what he needed. When Carmine was busy listening, he had little time to think, little time to dwell on the things that kept him awake at night.

It wasn't until they had pulled onto his street and the car slowed near his house that it struck Carmine—he never gave the guy directions. "How do you know where I live?"

"You're shitting me, right?" he asked. "You're a DeMarco. Your family is like royalty, and even a fucking British hobo knows where Buckingham Palace is."

Carmine shook his head. He should have known. "Thanks for the ride."

"Anytime, man. I'm Remy, by the way. Remy Tarullo."

Carmine opened the car door but froze when that name struck him. "Tarullo."

"Yeah, like the pizzeria over on Fifth Avenue."

"Any relation?" Carmine asked.

Remy nodded. "My pops owns the place."

Carmine's mouth went dry. He suddenly felt like he couldn't swallow. He hadn't been there in a long time, but he knew the place well.

"I don't go around there much, though," Remy continued. "Pops doesn't really agree with my life, if you know what I mean. Well, hell, never mind. I guess you don't know. Yours is a part of this. You don't have to deal with him looking at you like you're a disappointment, like you're fucking up everyone's life being a part of this."

Carmine said nothing, because Remy was wrong. He knew that feeling well.

"Anyway, I'm rattling on here," Remy said, tinkering with an old gold watch around his wrist. "Sorry, man. Just a sore spot, especially since what happened to my little brother."

Those words made his heart rate spike. Dean Tarullo. Carmine nearly forgot all about the boy from the warehouse. "What happened to him?"

"He got mixed up with the wrong people, I guess. Disappeared months ago."

"So he's missing?"

Remy's voice was quiet. "Yeah, but not the kind of missing that'll ever be found, if you get what I'm saying."

Gunshots flashed in Carmine's mind, the memory of Corrado silencing the boy forever infiltrating his mind.

"Yeah," Carmine muttered. "I know what you mean."

Haven sat on the green metal park bench, watching the activity all around her. She had just gotten out of her last art class and her final project lay beside her, the canvas carefully wrapped and secured in brown paper.

It surprised Haven how therapeutic painting turned out to be, two weeks of art doing what three months of waiting and crying couldn't begin to touch. It opened up a part of her, exposing her nerves for the world to touch. Drawing was technical, the lines and details needing to be precise, but she could let go while painting and pour her emotions into it. Each piece of artwork held special meaning, but she knew others would look at it and see something entirely different.

She enjoyed that about art, like it held a hidden code only she had the key to. She was telling her story, getting out every gritty detail of her tortured life, but people were none the wiser. She could never tell the world, but there was nothing that said she couldn't show them . . . as long as they didn't know what they were looking at.

Haven sat there for a while, enjoying the peaceful spring evening, before gathering her things and heading across the street to the apartment. It was approaching dusk, and Dia would already be home from her classes. They had made plans to go out to commemorate the end of her workshop, but Haven didn't feel much like celebrating. She felt another void deep inside now that it was over.

She reached their building, walking into the lobby as the elevator opened. A man stepped out of it wearing a black baseball cap and spotted her, holding the door.

"Thank you," she said, smiling politely.

He nodded. "Don't mention it."

She stepped into the elevator and pushed the number 6 button, humming to herself as the elevator dinged with each floor. She strolled down the hallway to the apartment, finding the door wide open with Dia in the living room. She held a small brown box up, shaking it zealously before holding it to her ear. Her hair was a soaked mess of colored streaks sculpted on top of her head, chemical fumes from hair dye potent in the air.

Haven shut the door behind her and dropped her canvas beside the door. "What in the world are you doing?"

Dia swung around, startled, and smiled sheepishly for having been caught. "Just trying to figure out what's inside."

"Why don't you just open it?"

"Because it's not mine," Dia said, holding it out. "It's yours."

Haven gaped at the box. "Where did it come from?"

"A guy just dropped it off a second ago."

She blinked a few times. "The mailman?" Who would send her a package? Dominic? Tess? Maybe Celia?

"Actually, I think he was a police officer."

Haven stared at her as those words sunk in. "Did he tell you he was?"

"No, he didn't say much, just asked if you lived here and left the box. I should've asked him, but I didn't think about it. He would've had to tell me, you know. They can't lie when you ask them." Dia thrust the box forward. "I need to go wash my hair. I'll be right back."

Haven looked over the cardboard box, seeing no labels, nothing but a piece of packaging tape securing it closed. She cut the tape with a knife and opened the flaps, her brow furrowing.

Inside was a large clear plastic bag labeled EVIDENCE, holding a normal-looking notebook. Haven picked it up, along with a piece of paper addressed to her from the Department of Justice office in Chicago.

Miss Antonelli,
We send our sincerest regrets for the inadvertent seizure of your journal. It was done in error and has been returned to you in the same condition as when it was confiscated. Again, please accept our apologies. We appreciate your understanding.

Special Agent Donald Cerone
U.S. DOJ

She blinked in shock and tore the notebook from the bag. She couldn't breathe as she scanned the pages of jumbled writing, her deepest, darkest secrets on display in front of her eyes. They had seen them. They had read them. They knew where she had come from. They knew what she was.

"What is it?" Dia asked, returning from her room within a matter of minutes. She rubbed her wet hair with a white towel, streaks of color now staining it.

"It's, uh . . . a notebook," Haven replied. "They took it when Dr. DeMarco was arrested."

"Ah, damn. I thought it was something cool." Dia pouted for a second before perking back up. "So, are we going out tonight?"

"I'd rather not," Haven said, still staring at the notebook. "It's been a long day. Maybe tomorrow?"

"Tomorrow I'm going to go to Durante for spring break, remember? You can come along if you want. We could hang out down at Aurora Lake."

The thought of going back to Durante made her head pound even harder. She wasn't ready to see that place again. "Maybe next time."

"Rain check, then," Dia said. "After I get back, we're going to celebrate."

A strong breeze blew through the abandoned ranch house in Blackburn from an open window on the first floor. Desert sand swirled along the wooden walkways like mini cyclones, sullying Corrado's dress shoes. His nose tickled as he breathed in the soiled air, the scent of festering mildew mingling with the dust. It blanketed everything visible like a dull, gray shield, tarnishing colors and hiding the otherwise obvious flaws in the house—the old bloodstain on the floor in the foyer, the gashes in the wood from where someone had once been chained to the banister like a dog.

It appeared like just another forgotten stop along the desolate highway—nothing special, nothing out of the usual hidden beneath the layer of filth—but Corrado knew the truth. He had heard the stories and witnessed enough first hand to know the seemingly innocent house was practically a portal straight to Hell.

And the gatekeeper, he knew, had been his own sister.

The place hadn't been touched in months, not since the day three people had died in the adjacent stable. He had done a quick clean-up job, ridding the grounds of everything incriminating, but the rest was to be left to Haven, the next of kin.

The estate was nearly settled, every penny of the Antonelli's money transferred to an account for the girl. All that was left to deal with were the possessions, Katrina's love for material things evident in the clutter.

Corrado wasn't a superstitious man. He would often have to restrain himself from mocking Gia DeMarco during one of her delusory outbursts, but being there, strolling through the dead-silent house, he could feel the evil that still resided in it. It suffocated him, the air thick with hatred and bad intentions. It clung to everything, desperate and unyielding, trying to find its way inside him so it could live on.

He was too strong, too stubborn, to let it seep into his lungs or burrow in his chest. Instead it skimmed the surface, bristling his hair as it crawled across his skin, unforgiving and stifling. He had killed his sister, disposed of her, but the demons that possessed her, the pride and envy and vengefulness and bitter rage, remained. And he could feel it all around him, shoving against him, trying to force him back out with each step he took.

Doing his best to ignore the sensation, he spent the next hour going through the house, sifting through desk drawers and scouring rooms, looking for anything the girl might want. He thoroughly tossed the place, turning furniture upside down and destroying things with no regard in his search. He came up empty in the way of personal effects, but he found a bit of hidden cash and some jewelry he could sell for her. The rest wasn't salvageable in his eyes, nothing worth saving.

No photographs. No mementos. No nothing in the way of admitting she was family or that anyone who ever lived in that home cared she existed.

He was in a downstairs closet, throwing things around, when he hit a wall panel and knocked it loose. He kicked it aside, peering into the hole, and caught a flash of something silver. He reached inside, felt around, and grabbed a handle, having to use some force to yank it out, a heavy cloud of dust coming with it. Corrado coughed forcefully as it infiltrated his lungs, his eyes stinging.

After stepping back out of the closet, Corrado surveyed the object with puzzlement. It was a vintage Halliburton aluminum briefcase, heavy and expensive. Age had dulled the outside, but it held sturdily together.

He tried to pry it open to no avail, striking at the lock, before conceding and throwing it to the floor. He considered leaving it there, frustrated, but something nagged him not to. It had clearly been hidden away for years, maybe decades. He couldn't fathom what the briefcase contained that warranted such protection.

It was a riddle to him, a puzzle . . . a mystery he needed to solve.

Giving up, he snatched it from the floor again and headed outside, tossing it into the back seat of his rental car. He stared at the house, still feeling his skin trying to slink away. Dusk had come upon him, nighttime approaching fast as the sun dipped behind the desert cliffs. After debating for a long moment, he went back inside and gathered some books and clothing in the room with the open window. Finding a container of paint thinner in the cellar, he splashed a bit on the belongings before pulling a book of *Luna Rossa* matches from his pocket. He struck a single match and stared at the flame briefly before tossing it onto the pile.

It ignited swiftly as Corrado made his way back out to the car, leaving the front door wide open. He pulled away from the property, heading for the highway out of Blackburn. There was enough wind blowing and dirt in the dry air to cover his tire tracks, enough oxygen in the house to be certain the entire thing would go up in flames. Given the isolated location and the darkening sky, it would be hours before someone spotted the smoke, sufficient time for it to burn to the ground.

An orange glow lit up the bottom floor of the house when Corrado glanced in the rearview mirror. Mixing with the burn of sunset, it illuminated the ground surrounding it. The tension in his muscles receded as he watched it, the clawing at his skin fading away.

A small smile lifted the corner of his lips. What better way to send the evil back to Hell than a fiery grave?

13

While Dia was on her way to Durante to visit her parents, Haven awaited a visitor of her own. She sat in the living room of the quiet apartment, the notebook from the federal agent laying on her lap. She had flipped through it countless times, rereading passages as she hoped the words would somehow change.

They weren't, though. Every time she looked at them, they seemed to get worse. It was all there in black-and-white, everything she had promised to never tell spelled out with utter simplicity.

She felt like she was going to be sick.

There was a knock after a while, firm and determined. Haven set the notebook down and opened the door, her heart hammering against her rib cage. Dr. DeMarco walked in without a word and she closed the door behind him. "I'm sorry to bother you . . ."

"You're not bothering me," he said, pausing in the living room. His eyes lingered on the wall splattered with art and photos before he turned to her. "I'm glad you called. Where is it?"

She pointed to the table where the notebook lay. "I had no idea they had it."

Dr. DeMarco picked it up and sighed. "I did."

She gaped at him. "You knew?"

"Agent Cerone showed it to me. He thought I would crack if I knew what you'd written."

Her stomach dropped so hard it was like she had taken a ten-story fall, stopping just shy of slamming into the concrete. She swayed, needing to sit down. "You read it?"

"He read a few passages to me, but I couldn't help that."

Her head swam as she ran through possibilities of what he might have heard. "I'm sorry. I really am. I was upset when I wrote some of it and—"

"Don't apologize," he said, shaking his head. "You have every right to feel how you feel."

"But they know the truth," she said. "The government knows about me now."

"Yes, but there's nothing they can do about it. You have an expectation of privacy with your diary. They can't use any of it without your cooperation."

Those words sent waves of relief through her. "They can't?"

"No, but it doesn't mean they'll forget about it either. The journal may be inadmissible legally, but there are other ways for them to utilize it. And trust me when I say they will. They already are."

"How?" she asked. "What can they do?"

"Exactly what they've done." He held up the notebook. "He didn't drop this off out of the kindness of his heart. He did it to get to me . . . to prove a point."

"What point?"

"It doesn't matter," he said. "It's between me and him."

His voice was quiet, his tone clipped. She didn't ask any more questions. She knew she wouldn't get any more information from him.

"Do you have any more notebooks?" he asked. "Any more diaries?"

She nodded hesitantly. "A few."

"Get them for me."

A few turned out to be closer to a dozen. She lugged them out from her room and set them on the small table in front of Dr. DeMarco. He eyed them thoughtfully, surveying the covers, but he didn't open a single one. "These will need to be destroyed. They're too dangerous to keep laying around."

"But you said they can't use them," she said.

"You're right, but it's not just the police you have to worry about. Some of this information, if it falls into the wrong hands, would be like handing an atomic missile to a deranged man." He paused, shaking his head. "Completely catastrophic."

She didn't argue. She wouldn't. She *couldn't.*

Dr. DeMarco turned away from the journals after a moment and strolled over to the window. He looked out at the street below, the early evening sunshine bright on his face. "They know where you're living now, so I suspect this is just the beginning."

"I don't know how they found my address," she said. "I tried to lay low like Corrado told me to do."

"You didn't do anything wrong," Vincent assured her. "It was all me."

"You?"

Vincent pointed at his foot. "I forgot they were monitoring me."

Haven's gaze drifted toward the GPS monitor around his ankle, the small scar on her back weirdly itching as she thought of the chip she used to have under her skin. "They tracked you."

"Yes."

"So they know you're here now."

"Yes," he replied. "They'll be keeping an eye on this place now that they know for certain you live here. Dia confirmed it when they dropped off the box."

"But . . . why? Why can't they leave me alone? I haven't done anything."

"True, but I have."

His explanation made little sense to her.

"We should think about moving you," he continued. "The choice is yours, obviously, but I think Corrado will agree with me when I say you'll be in much better shape if you drop far off their radar until all of this blows over."

"If I don't move?" she asked. "What then?"

He waved her over to him. Slowly, she stepped in his direction, hesitating beside him at the window. He motioned across the street at a man lingering near a tree, a cell phone to his ear as he casually kicked some acorns on the sidewalk. It was nothing out of the ordinary to her. The guy was vaguely familiar, a neighbor she assumed—the one with the hat who held the elevator for her.

"Meet Agent Cerone," he said quietly. "And if you don't move, expect to see a lot more of him."

The vast RICO indictment was neatly arranged on the desk, the small bold typeface spelling out more than twenty years of criminal conspiracy. There were thirty-two counts total, hinting at involvement in dozens of crimes. Murder, assault, kidnapping, extortion, gambling, loansharking, theft . . . the list formally and apathetically detailed the violence and mayhem that had ruled the windy Chicago streets for decades, as if they were outlining something as simple as a shopping list.

> On or about March 20, 1988, in Chicago, the defendant, Corrado A. Moretti, together with others, intentionally caused the death of Marlon J. Grasso. On or about April 13, 1991, in Chicago, the defendant, Corrado A. Moretti, together with others, intentionally caused the death of . . .

On and on it went for forty-eight pages.

Corrado had spent the good part of the past hour silently reading through the charges, reliving the moments he could easily remember and a few he wished he could forget. He took it all in, absorbing the summarized case, and felt nothing even close to distress except for a simple phrase on the first page that troubled him:

> Trafficking in persons for servitude . . .

"This is wrong," he said, glaring at the words. "I never did that."

"Which part?"

Looking up from the pile of papers, Corrado eyed his lawyer across the room. Rocco Borza sat at a small round table, studying the hundreds of documents and photographs sprawled out in front of him. Three others worked alongside him, silently and studiously sifting through the stacks. Mountains of evidence surrounded them like thick fortress walls, threatening and mocking, the only thing standing between Corrado and his future.

Somewhere in their midst, tucked into the boxes or hidden in the audiotapes, lay the final nail that could be pounded into his coffin, taking his life away. Their job was to find it and make it disappear.

Exasperated, Corrado stood and strolled to the window, peering down at the street below. The office was located on the fifteenth floor of a newly remodeled skyscraper in the heart of downtown Chicago. People appeared to be little more than flecks of colored dust at this distance, tiny pests doing their best to not be squished as they went about their days.

"All of it," Corrado muttered. "Every bit of it is wrong."

A sharp, sudden laugh echoed through the room, cutting off as quickly as it had sounded. Corrado didn't turn around or try to figure out which man it had come from. It wasn't worth it. He would only want to kill them for mocking him, and the last thing he needed was another death on his hands.

Besides, if his life hadn't been on the line, he would have likely laughed, too.

Corrado had little hope of finding help anywhere in that room. The indictment, while vexing, mostly rang true. The government had done their homework. His only saving grace would be sabotaging their case.

"Do you want to take these audio recordings home to listen to them?" Mr. Borza asked after a moment.

"Depends," Corrado said. "How many are there?"

His question was met with silence. Corrado turned around, glancing at his lawyer, and saw the man peering into a massive box. "Two hundred and twenty CDs, I believe."

Corrado blinked rapidly as he took that in. Two hundred and twenty, each one eighty minutes long. "That's almost three hundred hours of recordings."

"That it is," Mr. Borza said. "Had they included Vincent's, it would be double that."

The prosecution had been granted its request to separate Vincent's and Corrado's cases under the assumption they had a better chance of a conviction that way. Mr. Borza opted to defend Corrado, likely because he was terrified of rejecting the man. And while Corrado sympathized with his brother-in-law, having to start over on a defense with his life on the line, he certainly wasn't upset about the new development.

For Corrado suspected Vincent was a man who had already given up hope.

Corrado let out a deep sigh as his cell phone started ringing. He pulled it from his pocket, shaking his head when he saw it was his brother-in-law. *Speak of the devil* . . . "Yes?"

"We have a bit of a predicament with the girl," Vincent said, pausing before adding, "again."

Frustrated, Corrado rubbed his hand down his face. She had turned out to be more of a problem than he originally thought she would be. "I'll be there as soon as possible. Tomorrow, maybe, or the next day. Keep her out of trouble until then."

He hung up, turning back to his lawyer. "Get them to throw out the recordings. There's too many for me to go through."

Mr. Borza shook his head. "It won't be easy."

"I didn't say it would be," Corrado replied. "But do it anyway."

Drops of rain trickled from the overcast sky, just enough moisture to annoy Vincent. He sat behind the wheel of his car, listening to the rubber of his wipers scraping against the mostly dry windshield. Wincing, he turned them off, only to turn them right back on again. Back and forth he went—on and off, on and off, until he finally said the hell with it and turned them off for good.

His car idled in a vacant section of the park in Charlotte, tucked in along some trees that led to a jogging path. Even with his headlights off, Vincent could see the rugged dirt trail weaving past, disappearing into a dark section of woods.

Perfect place to hide a body, he thought.

After a few minutes, a bright glow turned the corner nearby, a car slowly driving straight toward him. He cringed as the headlights shone right through his windshield, blinding him temporarily until they turned off. Vincent blinked a few times, trying to clear the sudden colored splotches from his vision, as the car came to a stop a few feet in front of him.

Vincent didn't hesitate, anger and frustration fueling the adrenaline rushing through his veins. He climbed out of the driver's seat, the evidence bag containing Haven's notebook gripped tightly in his hand. His feet carried him briskly toward the other vehicle as the door opened, a man stepping out. The guy started to speak, a single syllable barely escaping his lips before Vincent was upon him, shoving him back against his car. He thrust the notebook against his chest so hard he nearly knocked the wind from the man. "You have some nerve, Agent Cerone."

"Ah, Vincent, I don't think—"

"Doctor," he spat, cutting him off immediately. "I've told you before—it's *Doctor* DeMarco."

"Vincent," he said again. There was no humor in his eyes, no yielding in his expression. "I don't think assaulting a government official is in your best interest."

"Oh, now you want to play by the rules?" Vincent asked. "You never seemed very concerned about that before."

"Nonsense." Agent Cerone pushed Vincent's hands away, shoving the notebook into his chest in return. "Let us act like real men, shall we? Use our words and not our hands? Or is that too difficult for the likes of you?"

Vincent glared at him in the darkness as he took a step back, putting necessary space between them. "Leave my family alone."

"Family?" Agent Cerone let out a bitter laugh. "Strange choice of word given the circumstances, isn't it?"

"She's a part of my family—always has been and always will be," Vincent said. "Just because you can't comprehend that, because you can't get it through your thick skull that we actually care about her, doesn't mean we're wrong."

Agent Cerone scoffed. "The fact that you actually think you're right—that you think this situation is okay—astounds me."

"Don't talk about things you know nothing about."

"Oh, I know plenty. I read the journal, remember?"

"You invaded her privacy! You stole her thoughts!"

"So?" he replied. "It doesn't make any of it less true."

"Maybe," Vincent countered, "but tell me something, Agent Cerone. Do you have any deep, dark secrets that you'd do anything to keep the world from finding out? Even kill to keep it from being exposed?"

"Are you threatening me?"

"No," Vincent said. "I'm just trying to make you understand."

"Understand what?"

"That you have to leave her alone," Vincent said, taking a step forward again, getting right in the special agent's face. "You won't get her. You can't have her."

"Why not?"

"Because . . ." Vincent's eyes instinctively darted toward the dirt path. ". . . Because if you do, she'll die."

Agent Cerone stared at him blankly. "Now *that's* a threat."

"No, it's not." Vincent shook his head as he turned away from the man, wiping the stray raindrops from his face. "But it is a guarantee."

"You really want to do this?"

Haven stood beside the Mazda later that week, staring down at the faded lines of the parking lot. She could feel Corrado's piercing eyes from the other side of the car, stabbing through her with his doubt. He looked exhausted, but judgment was clear in his tone. He didn't believe she could do it.

"Yes," she replied. "I do."

He continued as if she hadn't spoken. "I can make alternate plans if you're not sure about this. I have the resources to keep you hidden away."

"No, I'm sure." She shook her head. The last thing she wanted was to drop out of civilization again. There was no point going forward if she couldn't *live*. "I want to go. It's my choice, right?"

"Right," he said, still staring at her with skeptical eyes. "I guess we'll be leaving then."

Haven avoided his gaze as she climbed into the passenger side of the car. All of her belongings were in boxes stacked along the back seat, her entire life once again packed up in the car. She had left a note on the kitchen table for Dia whenever she got home, saying her good-byes. She didn't say where she was going, no other explanation except she thought it was time for her to set out on her own. She promised to stay in touch but as Corrado pulled the car out on the road, heading toward the highway to leave Charlotte, she wondered just how plausible their friendship could be.

"You might want to get comfortable," Corrado said. "It's a long drive."

"How long?"

"Twelve hours, maybe."

She settled back into the seat and turned her head to gaze out of the window. "The trip to California last year took three days."

14

Carmine stood in a dank hallway, leaning against the wall beside a door. It was cracked open, the flimsy wood barely hanging on its rusted hinges. Muffled screams of agony rang out of the apartment, keeping Carmine locked in place. Whatever was going on inside of there, he didn't want to *see* it.

The prepaid cell phone in his pocket vibrated with a message for the second time that day. He slowly pulled it out, not having to look to know who it was. Sal had given it to him so *la famiglia* could constantly be in touch, the name untraceable and messages safe from wiretaps. It had gone off for the first time less than an hour ago with nothing but an address. He had dressed, slipping out in the middle of the night, and ran the few blocks to where he was needed.

But getting there and going inside were two different things.

He glanced at the new message on the phone.

Where are you?

He started to type a reply when the apartment door was ripped open from the inside. It slammed into the wall and Carmine jumped as a man stepped out. He was short and husky, a stern expression on his round face and a pair of bolt cutters slung over his shoulder. He said nothing, stalking away as Salvatore stepped out behind him.

"There you are," Sal said, eyeing Carmine.

"Yeah, I, uh . . . just got here."

"Ah, well, you missed the fun!" Sal said. "It's over now."

"Damn." Carmine slipped the phone back in his pocket, relief washing through him. "I got here as fast as I could, sir."

"It's all right, dear boy," he replied, throwing his arm over Carmine's shoulder. "You missed the demonstration, but you can still take notes."

He pulled Carmine into the apartment before he could object.

The place was vacant of furniture, the old wooden floor covered in grime. Sal led him to the bathroom and Carmine froze in the doorway the moment he caught sight of the body in the bathtub. The man's arm was slung over the side, his hand secured to the nearby sink with a pair of metal cuffs. He was stark naked and covered in blood, his brown eyes wide open and a look of sheer terror covering his pale face. Duct tape was wrapped around his head, completely covering his mouth.

A blue tarp carpeted the floor, catching the excess blood splatter, but most of it coated the bathtub and sink, the white porcelain wet with bright red. It smelled like metal, the sickening taste of copper tingling the back of his throat.

Carmine averted his gaze, trying to avoid the dead man's eyes, and Sal laughed at his reaction. "First dead body?"

"No," he said. "You know it's not."

"Ah, yes, Maura. How could I forget?"

Carmine flinched. He hadn't meant her at all. He had been referring to the incident in the warehouse but suddenly the image of his mother flashed in his mind.

Sal pulled him away from the bathroom when the other man returned with another guy in tow. Silently, the man removed the handcuffs and pulled the body from the bathtub, wrapping it in the tarp. The two of them picked it up and carried it from the bathroom. It was quick, done within a matter of minutes, with the precision of an expert craftsman.

"It helps to remember they're not people," Sal said. "They're vermin. Pests. We're just exterminating the cockroaches, *Principe.* Nobody wants to live in filth."

"It's awfully messy," Carmine said, his voice cracking.

"That it is, dear boy," Sal replied. "It isn't always, but some prefer it that way, and who am I to deny a man his indulgence?"

"You're the Boss," a stern voice said behind them. "If you prefer it cleaner, cleaner you'll get."

Carmine turned, eyeing the man from earlier. His eyes were yellowing, his skin ashy. There was hardly any life left in him.

"Ah, I don't mind," Sal said, glancing back at the bathroom. "It'll give DeMarco something to do."

The color drained from Carmine's face. "What?"

"Clean it up," Sal ordered, letting go of him. "Make sure it's in tip-top shape before you leave. We'll be out on my yacht. Feel free to join us when you're done."

Sal walked away, leaving him standing alone in the apartment. He headed out after a moment, going to the corner store to buy cleaning supplies. He stocked up on rags and gloves and bleach, and spent the next hour scouring the bathroom in the abandoned apartment.

When finished, Carmine disposed of everything in a nearby Dumpster before making the trek home, feeling more and more disgusted with himself with each step he took.

–––––––

Carmine stripped out of his clothes the moment he stepped in his house, discarding them without another look. He made his way upstairs and turned on the shower in the bathroom, waiting for it to turn hot before stepping under the spray. Steam consumed the room, his skin turning pink as the scalding water scorched his skin. He scrubbed every inch of his body, his chest aching as he fought with everything he had to bottle in his emotions. He forced it down, swallowing the feelings as he rubbed his outside raw, trying to wash away the filth that lurked beneath the surface.

Afterward, Carmine put on some fresh clothes and headed downstairs. The place was furnished now, the piano having been delivered just the previous morning. It sat in its place in the corner of the living room, a black vinyl cover safeguarding it. Boxes were scattered amongst the rooms, belongings strewn all over. It was a disaster, takeout containers layering the kitchen counters as trash piled up on the floor.

He opened the freezer door, ignoring the growl of his empty stomach as he reached for the bottle of Grey Goose vodka he had stashed there. Popping the top off, he brought it to his lips and took a swig, savoring the burn as it coated his throat. He needed it, hoping the alcohol would numb his body and clear his mind of what he saw that night. He wished it would kill the ache that had resided in him for what felt like forever, but he knew deep down nothing would make that go away. Part of him was missing, a gaping hole where his heart had once been. It was the part he had left behind with *her*, the part she carried with her wherever she went.

Charlotte? he wondered. Was she living with Dia? What was she doing with her time? The questions nagged him night after night, but he kept them to himself. Where Haven went and what she did was her business. He had no right to ask anymore. He had given that up when he walked away.

The crimson flower design stood out strikingly against the gold background of the massive banner. Haven stood on the sidewalk below it, staring up at it, fascinated by the way it swayed in the gentle breeze.

SVA, the logo said. School of Visual Arts. According to Corrado, it was one of the best art schools in the country. Haven had never heard of it, but that wasn't surprising—she only vaguely knew about New York City itself.

It's the largest city in the United States, she silently reminded herself. It's the city that never sleeps. It was the first place she thought of when contemplating leaving Charlotte. If she had to go elsewhere, she thought it should be there. After all, Carmine had said it was where people followed their dreams.

And dreams, at that moment, were all she had anymore.

The crowd moved around her as she stood in the way, but she couldn't tear her eyes off the school banner. Half of it was out of admiration, the other half sheer terror, because looking away from it meant having to look somewhere else.

Haven had gotten used to being around others over time, slowly adapting to living in society, but the atmosphere in the city intimidated her. She had encountered more people the past twenty-four hours than she had seen her whole life before then. People were everywhere—walking, running, riding, driving—a continuous flow of bodies rushing past her like a fast-moving river. And she could do nothing but stand still in the center, hoping with everything inside of her that it didn't sweep her away.

She said she could do it, that she was sure, but doubt crept in further the longer she stood there. The noise, the lights, the smells . . . her senses were on overload as she tried to take it all in.

Corrado stepped out of the building in front of her, a folder of papers tucked under his arm. He forced his way through the crowd and stopped in front of her, his presence drawing her attention. "You're enrolled for the fall."

Her eyes widened. "I am?"

"Yes," he said. "That gives you about four months to settle in."

Four months . . . it seemed so long, but it was no time at all. She had already survived that long since Carmine had left her.

The thought of him made her chest ache. She glanced back at the banner with a frown, wishing she could hear his voice. She wondered what he would think, what he would say if he were there with her.

Don't you fucking be scared, tesoro, was the likely culprit.

She got lost in that moment, sinking deep into her thoughts, but Corrado's next words pulled her right back to the surface. "I enrolled you under the name Hayden Antoinette."

Haven blinked rapidly. "What? Why?"

"Because it's close enough to your real name for you to recognize it, but further enough from it that hopefully nobody else will."

She started to argue, but Corrado silenced her with a pointed look. The ache in her chest grew. He had taken away her identity.

Time moved swiftly, days passing in an unyielding blur. Corrado rented a place for her on Eighth Avenue in the Chelsea neighborhood of Manhattan, a one-bedroom apartment on the first floor of a newly renovated brownstone. The other residence in the building, an identical apartment on the second floor, stood vacant.

"This is for you," Corrado said one afternoon about a week after arriving in New York, handing her a small package. Haven opened it, dumping it out onto her new kitchen table. He had furnished the place with the necessities, nothing fancy, but better than she imagined she would have. The couch, the tables, the lamps, the chair—every bit of it belonged to her, even though Corrado told her not to get attached.

"Don't keep anything you wouldn't be willing to walk away from," he had said. "When people are looking for you, you might have to run."

Run. If Haven was tired of anything, it was running.

She focused her attention on the contents of the package: a credit card, some identification, and a small black cell phone.

"My number's the only one programed into the phone," Corrado said as she picked it up and eyed it warily. "Call me directly if you need anything. I'll handle your bills, but you can use the card for any other expenses. It'll come straight out of your inheritance."

"My inheritance," she whispered, picking up the credit card and the driver's license, both adorned with her fake name.

"Yes, I finally settled the estate," he explained. "There was an unfortunate accident with the house, though."

She peered up at him suspiciously. "Accident?"

"It burned to the ground. Quite sad."

"I bet," she mumbled, shaking her head.

A small smile tugged his lips. "You don't need it, though. You have a nice place here. I'm sure you'll settle in fine."

The apartment was equally spaced between the two buildings that would hold her classes, a few minutes walk in either direction for her to get where she needed to go. Everything surrounded her, so she didn't need to venture far from her apartment, and there was no reason for her to drive anywhere.

She did venture outside, though, after Corrado departed for Chicago again. She spent the afternoons wandering the area, memorizing streets, getting to know the neighborhood. It was monotonous and predictable, the same routine again and again, but to her every day sort of felt like a new adventure. There were different people, different street vendors, and different activities going on all around. And she infiltrated the chaos, mingling amongst it all, completely unnoticed and out of the limelight.

It admittedly wasn't what she had expected. Even standing in the center, she still felt as if she were on the outside of it all, looking in. It was a familiar sensation that oddly put her at ease, numbing her anxiety as she faded once more into anonymity.

At least, when invisible, she remained safe.

15

The docks, Third and Wilson

Carmine stared at the message, heaviness in the pit of his stomach. He wanted nothing more than to delete it, pretend it never arrived, but he knew Sal would never accept that excuse.

And neither would Corrado, for that matter.

"There's a big shipment coming in by boat in a few days," Sal had said about a week ago. "They'll load it onto trucks then leave. The trucks will stay parked there, just sitting there all night, begging to be stolen. A crew comes in and takes their pick. Easiest job there is."

Carmine had blown it off at the time, figuring it had nothing to do with him. He hadn't been integrated into their hierarchy, hadn't been put into a street crew or assigned a *Capo*. Since the moment he had arrived, Sal had just used him for odd jobs, taking him wherever he went and involving him in his personal schemes, but this was different. This simple message—*The docks, Third and Wilson*—changed everything.

This wasn't just Carmine being dragged into other people's messes—this was him *creating* the mess. He was no longer the accessory after the fact. He was about to be the goddamn perpetrator.

Pulling a chilled bottle of vodka from his otherwise empty freezer, Carmine tore the top off and took a long swig, letting the burn make its way through his system. Liquid courage, people called it, but he was starting to think of it as Stupid Shit Serum. Grey Goose got him through quite a few rough nights since arriving in Chicago, giving him the strength to do things he was certain only an idiot would truly enjoy doing.

Tonight, he ventured to guess, would be one of those times.

He grabbed his gun from the top of the kitchen cabinet where he stored it and slipped it into the waistband of his jeans before leaving the house. His brand new Mercedes was parked in the driveway, shining under the gleam of the streetlight. He had leased it a week before, the same night he had had the conversation with Sal.

Carmine slid into the driver's seat, taking a deep breath before starting the car. The drive through town was quick—*too* motherfucking quick—and he pulled up at the docks just a few minutes later. It was dark there, barely lit by moonlight, but he could make out the rows of white delivery trucks parked behind a flimsy chain-link fence. The gate was secured with a chain and lock, but there was no sign of any security beyond that.

Carmine parked and surveyed the trucks, unsure of what to do or where to start. There had been no planning, no instructions, no explanations, but he knew without a doubt there were expectations. And if he didn't deliver, he would be the one to pay.

He climbed out of the car and started toward the gate when a car wildly whipped from behind a nearby building, sending gravel flying as it headed for him. The headlights were blacked out. Through the darkness, Carmine couldn't see who was driving.

Jumping back, his heart thumped violently against his rib cage as fear coursed through his body, fueled by strong adrenaline. He reached for his gun, terrified, as the car came to a sudden halt and the doors flew open. Two guys jumped out, one from the passenger seat and one from the back. The doors had barely closed again when the car was thrown into reverse, skidding backward before speeding away.

It happened fast, mere seconds passing before the two guys approached. Carmine had his gun by his side, his finger hovering on the trigger, when a voice cut through the night. "DeMarco? That you?"

Carmine loosened his grip on the gun, his shoulders relaxing a bit. "Remy?"

Remy Tarullo stepped out of the shadows and into a sliver of moonlight. He was dressed all in black, a ski mask loosely sitting on his head. "Hey, man! Good to see you again! Mr. Moretti said they were gonna be sending you out, you know, having you join the crew. Told us to show you the ropes."

Relief washed through Carmine, rinsing away his unnerving fear. He slipped his gun back away. "My uncle sent you?"

"Yeah. He's our *Capo*, you know . . . guess he's yours now, too." Grinning, Remy slapped him on the back. "You aren't nervous, are you?"

"No, I just . . ." He didn't know what to say. He was nervous, but he couldn't admit that. ". . . I figure it's better to not go at it alone."

"I get it," Remy said, pulling out a pair of gloves from his back pocket and slipping them on. He pulled his mask down, covering his face, before reaching into his coat for an extra set of both. He tossed them to Carmine, who put them on as Remy's friend did the same. "You don't happen to have any bolt cutters in your car, do you?"

"Uh, no," Carmine said, slipping the ski mask over his face. He suddenly felt short of breath, suffocated by the thick material. "I didn't realize I'd need any."

Remy shook his head slightly. "You really did come unprepared."

Understatement of the fucking year, Carmine thought. "Can't say I've ever stolen anything."

"No big deal," Remy said. "You probably never had to, being a DeMarco and all. You even get to shadow the Boss all the time . . . man, you don't know how many of us would kill for that chance."

There was no hostility to Remy's voice, but the words made Carmine's hair bristle. He didn't doubt there were people out there who would kill him if they thought it might get them closer to the top.

Remy looked around briefly, as if searching for something, before pulling some small tools out of his back pocket. He jogged over to the fence, easily and methodically picking the single lock. He ripped the chain off before shoving the gate open, him and the other guy running inside. Carmine was right on their heels, dashing inside the lot behind them.

"Split up," Remy ordered, waving at the two of them. "Check those trucks and tell me what you find. Make it quick."

The men scattered to different sides of the lot, gunshots cutting through the night air as they shot off the locks on the back of the trucks. Carmine followed their lead, pulling out his gun and aiming it. He winced when he fired his first shot, his hand shaking and throwing off his aim. He had to shoot it three times before he hit his mark, hearing shouts through the lot as the men shared their loot.

Carmine flung open the back of his first truck, squinting in the darkness to read the boxes. "Uh, laptops."

"Try the next one," Remy ordered. "Too risky. A lot of them can be traced."

Carmine moved on to the second truck, getting the back of it open with the first shot. "TVs."

"Hot-wire it."

Carmine blanched. He didn't know the first thing about hot-wiring anything.

The third man found a load of DVD players and broke a window to climb in the front of the truck. Remy looked over, seeing Carmine just standing there.

"Come on," he said, grabbing Carmine's shirt and pulling him to the front of the truck. "Break the window and get in."

Carmine did as he was told, having no time to argue. He

smashed the glass and unlocked the door, climbing inside. Remy pulled a flat screwdriver from his back pocket, passing it through to him. "Carefully put it in the ignition and see if it'll turn."

The truck on the other side of the lot came to life a few seconds before Carmine's did. Remy let out a laugh as the engine roared and shoved Carmine humorously. "See, man? Let me drive it to the spot. Follow us in your car."

Wordlessly, Carmine jumped out of the truck and ran back to his car. He ripped the mask off, taking a deep breath to steady himself as the two trucks tore out of the lot. Carmine followed them into traffic, staying right on Remy's bumper.

Sirens blared in the distance. The trucks pulled off the main road as the flashing lights rapidly approached, weaving through traffic. Carmine was on edge, watching his rearview mirror as he pulled into the alley behind them. Three cop cars flew right by after a moment and kept going.

Carmine exhaled sharply. *Too fucking close.*

They drove down some back roads deep into the south side, coming to a stop at a large warehouse. They pulled the trucks inside, out of view, and Carmine parked his car behind them.

"Woo!" Remy hollered, jumping out of the truck. His friend joined him, the two of them cheering and sharing fist bumps, before Remy turned to Carmine. "You feel that, man? That high?"

Carmine nodded and smiled, although it was a lie. All he felt was nervous energy surging through him. He was on the verge of being sick.

The three men spent the next hour watching the trucks being unloaded before taking their payment and driving away. The stolen trucks would be discarded at a chop shop, nothing going to waste. Every bit of it was salvaged and sold, melted down and concealed, so not a fragment of evidence remained.

"What a rush," Remy said, fidgeting excitedly in the passenger seat. "That's what I live for. The violence I could do without, but the stealing . . . there's nothing like it. There's no way I'm gonna be able to sleep tonight. I mean, fuck! It was a close one! Just a minute later and we would've gotten caught. Ain't that shit great?"

Carmine found nothing great about it.

"Let's go get a drink," he continued, not giving anyone else any time to speak. "I don't know about you, but I need something hard after the night we just had."

Finally something Carmine agreed with.

———

Luna Rossa was busy for a Friday night. Unlike the last time Carmine had been there, black sedans were merely sprinkled within the sea of other vehicles, cars and trucks of all types crammed into the lot. It looked almost like an entirely different place, loud hip-hop music blaring from the building.

"I've never been here," Remy said. "Lived in Chicago my whole life, been involved in this shit for years, and until tonight I never stepped foot in this place."

Carmine's brow furrowed. "Why not?"

"I don't know," he said. "Didn't feel right just walking in. Guys like us only get invited here when we've done something to piss Mr. Moretti off."

"I got invited by the Boss as soon as I moved here," Carmine said. "Looked like a different place that night. It was old school."

Remy laughed. "You know how the saying goes: When the cat's away, the mice will play."

The guard looked at them when they entered, his eyes narrowing as he scanned the three men, but he said nothing, merely tipping his head in greeting. They walked through the club, bass from the music vibrating the floor beneath their feet, sending energy spiking through Carmine's body. He found it relaxing, the chaos and noise so loud he could hardly think.

A booth in the back was empty. He slipped into it, barely having enough time to sit down when a woman stopped right in front of him. He looked up at her, their eyes connecting right away as her serious expression shifted with a smile. "DeMarco, right?"

It took him a moment to place her face . . . the same waitress who had served him last time. "Uh, yeah. Hey."

"You want your usual?" she asked. "Vodka?"

He was stunned she remembered. "Yeah, sure."

"And your friends?" She turned to them. "What can I get you fellas?"

They rattled off their orders—scotch for Remy and a beer for the other guy. The waitress walked off, returning with their drinks in a matter of minutes, and Carmine downed his before she even had a chance to walk away. She let out a laugh, holding her finger up to silently tell him to wait, and retrieved the whole bottle of Grey Goose from behind the bar. "Anything else you need, just let me know. My name's Eve."

"Thank you, Eve," Remy said, winking. "You can call me Adam."

Carmine rolled his eyes as the girl laughed before walking away. "That was fucking terrible."

"Hey, girls love that cheesy shit," Remy said. "I know my girl does."

"You have a girlfriend?" Carmine asked, pouring himself another shot.

"Yeah, her name's Vanessa. How about you?"

Carmine downed his second shot. "No, no one."

"Well, then." Remy took a swig of his scotch. "Lucky for you, Eve seems interested."

Remy pointed with his glass and Carmine turned his head, spying the waitress leaning against the bar. Her eyes were focused directly on him.

Sighing, Carmine turned back around and said nothing.

The night wore on in a haze as the alcohol flowed freely to their table. They drank the hours away, laughing and yelling and carrying on. Girls came by their table, flirting and giggling, mooching off their drinks instead of buying their own. Carmine hardly noticed, too drunk to even care.

Too drunk, in fact, to care about much of anything.

It was after midnight when the atmosphere suddenly shifted. The thumping bass from the speakers abruptly cut off, and the chaos of the crowd dulled to a murmur. Carmine looked around, tensing as his uncle casually strolled through the club, his hands in his pockets. He headed to his office but stopped at the entrance to the hallway when Eve yelled his name. She said something to him, pointing directly at their booth, and Carmine blanched as he turned around. *Fuck.*

Corrado diverted then, bypassing the hallway to head straight for them. "Carmine," he said, his eyes scanning the three of them. "Gentlemen."

"This is Remy," Carmine muttered, pointing at him. "And this is . . ." He hesitated. He didn't even know the other guy's name.

"I know who they are," Corrado said tersely.

"Mr. Moretti, sir," Remy said. "Great club you have here."

Corrado nodded, but offered no response to the compliment.

"We were just getting a drink," Carmine slurred. "You know . . . or two."

"I see that," he said. "You guys just be careful getting home."

"Yes, sir," Remy said. "Thank you."

Corrado's eyes lingered on Carmine for a moment before he walked away, disappearing down the hallway.

Remy shook his head, gulping the last of his drink. "Man, he's intense as fuck."

Carmine laughed bitterly. "You're telling me."

Thump. Crash. "Shit!"

Haven's eyes shot open at once at the noise. Disoriented, she stared at the low ceiling above her bed, surveying the textured white paint as if it could somehow tell her what happened. Sunlight streamed in the small window across the room, sweeping across the faded wooden floor. It was warm, almost peaceful, and all was silent for a long moment.

Had she imagined it?

She started to close her eyes again when another bang rang out. Following it was the clicking sound of high heels against wood, accompanying a woman's frustrated growl. Confused, Haven's stomach twisted as she threw the covers off and climbed out of bed. She walked through the apartment at the same time the high heels started along the floor above her, following her direction as they made their way to the staircase.

Quietly, Haven unlocked her front door and peeked out as the woman started down the stairs. She was tall and curvy, her long hair an unnatural burgundy shade. She lugged two empty cardboard boxes with her and dropped them in the small foyer right outside of Haven's door.

Haven didn't want to be caught spying, but the woman saw her before she could slip back away.

"Hey there!" she said enthusiastically. "I'm Kelsey."

"Hav—uh, den." She cleared her throat. "Hayden."

"Do you live here, Hayden?" Kelsey asked, pausing to take a breath but not long enough for Haven to actually answer. "Thank God you're a *she* and not a *he*. I was totally convinced I was going to be living above some creepy bald dude with a potbelly who smelled like beef jerky and cheap beer. Yuck. Could you imagine? Ugh, I bet you were worried about the same thing, some pervert tromping through here all day and night. Am I right?"

Haven smiled timidly. She hadn't even considered it. The thought of someone moving into the vacant second floor never crossed her mind. She had assumed Corrado rented the entire building.

"So what do you do?" Kelsey asked, raising a perfectly arched eyebrow. "Are you a student or something?"

"Uh, yes," she replied. "I go to the School of Visual Arts."

Kelsey's eyes widened. "No shit? Me too!"

Haven was taken aback. "Really?"

"Yes, really," Kelsey said. "I'm majoring in graphic design. You?"

"Painting."

"Fine arts? Ugh, I could never do that." Kelsey waved her off dismissively. "So have you gone to orientation yet?"

"No." Haven frowned. She had been putting it off, her nerves getting the best of her. "I should probably do that, though."

"Totally," Kelsey said. "I was about to head over there myself. We can go together! Everyone needs a walking buddy, right?"

"Right." Haven glanced down at herself, still wearing her plaid oversize pajamas. She hadn't even brushed her hair yet. "I need to change first."

"Me, too," Kelsey said, scrunching her nose in disgust. "I can't go out looking like this. I broke a sweat and didn't even enjoy myself doing it."

Kelsey immediately turned, leaving the empty boxes where she had discarded them as she bolted back up the narrow stairs.

———

Twenty minutes later, Haven sat on the bottom step in the foyer, freshly showered and dressed in a pair of jeans and a red tank top. She tinkered with her keys as she waited, listening to the noise from above as Kelsey stomped around her apartment. Her loud footsteps echoed through the old building, the flimsy floorboards creaking and groaning. The building, although freshly remodeled, showed signs of its age.

Haven waited, and waited, and waited some more. Another twenty minutes passed, and she was about to give up, when the sound of Kelsey's high heels started clicking her way. Haven stood and glanced up the stairs, studying the girl as she approached. Her clothes were pristine, vibrant and crisp as if they had never been worn before. Her lips shone brightly from gloss, her eyes masked with dark makeup. She was a pretty girl, but Haven thought she looked much better without all of that covering her face.

"Ready?" Kelsey asked.

Haven nodded. She had been ready.

Although she wore six-inch high heels, Kelsey walked confidently, her steps effortless, her stride long. Haven strolled along beside her, listening as the girl prattled on and on about everything. By the time they reached the school a few blocks away, Haven knew all she needed to know about Kelsey—an only child, the daughter of a congressman, she had failed out of NYU and decided to give art school a chance after her parents forced her to move out to teach her responsibility.

"So, yeah . . . my dad says I only get three strikes before he cuts me off, and failing out of NYU was number two."

"What was the first strike?"

She shrugged. "Being born?"

Haven's expression fell as she blinked a few times, those words striking her hard. She certainly could relate. "You really feel that way?"

"Sometimes," Kelsey replied. "I've always had a strained relationship with my parents. My dad's never here in New York and my mom, well . . . if I'm not on the bottom of a wine bottle, she's not interested."

"That's, uh . . ."

"Pathetic?" Kelsey laughed. "I know it is. And first strike was actually probably when I almost failed graduating from high school. I was boy crazy and skipped too much. That's over with, though. I'm committed now. I don't have time for a boyfriend."

The two of them stepped inside the building on 23rd Avenue, following the signs to the busy registrar's office to have their student IDs made. Haven stared at hers when it was finished, ignoring the wrong name and instead focusing on the fact that her picture was prominently displayed on a badge granting her admission.

For the first time in her life, she was a student at a school.

The afternoon was chaotic as she went from building to building, meeting the administration and other students. Overwhelmed,

Haven's palms sweated and heart raced as they showed her the studios and enrolled her in classes, explaining the requirements as they took her around to the various galleries. Mandatory volunteer hours, optional summer sessions, semi-annual galas, and monthly counseling sessions . . . her anxiety skyrocketed, but it seemed to melt away the moment she stepped into the school's library.

Tall stacks of books surrounded her, towering above her, welcoming her in to their familiar embrace. It reminded her of life in Durante, a time and place she had tried not to dwell on during the weeks as she settled into New York. Her life was starting anew—new people, new places, new things, new chances—but the old seemed to still have a strong grasp on her heart, squeezing and constricting, forcing her to hold back, longing and yearning for the love she had left behind, instead of looking ahead.

She lost Kelsey somewhere in the bustle of the day and ran into her again hours later as the sun was setting, the long day coming to an end. Kelsey stood in the lobby of the fine arts building next to a guy with spiky blond hair, her hand pressed against his chest, her face lit up with intense fascination.

They separated after a moment, the guy jogging past Haven and out the door. Kelsey stood there, silently fidgeting as she bit down on her bottom lip, but she let out a squeal when she spotted Haven. "My God, did you see him? Wasn't he gorgeous?"

"Uh, sure," Haven said, glancing out the massive glass windows at the boy standing on the sidewalk with a group of friends. "Who is he?"

"His name's Peter something-or-other. He's a senior! He asked me for my number, so of course I gave it to him. God! Do you think he'll call? I hope he calls."

Haven looked at her incredulously. "I thought you didn't have time for a boyfriend."

"I don't," she said, waving her off with a laugh. "I can date, though. No harm in that. Besides, a girl has to have some kind of fun, right?"

Rhetorical question, but Haven shrugged in response anyway.

"What about you?" Kelsey asked as the two of them headed out on their way back home. "Do you have a boyfriend?"

The innocent question, asked offhandedly, was like a sucker punch to Haven's chest. It was the first time someone had asked her that. "Not anymore. I did, but . . . not anymore."

Kelsey's elated expression dimmed. "Ah, bad breakup?"

"You could say that."

Kelsey shook her head. "You're better off without him, whoever he is."

"Carmine," Haven mumbled. Something about saying his name aloud, acknowledging he existed . . . that they had once existed together . . . loosened the tight knot in her gut just a bit.

"Breakups suck," Kelsey said. "I've never really been a one man kind of woman because of that. My dad always says 'don't put all your eggs in one basket, honey,' so I figure, why put all my hope in one man? I like to play the field a little, see what's out there."

Haven would come to learn during the next few weeks, as she got to know Kelsey more, exactly how much of an understatement that was.

Every few days there was a new love interest, boy after boy coming in and out of the apartment above hers. Peter, Franco, Josh, Jason . . . Haven stopped keeping track eventually. She would hear them tromping along upstairs behind Kelsey, the sound of their heavy footsteps echoing through the connected apartments, and she would smile politely if she ran into them in the foyer, but she didn't bother to say hello.

The faces all blurred together over time, a mash-up of a man Haven had no interest in getting to know.

School started during those few weeks. Classes and studio sessions swallowed up Haven's time—painting, drawing, and art history taking up most of her days. After school was over, instead of heading home, she would go to the library and lose hours inside those thick walls, drowning in books and studying text. It monopolized her attention, but she flourished under the stress.

For yet again in her life, she had a strict schedule. Yet again, she had a list of things to do, and if it wasn't done she knew there would be consequences. Failing wasn't an option because, in Haven's world, failing was as good as giving up on life.

16

The knock on the office door was so timid Corrado barely heard it over the music in the club. He ignored the faint tapping, his gaze trained on the dingy briefcase on the desk in front of him.

After a minute or so, another knock sounded. Still weak. Hesitant. Again, Corrado ignored it.

Mafiosi knew they were supposed to carry themselves with confidence, especially when dealing with the most dangerous of men. He didn't care if his men were staring down Lucifer personally, surrounded by brimstone and hellfire leading them straight to eternal damnation. They needed to keep their composure, be prepared to fight, and never *ever* let their fear show. The streets were ruthless and their rivals wouldn't hesitate to make a move at the first sign of weakness. Vulnerabilities were exploited, and the worst thing they could do was come off as uncertain. It didn't matter if they were wrong—they needed to always appear right.

And Corrado, most certainly, was *not* convinced.

It took a while for the third knock to come. It was louder, more determined. "Come in," he yelled, sitting back in his chair and glancing at his Rolex as Remy Tarullo entered, tentatively shutting the door behind him.

"You wanted to see me, sir?"

"I did," he stated. "I told you to be here at nine. It's nine oh three. You're late."

"But I was here," he said defensively. "I was out in the hall."

Corrado raised his eyebrows. "You have the audacity to make *excuses?*"

"No, I, uh . . ."

"I'm not interested in what you have to say. It's meaningless to me. I don't care if you're run down in the parking lot. You had better drag your mangled body in here with enough time to be in my office when I *tell* you to be in my office. Nothing short of death is reason enough to be late. Do you understand me?"

"Yes, sir."

Corrado could smell his fear. It reeked, filling the office with the sickly-sweet scent of sweat and panic. Remy was tall and skinny with shifty eyes, but they were more about his sudden fear and less about deception. Was he hiding something? Maybe, but he didn't let it show. He had been called into a *Capo's* office—a wise man knew those situations didn't often end well. But he came, shoulders square, head held high.

What he lacked in brains he made up for in guts.

Remy was a decent earner and good at what he did, never once getting caught, which was why he had entrusted Carmine to his crew.

"Word around is you're the best at picking locks," Corrado said.

"Uh, yes," he said. "Not to brag or anything, but I've yet to find a lock I couldn't pop on the first date."

Remy grinned, trying to break the tension, but Corrado didn't find it funny. He just stared him over, pondering whether he was the right one for the job.

Tense silence ensued. Remy stood in place, making no move to sit. "Aren't you going to have a seat?" Corrado asked.

Remy's eyes darted to one of the empty chairs, but he still didn't move. "You didn't invite me to sit down, sir."

Maybe he was smarter than Corrado originally thought.

"Can you get this open?" he asked, turning the briefcase around to face the boy. Remy took an immediate step forward, his eyes narrowing as he studied the small lock.

"Uh, yeah, I think so."

"Think so or know so?" Corrado asked. "If you're not certain, turn around and walk out that door. I'll find someone better equipped to do the job for me."

Remy cleared his throat. "With all due respect, sir, there is no one better equipped. If I can't get it open, nobody will."

Touché. Corrado nodded, motioning toward the briefcase, silently permitting him to prove his worth. Remy eyed the lock for a moment before reaching into his pocket and pulling out a small tension wrench and a pick. Corrado watched, fascinated that the boy carried them with him. "Do you make it a habit to keep tools in your pocket?"

"Yes," he replied. "You never know when you might need to pick a lock or hot-wire a car, so I try to keep what I'd need on me just in case. Same reason you always carry a gun, I'm guessing."

"Do you carry a gun also?"

"Not always," he admitted. "I tend to only have it when I think my life might be on the line."

"Do you have one with you now?"

Remy hesitated. "Yes."

Corrado smiled at that and relaxed back into his chair, tapping his foot to the beat of the music from the club. Two songs from *Sinatra's Greatest Hits* passed before Remy made any progress, a smile lighting the boy's face as he finally jimmied the lock. The briefcase cracked open, not wide enough to see inside, but enough for Corrado to take over.

Remy returned his tools to his pocket and took a step back. "It's all yours."

"You're not going to ask me what it is?"

"No."

"You're not at all curious?"

"Well, of course, but it's none of my business," he replied. "If you wanted me to know, you would've told me, right?"

"Right." Corrado stood up, motioning for the boy to follow

him as he stepped out of the office and met up with one of the security guards in the hallway, standing watch outside the office door. "Tell the bartender Tarullo's drinks are on the house. Anything he wants, he gets—no questions asked."

The guard nodded. "Yes, Boss."

Corrado stepped back into his office, shutting the door and locking it before strolling over to the desk. He pried the briefcase open and blinked rapidly as he eyed the contents.

A lone VHS tape.

Corrado had considered a lot of things—guns, money, gold, even body parts—but an old movie had never crossed his mind.

The worn carton encasing it crumbled as soon as he picked it up. He tossed that part aside and surveyed the black tape, finding no label. It was seemingly blank, but Corrado knew better. Someone had gone to great lengths to hide that videotape.

Stepping back out of the office, he looked at the security guard again. "Fetch me a VCR."

The man's brow furrowed. "A VCR?"

"Yeah." Corrado waved him off impatiently. "Make it fast."

Twenty minutes passed, then thirty, and finally forty-five before the guard returned with a used VCR cradled under his arm. He passed it off to Corrado, who took it into the office and closed the door. Plugging it in, he hooked it up to the small television on the corner of his desk that displayed the security feed.

Immediately a movie started playing, a cartoon with a princess and an obnoxiously catchy tune blaring in the background. Corrado grimaced and ejected the tape, throwing it aside before carefully inserting the one from the briefcase.

Nothing happened for a moment; the numbers on the VCR counted away, but the screen remained as black as night. Corrado was about to give up, feeling duped, when the screen flickered and up popped a face he hadn't seen in years.

Frankie Antonelli.

The footage jumped and rolled. Corrado pushed the tracking

button, trying to straighten it out, but nothing helped. He gave up and sat back in his chair as Frankie started to talk, the sound cracking and buzzing when he turned up the volume.

"I, uh . . . I've never been a religious man. I come from a religious family, my pop's a devout Roman Catholic, just like my granddad back in the old country, but me? Naw, I never believed it. I don't believe in prayer or salvation, don't believe in Heaven, but I do believe in Hell. I got to. I live in it."

Frankie ran his hands down his face as he paused. "I don't believe in confession . . . you know, asking for forgiveness and all that . . . but I get why the guys do it. We ain't never gonna be forgiven for the shit we do, but it eases the conscience. It's hard to walk around every day, carrying so many secrets. And I got secrets. I got plenty of sins in my book. And I ain't asking to be forgiven for them, I ain't asking to be saved, but I gotta get them out. I can't carry them around anymore . . . not when I spend every day in this Hell, staring at them in the face."

Corrado's stomach dropped, coldness creeping through him. He felt the urge to eject the tape, throw it in the trashcan and set it on fire. What kind of wise guy—what kind of *man of honor*—breaks his vow of silence on video? He was disgusted, disgruntled, and downright angry.

But another part, deep down inside, rendered him immobile. Maybe it was curiosity, or maybe instinct, but something forced him to keep watching the tape.

For the next thirty minutes, Corrado stared at the screen, stunned speechless as a man he once considered a mentor, a friend, a brother, who turned into a traitor, a coward, a rat, spilled a secret that shocked even him. He had seen it all, he had done it all, but the words Frankie spoke, the horrific truth that spilled from his lips, was something Corrado couldn't begin to fathom.

Unimaginable. Appalling. He felt sick.

Corrado's disgust only grew with each word, his contempt now unwavering. Everything he believed, everything he knew, had been put into question by a shaky half hour of spineless confession.

"So, yeah, that's the truth," Frankie said quietly, shaking his head as if in disbelief at his own words. "I have to live with what I did . . . what I helped do. I ain't gonna apologize for it, or like I said, ask forgiveness. I had to do what I had to do. But I carried it with me for a long time, and I couldn't carry it anymore.

"If someone's watching this, I'm probably long dead. I won't be surprised if it's this that gets me killed. I've been feeling it lately, the feeling that something's going down that I don't know about, so maybe it's only a matter of time before this comes out. And maybe I deserve to die for this, but I ain't the only one. No, if this is how it ends, if this is how I escape from this Hell to go to the next, I hope the devil goes down with me, too. It's only fair, since he controlled it all."

Frankie leaned forward and shut off the camera. Corrado stared at the black screen, the office swallowed in uncomfortable silence.

Shell-shocked. It was the only word to describe how Corrado felt.

Getting his bearings straight, he ejected the tape and locked it in a desk drawer. He unhooked the VCR and grabbed the cartoon, meeting the security guard in the hallway once more. "Where'd you get this?"

"Stole it," he said. "Broke into a few houses down the block until I found one."

Corrado shoved it back to him. "Return it."

The guard blanched. "What?"

"You heard me," he said. "What kind of jackass steals from a little girl?"

17

Time heals all wounds. *Il tempo guarisce tutti i mali.* It's been said time and time again, but what they don't talk about are the jagged scars left behind. What they don't tell you is that sometimes, when ignored, the wounds fester.

What started as a scratch, barely scraping the surface, will turn into a gaping gash, ripping and tearing at the flesh, until all that is left is a jumbled mess of frayed nerves and broken organs. The pain demands to be felt, and you don't even notice until it is too late. Until it cripples you, bringing you to your knees.

Carmine drank every night as the heartache lingered, some-times consuming so much that he blacked out. His days were full of agony, his nights no better as he relived everything in his dreams. The only time he escaped was when he got lost in the blackness. Every night as he slipped into unconsciousness, he prayed that if he did wake up, he would finally forget everything. He just wanted to fucking *forget*.

It never worked, though. Every morning he would awaken and feel even worse than the night before, the cycle starting all over again. He was spiraling out of control, but he didn't care. It didn't matter what happened to him anymore . . . all he wanted was some *peace,* no matter the cost.

He went out almost every night to *Luna Rossa* with Remy, the loud music and crowds distracting him from his thoughts long enough for the alcohol to take hold. He met others, some that might have been good friends under other circumstances, but none of them could get past that wall he had built. And seeing Remy with his girlfriend, a thin redhead with blue-green eyes, didn't help Carmine ward off his grief. It reminded him of what he had lost, what he had left, what he needed, but what he could no longer have.

Carmine kept it together in public, playing that part expected of him, but when he was alone the crack in his façade deepened.

It was early evening when Carmine staggered out of his bedroom, bare chested with his baggy jeans hanging loosely from his hips. He tightened his belt, moving it down another notch, as he made his way downstairs. He stepped over some clothes laying in the hallway as he headed to the kitchen. The air-conditioner wasn't working, the house stifling and air hazy. It burned his chest to take a deep breath, his head pounding as he poured sweat.

His stomach growled loudly, pangs of hunger striking his sides. Opening the fridge door, he pulled out a carton of leftover Chinese food. He eyed it suspiciously, trying to remember when he had ordered it, before shrugging it off and grabbing a fork.

He grabbed a stack of mail from the counter as he ate and sorted through it: bills, notices, junk, shit that wasn't even addressed to him. He picked up a cream-colored envelope, seeing his name written neatly in cursive on the front. Tearing it open, he pulled out the card, reading the gold inscription on the front.

Dominic DeMarco and Tess Harper request the honor of your presence at their wedding on October 27 . . .

There was a knock on the front door, fierce pounding that echoed through the silent house. Carmine didn't bother to investigate. Instead, he leaned against the counter as he stared at the invitation, hardly tasting the cold noodles he forced down. A wedding. His brother was getting married.

The pounding continued, harder and louder, before the front door thrust open. Sunlight streamed through the foyer briefly and then the door slammed.

"Carmine?" Celia shouted.

"In here," he mumbled, his mouth full of food. Footsteps veered in the direction of the kitchen, Celia appearing in the doorway within a matter of seconds.

She paused, staring at him with wide eyes. "What are you doing?"

"Eating." He held out the carton. "Want some?"

Celia let out a frustrated groan as she reached for the switch on the wall. The bright light was harsh and Carmine squinted, trying to shield his eyes. "Christ, is that necessary?"

"Necessary?" Celia's voice was laced with bitterness and disbelief. "It's called electricity, Carmine. It's a part of civilization. Of course it's necessary! But honestly, I'm surprised the lights work around here. The telephone certainly doesn't seem to."

Carmine sighed but kept his mouth shut. He wasn't in the mood to argue.

"Look at this place," she said, crinkling her nose. "It's disgusting! It reeks!"

Again, Carmine said nothing. He watched as his aunt started tearing apart the kitchen, throwing away trash and gathering dirty dishes. His feet stayed planted in one spot as she cleaned, muttering under her breath in frustration.

After the kitchen was decent, she turned to him with a glare. "I can't believe you have *nothing* to say. When did you stop caring?"

"Is that what I did?" he asked quietly. "Stopped caring?"

"That's how it seems."

He stared back at her. The ache in his chest, dull when he had woken up, grew stronger as they stood there. "I wish that were true."

She scoffed, but the sound of a cell phone going off in another part of the house silenced her. Carmine pushed past her and strolled to the living room, snatching it off the couch cushion where it lay.

"So the phone *does* work," Celia said. "I'm shocked."

"Not now." Carmine shook his head. "Just . . . not now."

"Is the whole house destroyed?" she continued, ignoring him.

"If the downstairs in this bad, I'd hate to see upstairs. Do you at least have clean clothes? Are you doing laundry? Are you *bathing*?"

"Of course I am," he snapped, unable to take her questioning on top of everything else. "Why don't you go nag someone else? I've had more than enough of you interrogating me."

"I'm not interrogating you," she replied. "It's just that this place is a disaster! It feels like an oven in here."

"I've been busy."

"Too busy to pick up after yourself?"

"Yes."

"Too busy to open a window?"

"Yes."

She stared at him, not satisfied with his answers. "What's really going on, Carmine? What's happening with you?"

He laughed dryly. "I have things to do, Celia. I don't have time for this."

"Fine," she conceded. "This conversation isn't over, though."

After Celia left, Carmine threw on a shirt and shoes before heading back into the kitchen. He glanced in the freezer, frowning when he saw it was empty—no food, not even any ice, and more importantly, no vodka. He entertained the thought of stopping by the store to grab a bottle when his phone beeped, reminding him he had an unread message.

Hit Sycamore Circle tonight.

Carmine stared at it with dread. Sycamore Circle was in the north side of the city, an area he knew vaguely but only by name because it was well-known Irish territory. *La Cosa Nostra* respected the boundaries in Chicago, imaginary or not.

Carmine grabbed his gun before heading out of the house. He hopped in his car and started on the road to the north side of the city when his phone rang, Remy calling and telling him to pick him up along the way. Carmine detoured a few blocks to Remy's house, honking the horn as he pulled into the driveway of the modest sky-blue house with the large porch and flimsy chain-link fence. A pit bull puppy ran in circles in the grass, yapping frantically at the intruding car.

Remy came out right away, flying off the porch and leaping over the fence before stealthily sliding into the passenger seat. The smell of marijuana lingered on his skin and clothes, the man's eyes completely bloodshot.

"Man, this is crazy," Remy said, relaxing into the seat as Carmine pulled away from the house. "Irish 'hood? Shit's about to get real."

Carmine sighed. "Let's hope not."

The sun set as they drove to Sycamore Circle, meeting up with the other guys about a block away. They scoped it out, lounging in Carmine's car with binoculars as music played from the speakers. Remy pulled out a blunt, lighting it and taking a long hit. He held it out and Carmine promptly grabbed it from him, dropping the binoculars. He couldn't remember the last time he had smoked, the drug infiltrating his system and relaxing his taut muscles. Relaxing back into the seat, he closed his eyes, all of his worries leaving in a slow exhale of smoke.

The job was quick and easy, in and out in minutes. Not a single shot was fired, not a drop of blood spilled as the men surrendered the trucks without a fight. They had caught them off guard and completely unprepared. The last thing they had expected was for Sal to make a move in their territory.

———————

Night had fallen long before, the air stifling from the late summer heat wave that had been tormenting Chicago for days. Corrado was sweating profusely, his back completely soaked, but he didn't dare remove his suit coat until he was safely inside his residence. He let it drop to the floor right inside the door, exposing his white button-down that was splattered with fresh blood. He quickly unbuttoned it, wanting to dispose of the offensive material before anyone saw, but the light gasp from the stairs told him he was too late.

Busted.

"I thought you'd be in bed," he said without even looking at her, more to explain than apologize.

"I was," Celia said softly. "I couldn't sleep."

He removed his shirt before making his way to the living room. He lit the fireplace swiftly, tossing the garment in. Burning soiled clothing and disposing of incriminating evidence was something he did so often he could accomplish it in his sleep.

He could sense Celia behind him, following, watching. He could also sense her trepidation, and he didn't like it. Celia always found a way to understand.

"Is something bothering you?" he asked. "You don't usually wait up."

"I was worried." She paused. "Well, I *am* worried."

"It's ridiculous for you to lose sleep," Corrado replied. "I'm fine."

"I know," she said. "It's not you I'm worried about."

Corrado watched as the flames consumed the shirt before turning to his wife. A frown tugged her lips, the subtle wrinkles forming on her face more noticeable tonight. He had just seen her a few hours before, but she appeared to have aged years within a single day.

His beautiful wife—he wanted to take her anxiety away.

"I'm hurt," he teased, running the back of his large hand along her warm cheek. "My wife doesn't worry about me? I must be doing something wrong."

He leaned down for a kiss, hoping her soft lips would help erase the brutal memories of the day, but she pulled away with a dramatic sigh.

"I'm serious, Corrado. I know you can take care of yourself."

Celia grew quiet, her frown only deepening. Corrado knew there was so much more she wanted to say.

"But?" he asked. "I know you're not finished."

"But Carmine's a different story."

Corrado exhaled exasperatedly. He should have known. "Not again, Celia. Please."

"He's new to all of this," she said, ignoring his pleas. "I worry about him."

"He'll figure it out," Corrado said. "He has no choice."

"I know, but he's hurting," she continued. "You should've seen him tonight."

Corrado shook his head. "It's not my problem."

"Not your problem? You're his *Capo*!"

"And I make sure he does what he needs to in the business," Corrado said. "His personal life is none of my concern."

"But—"

"But nothing," Corrado said, cutting her off. "I have my own issues to deal with right now. You know that."

"I know, but he's falling apart."

"There's nothing more I can do," Corrado insisted. "And quite frankly, your meddling is only hurting him more."

"He's my nephew, Corrado. I'm asking you to help him."

"I am." He shook his head. Their definitions of help were vastly different. "I'm helping him the only way I know how."

"By forsaking him?"

"By making him stand on his own two feet."

"But he's not." She hesitated as if she weren't sure what to say. "There's something going on with him. I don't know what it is, but it's not right."

"Becoming one of us," Corrado said quietly.

"No, it's more than that." She sighed with frustration. "It's hard to explain. I don't like the people he's involved with. Why can't he work with you personally?"

Corrado let out an abrupt, bitter laugh. "Have you forgotten what I do, Celia? Do you need me to remind you?"

He could tell she tried to fight it, but a look of disgust briefly passed over her face. It twisted his stomach with guilt, having to strike her that way.

"The stealing is a lot safer than the rest," Corrado continued. "And the kids he's working with are harmless . . . relatively speaking. You don't have to agree with me, or even like it, but I hope you'd at least respect it. Respect *me*."

"I do."

"Then drop it," he said. "I'm doing all I can."

Celia said nothing. Her lack of response told Corrado he had won that round, but he knew there would be more battles. More requests, more denials, more conflicts. His wife was just as determined as he was stubborn.

"I'm starving," he said, hoping to change the subject as he headed for the kitchen. He had been busy all night and hadn't had time to eat. "Can you make me something?"

Celia scoffed. "I'm going back to bed. If you want to eat, I'm sure you can *help* yourself. You've never relied on anyone else before, remember, so why start now?"

18

"We have a problem."

Corrado shook his head as he stood by the window of his lawyer's office. "Don't tell me that. I came here because you said you had good news."

"I do," Mr. Borza said. "Well, I did, but it seems petty now in comparison."

Sighing, Corrado turned to him, not in the mood for guessing games. This case was proving to be harder than his others to shake. "Just be out with it."

"We got your arrest record thrown out since it would bias the jury. All previous trials resulted in not guilty verdicts or dropped charges."

"That's good," Corrado said. "It's progress."

"Yes," Mr. Borza agreed. "The prosecution's barred from mentioning any of it. Your criminal record, on the other hand, is still in, but it's squeaky clean."

"I know," Corrado said. "What else?"

"The judge ruled the wiretaps at the club weren't covered by the warrant, so those tapes are inadmissible. I'm still working on the ones from your home. The crime scene photographs were thrown out, since they would unfairly incite the jury. Being guilty under RICO is a far cry from being a cold-blooded murderer."

Not as far of a cry as the man thought. "Anything else?"

"Tommy DiMica and Alfredo Millano are both off the witness

list. Seems Tommy recanted his story and now says he doesn't even know you, and Alfredo was assaulted a few days ago in his jail cell. He's alive, but in no condition to testify."

Corrado nodded. He knew those things already. Tommy and Alfredo were both former *La Cosa Nostra*, and men who turned against the oath had to pay the price.

"So what's the problem?" Corrado asked. "Seems their case is falling apart."

"The problem is there's a new name on the list."

Mr. Borza picked up a piece of paper and held it out to him. Corrado took it and scanned the list, the name at the bottom jumping off the page:

Vincenzo Roman DeMarco

Corrado said nothing as he stared at it, forcing himself not to react.

"It's possible they're planning to subpoena him and he'll just plead the fifth," Mr. Borza continued.

"Or he's testifying against me to save his own ass."

"A plea bargain," Mr. Borza said. "I'm not certain, since I'm not on his case anymore. I'll request a deposition, of course, but in the meantime I'll see what I can do about getting this to go away permanently."

Corrado looked away from the paper and handed it back to the lawyer. "No."

"No?"

"Let me handle it," Corrado said, turning to the window once more. "I'd rather you not breathe a word about it to anyone."

The loud shrieking echoed through the room. Haven reached beside the bed, slapping the alarm clock to silence it. She was exhausted, her body weary, and entirely too comfortable wrapped in the comforter for her to even consider getting up. A strange buzzing noise met her ears but she did her best to block it out, not caring enough to investigate. She assumed it came from upstairs in Kelsey's apartment, and if that was the case, she probably didn't want to know what it was.

It stopped eventually and silence overtook the room. The moment she finally slipped back to sleep, a succession of bangs jolted her awake. Groaning, she hauled herself out of bed.

"Wake up!" The thick door muffled Kelsey's voice. "I *know* you aren't still in bed! Do you *see* the time? Up, up, up! Rise and shine!"

"Calm down," she yelled, her voice scratchy. "I'm awake!"

"You better be!"

Kelsey obnoxiously pounded a few more times even though she knew Haven was on her way. Sighing, she unlocked the door and pulled it open, immediately having a coffee cup thrust in her face.

"Here," Kelsey said. "It's probably cold now since you took so long."

Haven rolled her eyes, knowing she had bought it right down the street. "Thank you," she said, bringing it to her lips and taking a sip. The hot liquid made her tongue tingle as it burned, but she drank it eagerly anyway.

"You're welcome." Kelsey stepped past her into the apartment, watching her with a peculiar look on her face. "From the look of you, though, you probably need about ten more of them. Did you get *any* sleep last night, honey?"

"Some," she said, shrugging as she continued to drink her coffee—straight black, just as she preferred. It was the opposite of the one in Kelsey's hand, which she ordered every morning like clockwork on the way to school—venti soy chai latte, four pumps, no foam, extra hot. Haven had no clue what any of that meant.

"Some." She echoed the word, her expression telling Haven she didn't believe it. A smile crept on to her lips after a second, a sinister twinkle in her eye. "Did you have company last night? A guy, maybe?"

"Of course not!" Haven said quickly, looking at her with disbelief as the blush rose onto her cheeks. "I would never do . . . *that*."

"Pity," Kelsey joked. "You could use a good fuck to loosen you up."

"Kelsey!"

The two girls had easily become what most people would consider best friends, despite the fact that they were polar opposites in nearly everything. Kelsey grew up lavishly, never having to clean or even wear the same outfit twice. She had had the type of childhood where she asked for a pony and actually got it, whereas Haven had been doomed to sleep in the same grungy stables as one.

Kelsey loved going to crowded parties and got her news from trashy gossip magazines. Haven preferred staying home and losing herself in books. But still, something about her put Haven at ease. She reminded Haven of the life she had left behind, the one that part of her still yearned to belong to . . . the life she had nearly built with Carmine.

It still hurt her to think about, a burn in her chest constantly reminding Haven that a part of her soul had been torn away. It was a piece he had taken with him, one that would always be wherever he was.

Most days she could think of Carmine fondly, remembering things they had done together and everything he had said, but it wasn't always that way. There were still times when she questioned if she would ever smile again, worried the pain would one day swallow her whole.

"Hey!"

Haven glanced at her friend as she waved her hand in front of her face. "Huh?"

"Haven't you been listening to me? Jesus, girl, get yourself together. We have a long day ahead of us. You can't space out on me." Kelsey looked around. "Where's your phone? I tried calling you on my way here but you didn't answer."

"Really?" she asked, unable to recall hearing the phone ring.

"Where were you, anyway? You aren't a morning person. Usually I have to drag you out of bed."

"Oh, I just got home," Kelsey said. "Stayed at Derrick's last night. We—"

Haven held her hand up to stop her. "Enough said."

"Jealous wench." Kelsey scrunched her nose as she surveyed Haven. "Find your phone, and get dressed while you're at it. There's no way I'm going *anywhere* with you looking like that."

Rolling her eyes, Haven headed for the bedroom. "Always so bossy."

"One of the many reasons you love me," she yelled.

Haven took sips of her coffee as she headed into her bedroom, spotting the black phone laying on the bed. *Three missed calls* lit up the screen, the first two from Kelsey, and she froze when her eyes fell upon number three. She stared at the name as her heart pounded forcefully, the blood furiously rushing through her veins.

Corrado Moretti

"You don't have any liquor?" Kelsey hollered through the door. "What are you, a nun?"

Haven set her phone down, laughing, as she walked to the dresser. She dressed quickly, pulling her hair up to get it off her neck.

"Never mind," Kelsey yelled. "I'll get some upstairs!"

Haven shook her head and glanced at the clock, seeing it was a few minutes before ten. Sitting on the edge of the bed, she grabbed her phone again. Her hand shook nervously as she scrolled through her contacts, stopping when she reached Corrado's number.

It rang a few times before she heard the click. "Hello?"

Haven breathed a sigh of relief at the soft, feminine voice. "Hello, Celia."

"Haven!" she gasped. "It's been a while!"

"I know." She immediately felt guilty. "I've been . . . busy."

"No need to make excuses, kiddo. I just worry about you."

"I know you do, but I promise I'm fine," she said. "Is Corrado there? He called this morning."

"Did he?" she asked, surprised. "He stepped out earlier, said he had some things to take care of."

"Oh, okay," she said. "Can you tell him I called?"

"Sure, sweetheart."

"Thank you," she said quietly, suddenly feeling queasy. She bit her lip, trying to hold it back as she said good-bye and hung up the phone. She had a long day ahead of her and needed to keep it together.

She grabbed her things and headed back out to find Kelsey in the living room, staring at one of the paintings on the wall. "What do you see?"

Jumping, Kelsey turned as she clutched her chest. "I see a girl who needs to get laid," she said sarcastically as she surveyed Haven again. "She also needs some makeup for those bags under her eyes and a pedicure if she's going to wear flip-flops."

The girls departed, taking a taxi the few blocks to the Rainbow Art Center. Every semester they were required to do five hours of volunteer work, whether in a gallery or library or out in the community. Haven was excited about the opportunity to help, while Kelsey seemed to be dreading it more than anything.

Kelsey pulled the lid off her cup and gulped her drink as she started toward the entrance of the building. "Remind me why we're here again."

"You said they were easier to deal with than the artsy-fartsy intellectual types who spoke in haikus and took themselves way too seriously," Haven said, recalling her exact statement.

"That's right." Kelsey smirked. "Never trust a man in a beret with a French accent. He's either gay or a con artist. Trust me on this."

Haven shook her head, not even wanting to know the story behind that.

Chaos reigned, screeching voices and thunderous footsteps dominating the building. The moment the door shut behind them, a form came right for Haven. She braced herself as a little girl slammed right into her legs. Snotty nosed and wide-eyed, the child stared up at her with a mixture of confusion and fascination.

She smiled at the little girl adoringly, her thick dark hair fanning in her face and partially shielding her view. "Uh, hey, sweetheart."

The little girl said nothing, just continued to stare.

"They're animals, I swear," Kelsey muttered. Haven glanced over and laughed when she saw she had two little boys running around her legs, hindering her ability to walk. "It's a good thing I like the zoo."

A lady approached them, unfazed by the madness, and smiled warmly as she wrangled the children. "You must be the volunteers," she said, pulling the little girl away. "This is Emma, by the way."

"Hello, Emma."

The little girl smiled at the sound of her name before scampering away and joining the others. The teacher, Mrs. Clementine, showed them around before calling the class to order with a loud whistle. The noise echoed through the room, bouncing off the walls and stilling everyone immediately.

"In your seats," she declared. They started to oblige and Haven jumped into action, helping hand out the art supplies.

The Rainbow Art Center was attached to the local community center, where they taught free art classes for underprivileged children. The name struck Haven as ironic, because there was nothing bright or colorful about the place. The walls were a drab gray color and the paint was chipping, the building falling apart.

Most of the kids who came to the center had no families, every one of them deemed at-risk by the state. So young and innocent,

Haven knew they were all only one step away from living the life she had once lived.

They spent two hours painting and drawing with the kids. By the time class was over, Haven was worn out. Their caregivers trickled in to pick them up, and Emma met Haven at the door, smiling brightly as she held her paintings.

"I made you!" she exclaimed.

Haven laughed and took it, gazing at the distorted stick figure with the abnormally large head and big brown hair. There was a large red mouth on the face and a big yellow sun taking up half of the sky.

Haven smiled. "Beautiful."

"You can keep it."

"Thank you," she said. "It's really good."

Emma's eyes lit up. "Can I be an artist like you?"

"Absolutely," Haven said. "You can be anything you want to be."

19

Carmine stuck a screwdriver in a delivery truck's ignition and tried to turn it, but nothing happened. It wouldn't budge.

Groaning, he yanked it back out as another truck sped from the lot, spraying his windshield with loose gravel. He used the screwdriver to jimmy open the ignition, cracking the plastic cover as he forced it off, and pulled the red power wires from the cylinder. He stripped them quickly before tightly twisting the two of them together. The lights on the dash immediately turned on as the radio came to life, a heavy rock song rattling from the cheap speakers. Carmine grabbed the brown starter wires next and stripped them, immediately striking them hard against the red ones.

Mistake.

It sparked, a strong jolt of electricity burning his glove-clad fingers. He dropped the wires and cursed loudly as someone banged on the side of the truck.

"Come on, man!" Remy yelled. "Get that shit started!"

Frustrated, Carmine grabbed the brown wires again and held his breath as he touched them to the others. It sparked once more, but the engine roared to life before Carmine was forced to let go. He shook his hand, trying to wave off the pain as the truck idled. He had had to resort to hot-wiring a few times when the old screwdriver-in-the-ignition trick failed, but he had yet to figure out how to do it without damn near electrocuting himself.

Remy jumped up on the side of the cab and looked in. Even though his face was concealed by a black ski mask, Carmine could tell he was grinning with pride. "That's how you fucking do it, man," he said, reaching through the window to punch him on the shoulder. It was playful, but Carmine winced at the blow. "Drive it to the spot, will you? I'll meet you there."

Before he could object, Remy snatched Carmine's keys from his lap and ran off. Carmine put the truck in gear, knowing he had no other choice, and sped from the lot near the docks by Lake Michigan. His heart pounded ferociously as he pulled into the busy Chicago streets behind his Mercedes, his eyes surveying the other cars for signs of trouble. Distracted, he lost track of Remy as he hastily weaved through traffic, squeezing into tight spots where the delivery truck wouldn't fit.

It took nearly a half hour for Carmine to reach the secluded warehouse on the outskirts of town. The other delivery truck was already parked behind the building when he arrived and was being unloaded by a few associates of *La Cosa Nostra*. Carmine pulled in beside it and climbed out from behind the wheel, standing along the side to watch as the men wordlessly went to work.

It fascinated him how the drop-off ran fluidly like a well-oiled machine. Everyone had a job and everyone did their part, like runners in a relay race. It was habitual, a routine he had fallen into as he slowly submerged himself into life as a member of a street crew. Every week it was the same thing, the same schemes with the same guys, but in different locations around the city. And while it hadn't gotten better, and Carmine ventured to guess it never would, he had learned the art of detachment—being able to step out of himself for a moment and look the other way.

He was fractured, one half of him the still slightly naïve boy who drank himself unconscious to try to forget, the other half the man, numb to everything, who just went through the motions day after day. It was that man who went out at night and did the things that were expected of him—the theft, the violence, the deception—but it was the boy, heartbroken and disgusted, who woke up in the morning to face the aftermath.

It took about an hour for the trucks to be unloaded. Afterward, the owner of the warehouse handed Carmine an envelope of cash. He glanced inside, stealthily counting the bills, before slipping it in his pocket with a nod. He strolled away, the transaction complete, and hesitated outside the warehouse. His eyes scanned the dark property and he was about to start panicking when his Mercedes sped up, coming to a halt a few feet from him.

"What the hell took you so long?" Carmine asked when Remy climbed out. "It's been over an hour."

"Had something I needed to take care of," he replied, tossing Carmine's keys to him. "The car's nice, man. Runs smooth. You're a lucky bastard."

"It's all right, I guess," Carmine muttered, getting in the driver's seat while Remy slipped in beside him. "What was so important you ditched the job for it?"

"I didn't *ditch* the job." Remy laughed. "I just took a little detour, that's all. And it was nothing, really. Just had to pick something up from Vanessa. You know how it is."

Carmine didn't press him to elaborate. He figured if Remy was being evasive, he probably didn't want to know.

Haven let out a deep sigh as she headed into the brownstone, fumbling with her keys. She had been at a school function half the night, but slipped out as soon as she could get away with leaving. Exhaustion infiltrated every cell in her body and slowed her steps to a snail's pace. She grabbed the knob on her door, her brow furrowing when it turned right away. Her heart thumped erratically, realizing it was unlocked.

Silently, carefully, she stepped inside, horrified to see her drawers open from being rifled through. She pulled out the container of pepper spray she usually carried before tiptoeing through the dark apartment. She stepped into the quiet kitchen and reached for the light switch, but the moment her fingers touched it, a thump rang out upstairs.

Haven's heart stalled as she looked at the ceiling instinctively. The hairs on her arms stood on end as a strange feeling crept through her, the sensation that she wasn't alone nearly buckling her knees.

She stood as still as a statue, trying to convince herself she had been hearing things, when an unmistakable crash upstairs registered with her ears. She gasped, trembling, as she heard footsteps, originating in Kelsey's bedroom and heading down the hall. They were heavy, clomping against the wooden floor as if weighed down by steel. It reminded Haven of how Michael used to walk, the sound of his boots in the house as they sat in the dank cellar awaiting punishment.

She debated briefly as the footsteps started down the stairs, dizzy from the flood of memories. He was too close for her to make an escape undetected, so she slipped into a hallway closet and quietly shut the door.

The footsteps drew nearer, entering her apartment and walking right past where she hid, disrupting the natural light. She held her breath, not daring to move a fraction of an inch while they were there. The apartment was a flurry of noise as they shut drawers and moved things around, breathing heavily but never speaking.

It felt like an eternity before they left again. Haven heard them exit the building and she slipped out of the closet, even more stunned at her apartment this time. The chaos she had encountered minutes earlier was gone, everything back in its place, cleaner than she had left it that morning. Even the front door had been meticulously locked again, leaving no sign that anyone had even been there.

———

Carmine stepped into *Luna Rossa,* nodding to the bouncer before making his way to the back where his crew huddled around a large booth. He started toward them but barely made it a few feet when someone stepped directly in his path. "Come with me."

Carmine blanched as Corrado motioned toward the door. He had his coat on, a small flash of silver gleaming from his belt when he moved. Gun.

"What?"

"Just come on."

Carmine hesitated but followed his uncle out of the club, slipping into the passenger seat of his car as Corrado climbed behind the wheel. He started it up without hesitation, throwing it in gear and speeding from the lot.

"Where are we going?" Carmine asked. Had he done something wrong?

"A few Irish have been hanging out on Clark Street, harassing the owner of the pawn shop on the corner."

Carmine eyed him peculiarly. "And?"

"And we're going to make them go away."

Carmine's stomach dropped. Work. He hadn't been on a job with Corrado before, and he wasn't looking forward to going on one now. "I'm guessing they're there now?"

"They're playing the video poker machines," he said, his voice dripping with disgust. Corrado hated gambling, he had learned, even though a lot of his money came from underground sports betting.

They were silent the short drive to the store. Corrado pulled right up to the curb and got out without a word. Carmine followed him inside, immediately hearing the ruckus in the back. The men shouted and laughed, their thick Irish accents echoing through the shop as they banged against the machines.

Corrado walked straight to the back, taking a direct path to them. Carmine cut along the front, slipping down a side aisle out of view to sneak up behind them.

The men saw Corrado coming but barely had enough time to react before he grabbed the back of a guy's head and slammed it

into the machine. He cried out with the loud crunch, blood pouring from his face as his nose shattered. He grabbed it, staggering
when Corrado let go of him.

Corrado stealthily reached for the man's gun the same time
the second Irish pulled out his own. They aimed at each other simultaneously as Carmine stepped out of the aisle behind the guy,
flicking off the safety of his pistol.

Carmine pressed the muzzle against the back of his head. He
tensed when he felt it, his hand shaking slightly. Corrado grabbed
his own gun from his coat with his other hand and pointed it,
too. The Irish man hesitated but slowly raised his hands in the air,
taking his finger off the trigger. Carmine disarmed him and took
a step back.

Corrado put the first guy's gun in his pocket, keeping his own
cocked as he stared him down. "If I ever hear of you coming back
here, I'll do more than break a nose. Do you understand?"

"Yes."

"Be sure to tell O'Bannon I said hello," Corrado said, his cold
tone causing goose bumps to spring up on Carmine's skin. "Now
go."

They hesitated, looking dumbfounded as they stared at Corrado, and Carmine groaned. "You heard the fucking man. He said
go, so go, motherfucker."

They shot Carmine angry glares before scurrying for the exit.
One of the men lingered at the door, though, turning to eye them
with anger. "You want us to stay out of your territory, tell your boss
to stay out of ours."

"We don't step foot in your territory," Corrado said. "Ever."

The man shook his head. "You sound like you actually believe
your lies."

They were lies. Carmine himself had raided Sycamore Circle,
so he knew for a fact they had crossed the imaginary lines.

Corrado sighed when they finally left, sliding his eyes to Carmine. "You and that mouth. The elders believed we should be

gentlemen in how we spoke and always presentable in how we dressed. How hard is it to put on a suit?"

Carmine glanced down at his clothes. He had on jeans and a black button-up shirt, nothing out of the ordinary. "Suits are for weddings and funerals."

"So I suppose you'll be wearing one on Sunday, then?"

Carmine tensed. "What's Sunday?"

Corrado started to comment but his phone rung and stopped him. He pulled it from his pocket and glanced at the screen.

"Make him pay up," Corrado said, motioning toward the man working the counter. "A couple thousand."

Carmine nodded hesitantly as his uncle turned away, bringing his phone to his ear to answer it. "Hello? Is everything all right?"

He knew immediately from the casual greeting that it was a personal call. He watched with confusion as Corrado bolted out of the door—he wasn't the kind of person to take a personal call while on business.

He shrugged it off, nothing about the day making much sense, and headed to the front. "You got money for me?"

"I have some," the man said.

"How much is some?"

"Uh, about five hundred."

"You've gotta be fucking kidding me," Carmine said, stepping behind the counter where the man stood. Carmine spotted a baseball bat hidden near the register for protection and grabbed it.

"Okay, maybe a thousand," the man said quickly, backtracking. "Yeah, I have a thousand."

"It's twenty-five hundred," Carmine said nonchalantly, stepping back out from behind the counter.

"I know, but I don't have that right now," he said. "My kids have summer camp, and my wife's pregnant. I can have it next week, but I just don't have it all today."

Carmine walked through the shop as the man fumbled with the safe and pulled out a stack of bills. His hand shook as he counted them out, and Carmine tried to fight back his guilt. They were just innocent people, caught in the middle and trying to make a living, but if it wasn't them extorting the cash, it would be someone else. Someone less civil, who would demand a whole lot more.

Besides, he thought, it was better than the alternative. If he weren't robbing people of money and possessions, he would be robbing them of their lives, and he would much rather take what could be replaced.

"Not good enough," Carmine said, swinging the bat with as much force as he could. It slammed into the glass display case, shattering it and sending shards flying everywhere. He threw the bat behind the counter, nearly hitting the man with it, and grabbed the cash.

Carmine walked out, unable to even look at the shop owner, and opened the passenger door of Corrado's car. He climbed inside and saw his uncle was still on the phone, a serious expression on his face as he listened to whomever was on the line.

"I'll be there in the morning," he said, pulling away from the curb. "Yes, I'm sure. I'll notify you when I land."

He sighed exasperatedly as he ended the call and glanced at Carmine. "How much did you get?"

"A thousand."

"That's it?"

"That's all he had."

Corrado reached over, snatching the cash from him. He counted it out, barely paying attention to the road as he sped through the city.

Carmine's curiosity got the best of him after a bit. "Are you taking a trip or something?"

"Or something," he responded, tossing a single hundred dollar bill at Carmine and shoving the rest into the center console. "You're too soft. He would've given you more."

"I lost my temper and smashed one of his displays," he said. "I figured I cost him more in damages than he owed."

"Fair enough," he responded as he pulled back into the parking lot of the club. "You need to learn to control your temper."

"I'm working on it," he said, eyeing his uncle suspiciously. He seemed distracted, his eyes darting toward the clock on the dashboard. "Where are you going?"

"Somewhere I'm needed," he said, evading. "*Where* doesn't matter. But I have to leave right now to be back in time for the wedding, so you need to get out."

"Wedding," Carmine muttered, the word striking him. Sunday was his brother's wedding.

"Yes, wedding." Corrado reached over, opening the passenger door and waving his hand dismissively. "Out."

Carmine got out of the car and slammed the door. He watched as Corrado hit the gas and sped off, tires squealing. His words played through Carmine's mind, an odd feeling coursing through him. *Where doesn't matter . . .*

His head started to pound again, the ache in his chest intensifying, and a sinking feeling hit his stomach as Corrado's car disappeared from sight.

"Haven."

————

It hadn't taken Carmine long to make up his mind after Corrado's car pulled away. The moment his uncle turned onto the road, he reacted on impulse. Sprinting to his car, he unlocked the driver's side door and slipped inside. Tires squealed as he hit the gas, flying out of the packed parking lot and into traffic within seconds.

The roads weren't congested at that hour, but Carmine didn't see his uncle anywhere, so he drove in the direction of their neighborhood hoping he went home first. The moment he pulled onto the street, he saw the Mercedes idling in the driveway.

Carmine parked a few houses down and turned off his headlights to wait. Corrado came outside a minute later with a black duffel bag and glanced around cautiously before getting back into his car. He pulled out of the driveway and sped down the street, and Carmine waited a few seconds before starting on the road. He slipped in behind another car, weaving through traffic in the direction of the airport.

He stayed back as far as possible, making sure there were cars between them so not to raise suspicion. He lost Corrado's car twice but each time caught back up, having a general idea of where he was going, until he unexpectedly pulled down a side street a few miles into the trip.

Carmine slowed, unsure of what he was doing, but followed his uncle. They drove along a few vacant roads before cutting down an alley, and Carmine slammed the brakes when he turned and nearly rear-ended Corrado's car.

His heart pounded forcefully when he realized it was a dead-end. Corrado's driver's side door hung open, no sign of him anywhere. Before Carmine could shift the car into reverse, his door opened and someone grabbed him. It happened fast, the movement startling him, and the car stalled from his haste. He had enough time to pull the emergency brake, not wanting it to roll, before he was yanked out into the alley and thrown against the side of the car.

"What are you doing?" Corrado asked, pressing the muzzle of his gun underneath Carmine's chin.

He shook, stunned. "I, uh . . . fuck! I don't know. I just thought . . ."

"You aren't paid to think," Corrado said. "You're paid to follow orders and I don't recall telling you to follow me."

"You didn't tell me not to, either."

"What did you say?" The sound of Corrado's finger releasing the safety of his gun sent a cold chill down Carmine's spine. "I'm tired of your disrespect."

"I didn't mean it! I just . . . had to know. I had to see, Uncle Corrado."

Corrado froze briefly, not moving or making a sound.

"You think I won't kill you because you're Vincent's child?" he asked, his voice menacingly quiet. "Do you honestly believe I'm *that* soft?"

"No, sir," he said quickly, squeezing his eyes shut at his words. "I didn't mean any disrespect."

Corrado put the gun away and let go of Carmine. "There's no justification for you following me. Where I'm going doesn't concern you."

"Doesn't it?" he asked, trying to stop trembling as he stood up straight. "If you're going where I think you're going—"

"What did I just say?" Corrado asked. "I told you in Durante to make your decision and you did. You need to be a man of your word."

"So I'm right?" he asked exasperatedly. "You're going to her?"

"You have *no* right to intervene."

"I'm not trying to intervene," he said, shaking his head. "I just . . . Christ, I wanna know where she is, what she's doing. Why the fuck you're running off in the middle of the night. Is something wrong? Is she hurt or something?"

Corrado stared at him as he rattled off questions, his expression blank, but Carmine could see the annoyance in his eyes. He knew he shouldn't have been questioning him, but he needed something, *anything* . . . just a bit of information to keep him going.

Glancing at his watch, Corrado sighed impatiently. He looked as if he were going to speak and hope swelled through Carmine, but it was trampled when he instead raised his gun again. Carmine recoiled as his uncle fired off two shots in his direction, the unexpected noise startling him. Carmine turned to look incredulously, seeing the driver's side tires of his car rapidly deflating.

"If you're going to tail someone, at least be discreet about it." Corrado placed the gun back in his coat. "Call for a tow truck and go home. I don't need you slowing me down any more than you already have."

"Just fucking great," Carmine muttered as his uncle walked away.

Corrado paused. "That's an order, Carmine."

20

Haven nervously watched the clock, waiting for the black rental car to slowly pull up the street. It parked in a free spot directly in front of the brownstone, and Corrado climbed out, fixing his tie and looking around before heading inside. He tapped once on her door, patiently waiting for her to open up.

She started stammering as soon as he entered, trying to explain what had happened, but he held his hand up to stop her. She flinched from the sudden movement and he froze. "I have no intention of harming you."

Haven stood still by the door as he checked out the place. The apartment appeared undisturbed and Haven felt ridiculous, wondering if Corrado had flown out for nothing.

"Is your upstairs neighbor home?" he asked.

"Uh, no, not yet," she said. "Kelsey stayed with a guy last night."

"Look around and tell me if anything has been taken," he said. "I need to check her apartment and make sure neither of you have been bugged."

"Yes, sir."

She sorted through things, taking inventory, and found nothing missing. Even the cash she kept in a drawer was still there. *Always use cash,* Corrado had said, *never leave a paper trail.*

Corrado came back downstairs after a bit, leaving the door open a crack as he lingered near it. "The place is clean. Anything missing down here?"

"No," she replied. "I don't really own anything valuable, though."

"Value doesn't always equal a monetary amount," he said. "No diaries?"

She shook her head before it dawned on her. "Oh, crap!"

Darting into the living room, she scanned the bookshelf and breathed a sigh of relief when she saw the worn leather book amongst the others. "I have Maura's."

Haven turned to him and started to speak, to ask what she should do, when the front door thrust open, catching Haven off guard. She gasped as Corrado turned, reaching into his coat for his gun. He clutched it but didn't pull it out as Kelsey appeared in the doorway, her eyes darting between Haven and Corrado.

"Who's the DILF?" she asked, leaving the door wide open as she motioned toward Corrado. Her eyes scanned him, a small smile coming upon her lips.

Haven's cheeks flushed. "Kelsey . . ."

"Is this your missing friend?" Corrado asked. "The one that lives upstairs?"

"Missing?" Kelsey's brow furrowed. "Are you a cop or something?"

Corrado glanced at her. "Do I look like a cop?"

"Sort of," she said. "I mean, you *do* have a gun."

Corrado immediately removed his hand from his weapon, covering it again with his coat.

"He's . . ." Haven started, unsure of how to explain it.

"Corrado," he said, finishing her statement as he politely held out his hand.

"Kelsey," she said, shaking it. "Obviously you already know that, though."

"Yes. If you'll excuse me, I need to make a phone call."

He walked to the kitchen, pulling out his phone. The moment he was out of earshot, Kelsey jokingly punched Haven's arm. "Where the hell did *he* come from?"

"Uh, I've known him for a while," she mumbled.

"I'm not gonna lie—I was hoping you wouldn't go home alone last night. I hoped you'd get some of that stiffness knocked out of you, if you know what I mean, but how did you pull *that*?"

"You think we . . . ?" Haven was stunned. "No way! He's married!"

"So?" She shrugged. "A man like that needs more than just one woman to take care of him. I can't believe you spent all night with him and *still* didn't get laid."

"Why do you think I spent all night with him?"

"You have the same clothes on from yesterday," she said, as if it were the most obvious thing in the world. "Did you at least blow him?"

"Kelsey, shut up!"

"You're such a prude," she said, smirking. "If you won't, can I?"

"No!" Haven shook her head furiously. "Oh, God, why would you want to?"

"Are you seriously asking me that?" she asked. "Are you *blind*? He has that whole mysterious and dangerous look about him. There's no way a man like that isn't well endowed."

"Stop!" she hissed.

Kelsey rolled her eyes. "Oh, relax. I get it. You have no interest in men, except for Cartman . . ."

"Carmine," she corrected her.

"Cartman, Carmine—same difference. I've known you a few months now, honey, and I've yet to see that guy. He doesn't call, he doesn't write, he doesn't visit. He may as well be a ghost, but that fine specimen in the kitchen? He's real, he's tangible, and there comes a point where you have to give up the fantasy for the reality." She paused and glanced down the hallway as Corrado headed back in their direction. "And it doesn't hurt when the reality looks a hell of a lot like my fantasy."

Corrado stepped in the room, slipping his phone in his pocket as he gazed at Haven. "You should be safe here, but I'm going to have the locks replaced."

A tense silence fell over the room as Kelsey's eyes clouded with suspicion. "Did something happen?"

"Someone broke in," Haven mumbled. "They were here when I got home."

Kelsey's eyes widened. "Did they get anything? Did they hit my place, too?"

"She scared them away before they could make it that far," Corrado chimed in. "No harm done."

Haven nodded, confirming the lie. She looked at the clock as another bout of tension swept through the room. "I need to get ready. We have somewhere to be."

"I'd rather you skip it today," Corrado said.

Haven shook her head. "I can't."

He gave her a curious look. "Can't, or won't?"

"Won't."

He nodded as if he had expected that answer. "Proceed, then."

Haven left the two of them alone in the living room to get dressed. Kelsey was sitting on her couch eating when Haven returned, but Corrado was nowhere to be found.

"He stepped outside," Kelsey said before Haven had a chance to ask. "Got a call from what I assume is his wife. Major mood killer."

Haven shook her head. "He's not your type. He's a serious person."

"I noticed," she said. "He's intense. You're not in, like, WITSEC are you?"

"What?" Haven asked.

"WITSEC. You know, witness protection, where the government gives you a new identity so gangsters can't find you?"

Haven cracked a smile at the irony, considering it had been the gangster to give her a new identity to hide from the government. "No, it's not like that."

"So how come I've never seen him here before?"

"He doesn't live around here."

"Where does he live?"

"Why are you so nosy?"

"Because I am," she said, laughing. "How did you meet him?"

"He's a . . . friend of the family."

"Really? He looks really familiar, like I've seen him somewhere before," she said, standing. "It's strange. He *is* a cop, though, right?"

"Why the questions?" Haven asked.

She shrugged. "I'm just trying to figure out who he is. Is it a crime to want to know about my friend's life? You don't talk much about it."

"There's not much to tell."

Kelsey rolled her eyes. "Whatever, let me get dressed and we'll go."

Corrado's car was gone when they headed outside. They shared a cab in silence to the Rainbow Art Center and spent the morning cleaning the place, organizing everything and gathering up all of the kids' artwork. They carefully framed them all and spent two hours affixing the paintings to the wall and decorating for a party. Kelsey left at one point to get snacks and drinks as Haven blew up balloons. She turned around to get something, nearly colliding with someone standing there. The person grabbed her shoulders as she screamed, caught off guard.

"Relax," Corrado said. "It's just me."

"How did you know where I was?" she asked.

He raised his eyebrows. "You think I don't keep tabs on you?"

"Well, sure, but I didn't know how closely."

"Close enough that I could find you at any given moment," he said. "It's my job to know. It's nice what you do here, by the way."

"Oh," she said, flushing. Was that a compliment? "Thanks. I enjoy it."

"I imagine you do," he said. "Maura did similar things. She always said if she helped just one person, it would have been worth the sacrifice."

"She mentioned that in her journal," Haven mumbled. "I feel the same way."

"So you understand why Carmine left you, then?"

Haven cringed from the question, not expecting it.

"Vincent fought to ensure Carmine didn't turn out like him, but at eighteen he made the exact same decision his father did anyway," Corrado explained. "It's logical they'd worry what happened to Maura would happen to you, too. What they fail to realize, though, is the main thing Maura tried to teach them. *Cambiano i suonatori ma la musica è sempre quella.*"

"What does that mean?" she asked.

He didn't answer for a moment as he wandered through the room, his attention focused on the juvenile paintings. It was weird watching him. Haven never took Corrado as someone who would be remotely interested in those sorts of things.

"You read her journal, so am I correct to assume you know I failed her?"

"Failed her?" she asked hesitantly. "She didn't see it that way. She said you were always fair to her, even when she was . . . you know . . . in your home."

"I could've done more."

"Can't we all?" she responded. "We're only human, after all."

"You're a lot like Maura, but there are some differences. She wouldn't have stood here and held a conversation with me, that's for sure, and she would've certainly abandoned her plans the second I demanded." He paused, smiling with amusement. "Regardless, I see why they'd worry, but just because a person's situation changes, doesn't mean *they* change. It doesn't matter if you're in North Carolina or California or New York or Illinois—you are who you are. That's what I meant by it."

The door swung open then, sunlight filtering in from outside.

"Have you ever been in a Wal-Mart?" Kelsey hollered, coming in the room and dropping bags on the floor. "That place was a madhouse. I felt like I stepped into some alternate universe where banana clips and blue eye shadow are still in style. And Jesus, what's with all the big hair? I'm surprised I made it out alive! Half those women looked like they could eat me for supper! And I swear, I saw a minivan in the parking lot with one of those honor student bumper stickers, and the woman driving had on . . ." She glanced over, her words faltering when she spotted Corrado. ". . . Mom jeans. Hello, there."

"Hello," Corrado replied. "I'll let you ladies get back to your work."

He strolled away, stepping outside as he pulled out his phone.

"Personal bodyguard?" Kelsey asked, a mischievous twinkle in her eyes. "Is this like the *Bodyguard* movie, steamy affair included?"

"No. I told you, it's nothing like that."

"Pity." She shrugged and started digging through the bags, setting up the snack table. They ordered pizza and Haven fixed the punch when people arrived, the children excitedly running in while their caretakers lingered off to the side. Some didn't even bother to stay, instead dropping the children off at the curb.

Corrado stuck around for the party, watching warily, so quiet and stoic most barely noticed his presence. Others, however, cast him suspicious looks as they kept their distance. Haven smiled, realizing they likely thought the same thing Kelsey had—he was a police officer.

It was chaotic with so many kids running around, and Haven did her best to keep everything under control as they held a ceremony and handed out certificates. When it was over and time to go, Haven gave each kid a hug, telling them the same words that had been spoken to her at their age. Words she had lost focus of in the midst of all the heartache, but words both Maura and her mother had wholeheartedly believed.

"Never lose hope," she said. "You're special and meant to do great things in the world. I believe in you."

Kelsey offered to walk one of the kids home as Haven cleaned up the mess. She could sense Corrado's eyes on her but ignored him the best she could, trying to finish what she needed to do.

Corrado cleared his voice. "Were you attached?"

"To what?"

"Those children."

"Yes," Haven said quietly. "They reminded me of myself."

"Strange how those things work. Doesn't matter where you go—there will always be someone." Haven nodded and reached for the large black trash bag, but Corrado grabbed it. "I'll get this for you."

"Thanks," she mumbled. "The Dumpster is out back."

Haven finished cleaning up and grabbed her things before heading for the parking lot, finding Corrado's empty rental car parked by the door. She started around the building to see if he was still at the Dumpster. She froze when she saw him behind the parking lot with a man, the driver's side door open on a black car with New York tags. The man had his back to her, so she couldn't see his face, but his body language told her it wasn't just casual conversation.

The man climbed in the car after a second, tires squealing as he sped out of the opposite side of the parking lot.

Corrado approached. "Do you need a ride?"

"I can walk," she said. "It's just a few blocks."

"Nonsense." He waved her off dismissively. "Get in the car."

Corrado didn't speak at all during the drive. Not long after they arrived, someone showed up to change the locks on the brownstone.

"I have some things to handle, and I need to get some sleep," Corrado said, handing Haven a new set of keys. "I'll be leaving tomorrow to make it to the wedding."

Wedding? "Someone's getting married?"

"Dominic and Tess," Corrado said, eyeing her peculiarly. "Didn't you receive your invitation?"

She shook her head slowly. "No. I had no idea."

His expression flickered, a frown on his lips. "I must've forgotten to send it. There's still time, though, if you'd like to send a gift. I'll stop by in the morning before I leave to pick it up, if you want to go get something."

"Okay," she said, not knowing how to respond to that. "Thanks, I guess."

"I suppose you're welcome," he responded. "Have a good evening, kid."

21

Carmine sat alone in a booth in the back of the club, shot glasses scattered along the table in front of him. He could feel the alcohol flowing through his veins, diluting his blood stream and hindering the thoughts from flooding his brain. They still came, a slow trickle of memories washing through him, but he found it easier to tolerate in smaller doses like this.

It still hurt, though. It was still a constant reminder of what could have been but wasn't, and as far as he was concerned, never would be. There were reminders everywhere: in the deep brown of the wooden table that resembled the color of her eyes, in the twinkling of the club lights that made him think of catching fireflies, in the melody of the song playing that sounded vaguely like the one she used to hum.

She was everywhere, yet nowhere, and every second that passed felt like walking away from her all over again. No matter what he did, no matter what he tried, he couldn't forget. The memory of Haven haunted him.

He downed the last shot on the table, closing his eyes as he savored the burn, hoping it would finally be the one to kill the pain.

If someone years before had asked Carmine what life in Chicago would be like, he would have given them some cliché answer about money, power, and respect, but he knew better now. *La Cosa Nostra* wasn't about any of that.

As Sal sat comfortably, pointing fingers and calling shots from his twelve-million-dollar mansion while drinking the best scotch money could buy, the men carrying out the jobs were barely scraping by. They were risking their lives for people who just stood by while they struggled, not caring what happened to them as long as they handed over a cut of their *take*.

It was all about *paying tribute*. If a group of guys hijacked a shipment, right off the top more than half went into the pockets of the administration. After giving the associates their cut and paying off everyone who looked the other way, each man was left with barely enough to pay their rent.

A *taste*, they called it. Everyone always wanted a taste. They claimed, as a family, that they all worked as one. They said it was a matter of respect. They said it was the honorable thing to do.

As far as Carmine was concerned, it was utter bullshit.

Where was the respect in being summoned out of bed at three in the morning to watch a man get his head bashed in because he borrowed money he couldn't pay back? Where was the respect in burning some man's house down, taking away everything he had worked for his entire life, because he gave the Boss a look he didn't appreciate? Where was the respect in intimidating a seventeen-year-old girl and threatening to kill everyone she loved because she witnessed something she shouldn't have seen?

Assault, extortion, hijacking, kidnapping, robbery, bribery, gambling, chop shops, prostitution, corruption, arson, coercion, fraud, bootlegging, human trafficking, and murder . . . where was the respect in *any* of it?

He sure didn't fucking see it.

"Bad night, man?"

Carmine glanced over as Remy slid into the booth across from him. "You could say that."

Remy motioned for the waitress and asked her for a rum and Coke, taking it upon himself to order Carmine another shot of vodka.

"I figured," Remy said. "You got that look about you tonight, that 'I've seen shit that can't be unseen' look."

Carmine pushed the empty glass aside with the others. "Doesn't mean I can't try to forget."

"True, but you're doing it the wrong way. Alcohol is a downer. As if this all isn't depressing enough, hitting the bottle just drags you further down. You go from being a moody bitch to a miserable cunt, and nobody likes a miserable cunt, DeMarco. Not even me, and I love everybody."

Carmine managed a small laugh at that. "It numbs me."

"Yeah, I'm sure it probably numbs you enough that you won't feel the concrete shattering your bones when your depressed ass leaps off the top of Sears Tower," he said. "But you should never jump unless you know you can fly, or at least float. Nobody wants to fall. That's how you end up hurt."

Carmine stared at Remy as he tried to make sense of his words. He wasn't sure if he was just too damn drunk or if the man intentionally talked in code. "I can't decide if you're a genius or if you're just a fucking rambling idiot."

"Why can't I be both?"

Carmine shrugged. Maybe he was.

"Anyway, you wanna know how you really unsee?" Remy asked. "How you really forget?"

"How?"

"Instead of dragging yourself down more, lift yourself up. You don't wanna be numb, man. You wanna be happy."

Carmine shook his head. *Happy.* He remembered a time he felt that way. "That ship sailed a long time ago."

"Oh, that's where you're wrong." A sly smile turned Remy's lips. He leaned across the table, closer to Carmine, and whispered conspiratorially, "I think it's time I introduced you to Miss Molly."

"Molly?"

Remy nodded. "She's beautiful. Just one night with her will change your life."

———

It was strange, abrupt yet slow moving. One second there was nothing and suddenly it was there, tiptoeing through his veins. There wasn't an intense rush of sensation, blinding and all consuming. Carmine didn't feel like he was sky high. No, for the first time in quite a while, he felt like he had his feet firmly planted on the ground.

He tried to find the words to describe the feeling, but none existed. It was new, yet somehow familiar, like a combination of everything good that ever lived inside of him. It was his mother being alive. It was being in love with Haven. It was playing football, and going to college, and having a future. It was forgiveness. It was understanding. It was all that was wrong suddenly becoming right. It was sunshine, and light, and spewing goddamn rainbows. It was walking on water before turning it into wine. It was Heaven. It was bliss. It was being blind for a lifetime and suddenly being able to see. It was freedom. It was happiness. The stars had aligned and wham bam . . . motherfucking world peace.

"What is this shit?" Carmine asked, rubbing his nose absently as he eyed the remnants of the white powder on the table. It glistened like flecks of glitter under the club lights, mesmerizing him. His senses were heightened, the notes of the music echoing from the speakers rippling across his flushed skin before sinking in.

He wasn't sure why, but he suddenly yearned to play the piano again.

"I told you—Molly," Remy replied. "Pure powder MDMA."

Carmine smiled to himself, the first genuine smile to grace his lips in months, and he felt a burst of gratitude. Molly was beautiful. She was ecstasy.

Literally.

He had heard of it, of course, mainly being taken in pill form, but he had never encountered it before. Ecstasy hadn't yet infiltrated his small North Carolina town as it had in the big cities.

"So how do you feel?" Remy asked. "Still numb?"

Carmine shook his head. Numb was the complete opposite of the sensation stirring within him. It settled deep in his chest, filling the gaping hole as it wiped away the pain, the ache, the heartbreak. "I feel like I could take on the world and actually fucking win."

Remy laughed as he picked up his glass of rum and Coke and drank the last bit. "Yeah, well, you can't. The world will still destroy you, my friend, so don't do anything stupid . . . not if you wanna live to see another day."

Standing, Remy reached into his pocket and pulled out a small baggy filled with the glittery white powder. He dropped it on the table in front of Carmine. "My treat. Just use it sparingly, okay? A little goes a long way."

Carmine picked it up, concealing it in his palm. "Thanks."

"Don't mention it." Remy took a step before pausing. "Seriously, please don't mention it, man. I'd rather people not know, you know."

"I understand," Carmine said, staring down at the packet stashed in his hand. Their bosses frowned upon drugs. The men up top may have looked the other way and arranged exchanges off the record to make a quick dollar, playing invisible middlemen in a bigger game, but they were never to get their hands dirty in the drug trade. It was too dangerous—too many people involved, too much publicity, too much risk for exposure. It was one of their biggest rules, second only to keep your fucking mouth shut and never rat on your friends.

22

The tan rectangular building stood on the corner of a quiet intersection, spanning nearly half a city block. The outside was modest, with brown archways and bright green grass, a sign along the front displaying THE ROSEWOOD HALL in casual script.

Carmine expected something flashier. He always took Tess to be the kind who would demand white horses and a gold-plated dance floor at a remote location, not a simple wedding hall in the middle of Chicago.

He glanced down at his invitation once more as he leaned against the building, triple checking he had the right place before shoving it in the pocket of his black slacks. He watched in silence as the lot filled with cars, surprised at the amount of people arriving for the wedding. He didn't recognize half the guests, which unnerved him. Everyone had moved on with life, met new people, and made new friends, but he was just him . . . still the same Carmine DeMarco.

That was how it seemed, anyway. So much had changed but yet nothing felt different. He was back to being that teenage boy, all alone with no one to talk to—no one to confide in. Instead, he buried everything deep inside, concealing secrets and hiding the truth from everyone—sometimes, even from himself—as he waded through reality, refusing to accept half of it was his life.

It was a nice day in Chicago, the temperature hovering around seventy degrees, but sweat uncomfortably gathered along his back and made his shirt stick to him. On edge, he contemplated leaving, although he knew he shouldn't. He *couldn't*. He had disappointed a lot of people in his life, made plenty of fucked-up choices at the drop of a hat, but bailing on his only brother's wedding would certainly top the list.

Even if that brother probably didn't care if he showed up.

Sighing, Carmine reached into his pocket for his flask and took a swig. The hot liquid burned his throat, the flames eating away at his chest. He took another drink when someone called his name, the sharp voice startling him. He choked on the vodka, coughing as he put the lid back on it.

"What?" he rasped as Celia approached.

"Was it necessary to bring *that* along?" she asked, motioning toward the flask.

He rolled his eyes as he slipped the flask away. "Is your husband here?"

"No, I haven't heard from him today." She frowned. "I don't know if he's going to make it."

Carmine's stomach sunk. "Is he still with *her*?"

"Who?"

"Don't treat me like an idiot, Celia. You know who."

She eyed Carmine warily. "What makes you think he's with *her*?"

"I don't *think*. I know."

"I'm not sure," she replied. "I know as much as you do, kiddo. He left, and I don't know why or where or when he'll be back. I do know, though, if he shows up and sees you drinking, he's not going to be very happy."

Vincent yelled from the front door of the hall, saying the ceremony was about to start, and Carmine pushed away from the building. They headed inside quietly, going straight through to the courtyard in the back. A long aisle was set up, surrounded by dozens of white chairs in rows. Celia dragged Carmine to the front, forcing him into the seat beside her.

The ceremony went by quickly. Carmine barely heard any of it as he fidgeted and tugged at his tie, looking around for any sign of his uncle. The moment it was over, they went inside for the reception, and Carmine headed straight for the open bar. He took a seat, barking for the bartender to get him some vodka, and he downed two shots back-to-back as soon as they were set in front of him.

The bartender poured him another, shot after shot flowing until Carmine's vision was a bit hazy. The celebration went on behind him, music playing as people danced and cheered, celebrating Tess and Dominic's union, while all Carmine enjoyed was the familiar numbness creeping through his limbs.

Another shot was poured—number five, maybe six—when the stool beside Carmine shifted. Tensing, he glanced over as Dominic sat down, loosening his bowtie. He didn't look at Carmine or even acknowledge him as he told the bartender to pour him a shot, too.

Dominic downed it in one swallow and grimaced, motioning for his shot glass to be filled again. "I don't know how the hell you drink this straight from the bottle, Carm."

Carmine threw his back when the bartender approached. The man filled them both up, giving a small nod as he set the bottle between them on the bar.

About fucking time he gets the hint.

"Your body gets used to it after a while," Carmine said. "I barely feel the burn anymore. It goes down like water."

"Huh," Dominic said, throwing his vodka back. He grimaced once more, a rumble escaping his chest as he slammed the shot glass down on the bar. Carmine chuckled and filled them both back up, but Dominic just stared at his glass. He picked it up after a moment, swirling the liquid around as if deep in thought.

"Go ahead and say it," Carmine muttered.

"There's no point," Dominic said. "Your misery takes the fun out of it."

"I'm fine," he insisted, grabbing the liquor. He went to pour himself a shot but stopped, instead just tipping the bottle back.

There was no point in pretending—they both knew he would drink the entire thing, anyway.

"You know, none of us hear from Haven anymore," Dominic said, picking up a coaster from the bar and putting it on its corner, attempting to spin it.

"Did something happen?" Carmine asked. "She's okay, isn't she?"

"I'm sure if something was wrong, we'd know. Corrado keeps up with her."

"What about Dia?" he asked. "Doesn't she see her, too?"

He laughed humorlessly. "No. She went home for spring break and when she got back, Haven was gone. You'd know that if you still talked to her, by the way."

Carmine was stunned. "Dia doesn't call me, either."

"That's because she's afraid you'll flip out. She thinks she failed because Haven left, but I told her what happened was supposed to happen. You pushed the little birdie from the nest, and she did exactly what she was always meant to do."

"What's that?" Carmine asked.

"She flew."

A smile tugged Carmine's lips at those words. *She flew.* "I'll drink to that."

"You'll drink to anything."

He raised the bottle. "I'll drink to that, too."

Dominic stood up and walked away, rejoining his table at the front of the room with Tess and Dia. Carmine stared at the bottle of liquor in his hand, realizing his brother had just done the one thing he had been too stubborn to do—concede.

Carmine hesitated before getting up and strolling over to their table. He paused beside it, his eyes silently scanning them, before slipping into an empty seat.

Dia tentatively smiled from her seat beside him. He gave her a small smile, the warmth and acceptance in her expression comforting.

The three of them talked about weddings and families and the future, but Carmine didn't say much. There really wasn't anything he could say. His future was set in stone and it wasn't anything to gush about, or anything he could even share. It was nice, though, being around them again. There was no anger or resentment, no guilt or blame for the things that happened, or the ones that didn't. There was nothing but love and friendship at the table, and even some long-overdue sympathy.

Vincent came over for a few minutes, laughing and joking around. Carmine felt a strange sensation brewing inside as he watched them. They were his family—his *real* family—the ones who had been through it all with him.

But still, even then, he felt the void, the part that was missing. He felt her absence, when he wanted nothing more than her presence.

And, if he were being honest, he felt something else then, too . . . a craving for the sensation he had had the night before.

––––––––

The Rosewood Room was near the Children's School of Music and just down the street from an old closed down theater, one that used to play movies for a quarter in the summer of 1972.

Vincent had been just a kid at the time, slightly rebellious yet highly impressionable. He would often leave his house on Felton Drive, two blocks past where he later settled with his own family, and slip away to that theater without his parents knowing. It was at a time when he and Celia came and went as they pleased, not long before the brutal underground wars broke out that changed everything. Before their parents tightened their grip and started monitoring their every move . . . before they came to the realization that they needed to.

His mother had been strict and maybe already a bit delusional, refusing to let them watch television, not wanting to poison their minds, so he would lie whenever she asked and tell her he was going to the park with friends.

The Godfather came out that year. Vincent saw it one cloudy Tuesday afternoon in July, sitting in the back row of the packed theater. Those three hours altered his life, turning everything he thought he knew upside down.

Until then, he only had a vague understanding of the Mafia, based on the things he had witnessed and his mother's volatile rants. He thought it was a club, maybe part of a union, considering he had seen his dad take money from Teamsters. But reality made itself known that day, playing out on the massive flickering screen.

Vincent had been so fascinated by the film, so rocked to the core, that he hadn't noticed a dozen of his father's close friends sitting in the audience with him.

He ran home that afternoon with a million questions running through his head, absentmindedly navigating a path he knew by heart. Two blocks over, one block down, cut through the small alley the next street over, then it's only four more blocks south to his home. He could zigzag through the streets without thinking, making it there within minutes.

And years later, as Vincent strolled away from the wedding hall after taking one last look at his family, his feet seemed to instinctively remember the way. He walked past the old theater, surveying the boarded-up windows and crumbling bricks, and he thought back to that day he watched *The Godfather*. He intended to question his sister when he made it home, but he never had the chance.

As soon as he opened the front door of his house and ran inside, his father's boisterous voice rocked the downstairs. "Vincenzo Roman!"

Vincent's feet immediately rooted to the floor as he cringed at the sound of his full name. Glancing in the direction of his father's voice, he saw him standing in the doorway to his office. His heart beat wildly. *Not good, not good.* "Yes, Dad?"

"We need to talk."

Antonio disappeared inside his office. Vincent stood there for a second, intentionally delaying, before forcing his feet to move that way. He took a seat in front of his father's desk.

"So what did you do today?" Antonio asked, leaning back in his chair, his hands clasped across his bulky chest.

"Went to the park."

"The park, huh?"

"Yes."

"And how was the park, son?"

"Fine."

"And you were there all afternoon?"

"Yes."

"Did you enjoy yourself?"

"Yes."

"Fascinating," Antonio said. "I do wonder how you did it, though, being in two places at once. You see, I got a call a few minutes ago that you were at the theater this afternoon, and I know you wouldn't lie to me, right?"

The color drained from Vincent's face. Antonio stared at him intently, waiting for an answer that never came.

"You can't think I won't know these things, that I won't find out," he continued, realizing Vincent intended to remain silent. "I got eyes and ears all around this city. Someone can't take a piss in my neighborhood without it getting back to me. And I don't like the fact that my kid, my only son, thought he could get one over on me. Do you think I'm an idiot? You think your father's a *jamook*?"

Vincent shook his head feverishly. "Of course not."

"You got questions, you want to know things? You come to me. You don't go out there and get information from everyone else."

"Yes, sir." Vincent paused, thinking that over. "I just wanted to see a movie. I didn't realize . . ."

Antonio stared at him as he trailed off, letting out a deep sigh as he leaned forward. "Look, son, there's this saying—fortune favors the bold. If you want things, if you want to be successful, you have to take chances, you have to accept risks. You have to, you know, do some things that maybe other people won't do. Life, it's kind of like a game of chess. You know about chess, right?"

Vincent slowly nodded.

"So you know the king is the most important player. As long as he's standing, the game continues. And that's just like in life. You want to be the king, even if that makes you the biggest target. The king, he's the key to it all, make or break. You never want to be a pawn or a rook or a knight. You never want to be disposable, just another piece in the way. You want to control the game. You get what I'm saying?"

He nodded again.

"So since you know chess, you also know the real truth," Antonio said. "The king dictates the game, sure, but the queen? She holds the real power. Which is why we aren't going to tell your mother about what you did today. She doesn't need to know you lied and broke her rules, because the queen won't be quite so understanding. *Capisce?*"

"Yes, Dad."

Vincent stood to leave and made it halfway to the door when Antonio called his name. "How was it, son? *The Godfather?*"

He glanced back. "It was the best thing I've ever seen."

Antonio smiled, a genuinely elated smile, before waving him away.

And as Vincent strolled through the streets of Chicago years later, he could still remember that look of pride on his father's face. It wasn't a look he received often—mostly it was disappointment as he forced harsh lessons upon him growing up, lessons he carried with him his entire life. Some good, some bad, but every one of them had somehow changed him. They had turned him into the person he was—a man ripped apart by the concept of loyalty.

He walked the first three blocks easily, slowing his footsteps as he approached the alley. Something in the back of his mind urged him to take the long way around, but he ignored that pesky voice, shoving it back as he continued on. He stepped into the alley, strolling down the narrow path as he looked between the old tall buildings, desperate for renovations.

About halfway down he paused, kicking around at some loose gravel on the ground. He ran his fingers along the worn siding of a business, the brick crumbling a bit in his hand. He let out a deep sigh as he felt the ridges and gashes, his chest tight with anxiety.

"Vincent."

Vincent looked over as Corrado strolled down the alley toward him. His suit was wrinkled, his eyes tired, and a small gift box wrapped in bright green paper was tucked under his arm. "You missed the wedding, Corrado."

"I know," he said. "I just got back from New York."

"Business?" Vincent asked. "Amaro family? Geneva? Calabrese?"

Corrado shook his head. "More like Antonelli."

Vincent's brow creased. "Haven?"

"No reason for concern," Corrado said, dismissing his inquisitive look as he looked around the dingy alley, shifting the present to under the other arm. His eyes settled upon the brick wall behind Vincent. "It was right here."

"Yeah, it was."

It was in that spot, more than a decade earlier, when Vincent's world violently collapsed. He felt the pressure of it pressing on him, the memory weighing him down. Whenever he blinked, in that split second when blackness took over, drowning out his senses, he could still see it—ashy pale skin, lifeless eyes, copper colored hair drenched in red. Terror coated her face, a horrifying mask of questions with no answers . . .

Why her? Why them? Why now?

They were things he had wondered for years, things he thought he had figured out when he murdered Frankie Antonelli. But standing there, the questions still lingered.

Why?

"It's peculiar, isn't it?" Corrado asked. "The thirst for revenge? It's easy to dismiss the things we do, but it's impossible to forget the things done to us. We never think about their families, but when it's ours, we never get over it. We carry that grudge forever."

"I think about them," Vincent said. "I always consider their families."

"Did you think about Frankie's?"

Vincent hesitated. "No. I was only thinking about mine back then, but I do now. Every day."

"That doesn't count," Corrado said. "The only relative he has left is Haven, and I assure you she isn't grieving that loss."

Vincent thought that over. "You've honestly never considered their families?"

"Never," Corrado said, staring at him pointedly. "My conscience is clear, Vincent. I carry no regret, and I don't want to start now. It's why, with God as my witness, I'll never pull the trigger unless I'm absolutely certain the world is a better place without them."

"You're lucky," Vincent said. "Every time I think I clear my conscience, something else comes about."

"That's because you're letting yourself be a pawn."

A bitter laugh forced itself from Vincent's chest. "I was just thinking about the day my father told me to be a king and not a pawn. But he failed to tell me there could only be one king. The rest of us, well . . . we can only do what we can do."

"You're missing the point," Corrado said. "Being the king isn't always about having the title. Sometimes the title is a ruse. You want control? You need the upper hand, but you never let them see you have it until you're ready to make your move."

"And what if the only moves I have left break the rules?"

He shrugged. "Depends on whose rules you break."

Corrado took a step back and nodded before strolling away.

After he was gone, Vincent turned back to the building, running his hand along the crumbling brick once more. "I'll see you later, Maura. *Ti amo.*"

Vincent strolled out of the alley and down the block toward the pizzeria. John Tarullo stood outside the front door, sweeping the large welcome mat with a cornhusk broom. He glanced up, nodding stiffly in greeting. "Dr. DeMarco, I hear you have a son getting married today."

"Yes. Dominic."

"I hear he's a good kid."

"He is," Vincent replied. "Both of my sons are good kids."

Tarullo looked at him warily, raising his eyebrows. "I hear your Carmine is friends with my Remy."

"Ah, but that doesn't mean they're bad kids," Vincent said. "Maybe just a little misguided. I was the same way, and you wouldn't call me bad, would you?"

"No," he said at once, but Vincent could see the truth in the man's eyes. Yes, yes, an unadulterated hell yes.

Vincent let out a laugh as he walked away.

––––––––

Carmine sipped his drink, lounging in the white wicker chair as he listened to his friends and family chatter on. He relaxed, almost enjoying himself for once, until a gruff throat cleared right behind him.

He stiffened at the sound.

"This is for you two," Corrado said as he reached across the table, holding a box wrapped in shiny green paper. Carmine turned to face his uncle, who looked exhausted but otherwise fine. "I apologize I missed the ceremony, but I had unexpected business."

"Thanks, Unk," Dominic said as he took the gift. "It's understandable."

Corrado walked away without even looking at Carmine. Carmine watched as he approached Celia, motioning for her to follow him. Corrado's eyes darted around nervously and Carmine's heart pounded rapidly when Dominic's voice rang out. "Twinkle Toes."

Carmine turned to him so quickly he nearly knocked over a glass of champagne, wondering why he had said that name, and saw he had pulled the card from the top of the gift.

"Read it to us," Tess demanded.

Dominic sighed. "*Dom and Tess, I wish I could give you this in person, but I'm tied up with things here. I bet Tess looked beautiful in her dress. Maybe someday I'll get to see pictures of it.*" He paused, glancing at Tess. "She's right, babe. You're always beautiful but especially today."

Smiling, Tess waved for him to continue.

"*It's hard to believe it's been so long since we've talked. I'm doing okay and have been busy, but I won't bore you with details. Please tell everyone hello for me the next time you talk to them, and tell them I miss them. I hope college is going well for all of you.*"

He looked up. "Twinkle Toes says hi and said she misses you motherfuckers. She hopes you aren't fucking up in school."

Carmine cracked a smile as his brother glanced back at the note. "*I don't know what you're supposed to give for weddings. Someone told me people register at stores for household things, but I didn't think Tess would want a blender. So I got something both of you can enjoy. I'd suggest opening it in private, but I don't think she'll be embarrassed either way.*"

Tess snatched the box from Dominic, tearing the paper off and opening it. She glanced inside, shifting some tissue paper around, and laughed. "I knew it."

"Holy shit, Twinkle Toes is kinky!" Dominic reached for the box and pulled out some lingerie, drawing attention as he waved it around. Tess grabbed it, her cheeks tinged red as more people looked, and threw it back in the box.

"You're such a douchebag sometimes," she said, storming away. Dia smiled and excused herself, following her sister.

"Looks like she was wrong," Dominic said. "Tess was embarrassed."

"Didn't realize it was possible," Carmine said.

"Me, either. I'd send her a thank-you note for that, but she didn't say where she was living."

She didn't, Carmine realized. No indication at all of where she was.

Dominic got up to go after his wife and Carmine sat there for a moment, finishing his drink alone as reality crept back in, ruining his brief moment of contentment. He left the wedding hall, not bothering to say good-bye to anyone, and took the long way home. He strolled down the street to his house, slowing as he spotted his father sitting on the bottom step. His brow furrowed as he drew near, seeing the lit cigarette between his fingers. "When the fuck did you start smoking?"

Vincent shrugged, flicking his ashes on the concrete. "When did you?" he countered, pointing at some old cigarette butts littering the yard.

"They're not mine," he replied. "Most of them, anyway. Remy smokes."

"Ah." Vincent pulled out a pack of cigarettes and handed one to Carmine along with a lighter.

He lit it, taking a drag as he stared at his father. "It's kinda fucked up to be smoking with you, a *doctor*."

"I'm not a doctor anymore." He let out a bitter laugh. "Can't have a suspected member of *La Cosa Nostra* wielding scalpels."

Carmine felt guilty for bringing it up. "Sorry."

Vincent raised his eyebrows. "Did you just apologize to me?"

"Maybe."

Vincent smiled. "Yeah, I'm sorry, too. It doesn't really matter, though—not anymore. It is what it is."

"Can you get reinstated after the trial? Go back to practicing medicine?"

He cut his eyes at Carmine incredulously, not bothering to entertain the question. "I actually started smoking after your mother died. I drank, too. *A lot*. That's the biggest reason I couldn't face you kids for almost a year. I know you blamed yourself, and it *was* difficult to see you, but I didn't want you to see me, either."

"What changed?" Carmine asked curiously. It was something he had always wanted to know, but a question he had been too damn self-absorbed to ask. "What made you pull yourself together?"

Vincent took a long drag. "I tried to murder Haven."

That response made Carmine choke on a puff of smoke. "What?"

"The night I killed the Antonellis, I tried to kill her, too. My gun jammed and she slept right through it. But I realized that night your mother would have been disgusted. I wasn't doing her memory any justice. So I pulled myself together before anyone else got hurt."

Carmine tossed his cigarette on the ground and stomped it out. He wasn't sure whether it was the smoke or his father's admission, but his chest suddenly ached. Reaching into his pocket, he pulled out the flask and took a drink, trying to dull the pain. Vincent watched him curiously so he held it out to him, offering his father some. He hesitated but threw his cigarette down and took it. He grimaced from the hot liquid, but it didn't stop him from taking a second swig.

"I've failed you a lot, withheld when I should've been honest, and it's to the point where all I have left to give is the truth," Vincent said quietly. He looked like a broken man, utterly defeated. "I remember the face of every person I've killed. I see them everywhere I go, and I know they aren't there, but the memory of what they looked like in their final moment lingers. The fear, the anger, the heartbreak—it follows me everywhere. I remember the way your mother looked, too. The way she looked when I saw her that night in the alley."

"So do I," Carmine said. "I remember the sound of her screams."

Vincent looked at Carmine curiously, apprehension in his eyes. He had never talked to him about that night, the memory too painful to verbalize. The only person he had told was Haven, but standing there with his father and taking in his broken expression, it felt necessary.

Sighing, Carmine closed his eyes as he sat beside him on the step, running his hand through his hair nervously as he recalled detail by detail what happened that fateful night. From the moment they stepped out of the piano recital to waking up in the hospital, every ounce of pain came out through his words.

"I can't remember what they looked like, though," Carmine said. "I've tried to imagine the killers hundreds of times, but it's a blur. The man with the gun, I don't think he ever looked at me, and the other, his face is always fucking distorted."

"Did they say anything?"

"*Shut her up! Do it quick!* That's it."

Vincent sat quietly and took it all in, his head bowed. "You almost bled to death. I was so angry at her that night, and the whole time she was dead and you were lying behind a Dumpster."

"It wasn't your fault," Carmine said. "The only people to blame are the motherfuckers with the guns in the alley that night."

Vincent cleared his throat. "I suppose you're right. I sometimes wonder if I could've stopped it, though."

"Yeah, well, Mom would tell you that's fucking bullshit," Carmine said, earning an amused look from his father. "Well, not in *those* words, but you know what I mean. Like you said a bit ago, it is what it is. I mean, often this past year I've wondered if we could've saved Haven a different way, so I could be with her wherever she is . . ."

"New York," Vincent said as he trailed off.

Carmine eyed him curiously. "New York?"

"I don't know exactly *where*, but she's in New York somewhere."

A smile tugged the corner of his lips. She went to New York like they had talked about. "The point is, I've learned it's senseless to wonder. I did what I did, you did what you did, and we are where we are. We just gotta do what we gotta do."

"You know, you mask it with the alcohol and profanity, but you've grown up quite a bit this past year."

"Yeah, well, I don't think Corrado would agree with you," Carmine said. "He threatens me at least once a week. I'm just waiting for the day he catches laryngitis and can't say, '*I'll kill you,*' so he just does it instead."

Vincent laughed, shaking his head. "He's threatened to kill me before. I've threatened to kill plenty of people, too, like Haven. It's how we're taught to control people, so it becomes second nature. Most of the men we deal with fear nothing except death."

"You know, it's fucked up how nonchalant you are talking about killing the girl I love."

"You still love her?" he asked curiously.

Carmine nodded. "I think I always will. Regardless of all this bullshit, she'll always be my hummingbird."

"Hummingbird," Vincent echoed. "Why do you call her that?"

"Uh, I don't know. Kinda just came out one day and stuck."

"Your mother would've loved that nickname." Vincent smiled to himself. "I haven't seen any in ages, but in the summertime hummingbirds used to swarm the tree in the backyard. Maura loved them; the way they could hover and fly backward and never tire. She was convinced the souls of the pure and innocent lived inside of them, and that's why they defied nature."

Before Carmine could respond, his phone chimed. He tensed when he saw the familiar message:

The docks, Third and Wilson.

Carmine slipped the phone back away. "Guess I gotta go."

Vincent nodded as he lit another cigarette, not appearing surprised, and made no move to get up.

"You wanna go inside?" Carmine offered. "It's still your house."

"No, I'm just going to sit here for a few minutes and then be on my way."

"Okay, then." Carmine started walking away. "I'll see you later."

"Carmine?" Vincent called out.

Carmine looked back, seeing the serious expression on his face. "Yeah?"

"I love you, son," he said quietly, taking a drag from his cigarette. "I don't think I've told you that since you were eight, but I
do."

"I love you, too," Carmine replied, his father's words putting
him on edge. "Look, don't go do anything stupid, okay?"

Vincent chuckled. "I won't do anything you wouldn't do."

"Yeah, well, *that* scares me, because I do some fucked-up shit."

"Go." Vincent waved Carmine off. "You know you can't be late
when you're called in. Don't worry about me."

"Whatever you say," Carmine mumbled, heading for the car.
"Bye, Dad."

"Good-bye, son."

23

Carmine stood stoically on the long wooden dock one Sunday afternoon, dark sunglasses covering his eyes from the blazing sunshine. He was hesitating, telling himself he may have the wrong place, but the words *The Federica* etched on the side of the boat in front of him were a clear giveaway that he had the right one.

Five minutes passed, maybe ten, as he stared at the yacht in silence, not wanting to go any farther. Last night's alcohol still simmered in his bloodstream, the remnants of Molly lingering in his veins. The buzz had faded away, though, as the onset of a headache made itself be known. He had been up until almost sunrise, partying with Remy and the other guys in his crew. He had just gotten home and climbed into bed when Sal called, telling him to report in at exactly one o'clock.

Business? Personal? Carmine wasn't sure. What he did know, though, was he had no interest being there either way.

A car pulled up behind him, parking in the grassy lot beside Carmine's Mercedes. He turned, watching his uncle climb out and head toward him. Corrado wore a white V-neck shirt, khakis, and a pair of tan loafers. Carmine's brow furrowed as he stared at the man's shoes.

"Something wrong?" Corrado asked, approaching him on the dock.

"No." He shook his head. "I've never really seen you so casual before."

"It's Sunday," he replied, shrugging as if that were a good explanation. "Celia is spending the afternoon with her mother so I thought I'd join Sal today."

"Oh." Carmine looked away from him, his gaze turning back to the yacht. "What are we doing here, anyway?"

Corrado didn't answer. Instead, he walked away, stepping onto the yacht and plopping down in a vinyl chair. Carmine remained still for a moment before joining him, taking a shaky step onto the polished wooden deck. He held tightly onto the railing to stabilize himself, the yacht swaying lightly. He was about to take a seat beside his uncle when Sal surfaced from inside, dressed even more casually than Corrado. Hairy legs hung out from the bottom of a pair of plaid shorts, a white undershirt clinging tightly to his oversize stomach. For once, Carmine felt like he almost fit in wearing his jeans and t-shirt.

"Principe!" Sal said excitedly, his eyes drifting from Carmine to Corrado. "Ah, Corrado! I'm glad you could join us, too! We're just waiting for one more."

Carmine eyed him anxiously. "Who?"

Sal nodded toward shore as a black sedan pulled up. Coldness rushed through Carmine as if there were ice in his veins as the man stepped out. The scar on the side of his face gleamed in the sunlight like a bright, sinister warning sign pointing to danger ahead.

Carmine's headache kicked in full-force, the pounding blinding as he clenched his teeth together to stop from saying anything. Instead of reacting, he forced himself to sit down in the vacant chair beside his uncle.

Carlo stepped onto the yacht, walking with determination, an aura of conceit enshrouding him. It was evident in his stride, and his smile, and his stance—the man believed he was invincible.

"I hope I'm not late," Carlo said.

Carmine glanced at his watch: 1:13 P.M. They were all late, technically speaking.

"No, no, of course not," Sal said, smiling gleefully as he slapped Carlo on the back. "It's just good to see you."

They set sail a minute later, navigating out toward an unoccupied area where nothing surrounded them but the calm, dark waters of Lake Michigan. Carmine remained tense, every muscle in his body rigid, as the men grabbed fishing rods and cast them in the water. They lounged and shared laughs, steadily sipping alcohol.

"So, we have a bit of a situation," Salvatore said eventually, his nonchalance shifting to seriousness. "We have another traitor that needs dealt with. He can't see it coming, and he's going to trust few at this point. You understand the gravity of the situation?"

"Of course," Corrado responded at once. "The rats have to go."

Salvatore turned to Carmine, his eyebrows raised inquisitively. Carmine nodded, unsure of why he was asking him, but he wasn't going to question it. His job was simply to agree. "Yes, sir."

"Good," Sal said, pulling out a cigar and clipping off the end of it, "because I need Vincent taken out as soon as possible."

Carmine's blood ran cold, his heart stopping for a fraction of a second. *Vincent?* It couldn't be so. He couldn't mean his father.

"It's unfortunate, but we have sources saying he's been feeding information to the Feds," Sal continued as he lit his cigar, savoring the first puff. "His father, Antonio—God rest his soul—was one of the greatest Boss's in the history of the organization. Vincent turning is a notion I wouldn't suggest if I weren't one-hundred percent sure."

Salvatore paused, glancing at Corrado, and Carmine held his breath. He waited for his uncle to defend him, for him to talk Salvatore out of it, to make him see logic that Vincent DeMarco would *never* jeopardize his family.

But the moment Corrado opened his mouth, Carmine's hope disintegrated. "I'll handle it."

"He'll expect you," Salvatore warned. "He knows you're the best."

Corrado started to respond, but another voice silenced him. "What about the boy?" Carlo asked. "Why not him?"

"Me?" Carmine asked incredulously. "I can't—"

"Can't?" Sal countered, his eyes darkening. "Are you refusing?"

"With all due respect, sir, Vincent has a lot of experience," Corrado said. "Carmine's still an amateur."

"True, but he wouldn't fire on his son, especially one who looks strikingly close to his wife. It would be like Maura dying all over again. No, Carlo's right. Carmine's perfect."

Carmine stared at them with shock, not knowing how to react. The fact that Salvatore would use his mother's memory to his advantage in his violent twisted game made him sick. There was no way he had just been ordered to murder his own father. It was unfathomable. "I'm supposed to kill my father?"

"A traitor, Carmine," Sal said sharply. "Your order is to eliminate the threat. It's about time you've proven your loyalty, anyway. You should've been made to do it long ago, but I didn't press the issue because of who you are. In fact, I've tolerated a lot I shouldn't have because of your last name, but I won't tolerate it any longer. Your grandfather would be rolling over in his grave right now."

"He would," Corrado chimed in. "Antonio would've never stood for this."

"So do what's expected of you," Salvatore continued. "Earn some respect back for your bloodline."

"But—"

Salvatore shot Carmine a look of murderous rage, silencing him abruptly. The atmosphere shifted once more to nonchalance as Sal puffed on his cigar with ease, turning his focus back to his fishing rod.

Two hours later the yacht docked again, and Carmine was the first one off the boat. He started down the dock in a stupor and heard Corrado follow, but he didn't turn around. Seething, he headed straight for his car when Corrado grabbed him.

"Get off of me," he spat, shrugging away from his uncle.

"Relax," Corrado said. "You did good."

Carmine laughed bitterly. "You expect me to *relax*? Maybe you can kill your own fucking family with no remorse, but I can't! How the hell could you agree with him? I thought you knew my father better than that!"

"I clearly know Vincent better than you do," he said. "You're ignorant if you believe he didn't know this would happen."

"You're saying he *planned* for this? What fucked-up world do you live in?"

"The same one you live in," Corrado said calmly, reaching into his pocket for his phone. "But it's a moot point, because you won't be killing anyone, Carmine."

"That's news to me, considering I was just *ordered* to. What am I supposed to do?"

"You're supposed to go home."

Corrado turned away and got into his car, leaving without another word. Carmine headed home, pulling into the driveway a few minutes later. The house was warm, the air-conditioning still broken. Carmine grabbed the bottle of Grey Goose from the freezer before strolling to the living room, flopping down on the couch and kicking off his shoes.

Time passed as he sat there staring at the floor, his frantic mind trying to sort through his options while he attempted to drown it all out with liquor. It surged through his body, but it didn't extinguish the ache in his heart.

Best-case scenario, Carmine thought, his father got away and he never saw him again. Worst-case scenario, he ended up dead, possibly at Carmine's hands. Violence, mayhem, murder, bloodshed, fucking annihilation—he wondered if there was any way to avoid it anymore.

Later he still sat hunched over, gripping his hair with the empty bottle of vodka at his feet. He was still lucid, hadn't even come close to drinking enough to black out. He got up when the sun set, the house cooling off a tad bit and growing darker. The cool wooden floor felt good against his feet as he strolled toward the kitchen, his head throbbing as he scoured the cabinets for more alcohol. He grew aggravated when he found none, slamming a cabinet drawer angrily as he grabbed his phone. Scrolling through his numbers, he stopped at Remy.

"Yeah?" Remy said, answering on the first ring. "What's up?"

"I need Molly."

Remy's laugh lit up the line. "I'll be right over, man."

Molly became Carmine's nightly companion.

While she finally made him feel alive again, filling that void deep inside of his chest, she proved to be both a blessing and a curse. She gave him something to focus on, something to look forward to, but at the same time she lured him deeper into a vast pit of darkness. Because when Carmine was high, he couldn't possibly be higher, but when he came down, when the drug wore off, leaving him to face life once more, he found himself much deeper than he had ever been before.

Depression took over, suicidal thoughts bombarding his mind. Reckless and unstable, he couldn't think straight or function normally.

He grew desperate for the sensation, seeking her out more often to delay the unavoidable come down. It got to the point where he was constantly high, everything falling to the wayside in his quest to *feel.*

His downward spiral was abrupt, a twelve-story fall straight to the ground.

The Novak Gala, held twice a year in an upscale gallery just north of Chelsea, always drew the most elite art patrons. Hundreds gathered to celebrate local artists, from the professionals to the blossoming post-graduate students at the surrounding schools.

Pieces were auctioned off for charity, supporting art programs in the underfunded public schools, and the media always took notice of the up-and-coming talent. It was a highly anticipated event in the community, but possibly even more so for the students at SVU.

For at every event, some lucky undergraduate students were given the opportunity of a lifetime: the chance to show their work. Students were given a topic and had to submit a single piece of art to be judged by the administration. The competition was stiff— out of the three thousand submissions, only the top twenty were chosen. The odds of being picked were less than one percent, but it didn't stop the students from giving it everything they had.

November faded fast, weeks passing, and with it came the deadline for submission to the judging panel. The theme for the winter gala was "coldness" and Haven stayed busy, creating scene after scene of dramatic landscapes—ice, blizzards, and freezing rain— before finally settling upon a painting of a field with falling snow. Simple, but beautiful, the white mingling with the fading green. She spent Thanksgiving holed up in her small apartment, surrounded by warmth from the oversize metal radiator, perfecting her painting, as she ate dinner straight out of the carton from the local Chinese delivery place. She hardly noticed it was a holiday, too engrossed in her work, too determined not to dwell on those things.

When the school reopened the Monday after Thanksgiving, Haven turned her project in to her Painting I professor, Miss Michaels. She studied it for a moment before nodding. "I'll be sure to submit it this afternoon."

"Thank you," Haven said, smiling proudly as she took one last look at her painting. She could see no flaws, everything precise, numerous art techniques she had learned portrayed. She couldn't imagine what more they would want.

"You're welcome, dear."

Haven hurried home after class that morning, bundled up in a thick tan coat, to find Kelsey rushing out of the brownstone. Haven's brow furrowed. She purposely had no morning classes so she wouldn't have to be up at that hour.

"I'm heading to the studios," Kelsey said, answering Haven's question before she could ask it. "I totally forgot submissions were due. I haven't even started mine!"

Haven stared at her with shock, blinking a few times. "Uh, good luck."

Kelsey gave a halfhearted wave before taking off, running down the street.

———

Two weeks later, as class was dismissing, Miss Michaels handed out envelopes to each of the students. The room filled with the rumbling of murmurs and the sound of crumpling paper as her classmates discarded their letters in the trashcan on their way out the door.

Rejections, from what Haven could tell. It made her nerves flare.

Haven opened her envelope carefully, smoothing out the crease in the paper as she read the letter the whole way through.

> We appreciate your effort . . .
> The competition was stiff . . .
> So much talent . . .
> We regret to inform you . . .
> Better luck next time . . .

Haven slowly absorbed the typed words, disappointment setting in when her eyes scanned the last sentence.

> Your submission ranked number 348.

Nowhere near the top twenty.

"You okay, dear?"

Haven glanced at her professor as she refolded the letter, sliding it carefully back into the envelope. "I don't understand what was wrong with my painting."

"Nothing, technically speaking," Miss Michaels said. "It just wasn't what they were looking for."

"Why?"

"You see, you took the assignment literally, and while there's nothing wrong with that, it made it lack the one thing they truly wanted."

"What's that?"

"Soul," she replied. "You could look at your painting and think coldness, but you couldn't feel it. And that's what's important. Your paintings should make people feel something, even if they have no idea why."

24

Time is a peculiar thing. A moment can feel like an eternity, while sometimes months can pass and seem like no time at all. It's unreliable, and fickle, but it's the most constant thing there is. *Time*. No matter what you do, you can't stop it. The clock will continue to tick away, minutes passing into hours, hours into days, until suddenly you are standing there and it's already a year later.

Christmas had arrived, twelve months passing since the day Carmine walked out the door in Durante. It had been a year marked with violence, with uncertainty, where doubt constantly lingered over his head like a stubborn storm cloud.

And the time showed on his face—his expression harder, his skin thicker, and his eyes bleaker, unfriendly and guarded. But in Carmine's mind, he had difficulty reconciling that he had been away from his former life for so long. To him, it seemed like just yesterday he had seen Haven, just a moment ago he had heard her voice or listened to her laugh, that he had kissed her lips or made love to her. The time that passed had been a mere hazy blip for him, the blink of an eye, a single steady heartbeat, but the weariness in his bones carried the truth.

He had managed to survive a year without her . . . the first, he thought, of a lifetime to come.

Although he was a man now, seeing things a person ought not see, doing things men should never do, deep inside of him the boy still loitered. He dodged his family, sidestepping accountability in lieu of living in a delusional world of his own—a world where he somehow convinced himself he could beat time, that he wasn't living his life dictated by the steady ticking of a clock, this one moving backward and not forward, counting down how many hours he had left on earth.

Because living the life he did, it was only a matter of time before death came knocking at the door, prepared to take him away.

And it only sped up with each chime of his cell phone.

———

Sycamore Circle.

Carmine glanced at the message as he strolled barefoot through the downstairs of his messy house, sipping straight from a half-empty bottle of vodka. Sighing, he set his drink on the counter in the kitchen before calling Remy, tapping his foot impatiently as it rang and rang. No answer.

He tried calling twice more as he threw on a coat and some shoes, wanting to know if he needed a ride to the site, but each time he only reached voicemail.

The sky was completely black, void of stars that night, with a light dusting of white on the frozen ground. It had been a peculiarly gentle winter so far, only a few days of ice and snow—one of the few blessings Carmine counted in his life at the moment—but he could feel a storm brewing. The tips of his fingers tingled and his nose grew numb the moment he stepped out into the frigid night air. Shuddering, he slipped on a pair of black gloves and put the hood up on his coat before climbing behind the wheel of his car, blasting the heat as he drove to Remy's.

There was no sign of him at the house, no lights on inside and no cars in the driveway. Another call went unanswered so Carmine headed to the meet-up spot, assuming he would see him there. Two other cars hid in the shadows of the abandoned lot, just down from the spot where the trucks were parked, but neither were Remy's old Impala.

One final call to his phone went unanswered.

The men staked out the location for a bit, watching and waiting, but there was no movement, just as last time. The trucks stood alone, ripe for the picking.

Or so it seemed.

They moved in, cracking locks and shoving through the gate, the group of guys approaching the trucks. It was methodical and routine, quiet and easy, until suddenly it wasn't anymore.

Carmine shoved the back of a truck open, expecting to find it packed full of weapons, but instead he saw nothing. Nothing at all. His heart dropped into his stomach, his vision blurring from dizziness. Something was wrong. Something was terribly fucking wrong.

A single loud gunshot cut through the night, confirming his worst fears. He turned quickly, blood rushing furiously through his body, and watched as one of the guys from the crew dropped to the ground. A horrifying scream ruptured from the guy's chest, so loud and poignant it vibrated through the air around them.

"Man down!" somebody shouted. "Fuck! Man down!"

Before Carmine could even think to react, the shadows shifted and people appeared out of nowhere. Ten, or twenty, or maybe even thirty men descended upon them, gunshots ricocheting through the lot.

Men scattered as others dropped, bullets flying left and right around Carmine. He grabbed his gun and shot back, but he couldn't see to aim in the darkness. A bullet zipped by his head, searing pain ripping through his face as it grazed his cheek. He cursed and sprinted away, firing shots behind him into the lot. Skidding on a patch of icy snow, he lost his balance and fell, but managed to get to his feet again before another bullet struck near him.

He jumped in his car and sped away from the scene, his hands shaking and stomach churning. They hadn't caught them off guard that time. They had been ready, laying in wait in the shadows, on the offense instead of defense.

As he drove through town, weaving frantically through traffic, all he could think was that they had walked straight into a trap. Someone had tipped them off.

The wound on Carmine's face burned like fire, a trickle of blood running down his cheek. He pushed his hood off his head as he ran his trembling hand through his chaotic hair. Terror coursed through his body, overtaking the dullness he had managed to shroud himself with. He had gotten so used to feeling nothing unless it was manufactured, the craved effects of the intoxicants he repeatedly forced down his throat and up his nose, that the inherent emotion that hit him seemed to be triple fold. It was raw and real, his heart racing violently.

Had it been Sal? Did he want him dead?

Disoriented, he sped through the streets, going straight to the club to look for Corrado. He bypassed the security guard at the front door and headed straight for the back, making his way down the narrow hallway. It struck him as he reached the office door that the music was loud, hip-hop thumping from the speakers, the first sign that his uncle was gone. He pushed that aside, though, and feverishly pounded on the door anyway.

"Hey," a guard said, having followed him from the front. "You looking for Moretti?"

"Yeah."

"He ran out for a bit," he said. "He shouldn't be much longer. You can have a drink and wait."

Frustrated, Carmine stepped back into the club, grabbing a towel from the bar to hold against the wound on his face. Glancing around, he tensed when he spotted Remy sitting at a table along the side, surrounded by girls. Confusion and rage simmered deep inside Carmine's gut.

"Where the fuck were you?" Carmine spat, hastily approaching the table.

Remy looked up at him, his bloodshot eyes widening. "Shit, man, what happened to you?"

"What happened?" Carmine laughed bitterly, pulling the towel away. Blood seeped into the white material, the sight of it making Carmine even dizzier. "What happened is we had a fucking job tonight and you were nowhere to be found!"

Remy sat up abruptly, reaching for his phone. "Shit, shit, shit," he chanted, scrolling through his missed calls and messages. "I didn't hear my phone, man. I swear."

Carmine grabbed the closest chair and shook it, nearly knocking the girl sitting in it to the floor. She jumped up and Carmine took her seat, shaking his head. "Yeah, well, it was a fucking ambush anyway."

"No way!" Remy shook his head with disbelief. "The docks?"

"Sycamore Circle."

"Fuck."

Fuck. Carmine shook his head. *Fuck* was right.

"Look, man, have a drink or something," Remy said, standing up. "Let me check on the others."

"Give me what you've got," Carmine said, grabbing his arm before he could walk away. "I need . . . fuck, I need *something*."

Reaching into his pocket, Remy pulled out a small packet of powder. "You might want to take it easy on it. It's not what you're used to."

Carmine ignored him as he walked away. He dished some of the powder out onto the table and inhaled a bunch of it, breathing in line after line, carelessly, recklessly. He needed the excitement . . . needed the fear erased.

Relaxing back in the seat, he waited for it to hit. Two or three minutes passed before the euphoria washed over him, intense and blinding. He reveled in the sensation, letting out a shuddering breath of relief, and waited for it to level out, but it didn't. It grew and grew, mounting deep within him and overtaking every cell in his weary body until there was nowhere else for it to go. It seized his frantically pounding heart, slowing it so intensely that it nearly stalled the beats.

His breath left him in a whoosh as his entire body was swarmed in a sense of peace—no more fear, no more anxiety, no more *nothing*.

It overwhelmed him, too much, too fast, too intense. The burning in his cheek was replaced with pins and needles, his eyelids drooping so fast he nearly lost consciousness right away.

"Fuck," he muttered, running his hands down his face in an attempt to stay awake, smearing the blood from his wounded cheek.

The music suddenly stopped, the atmosphere shifting as the darkness in the club grew. It took over everything, consuming him, but a familiar voice cut through it and called his name. "Carmine!"

Carmine looked in the direction of the sound, blinking a few times, and saw Corrado's rapid approach. It seemed in slow motion, shuddering movements like a spastic strobe light. He tried to speak, but he couldn't get any words to form.

"Stay awake, kid," Corrado said, his voice calm and collected. Carmine started at him briefly, trying to obey, but the drug was stronger. Despite a crack across his face that sent stinging exploding under his skin, Carmine's heavy eyelids closed.

The club erupted in chaos, but Carmine was only vaguely aware before he slipped completely into the drug-induced blackness.

———

Beep . . . beep . . . beep . . .

What the fuck?

Carmine pried his eyes open, squinting from the harsh fluorescent lights. The beeping echoed through the small, secluded room, coming from a cardiac monitor to his left. The monitor spiked with each beep, coinciding with each heartbeat in his chest. It was strong, steady. He stared at it, following the wires straight to his body, surveying the IVs and tubes connected to his skin. He lay in an uncomfortable hospital bed, draped in a flimsy gown and covered with a white sheet.

Something moved on the other side of the room. Carmine turned his head, his attention suddenly shifting away from his own predicament. Corrado stood in front of the window, peering out at a large parking lot. He didn't turn or speak, his hands shoved in the pockets of his pants.

Before Carmine could make sense of any of it, the door to the room opened and a nurse walked in, followed by a doctor. The doctor, white haired and clad in a lab coat, carried a thick chart in his hands. He looked at Corrado with hesitation before turning his gaze to Carmine in the bed. "Mr. DeMarco, it's nice to see you awake."

"Uh, yeah." Carmine's throat was scratchy. He cleared it before speaking again. "What am I doing here?"

"You don't remember?" the doctor asked, glancing down at the chart. Carmine remembered going on the faulty job and then making his way to the club to wait for Corrado, but the rest was a black haze. "Well, you were brought in a few hours ago, unresponsive from an overdose."

"Overdose?"

"Your labs indicate a few drugs in your system, but you overdosed on heroin."

Carmine blanched. *Heroin?*

He absorbed nothing else as the doctor talked about Narcan and counteragents, drug rehab, and long-term side effects. Dread once more bubbled up inside of him, brewing in his bloodstream. His muscles were locked up, everything strained and painful. He felt like a fucking Mack truck had hit him.

"We'll run a few tests and have you out of here by tomorrow," the doctor said. "Until then, try to get some rest."

The man's eyes darted to Corrado again before he excused himself, the nurse leaving with him. The tension in the room quadrupled upon their exit. Carmine lay there, trying to find the words to address the situation, but Corrado beat him to it.

"The rules are simple," he said, still staring out the window. "We don't have many, but the ones we do, we expect to be followed. Stay away from drugs and stay out of the limelight. Which part of that didn't you understand?"

"I, uh . . . look, I didn't mean for it to go that far, I . . ."

"I don't want to hear your meaningless excuses, Carmine. How long have you been doing it?"

"A few weeks," Carmine admitted. "Two months at most, I guess."

"You guess?"

"Well, I haven't kept a fucking calendar or anything."

"You *will* talk to me with respect." The tone of Corrado's voice sent a chill down Carmine's spine. He wasn't speaking as family— he was addressing Carmine as his superior. "Do you understand?"

"Yes, sir."

"Good. And what in the world possessed you to do a job out at Sycamore Circle? Everybody knows that's Irish territory!"

"I, uh . . . I got a text." Carmine looked around for his phone, spotting his clothes laying in a heap on the floor. "I thought you ordered it."

"Must've been Sal," Corrado muttered to himself, shaking his head. "Three men were hospitalized, you know. One nearly died. And you just fled the scene . . . fled to go get high."

"I went to find you," Carmine said defensively. "It was an ambush. They were waiting for us."

"Of course they were. They warned us weeks ago."

Carmine said nothing. He didn't know what to say.

"Do you know the history between the Italian and Irish in Chicago?" Corrado asked, glancing at him and raising his eyebrows.

He nodded hesitantly, clearing his throat. "They hate each other."

"It's deeper than that," Corrado said. "We've clashed since before Prohibition, when John Torrio was building our empire.

He was diplomatic, believed just because we were criminals didn't mean we had to be savages. Bugs Moran, the underboss of the Irish Mob at the time, tried to kill Torrio. He was severely injured in an assassination attempt, which forced him to hand over control to Al Capone. Capone continued what Torrio started, but he wasn't above equal justice."

"An eye for an eye," Carmine muttered.

"Exactly," Corrado said. "Moran tried to kill Capone a few times but failed. He wasn't a very good hit man. A peace conference was called, where Capone said he believed Chicago was big enough for all of us. Said it was like a pie, where every gang should have their fair slice."

"Makes sense," Carmine said, even though he had no clue where the conversation was going.

"Makes sense to me, too," he said. "For a while, after that meeting, the bloodshed ceased, but it didn't last. You know what happened next, right?"

Carmine stared at him. "Uh, sorta. I was never good at history. I failed it in high school . . . both times."

Corrado laughed dryly. "This is the history that matters . . . *our* history. Moran started killing Capone's friends. Capone's patience wore thin until he finally decided enough was enough. He sent some men dressed as police into Moran's warehouse, lined six of his associates against the wall, and slaughtered them."

"Saint Valentine's Day Massacre."

"The bloodshed stopped after that. And it's only because we've respected those boundaries, because we've shared the pie, that we've had peace." Corrado paused. "All of this ends *now*, Carmine. If I ever hear of you touching drugs again, if it doesn't kill you, I will. I won't allow you to become a heroin addict."

"I didn't know it was heroin," he said. "It was supposed to be Molly, you know, MDMA."

Corrado turned from the window. "This is Molly? I thought you had a girlfriend by that name."

"You thought I was *seeing* someone?" he asked. "That's crazy."

"No, crazy is infecting your system with illicit intoxicants for a thrill instead of indulging in something safer, like a woman."

Carmine shook his head. "There's only one woman for me."

Corrado ignored that, turning to stare out the window once more. "This is the same room, you know. It's been remodeled, but it's where they kept you when you were shot. I felt déjà vu this morning, seeing you lying in that bed. The only difference is your father isn't here now. I can only imagine how he'd feel, seeing you treat your life so carelessly . . . a life Maura died to protect."

The beeping from the monitor was momentarily erratic at the mention of Carmine's parents. Shame seeped under his skin as his uncle continued his lecture.

"I need to be able to trust you, and so far, you've given me every reason not to. You can't continue to disrespect me, to disrespect the organization your grandfather helped build. It's bad enough your father . . ." Corrado trailed off, his posture going rigid. He stood frozen, a cold stone statue, and his voice matched it when he spoke again. "Don't tarnish the DeMarco legacy any further."

Carmine's voice was hardly a whisper. "Yes, sir."

Corrado strolled over to the hospital bed. "Where'd you get them, anyway?"

"Get what?"

"The drugs, Carmine. Where'd you get them?"

Carmine shook his head. "I, uh . . ."

"Tell me," Corrado demanded. "I want to know who's been supplying you."

"But I—"

"Tell me!"

A shuddering breath escaped Carmine's lips, with it the lone name. "Remy."

Corrado's eyebrows rose with question. "Tarullo?"

"Yes."

Before he could elaborate, Corrado's strong hand shot out

and wrapped around his throat. The cardiac monitor went wild, frenzied beeping filling the room as Carmine struggled to take a breath, his lungs burning, begging for oxygen.

"Rule number one," Corrado whispered, leaning close so he hovered over a thrashing Carmine, his mouth near his ear. "You never rat out your friends."

He let go, and Carmine inhaled sharply. Tears stung his eyes, his vision blurred as he watched his uncle head for the door. "I'll be back. I have to do some thinking on how best to handle you."

The sun was just starting to rise outside, blinding light filtering into the window as it bounced off the windshields of the cars in the parking lot. Seven in the morning, he guessed, maybe earlier.

Carmine lay there on the lumpy, uncomfortable bed for a while, humoring the nurses as they poked and prodded, taking vials of blood and checking vitals, before he decided enough was enough. Tearing the IVs out, ignoring the blood running down his forearm, he disconnected himself from the machines. Doctors rushed in as the cardiac monitor flatlined, gaping at him as he pulled on his clothes. He ignored their pleas to get back in bed, brushing past them and walking straight out of the hospital against medical advice.

He didn't make it very far. A block or so away, he strolled into a small tavern with a fluorescent OPEN sign flickering in the window. Head pounding viciously, eyes burning, and throat dry, he wanted nothing more than to drown in a drink.

"Just give me whatever's on tap," he muttered, reaching into his pocket and pulling out a few crumpled-up bills.

"Do you have ID?" the bartender asked. Carmine glared at him, making no move to answer. He wasn't sure if it was the look in his eyes—the I'll-fucking-cut-your-balls-off-for-a-drink glare—or maybe the blood on his ripped shirt, but something changed the man's mind. "Never mind. You look old enough to me."

He poured Carmine a beer, setting it on the bar in front of him, and wordlessly took the cash. Carmine picked up his mug and took a sip, grimacing from the bitter taste. He was about to take a second one—bigger this time—when someone grabbed him from behind. He flew off the bar stool and hit the floor with a painful thud, the beer spilling all over the front of him.

"What the fuck?" Carmine spat as the person clutched his arm and dragged him toward the door. He saw his uncle as he finally got to his feet again. "Corrado?"

"You walk out of the hospital to go to a bar?" Corrado seethed, pulling him onto the sidewalk and toward his Mercedes parked along the curb. Carmine tried to yank his arm away, but Corrado's grasp was too tight. He forced him in the passenger seat of the car before climbing in beside him and speeding away. "You nearly died last night."

"Yeah, well, I didn't. How the hell did you find me? Do you have a GPS chip planted on me?"

"Of course not," Corrado said. "Although maybe that's not such a bad idea. Is that what you want? Me to inject you with a chip like your father did your girlfriend?"

"Ex," Carmine muttered. "She's not my girlfriend anymore."

"Lucky for her," Corrado said. "That means she dodged a bullet . . . unlike you."

Carmine tried to keep a straight face as his uncle reached over, pinching his cheek where he had been shot. The wound stung almost as much as his harsh words.

Corrado drove the two of them past *Luna Rossa*, his eyes surveying the club. "I've owned *Luna Rossa* for decades, and until last night there wasn't a single incident here. Not one. Murderers and thieves come in and out of my doors every day, and it took a coward to blow my perfect streak."

25

Come home with me."

Haven looked up from the book in her lap as Kelsey burst into her apartment, half a dozen bags awkwardly juggled in her arms. Frazzled, she breathed erratically, her eyes so wide she appeared unhinged.

"What?" Haven asked. "Why?"

"Why?" Kelsey dropped her luggage on the floor by her feet. "Because it's Christmas, that's why. The semester's over, you have no work to do, so there's no reason why you can't come home with me."

Haven closed her book, sighing. "But it's Christmas."

"Duh, that's what I said." Kelsey rolled her eyes. "You shouldn't be here all alone. It's not right."

"What about your family, though?" Haven asked. "I don't think Christmas is really the time to bring a stranger home."

"Are you kidding me? You clearly don't know my family." Kelsey shook her head, laughing dryly as she muttered something quietly to herself. She turned back to Haven after a moment, her expression suddenly severe. "Seriously, come home with me. Please don't make me go alone."

Haven laughed. "They can't be that bad."

"Like I said, you don't know them," Kelsey replied. "So come meet them, eat Christmas dinner, and then we'll talk about whether or not they're bad."

Hesitating, Haven looked away from her friend. "I don't have anything packed."

"Do it now. The car will be here in ten minutes. That's plenty of time for you to pack. I mean, really . . ." Kelsey eyed Haven, scrunching up her nose. ". . . It takes less than that for you to get ready in the mornings."

"Fine." Haven tossed the book onto the couch beside her before standing. "I'll go."

"Awesome," Kelsey shouted as Haven walked into the bedroom. "And change your clothes while you're in there! You're totally not wearing sweats in public with me."

Rolling her eyes, Haven slammed the bedroom door behind her.

Ten minutes later, she reemerged with a duffel bag full of clothes and necessities, wearing a pair of jeans and a long-sleeved pink blouse that matched her Nike's. She pulled her wavy hair back into a ponytail and grabbed her coat, standing in front of her friend for inspection. "Better?"

"Good enough." Kelsey turned to the window as a horn blared in front of the building. "Oh, perfect timing! Car's here!"

Haven locked up the apartment before following her friend out of the brownstone, her footsteps faltering the moment she stepped outside. Along the curb in front of her sat a black stretch limo, the driver hurriedly taking Kelsey's bags from her to toss in the trunk. Kelsey thanked him with a smirk before turning to Haven. "What are you waiting for?"

What was she waiting for? She blinked a few times, squeezing her eyes shut tightly the last time, expecting the car to be gone when she reopened them, but it wasn't. It idled there, both Kelsey and the driver looking at her strangely.

"I, uh . . . nothing." Haven shook her head as she walked to the limo. She attempted to put her own bag in the trunk but the driver stopped her, prying it from her hands. "Uh, thank you."

"My pleasure," he replied, opening the back door for the two of them. Haven climbed in, the smell of fresh leather strong in the vehicle. The seats and floor were immaculate, not a speck of dirt anywhere.

"First time in a limo?" Kelsey asked, casually lounging in the seat.

"That obvious?"

"Maybe," she replied. "My father sends them for me all the time. 'Nothing but the best for my baby girl,' he says."

Haven smiled. "He sounds nice."

Kelsey's abrupt laughter bounced through the confined space. "Nice? Yeah, just wait . . ."

Her words made Haven's anxiety flare. "You said he's a politician, right?"

"Right. Good ol' senator from the great state of New York. Not like he actually *does* anything, though."

"What does your mom do?"

"Drinks wine and harps on people," Kelsey replied. "So basically the same as my father: nothing."

Even though it was only a few miles away, it took them nearly forty-five minutes in traffic to reach Kelsey's parents' estate, a large three-story mansion on the Upper East Side. Haven gawked at it as they pulled onto the property, admiring the manicured lawn with elaborate fountains. "You lived here?" she asked with disbelief. "Why in the world did you move to a tiny apartment?"

Kelsey sighed. "My father offered to get me a place nearby, but I wanted to live in Chelsea. We waited so long it was hard to find a place near the school, but he made a few calls and managed to get the apartment above yours."

Haven shook her head, too dumbfounded to understand as the limo came to a stop, the driver opening the door for them. He retrieved their bags when they climbed out, the front door to the house opening right away. Two men appeared, wordlessly taking the bags from the driver and hauling them inside.

A third man appeared then, strolling casually out of the front door. He wore a tie and coat, his dark hair perfectly sculpted, a few gray strands gleaming in the sunlight. He paused, eyeing the two of them intently. "Kelsey."

"Father."

"It's good to see you."

She muttered under her breath, the words inaudible but tone petulantly scathing, before she cleared her throat and replied. "You, too."

"I see you brought a friend."

Haven's cheeks suddenly grew warm as the attention shifted to her.

"Yeah, this is my neighbor, Hayden Antoinette," Kelsey said. "I invited her for Christmas."

"That was, uh, nice of you," he said. "Uncharacteristically so."

Kelsey narrowed her eyes. "I know how to be nice."

He ignored her statement as he stepped forward, holding out his hand to shake hers. "Hayden Antoinette, is it? Any relation to Marie?"

"Marie Antoinette?" Haven's brow furrowed as she shook the man's firm hand. Something about his grip, his commanding presence, made her nerves flare further. "Well, uh . . . she was a French queen, right? And I'm just, uh . . . well, I'm not royalty."

He let out a laugh as she stammered, her cheeks turning even redder. "I was just joking, dear. It's nice to meet you."

"You, too . . ."

"Cain," he said, letting go of her hand. "Just call me Cain."

"Just call me Cain," Kelsey mocked her father in a fake deep voice. "Are you done kissing ass now, Senator? Can we go inside?"

Cain swept his hands toward the entrance. "By all means, sunshine, go on in."

Kelsey grabbed Haven's hand and pulled her past her father. Cain watched them intently like he was studying their every movement, his gaze making Haven's hair bristle a bit.

She followed Kelsey, her eyes guardedly surveying the vast

house as they made their way upstairs. Kelsey showed her to the guest room, where Haven's bag already sat beside the bed. "My bedroom's right down the hall," she said. "The door on the end."

Kelsey left her there, and Haven took a seat on the large canopy bed. The guest room, the size of her entire apartment across the city, was adorned in various shades of burgundy and gold, the carpet beneath her feet vibrant white—so bright, in fact, she was almost afraid to move.

Haven unzipped her bag, reaching inside for the familiar leather-bound journal. Kicking off her shoes, she lay back on the bed and stared up at the see-through gold cloth draped above her, a frown tugging the corner of her lips. No matter how hard she fought it, attempting to keep a smile on her face, the sadness won out.

Christmas Eve. Tomorrow was Christmas day. And the next day, well . . . she didn't like to think about what December 26 marked.

Opening the book, she pulled out the piece of paper she had tucked inside and unfolded it, staring at the sloppy writing, haphazardly scribbled in the middle of the night last Christmas. She had read it so many times she could recite it word for word.

She got to the end, her fingers tracing the three simple words: *I love you.*

"I love you, too," she whispered.

A year later, she still did.

Carmine's brow furrowed as Corrado drove past the street that led to home. He cleared his throat. "Uh, I think you missed the turn."

Corrado's eyes remained on the road in front of him. He offered no reply as he reached for the radio, pressing the button to turn the music up. Frank Sinatra loudly vibrated the speakers, the song making Carmine's skin prickle. His heart banged against his ribcage, echoing in his ears.

Frank Sinatra tended to trigger something in Corrado.

Panicking inside, his paranoia spiked as Corrado drove onto some vacant roads, deep into a neighborhood Carmine hadn't been to in more than a decade. He had definitely fucked up and he knew there would be consequences, but he never thought it would be this. He never considered the fact that his uncle might get fed up. He never thought he might actually *end* him.

Carmine, until that moment, still believed he was invincible.

After driving for a few more minutes, Corrado slowed and pulled the car along the curb. Reaching over, he grasped the passenger side handle and flung open the door. "Get out."

Carmine's eyes darted around for some sign of life. Corrado wouldn't kill him if there were witnesses. "What?"

"I said get out!"

Carmine obeyed at the sound of his uncle's raised voice. He jumped out of the car and slammed the door, his frantic mind working fast. He thought about running, debating if he could evade him in the nearby alleys in the night, but he didn't have to act. Tires squealed and a cloud of smoke filtered into the air as Corrado hastily sped away, leaving him standing there alone.

Carmine stared at the red taillights as they faded into the night, partially relieved but even more baffled. "What the fuck?"

"Now, now," a voice said behind him, so close the hair on the back of Carmine's neck stood on end. "That's no way to talk here."

Turning around, Carmine instinctively reached in his waistband for his weapon but unsurprisingly came up empty. He had nothing, to be precise—no ID, no wallet, not even a penny in his pocket.

He stood frozen at that realization, his panic dissipating as he took in the cloaked form a few feet away. The first thing he noticed was the Roman collar, the bright white sliver of fabric shining brightly in the darkness.

Confused, Carmine glanced past the man and surveyed the massive brown building, taking in the ornamental front door and massive steps leading to it. Corrado had dropped him off in front of an old church.

"Sorry, sir," he muttered. "Or, I mean . . . your holiness?"

The priest smiled. "You may call me Father Alberto. What seems to be your trouble tonight?"

"Nothing. No trouble. I just . . ." Carmine wasn't sure what to say. *I just really kinda sorta fucked up my life and thought my uncle was about to kill me for it?* ". . . I need a phone. You wouldn't know where I could borrow one, would you? I mean, I know you wouldn't have one, but maybe you know someone who does?"

Father Alberto raised his eyebrows. "Why wouldn't I have one?"

"I don't know. I guess because you're one of those old school religious guys."

The priest let out a hearty laugh. "I'm Catholic, son, not Amish. I have no aversion to technology. Come, you can use my phone."

Motioning for him to follow, Father Alberto headed inside. Carmine hesitated before stepping into the church, his eyes darting around cautiously. The place was dim with a golden glow that was strangely warm and inviting. Carmine's nerves instantly eased a bit. At least, he thought, his uncle wouldn't kill him there.

He followed the priest to a small office in the back with a wooden desk taking up most of the space. An old white telephone sat on the corner, the twisty cord tangled. Picking it up, Carmine dialed Celia's number as the priest took a seat behind the desk. Carmine leaned against it, waiting as the phone rang.

The answering machine picked up on the fifth ring, and her cell phone went straight to voicemail. He tried them both twice before giving up.

"No answer?" the priest asked.

"No."

"Well, take a seat then." Father Alberto motioned toward a chair in front of his desk. "We'll chat while you wait. You can try your calls again later."

Carmine debated for a moment before plopping down in the chair. It wasn't as if he really had another option. With no money and no friends, it was either wait or start walking, and he was too damn exhausted for the second choice.

"Thanks," Carmine said. "For the phone and the seat."

"You're welcome. It is what we old school religious guys do, after all."

His voice was lighthearted and Carmine chuckled. "Sorry about that. I didn't know. I've never been into the whole church thing."

"Why not?"

Carmine shrugged. "Not really my scene."

Father Alberto stared at him peculiarly. "Do you believe in God?"

A question Carmine dreaded, especially coming from a priest. He briefly considered lying to placate the man but thought better of it, considering he was sitting in the middle of a church. He had evaded death twice that week. Something told him he wouldn't be so lucky the third time if lightning struck. "Honestly, I'm not sure. Maybe? But I've seen some bad shi—uh, stuff, in my life that makes me doubt anyone gives a fu—uh, damn, about us." Carmine's eyes widened when he realized, despite his best effort, he still cursed. "Shit. Sorry, Father. It's been a bad night."

Carmine was half expecting to be kicked out, but Father Alberto merely smiled. "You aren't the first to utter those words within these walls, and I'm certain you won't be the last. I'm more concerned by your negativity than your profanity."

"Well, you have a better chance of getting me to stop cursing than you do of changing the way I see things. It's hard to believe there's someone watching over us when so many good people get fucked over every day."

"Ah, that's an argument I hear often," Father Alberto said. "How can a God exist when it seems so many have been forsaken? But you fail to realize, son, without the bad we can't truly appreciate the good. Suffering teaches us to be better people. What we do in bad times measures how good of a person we really are."

Carmine let out a bitter laugh, slouching in the chair as he thought about how he had adapted. "I must not be a very good man, then."

"Oh, I don't believe that."

"That's because you don't know me. You don't know the things I've done."

"Then tell me," the priest challenged. "Change my mind."

Carmine scoffed. "I can't."

"Why not?" he asked. "Are you ashamed?"

"No." Carmine hesitated. "Well, yes, but that's not the point."

"That *is* the point," the priest said. "This is a safe place. Anything you say within these walls stays within these walls. The only thing keeping you from confessing your sins is your own reluctance to admit them."

"Because I'm screwed up. Who would *want* to admit that?"

"Someone without morals," he said, "which brings me back to you being a good man. The truly bad don't have a conscience, son."

Carmine pondered those words. The old man had somehow twisted things to his liking.

"If you don't want to discuss your past, why don't we talk about the future?" the priest suggested. "Maybe we can figure out why God brought you here tonight."

"God didn't bring me here," Carmine said.

"No?"

"No, the devil dropped me off."

Surprisingly, the priest smiled at that. "Is there a reason he did that?"

"Your guess is as good as mine, but I'm starting to think he might actually have a sense of humor."

Time passed as the two of them sat in the cramped office, going round in conversation about religion and life. Neither wavered, Carmine refusing to budge from his line of thinking, but he found himself feeling better the more the priest spoke. Something about the man's voice, the compassion in his words, put Carmine at ease. He started making small concessions, offering tidbits of truth as he skimmed the surface of his reality and shared the tiny shavings that came off the top.

The sun had already started to rise when Carmine tried his calls again, each one just as unsuccessful as before. He hung up the phone with a frown, realizing nobody would be coming to his aide.

"No answer again?" the priest asked.

"No," he replied. "I should get going. I have a long walk ahead of me."

"Walk?" The priest shook his head. "Nonsense. I'll give you a ride."

Carmine blinked a few times, surprised. "You have a car?"

"Of course," the priest said. "A telephone, a car . . . I even have a microwave, if you ever need to borrow one. What's mine is yours."

Carmine stared at the priest with disbelief. "Why didn't you tell me sooner?"

"You didn't ask."

Carmine stood, stretching his tired body as he ran his hands down his face. "We wasted a whole night here when you could've driven me home hours ago."

"Ah, I wouldn't say we wasted the night," Father Alberto said. "I rather enjoyed speaking with you. It was quite illuminating."

Carmine followed the priest out of the church and around the corner, where an old model Cadillac Deville was parked along the curb. He smiled when he saw it, eyeing the light blue paint and tan interior.

"This is yours?" Carmine asked.

"Technically it belongs to Saint Mary's, but yes," he replied. "A former parishioner donated it to the church ages ago. I want to say it's been nearly thirteen years."

"Christ," Carmine said, surprised it still ran, and smiled sheepishly when the priest gave him a peculiar look. "I'm just saying, you know . . . wow. My grandfather had one of these. He used to pick me up from school sometimes when I was a kid and drive me around. Pretty much the only memory I have of the man."

"Is that right?"

"Yes. He died when I was a kid, probably about . . ." Carmine paused as he did the math in his head. ". . . Thirteen years ago."

The priest smiled at him before climbing into the car and starting it. It hesitated, the engine roaring and car trembling as it sprung to life. Sighing, Carmine climbed into the passenger seat and rattled off his address, staring out the side window as they silently drove through town.

Father Alberto pulled the car into the driveway when they arrived. Carmine turned to the man, about to thank him, and noticed the look of awe on his face. Before Carmine could say anything, the priest burst into a loud, boisterous laughing fit. He laughed so hard tears sprung to his eyes, and he wiped them with the back of his hand as Carmine stared at him with confusion. "What's so funny?"

"The door is blue."

"Yeah, so?"

The priest shook his head. "I thought Vincenzo was joking."

Carmine's expression fell at the sound of his father's name. He could only gape at the man in shock.

"He truly did a terrible job painting it," Father Alberto continued, "but I commend him for doing it, nonetheless."

"You know my father?"

"Of course I do," the priest said. "It's no coincidence you ended up on my front steps tonight, son."

Carmine shook his head. What was this, a goddamn intervention?

"Merry Christmas." The priest smiled, waving good-bye. "And for the record, I've always suspected Corrado had a sense of humor, too."

26

Christmas on the Upper East Side turned out to be a more formal affair than Haven anticipated. No gifts were exchanged in the morning, no stories shared in the afternoon. At precisely three o'clock they all gathered in the large dining room, the four of them sitting at a table fit for a dozen. The staff served the meal, quietly and swiftly fixing each of them a plate before disappearing from the room.

Haven stared down at her food as the others started eating, her stomach in tight knots. Those people, the servants—didn't they have families? Why were they working there on Christmas?

Thoughts of the worst kind infiltrated her mind. They couldn't be, could they? A senator, a man of the law, wouldn't keep slaves in his home.

Would he?

The possible answer to that terrified Haven.

"So, Hayden . . ."

Haven looked up from her plate, turning to Kelsey's mother, Anita, down the table from her. Anita wore her dark hair in a tight bun on top of her head, a long string of pearls draped around her neck. She sipped from a glass of white wine that she had already refilled twice since they sat down.

"Yes, ma'am?"

"Tell me about your family."

Haven stared at her. "My family?"

"Yes, your family. I'd like to know why you're not with them on Christmas."

"Mother . . ." Kelsey hissed through clenched teeth at the same time her father muttered, "Anita, please."

"Relax, I'm merely curious," she said, waving them both off as she eyed Haven. "So, your family?"

"Well, uh . . . I don't really have one," she replied. "My parents are both gone."

"An orphan?" Anita gasped loudly, leaning closer to the table. "How tragic! How did they die?"

"Car accident," she answered right away, swallowing back the harsh truth that the only parent she really ever had took her own life to free herself from restraints . . . restraints put on her by the man who was supposed to be her father.

"So sad," Anita said. "What about your other family members? Brothers? Cousins? Uncles? Aunts? Do you have anybody?"

"That's enough, Anita," Cain said, his voice firm. "Drop it."

"Oh, get off it," Anita said as she took a sip of her drink. "You can't tell me you're not curious why a young girl has no place to go on Christmas."

"She has someplace to go," Cain countered. "She's here, isn't she?"

Anita scoffed. "Please, Cain. Nobody actually wants to be here. Not even our own daughter wants to be in this house."

"That's because you always give everyone the third degree," he said. "I don't even want to come here half the time because of your interrogations."

"Oh, don't give me that! That's not why you don't come home! Maybe you can lie to everyone else and have them believe the bullshit that comes out of your mouth, but not me."

"Bullshit?" Cain slammed his hand down on the table. "You want to talk about bullshit, let's talk about it."

Back and forth they went, bickering, slamming each other with harsh words. Kelsey continued to eat, completely unfazed, while

Haven flinched and cringed at their exchange of hostility. It went on forever until suddenly they both seemed to run out of things to say.

Silence strangled the room. Haven took a few bites of her food, forcing it down, grateful that was over.

Until Anita spoke again. "So Kelsey, sweetheart, how bad did you fail school this time?"

"I didn't fail," Kelsey said. "I made mostly As and Bs with one D."

"What was the D in?"

"Painting."

"How in the world?" Anita shook her head in disapproval. "Even a monkey could pass that class. Any idiot can slap paint on a canvas."

The words were like a crack to Haven's chest. She let out an involuntary gasp, stung by the insult. Cain's eyes darted from her over to his wife. "Dammit, Anita."

"Oh, you're a painter?" she asked. "I'm sure your work is lovely, dear. Just lovely. My daughter, on the other hand . . ."

The bickering started all over again.

Haven breathed a deep sigh of relief when dinner ended. Kelsey excused herself to use the restroom while Anita grabbed the bottle of wine and darted from the room, leaving Haven alone with Kelsey's father.

The staff came in to clear the table. Haven watched them curiously, forgetting Cain was there until he spoke. "They've been employed by my family for a long time."

Haven glanced at him curiously. "What?"

"The staff. They've worked for me for years, since Kelsey was a baby. Christmas is completely voluntary, but since they get paid double on holidays they usually all choose to work part of their shift."

"Oh." Suspicion washed through Haven. "How did you . . . ?"

"How did I know you wondered?" he asked, nailing her question right away. "I didn't grow up wealthy. My mother moonlighted as a dancer. My father was a conman. Needless to say, I know that look on your face well."

"What look is that?"

"The look of not understanding how life can deal someone such a crummy hand." Cain stood, tipping his head. "It was nice meeting you. You're welcome here any time."

He walked out, leaving Haven alone in the giant dining room. Kelsey returned after a moment, pausing in the doorway. "So?"

"So," Haven said, standing up, "maybe you weren't totally exaggerating."

Kelsey laughed. "Told you. Terrible."

Terrible? Maybe not, but they certainly reminded Haven of people she had tried to avoid since she was a kid.

Saint Mary's Catholic Church was a ghost town on a Saturday night, the rows of pews leading up to the pulpit vacant. The Bibles were all closed, tucked into their wooden nests, awaiting tomorrow's service when the words printed on their pages would once again become front and center in dozens of lives.

Lives that, when the moon shone in the night sky, casually and callously disregarded the commandments they swore to abide by in the Sunday morning sunlight.

Vincent slipped into the church under the cloak of darkness, shrouded in an oversize black hooded sweatshirt covered in thick snowflakes. He removed his hood once safely inside, exposing his dark unkempt hair. He hadn't had a cut in weeks, nor had he taken the time to shave—his scruffy hair coated his jaw while baggy jeans hung loosely from his waist. He appeared to be quite the opposite of the clean-cut doctor he once was.

He strolled up the aisle toward the front of the church, stopping near the massive organ to the left of the pulpit. It didn't take long, only a moment or two, before Vincent heard footsteps behind him in the church. They were subtle, undetectable to ears that weren't trained to listen to the dangers carried on the wind.

He hadn't seen Father Alberto in quite some time—not since he had spilled his soul, letting loose all of his deepest, darkest demons—but he needed the man now. He needed his guidance. He needed to know that sometimes it was okay to do something immoral in order to spare others from suffering. Two wrongs don't make a right, he knew that, but he couldn't help but wonder if maybe, just maybe, one inconceivable wrong could be forgiven if it set it all straight again.

Vincent bowed his head as he closed his tired eyes, sullenly making the sign of the cross. "Forgive me, Father, for I have sinned."

"What else is new?"

Vincent's eyes snapped open at the sound of the voice, low yet striking, entirely detached and frighteningly familiar. Guarded, Vincent's heart pounded as hard as a bass drum when he turned around, coming face-to-face with the last person he expected to encounter: Corrado.

"I almost didn't recognize you," Corrado said, standing beside the front pew a few feet away. "You haven't been stealing your son's clothes, have you? It's really not a good look."

Vincent eyed his brother-in-law suspiciously. Corrado seemed relaxed, his hands in the pants pockets of his black fitted suit as he stared at him, awaiting a response.

"How did you know I'd be here?" Vincent asked.

Corrado shook his head. "Lucky guess. You're quite predictable, to be honest. Just as predictable as your son."

"What are you doing here?"

"I could ask you the same thing, Vincent," Corrado replied. "Church sanctuary ended centuries ago. They can't offer you protection anymore. Well, maybe protection from God, but not from man. Nothing can protect you from man's wrath. Not the police and certainly not a priest."

"I didn't come for asylum," Vincent said. "I came to get advice."

"Ah, maybe I can help you, then. Please, continue. Forgive me, Father, for I have sinned. It's been . . ." Corrado raised his eyebrows expectantly as he trailed off.

Vincent glanced around. Corrado was blocking the main exit of the church. There was nowhere for him to go, no way to leave unless Corrado allowed him to pass. "It's been six months since my last confession."

"Six months," Corrado repeated. "I'm sure you have a bit of repenting to do then."

Vincent scoffed. "Probably not as much as you."

Corrado let out a laugh as he pulled his hands from his pockets. Vincent's hair bristled when he saw the black leather gloves. It was a sight he knew well, the sight of the man at work. He was like a reaper, a malicious spirit ripping the life from men before vanishing undetected, leaving no trace of himself behind.

Corrado's victims rarely knew what hit them. Most never even saw him as he snuck up on them in the night, firing a single shot through the base of their skull, severing their spinal cord and killing them instantly. It was neat and tidy, painless and quick. He was in and out and on to the next thing within a matter of minutes. Corrado wasn't in the business of torture . . . unless you made him mad.

When Corrado got angry, when he took things personally, a different side of him emerged. The ugly, green monster burst forth, ripping through his calm skin, and nobody was safe from his rage when that happened. He never made a mistake, never got sloppy, but the otherwise unruffled man was no longer merciful. He would tear a man to pieces, slowly, methodically, until everything left behind was no longer recognizable.

"Did Sal send you?" Vincent asked, trying to keep his voice even.

Corrado shook his head. "I came on my own."

Not business. *Personal.*

Corrado took a step forward then, tugging his gloves to make sure they were on tight, and Vincent instantly took a step away. He did it again, and again, and again, like the two of them were doing a deadly tango.

"I don't want to believe it," Corrado said, "but seeing you here—seeing you like *this*—I can't help but wonder if it's true."

"It's not how it seems," Vincent said.

Corrado shook his head. "It never really is, is it? But that's irrelevant, and you know it. You crossed a line, and it doesn't matter why you did it or what you planned to do on that other side, the fact that you went over there is inexcusable. *Lupo non mangia lupo.* How many times did we hear your father say that when he was alive? How many times? Wolves don't eat wolves. We don't turn on our own."

"You're right," Vincent said. "If you can't trust your own kind, who can you trust?"

"No one, according to your son," Corrado said. "*Non fidarsi di nessuno.* Did you even stop to think about how this is going to affect him? How this is already affecting him?"

Thoughts of Carmine made Vincent's chest ache. "Is he okay?"

"Of course he's not *okay*. He'll never again be okay! It's his job to kill you!"

Flinching from the hostility, Vincent took a few quick steps back. "You can't let him do it."

"I don't plan to." Corrado stealthily moved with him, not missing a beat.

A loud voice echoed through the cathedral then, stalling them both. Father Alberto stepped out of his office, scowling. Corrado backed up, putting some space between him and Vincent, as the priest swiftly approached. "Gentlemen, I'm not a man to judge, and I've never condemned you for your life choices, but there comes a point where enough is enough! You don't bring that into the house of the Lord. This is a place of worship, of love, of acceptance. We're always open, but only to those who check their sinning at the door."

"You're right." Corrado shoved his hands back into his pockets. "This isn't the time or the place for this."

"And what, exactly, are you two squabbling over?" the priest asked. "You're family!"

"It was a misunderstanding," Vincent said. "That's all."

"Right, a misunderstanding," Corrado agreed, clearing his throat. "If you'll excuse me, I should be going. I have business to handle later tonight."

Father Alberto raised his eyebrows at him. "I hope not too late. I expect to see you planted in one of these pews tomorrow morning."

"I wouldn't miss your service for anything, Father," Corrado said, looking from the priest to Vincent. "It'll all be finished before the sun comes up."

He turned, casually strolling toward the exit as if he had not a care in the world. Vincent and Father Alberto both watched, remaining silent until Corrado disappeared outside into the night. Vincent sighed, running his hands down his face in exasperation. *Not good. Not good at all.*

"Oh, Vincenzo, what have you gotten yourself into?"

"A situation with no way out," he said quietly.

"I don't believe that," Father Alberto said. "There's always a way out."

"Alive?"

Father Alberto was quiet, staring at the door Corrado had disappeared out of as he pondered Vincent's question.

"That's what I thought," Vincent muttered when the priest supplied no response. "I guess there are worse things to be than dead."

"Come to me, all you who are weary and burdened, and I will give you rest," Father Alberto said, quoting Matthew 11:28. "As true as that may be, I don't like you sounding so defeated. You should never give up."

"I'm not giving up, Father. I'm giving *in*. I've fought against the current for a long time, but in the end I got swept downstream anyway. And I can't keep swimming. I can't. I'm too damn tired to do it anymore."

"So, what, you just let yourself drown?" Father Alberto asked with disbelief.

"No," Vincent said. "I wait for someone to throw me a lifeline, and then I drift away."

"And what if no one does? Certain things are unforgiveable. Don't do anything you'll regret."

"I have faith I won't have to."

Father Alberto shook his head. "You look terrible, Vincenzo. Come, I have an extra cot in the back for you to get some sleep."

"I shouldn't."

"Then at least eat something and freshen up."

He wanted to refuse, but the thought of food and a shower was too tempting to resist. Following Father Alberto to the back, he scarfed down two sandwiches and a bag of chips as the man sat across from him, studying him with his concerned eyes. "Is there a reason you came here tonight?"

"Advice," he said. "My father used to have this saying: *chi tace acconsente*. I just wondered what you thought about it."

Chi tace acconsente. Silence gives consent. Antonio DeMarco believed if you wanted something, if you believed in something, it was your responsibility to fight for it. If you remained silent, if you just stood back and did nothing, then you had no one to blame but yourself when nothing happened.

"I believe your father was a wise man," Father Alberto said. "I may not have agreed with his choices, but I always admired his beliefs when it came to family and responsibility. And it's true—if you stand for nothing, you'll fall for anything."

Vincent's brow furrowed. "Is that scripture?"

Father Alberto smiled. "No, I believe it was Alexander Hamilton."

"Thanks, Father." Vincent stood. "I'll take that shower now, if you don't mind."

Father Alberto showed him to the small bathroom. Vincent stripped out of his clothes, sighing as he pulled the simple gold necklace from around his neck, setting it on a shelf beside the towels. He squeezed into the shower, the stall so tiny he barely fit inside, and scrubbed with a bar of unscented soap. After washing his hair, he got out and dried off, putting his dirty clothes right back on again.

Vincent walked away, avoiding Father Alberto and any sort of good-bye as he made the inevitable journey to the exit. He covered his head with his hood again when he stepped outside, his hair still damp. A nice breeze hit his face as he stopped on the top of the church steps and peered out at the empty street.

A chill ran through his body, but it had nothing to do with the cool night air.

"Corrado." He greeted him quietly, not bothering to look at the figure lurking in the shadows beside the steps. He knew he would be out here, waiting for him.

"Well, Vincent, we could call you a lot of things, but a coward certainly isn't one of them."

———

"Come on! We're running behind!"

Corrado stood in the upstairs bathroom, early morning sunlight streaming in the window as he stared at his reflection in the small mirror. He was already showered and dressed, but he had done little else to prepare for the day. Exhaustion infiltrated every cell in his body, clearly visible in the lines on his face. He studied them, surveying every mark and blemish, every gray hair on his head and every blood vessel in his tired eyes.

"Do you hear me, Corrado? We're going to be late!"

Celia stepped into the bathroom, frowning. Without saying another word, she walked up behind him and fixed the collar of his shirt.

"Twenty-seven years," he said, meeting her eyes in the mirror.

"We've been married for almost three decades and you still have to fix my tie most days."

She smiled. "It's hard to believe it's been that long."

"I know," he said, glancing from her reflection back to his. "I'm showing my age."

Celia laughed as he turned around to face her. "You're still as handsome as the day we met."

"And you're even more beautiful."

He leaned down and kissed her softly, enjoying the feel of her lips on his own. She broke the kiss within a matter of seconds, though, and wrinkled her nose when she pulled away. "You're quite a bit scruffier now, though," she said, rubbing the prickly hair on his jaw.

"I didn't feel like shaving," he said. "Don't have the energy today."

"You do look tired," she commented, her hand moving from his face to his hair. "Did you get any sleep at all?"

"Some."

"You got in really late last night."

"Yes."

He gazed at her, seeing the questions in her warm brown eyes. *Where were you? Where did you go? What did you do? Who were you with? Who did you hurt?* They were questions that nagged her, always on the tip of her tongue, but she would never ask and he was grateful for it. He didn't want to lie to her, and there was no way he could tell her he had stalked her only brother a mere few hours ago like he was prey, cornering him like a wounded animal in the same church they were headed to.

"Well, come on," she said, looking away from him. "We still have to pick up Mom, and you know she hates being late. If we don't hurry, she's going to complain the entire time."

Corrado stepped out of the bathroom, shutting off the light, and followed his wife out to the car. Neither said much on the drive to Sunny Oaks Manor where Gia DeMarco had resided for the past few years. Corrado was never fond of the woman and her harsh tongue, but he had the utmost respect for her.

When they arrived, Celia went upstairs to get her as Corrado waited by the entrance. He opened the car door when he saw them coming and Gia slid into the back seat of the Mercedes without acknowledging him. She scowled, her arms crossed over her chest.

Corrado shut the door, sighing, as Celia shot him a pointed look that said whatever they were about to endure was entirely his fault.

He would take the blame. It was the least he could do.

"You look nice, Gia," he said politely as he pulled out into traffic. "Is that a new dress?"

"Is that a new dress?" she muttered, mocking him. She stubbornly stared out the side window of the car, refusing to look in his direction. "I'm not a child, you know, and I don't appreciate being treated like one—especially by you. Antonio would have your head if he were still alive, God rest that bastard's soul."

"He would," Corrado agreed quietly. "Antonio would be severely disappointed."

"It really is a nice dress, Mom," Celia chimed in, glancing into the backseat with a hopeful smile plastered on her face. "That color blue looks fantastic on you."

"And other colors don't?" Gia asked, finally shifting position to look at her daughter. Her gaze scanned her, picking her apart piece by piece with her sharp eyes. "You shouldn't wear so much black, Celia. The darkness washes you out, and you look like you're in mourning. People are going to think you're unhappy. They're going to start wondering about your marriage. Is that what you want? For them to think you can't please your husband?"

"Don't be silly," Celia said, turning back around. "Everyone knows I wear black because it's slimming."

"Well, it doesn't appear to be working," Gia said. "Maybe you should try exercise."

Celia forced a laugh, but Corrado could tell from her expression that the insult stung. He reached over to grab his wife's hand, wordlessly comforting her.

They pulled up to a stoplight, traffic heavy despite it being early on a Sunday. Gia dramatically exhaled and Corrado glanced in the rearview mirror in just enough time to see her turn her stubborn eyes back out the side window. "I can't believe we're late. We're going to have to sit in the back."

"We always sit in the back, Mom."

"Because we want to, not because we have to," Gia said. "I hate when I don't have a choice. I should have a choice, you know. When your father was alive, everyone waited for us to sit first. It was a matter of respect. No one cares anymore."

Corrado sighed in relief when the light turned green.

The church was packed when they finally arrived, and Corrado had to park around the corner. He offered Gia his arm, but she refused and walked a few feet ahead of him, huffing the entire way. Celia tried to keep up with her mother but Corrado didn't bother, instead strolling slowly toward the church doors.

He slid into the back pew beside his wife a few minutes later, smoothing out his jacket. Mass had already started, Father Alberto standing up front preaching about love and forgiveness. Corrado remained quiet through the service, merely going through the motions, and he stayed in his seat when it was time for communion. When it was over and they were dismissed, Corrado was out the door before anyone else.

Celia and Gia joined him, lingering with the others and greeting friends. Corrado stood along the side, patiently waiting for them, when Father Alberto sought him out in the crowd. "I didn't see you at first, Corrado. I thought perhaps you were missing church today, after all."

"Of course not, Father," he replied. "We were just running a bit late."

The priest eyed him closely. "Will I be seeing you later this week?"

"For . . . ?"

"Anything," he said. "My door is always open, but as you know, I regularly take confession on Wednesday nights."

He was fishing, Corrado realized. He wanted information that Corrado wasn't going to give.

"Maybe," he replied. "The week's still young. There's no telling what may happen between now and then."

27

The run-down building was set back off the main highway. Massive holes littered the large gravel lot surrounding it, cars haphazardly parked every which way to avoid getting stuck in them. A fluorescent sign hung above the entrance, the word SINSATIONS flickering in hot pink letters.

"What are we doing here?" Carmine asked as he climbed out of the passenger seat of the black Mercedes. Corrado had dragged him out of bed at three in the morning, but he hadn't explained where they were going on the drive. Of all the places he considered, a trashy strip club hadn't been one of them.

"Business," Corrado replied, motioning for Carmine to follow him.

Carmine strolled through the parking lot behind his uncle. "Do you own this place, too?"

Corrado's footsteps faltered as he flashed Carmine an irritated look. "You clearly don't know me very well if you think I'd run a place like this. The owner pays a fee every month and we let them keep their filthy dump in our territory."

"Blackmail and extortion," Carmine muttered. "Nice."

Corrado laughed dryly. "It's a fair trade. No one messes with them because they pay their dues, and in exchange we utilize their facilities when necessary."

"What would you ever want with this shithole?"

"You'll see."

Bass-thumping loud music instantly assaulted them when Corrado opened the door. Carmine's ears started ringing as he stepped inside, grimacing from the stench. It smelled like stale sweat and liquor, with cigarette smoke lingering in a thick cloud. He coughed as he inhaled it, peering through the haze at the stage. Women danced around poles in platform shoes, their skin blindly glittering under the lights. Parts of them sagged as they bent over, letting men stuff dollar bills into G-strings.

No respectable human being would step foot in the place, and he realized that was likely the point.

"Stop looking," Corrado said, leaning closer to Carmine and still having to shout to be heard. "We're not here for pleasure."

"Funny," Carmine muttered, following him through the club. "If you think I'd ever have anything to do with bitches like that, then you clearly don't know *me*."

They headed into a back office and shut the door behind them to block out some of the noise. Corrado opened a cellar door in the floor and started down the stairs, but Carmine hesitated at the top when he heard a female's piercing scream. His heart nearly stilled at the sound as Corrado groaned. "Why isn't she gagged?"

She screamed again, the sound silenced right away.

Carmine slowly started down the steps, not wanting to aggravate Corrado by lingering behind. The thick cellar walls muffled the music from the club, a wordless vibration of bass coming from above. He looked around cautiously as the room came into view, shocked at the sight before him. Two people sat in chairs in the center of the room, handcuffed to metal chairs with burlap sacks over their heads. One was clearly a girl, wearing a gold-colored dress, while the other was clad in jeans and a t-shirt. Besides Corrado, there were two other *Mafiosi* in the room, watching from the sidelines just as he was now.

Carmine studied the captives, assessing the situation, when his eyes fell upon the guy's old, gold watch. Coldness swept through him as his heart dropped into his shoes. "No," he whispered to himself, horrified. He had seen that watch before. "God, no."

Corrado peered back at him, hearing his quiet declaration. Their eyes locked for a moment before Corrado motioned toward one of the guys in the back, who ripped the bag off of the girl's head. She glanced around in a frenzy, fear flashing across her face when she spotted them. Red hair fell into her face as her eyes locked on Carmine. He had to look away.

"Do you know her, Carmine?"

Carmine nodded slowly. "That's Remy's girlfriend."

Corrado laughed, the bitter sound sending a chill down Carmine's spine. "Her name's Vanessa O'Bannon. She's Seamus's daughter, and apparently also the one who supplied Remy with his drugs, filtering Irish product through right under my nose."

Corrado motioned toward one of the men, who took the bag off the other person's head. Remy's terrified eyes immediately sought out Carmine, tears streaming from them as he silently begged for help.

"What are the rules, Carmine? Recite them to me."

Carmine looked away from his friend and blinked a few times when that question registered. "Stay away from drugs and stay out of the public eye."

"Keep going."

"Uh, our women are off limits. And children."

"And?"

"Don't rat on your friends," Carmine said, regret bubbling up inside of him. "Keep your mouth shut and stay away from the police."

"What else?"

"Don't steal from each other. Give back to the organization. Always be available when called on, no matter what." Carmine paused. "That's it."

"You're wrong," Corrado said. "You missed one—an important one."

"What's that?"

"Never fraternize with the enemy."

Corrado reached into his coat and pulled out his gun. Without warning, a lone gunshot exploded in the cellar, the loud noise bouncing off the thick walls. Carmine jumped back as the bullet ripped through the back of Remy's skull, blood splattering the floor and walls around them.

The air left Carmine's lungs, his knees weak as a high-pitched, blood-curdling scream echoed through the room. Carmine couldn't move. His eyes were fixed on the polka dots of bright red now littering his white Nike's. His friend's blood . . .

Suddenly, unexpectedly, flashes of Nicholas assaulted his mind. For the second time, the overwhelming guilt of getting a friend killed consumed him.

Shell-shocked, Carmine watched as Corrado pointed the gun at Vanessa's forehead. Sobbing, tears coated her flushed cheeks as she violently shook. She squeezed her eyes shut tightly as Corrado pulled the trigger at close range, a subtle click ricocheting through the room.

Carmine felt the bile rising up and swallowed it back, not wanting to get sick. Vanessa continued to sob, her head down in defeat.

Grasping her chin, Corrado pulled her face up, forcing her to look at him. "I know where you live. I know where your father hangs out. I know where your little cousin Jessie goes to school. Your best friend Marie? I know where she works, and I've been to the church your grandmother plays Bingo at on Tuesday nights. You cross me again, you step foot near my club, and I'll kill every single one of them before I slit your throat in your sleep. *Capisce?*"

Vanessa nodded furiously, hiccupping, unable to speak through her cries.

Corrado removed her restraints and took a step back. "Walk out of here calmly and hitch a ride home. Don't speak a word of this."

Vanessa jumped up, stumbling as she scurried up the stairs.

Carmine watched in shock, his eyes darting between the door and his uncle. "You let her go? What if she calls the police?"

"She won't," he replied, putting his gun away before motioning for the other two men to dispose of Remy's body. They quickly wrapped it up in a blanket and carried the bundle up the stairs. Corrado supervised it, turning back to Carmine once the body was gone. "Clean up this mess."

Carmine ran his hand through his hair in a panic. "Me?"

"Yes, and make it fast," Corrado said, starting up the stairs. "You know, in case I'm wrong and she opens her mouth."

28

The long mahogany table filled the conference room, leaving hardly enough space for people to push out their chairs. It was cramped, the atmosphere stifling as Corrado breathed the same stale air as half a dozen other men.

He sat at the far end of the table with Mr. Borza to his right, the lone court reporter seated beside the lawyer. The federal prosecutor by the name of Markson sat on the left side with his two assistants, while a U.S. Marshal slumped half-asleep in a chair by the exit. Corrado wasn't surprised they had enlisted security, given the nature of the case, but he was a bit offended they thought one pesky man would be enough to keep everyone safe.

The clock on the wall read 8:23 in the morning, nearly half an hour past the time the proceedings were scheduled to start. Tension choked the silent room as everyone stared at the closed door, waiting for it to open, for something to finally happen. No one seemed to know what to say, neither side wanting to be the first to verbalize what was becoming evident:

Vincent DeMarco was a no-show for his deposition.

The clock steadily ticked away, another ten minutes passing before Mr. Borza cleared his throat. "I think we can all agree this isn't happening today."

"Just give it a little longer," the prosecutor said. "He'll be here."

"We've already given him thirty minutes," Mr. Borza argued. "He's clearly decided not to testify, after all."

The prosecutor scoffed. "If he doesn't show, it's because something's keeping him from being here."

"Like what?" Mr. Borza asked. "Traffic? A flat tire? Those are hardly good excuses."

"No, I mean something like your client."

"Oh, give me a break," Mr. Borza said, waving him off. "Mr. Moretti has been here with us all morning. You know that. He was here before even you."

"Maybe so, but what about last night or the day before? What about last week?" The prosecutor turned his attention to Corrado, his eyes ablaze with anger and suspicion. "When was the last time you saw Vincent DeMarco?"

Corrado didn't have a chance to consider responding. Mr. Borza shoved his chair back, slamming it against the wall as he stood. "You know very well my client is under no obligation to be here for this nonsense, much less entertain your absurd, paranoia-fueled questions! Contact me if your witness surfaces and we'll reschedule this sideshow. Otherwise, we're done."

The lawyer stormed out of the room, all spitfire and rage, while Corrado stood, as calm as could be. "Gentlemen."

"This has your name written all over it, Moretti," the prosecutor muttered, slamming a notebook closed as he gathered his things. "You won't get away with this. Mark my words. I'll have you off the streets by the end of the day."

———

Corrado wasn't home for more than two hours before his phone started incessantly ringing. He ignored it, not in the mood to humor anyone with conversation, but realized they weren't going to give up after the third consecutive call.

He answered with a sigh, hitting the speakerphone button. "Moretti speaking."

"We have a problem."

Corrado closed his eyes at the sound of his lawyer's voice. He was tired of hearing Mr. Borza say those words. "What now?"

"The prosecution filed for an emergency hearing on a motion to revoke bond based on evidence that you're a flight risk and a danger to society."

Leaning back in his office chair, Corrado ran his hands down his face with frustration. "What evidence?"

"Well, they're citing the fact that Vincent's missing. They've issued a warrant for failing to appear, but so far there's no sign of him here or at his home."

There wouldn't be, Corrado thought. They weren't going to find Vincent.

"It seems he found a way to remove his monitoring device," Mr. Borza continued. "They tracked it to a location here in Chicago, but it turned out to be a Dumpster. They searched it, just in case, but there's no sign of a, uh . . . you know."

"A body," Corrado said, finishing the man's thought.

"Yes."

Nervousness seeped through the phone, clinging desperately to every word. It made Corrado tense. Even his lawyer doubted things.

"That's hardly what I'd call evidence of wrongdoing on my part," Corrado said. "They're just looking for an excuse. Punishing me for my brother-in-law's sins."

"While that may be true, it doesn't mean it won't work," Mr. Borza said. "You're on trial for a statute they invented to be able to nail you for crimes you're only somewhat linked to. The government isn't above stretching things to suit them."

"So you're saying they'll be successful."

Mr. Borza hesitated. Corrado knew the answer before the man even said, "More than likely, yes."

While he wasn't surprised, given Mr. Markson's words from that morning, Corrado's stomach churned from the turn in events. "How long does that give me?"

"The hearing is scheduled for tomorrow morning. They wanted

to do it tonight, but I stalled a bit. It's better if you aren't present, I think, or they may detain you on site. Otherwise, they'll give you about forty-eight hours to surrender."

"So the weekend," Corrado said.

"Something like that."

Corrado was silent for a moment, mulling over the situation. Forty-eight hours wasn't enough time for him to do everything he needed to do. If they detained him, he could be gone months, or even years. Too much relied on his ability to remain out on the streets.

"Just do what you can," Corrado said finally. "I trust your abilities."

"I'll give it my all, but I can't work miracles."

Corrado let out a sharp laugh. "Are you insinuating only God can help me now?"

"Not at all. I'm just saying we may have to give them this battle and keep our eyes focused on winning the war."

Corrado pressed the button again, ending the call without giving a response. He sat there for a moment, rubbing the tips of his fingers together deep in thought, before standing up and grabbing his cell phone. He slipped it in his pocket and headed out of his office, passing his wife on the way to the front door.

"You're leaving?" she asked.

He kissed her cheek. "I have things to take care of. Don't wait up for me."

I think some people are born with tragedy in their blood. Mixed with the cells, the plasma, and the platelets are deeply hidden secrets they just can't escape. It's a part of them, passed down between generations, but it doesn't define them. It doesn't mean they're doomed. Like a smart man once told me, the nastiest fertilizer makes the most beautiful flowers grow.

Haven ran her fingers along the yellowing paper, tracing the handwritten words as she read the paragraph for the second time. She sat in the middle of her couch, legs crossed, with the leather-bound journal on her lap. Kelsey lounged in a chair across the room, her legs kicked over the side, as she flipped through channels, seemingly uninterested in anything on television.

After a moment, the familiar voice of Alex Trebek resounded through the room. "The author of the twentieth-century work *The Secret Garden*."

"Frances Hodgson Burnett," Haven muttered, looking up from the journal at *Jeopardy* on the screen.

Kelsey glanced at her when she answered, shaking her head as she changed the channel. "You're such a nerd."

Haven shrugged. If she meant that as an insult, she didn't take it as one.

Kelsey flipped through a few more before giving up, turning off the television and tossing the remote down. She grabbed a blue registration folder from the coffee table, eyeing Haven peculiarly as she sat back in the chair. "What are you reading, anyway?"

"Nothing." Haven closed Maura's journal. "It's just a book."

Kelsey stared at her for a moment, her eyebrow arched. "I gathered that much, Sherlock."

Haven stood and returned the journal to the bookshelf before grabbing the second registration folder from the table. "Don't worry about it."

Rolling her eyes, Kelsey opened her folder and started sorting through the papers. Haven followed her lead, taking out her schedule for the spring semester. School started back up in the morning, giving Haven another fresh start. She hadn't done too horribly in the fall, failing none of her classes, but some she had just passed by the skin of her teeth.

"So I'll drop Drawing II and pick up Writing and Literature with you," Kelsey said, reading over her schedule.

Haven glanced through hers. "I have that at eight in the morning on Tuesdays and Thursdays."

Kelsey grimaced. "Ugh, forget about it. How about Survey of World Art?"

"Nine-thirty, same days."

"Still too early."

"Sculpture?"

"Gross."

Haven laughed. "Well, all I have left is Painting II."

"When's that?"

"Monday, Wednesday, and Friday at noon."

A smile curved Kelsey's lips. "Bingo!"

Kelsey scribbled it down on a piece of paper as Haven put her schedule away, placing the registration folder back on the table. She settled back into the couch, crossing her legs once more, when a loud ringing ricocheted through the apartment.

"Phone's ringing," Kelsey said, picking a pillow up off the chair and tossing it at Haven. She caught it, tensing as her blood ran cold. Her eyes darted over to the bookcase where the small black cell phone lay, glowing and vibrating as it rang.

Besides Kelsey, there was only one person who had that number.

"Aren't you going to answer it?" Kelsey asked.

"Uh, yeah." Haven walked over to the phone, glancing at the caller ID even though it was senseless. Corrado's name shone brightly on the screen. Her hand shook as she picked it up, but before she could answer it, the ringing stopped.

Thirty seconds, then forty-five, then a minute passed until her phone chimed again, this time with a text message. Haven opened it, reading the simple message:

Call me.

The club on Ninth Street was packed, the sound of an old Frank Sinatra song booming from the massive speakers situated in the corners. Cigar smoke permeated the air, making Carmine's eyes water the moment he stepped inside.

Corrado had called him and told him to come down right away. He wouldn't elaborate as to why on the phone and that put Carmine on edge. Was it his father? Haven? Had something happened to her?

The last time he had been there, things hadn't gone over very well.

Slowly, he walked over to the bar. "Vodka, please."

The bartender raised an eyebrow. "Do you have ID?"

Carmine hesitated. *What the fuck?* "You know me, man."

"You're right," the bartender said, not sounding impressed in the least. "I do."

"Yeah, so are you gonna give me a shot?"

"Sure," the man said. "Just as soon as you show me some ID."

Carmine stared at him, stunned. "Are you fucking with me?"

The bartender sighed. "Look, I feel for you, but you know your uncle . . . I ain't losing my life just so you can drink. He said you were cut off permanently."

"This is fucked up," Carmine muttered, wishing he had *something* to soothe his frazzled nerves before he had to face Corrado. "Where is my uncle, anyway? He told me to meet him here."

"He's in his office," the bartender said, motioning toward the hallway. "You know which one it is."

Frustrated, Carmine pushed away from the bar and slowly made his way to the back. He knocked on the door and waited. The last thing he wanted was another fight with Corrado.

"It's open," Corrado yelled.

Carmine stepped inside. Corrado sat in his leather chair, nonchalantly flipping through paperwork. Not wanting to interrupt, Carmine wordlessly plopped down in a chair in front of his desk.

Corrado glanced up at him and stilled his movements. "Did I tell you to sit?"

"Uh, no."

"Then I think a man of reasonable intelligence can conclude you should still be standing. You're by no means a genius, but even a two year old can follow simple commands."

Carmine's mouth drew into a thin line as he tightly pressed his lips together, fighting hard not to respond to the insult. He should be used to it by now, but his temper still often got the best of him.

He stood back up.

"Now you can sit."

Motherfucker.

Carmine plopped back down, fidgeting as he drummed his fingers on the arm of the chair. A sheen of sweat formed on his brow, the lights in the room feeling too bright and uncomfortable. His heart hammered in his chest as he waited for Corrado to tell him why he had been called there, but the silence lingered on. Corrado returned to his paperwork, ignoring his presence.

Nearly twenty minutes passed—excruciatingly uncomfortable minutes—before his uncle looked up at him again. "Are you on something, Carmine?"

"No," he said, his eyes narrowing defensively. "I haven't. Not since . . ."

"And you better not," Corrado said. "It's unacceptable. Disrespectful. I've put a bullet in men for less than what you did, and . . ."

Sighing, Carmine slouched in the chair as his uncle went on and on, the same shit he had heard more than a dozen times the past few weeks. He knew it all—in fact, he knew it before the incident even happened—and he was getting tired of constantly being berated for his mistake.

He had paid enough, he thought, the aftermath something he would never forget.

His mind wandered then, drifting, until the sound of a phone

266 J.M. DARHOWER

ringing shattered his train of thought. Corrado immediately stopped talking as he glanced at it, his eyes darting straight to him, his expression severe. "If you say a single word, I'll make you suffer. Understand?"

He blanched, nodding, suddenly too terrified to reply.

"I mean it," Corrado warned. "Don't even breathe too loud."

Reaching for his phone, Corrado answered it as he brought it to his ear. "Hello, Haven."

And just like that, the air flew from Carmine's lungs. Corrado narrowed his eyes at him as he let out a shuddering breath, but he couldn't help it. The room felt smaller, stifling, suffocating.

He wanted to puke. He wanted to cry. He wanted to sucker punch his uncle and snatch the fucking phone from him just to hear her voice one more time.

But he did nothing. He merely sat there, staring across the desk, straining his ears in hopes to hear something, anything . . . just a part of her again.

"I just called to tell you I'd be away for a while," Corrado said. "It's nothing to be concerned about, but I may be out of touch for a few months."

Corrado was silent as he listened to her response. He pulled his phone from his ear after a moment, laying it on his desk as he pressed a button on the screen. Carmine's stomach sunk, figuring he had hung up, until he heard her sigh through the line. It was subtle, barely inaudible, but it was there. *Speakerphone.*

"How's school?" Corrado asked, sounding disinterested, his eyes glued to Carmine as he asked the question.

"It's, uh, good," Haven replied. "The new semester starts tomorrow. I'm all signed up for my classes."

"That's great." Corrado tapped his fingers against the desk. "I hope you're enjoying yourself and making friends."

"I am."

"Good," Corrado said. "I'm glad you're well. Take care of yourself."

"You, too, sir."

Carmine closed his eyes as his uncle pushed another button, this time ending the call. They sat in silence for a moment before Corrado addressed him. "I'm not going to be around to keep an eye on you, Carmine, so you better stay straight."

"Where are you going?"

"Jail."

Carmine blinked a few times. "What?"

"They're revoking my bail as we speak," he explained. "They think I had something to do with your father going missing."

After a strangled bout of silence, Carmine forced the million-dollar question from his lips. "Did you?"

Corrado waved his hand, turning back to his stack of paper-work. "You're dismissed, Carmine."

29

The moment Corrado stepped in his house later that night, the succulent aroma of marinara assaulted his senses. He took a deep breath, inhaling it as he strolled toward the kitchen. Celia stood in front of the stove, the sleeves of her blouse rolled up to her elbows and her usually pristine hair pulled back in a sloppy bun. A blue apron was tied around her, protecting her clothes from splatter as she stirred the homemade sauce.

Corrado silently watched her, a ghost of a smile tugging his lips. She hadn't heard him come in and continued to concentrate on her cooking, oblivious to her husband's presence. Corrado loved these moments, when Celia was in her element and the world around her faded away. She glowed radiantly, beaming like the sun as she floated along. It was what had drawn him to her in the first place—her ability to bring light into such a devastatingly dark world.

He would miss it. There was no doubt about it. His world would soon be a much colder place.

He let out a deep sigh, not wanting to think about what would come tomorrow, and Celia jumped at the noise. Dropping her spoon, she spun around and clutched her chest. "You scared me! I didn't know you were home."

Corrado's smile grew, but he said nothing as he took a few steps toward her. Carefully, he untied the apron from around her waist, and Celia eyed him skeptically as he tossed it aside. He reached up and tugged on the band securing her hair, making it fall loose. It was messy, an unruly wave cascading past her shoulders.

"What are you doing?" Celia asked as he took her hand.

"Taking you upstairs," he said, "and getting you out of those clothes."

She tried to dig in her heels to make him stop, but he was much stronger than her. "Corrado, hold on! I'm cooking!"

"So?"

"So my sauce might burn!"

"You can make more later."

"But the stove is on!"

"Who cares?"

"Who cares?" she asked incredulously as he pulled her toward the stairs. "What if it catches on fire?"

"Then I'll buy you a new stove."

"It could burn down the whole house!"

"Then I'll build you a new house."

She laughed with disbelief. "It'll burn down with *us* in it, Corrado."

He glanced at her, cocking an eyebrow. "Do you really think I'd let that happen?"

Her comeback was snappy. "Do you really think you could stop it?"

Corrado was momentarily silent, still clutching her wrist as they stood near the bottom of the stairs. He pondered her question. Did he think he could stop it?

"*Bellissima*, I'd stop time for you. I'd give you the moon and the stars; I'd learn to defy gravity. There's nothing I wouldn't do, nobody I wouldn't kill, if you asked me to. If you *needed* me to. Saving you from a fire would be nothing, purely instinct."

She stared at him for three beats, not budging, before her body relaxed and she gave in. It wasn't as if it was a hard decision for her—as much as Corrado would do for her, they both knew she would never deny him anything. Whatever he needed, come hell or high water, Celia would be there every step of the way.

Their hands linked together, Corrado took her upstairs to the bedroom. He shut the door behind them, locking out the cruel world that would tomorrow tear them apart, but today—*tonight*— it would just be her and him.

———

Hours later, Corrado descended the stairs and made his way to the dark kitchen. He turned off the stove and dumped the scorched sauce down the garbage disposal before rinsing out the pot. He scrubbed it for a minute but when it refused to come clean, he tossed the entire thing in the trashcan.

He headed back upstairs and showered, standing under the spray of hot water until it started to grow cold. He shaved then, using a thin razor blade under the bright lights of the quiet bathroom to remove the stubble along his sharp jaw. Afterward, he slicked back his thick hair before dressing in his most expensive black Brioni suit. With his Rolex affixed to his wrist and his Italian leather shoes on his feet, he wandered into the bedroom and gazed at his wife under the moonlight.

Celia snored lightly, snuggled up to his pillow. Corrado leaned down and kissed her forehead. "Sleep well, *bellissima*."

He made his way back downstairs, using his cell phone to call for a car service to pick him up. It only took the town car a few minutes to arrive, and another few minutes for them to make it through the city. He tipped the driver handily when they arrived and he climbed out, waiting for it to leave before he started to move.

He strolled into Metropolitan Correctional Center shortly before three o'clock in the morning, his head held high and a swagger in his step. He may have been there to surrender himself to a bright orange jumpsuit and confinement in a rat hole, but he saw no reason why he couldn't at least do it in style.

30

"Grip firmly, everybody, and use deep strokes. Up, down, up, down."

Strangled laughter echoed through the small art room. It sounded like someone was choking on air.

"Experiment with light and hard touches. Play around with it. Find out what feels good to you."

Kelsey leaned over, elbowing Haven as she whispered, "Do you think she does that on purpose?"

Haven's brow furrowed. "Does what?"

"That's it. Keep it up, guys. This is exactly what I like to see—your creativity exploding onto the canvas as I help you reach your peak."

Kelsey coughed loudly, trying to hide another laugh, but others in the class were less successful at containing themselves. The professor didn't notice, though, or if she did, she didn't react.

"Art's personal. It's just you and your tools, making something out of nothing. It's a sensual process. You're creating love."

"Yeah, definitely on purpose," Kelsey said. "Miss Michaels is freaky-deaky."

Haven felt the blood rush to her cheeks when she realized what the fuss was about. She dropped her paintbrush and stared at the random shapes and patterns on her canvas, everything suddenly looking sexualized.

"Beautiful work, Hayden. Absolutely stunning."

Haven smiled softly, her blush deepening as the professor stopped beside her station. "Thank you."

"It's truly my pleasure."

The rest of the class passed in a similar fashion, more immature snickering accompanying possible sexual innuendos. By the time they were dismissed twenty minutes later, Haven was flustered and about to jump out of her own skin.

She grabbed her things before bolting toward the exit, hoping to delay the inevitable awkward conversation with her friend, and made her way to the lobby from the seventh floor. Rushing out of the massive brick building, she collided with a form right outside the front doors. Haven bounced back from the force of it.

Monday was turning out not to be her day.

"I'm sorry," she said at once, pulling away from the guy in front of her. He seemed startled, his feet locked in place and eyes wide. They were a strange blue color, bordering on steel gray. His skin was dark tan.

"No big deal," he replied, letting go of her. His voice was high-pitched, a thick Brooklyn accent she heard often around New York. "You okay?"

"Uh, yeah," she said, taking a step back. "I'm fine. This happens all the time."

"What does?" he asked. "You running into strangers?"

"Yes."

He let out a laugh, his face lighting up to expose a set of clear, deep dimples. "Gives new meaning to hitting on people, huh?"

She smiled at his joke, grateful that he didn't seem angry. "I suppose so."

He started to speak again, but she didn't give him time. Hearing Kelsey's laughter in the building behind her, Haven blurted out another quick apology before dodging past the man and into the crowd on the street.

Painting II, also known as Art from the Heart, had become Haven's favorite class from the first day of the semester. It was the one hour where she threw caution to the wind and allowed herself to truly feel everything inside of her. There was no pretending. Not when painting.

Soul, the professor had said. And Haven gave it every ounce she had.

"Do you think Miss Michaels gets off on da Vinci?" Kelsey asked on Wednesday as they strolled out of class together. "Maybe *The Last Supper* is porn to her. She kept gushing about it today." She paused, crinkling her nose. "Gushing. Gross, now I'm doing it."

Haven rolled her eyes. "It's a religious painting. I doubt she finds it erotic."

"Okay then, *Mona Lisa,*" Kelsey said. "That's da Vinci, isn't it? Or wait, maybe it's Van Gogh. Picasso?"

"It's da Vinci," Haven said. "How are you an art student?"

"Totally other side of the industry," Kelsey replied. "I design things on a computer, unlike you folks who make love to a canvas."

"We create love on a canvas."

"What's the difference?" she asked dismissively. "Both sound kinky to me."

Haven shook her head, looking away from her friend as they stepped out of the building. Her eyes immediately locked with a pair of blue ones, the same guy from two days ago. He smiled at her, giving a slight wave, and Haven blushed from the recognition.

"See, I'm right," Kelsey said, noticing her suddenly flushed cheeks. "All of you artsy fuckers are turned on by it."

———

Friday, when leaving class, the guy was there again, just as he was the following Monday and Wednesday. The cycle continued with curious looks, polite smiles, and subtle waves every other weekday at precisely one o'clock. He was always lingering just outside the building like he was waiting for someone or maybe something.

On Friday two weeks later, Haven was asked to stay after class.

The halls were vacant by the time she left, the street clear of students. She walked out of the building as she situated her backpack, her footsteps faltering after a few feet. On the corner, leaning against the building, was the guy once again.

He glanced up as she approached. "Hey there."

Haven smiled politely. "Hello."

He pushed away from the wall and stopped in her path. "Remember me?"

"Yes." Her heart raced at the blunt acknowledgment. She already preferred it when he didn't say anything. "I didn't hurt you, did I? I'm honestly really sorry for it. I was in a rush and—"

"Relax," he said, cutting her off with a laugh. "You just ran off that day before I had a chance to talk to you."

"Oh." She eyed him warily. "About what?"

He shrugged. "About anything."

"Uh, okay."

They stared at each other for a moment, the air thick with awkwardness. Haven took a step to the side to go around him, but he spoke again before she made it that far. "So, can I walk you to your next class?"

She shook her head. "I'm done for the day."

He started to reply, but she was gone before he could say anything.

————

He tried again on Monday. "Can I get you some lunch?"

Another refusal. "I'm not really hungry, but thanks."

And again on Wednesday. "How about some drinks?"

She mumbled as she ducked past him, "I'm not thirsty."

Friday, just like clockwork, he was standing there. "Can I walk you home?"

"I'm not going home right now."

Monday, Haven was prepared. She stepped out of the building after class with Kelsey at her side, chatting away, but the guy was one step ahead of her. He pushed away from the wall when he saw them and paused in their path, focusing his attention on Kelsey. "Excuse me, miss. Can I cut in?"

Kelsey's brow furrowed. She was momentarily stunned into silence. "Cut in?"

"Yes," he said. "You see, I've been trying to talk to your friend for weeks, so, well, I'm a little jealous right now."

A smile slowly lit up Kelsey's face. "Oh! Absolutely!"

Kelsey turned to her and winked dramatically, barely containing her squeal as she skipped away into the crowd. Haven just stood there in disbelief as the guy smirked. "So, since your friend approves, can I walk beside you wherever you're going today?"

She shook her head. Unbelievable. "Why would you even want to do that?"

"Why wouldn't I?" he asked. "You're a gorgeous girl."

Those words sunk in and she gaped at him. He was flirting, she realized. He was flirting with *her*.

She shrugged hesitantly. "Uh, I guess. I mean, you can do anything you want. I can't really stop you, right?"

"Right." The word was drawn out in his accent. "Are you giving me the it's a free country spiel?"

"No. Well, yes . . ." She scrunched up her forehead. "It is, isn't it? Or at least that's what they say."

"Yeah, but I don't want to impose. I know I've been persistent, but I just wanted a chance to actually meet you. You can tell me no, and I'll never ask again."

There was a tinge of hurt in his voice that surprised her. She didn't want to be rude to the boy, but his presence alarmed her, the attention unnerving.

"You're not really imposing," she said. "I mean, we're just walking, right?"

"Right," he said again, looking away from her and shaking his head. A smile tugged his lips as he motioned for her to proceed. "Walking. After you."

Haven strolled down the street and he stayed in step beside her, his hands in his pockets and his gaze on the ground.

"So, where are we heading?" he asked.

"The library," she replied.

"The library isn't on campus?" he asked. "This is an art school, isn't it? Just art? Or do they have normal shit, too?"

She peeked at him curiously. *What kind of question is that?* "Just art, but I like to think it's pretty normal."

He shook his head. "I didn't mean it that way."

"I take it you don't go to school here," she said. "Otherwise, you'd know that."

"No, I'm not a student." He laughed to himself. "I walk by here all the time for work, though. I'm working down at the construction site on Sixth Avenue."

She eyed him curiously. His clothes were crisp and clean, an expensive watch on his wrist. "You don't look like a construction worker."

He smiled. "No, I'm more of the supervising type. I don't like getting my hands dirty if I don't have to."

Haven loosened up as they walked. He offered to carry her things and waited as she dropped off the books at the library before asking again if he could walk her home.

"Why?" she asked, standing in the middle of the sidewalk in front of the New York Public Library. People walked around them, casting glares for being in the way, but she wasn't budging. Not until he answered.

"Didn't you already ask me that?"

"Yes, but . . ." She paused. "You're being nice. People just aren't nice like that unless they want something."

"I am," he said. "I do want something, though."

Haven's eyes narrowed. "What?"

"To get to know you."

"Why me?"

"Why not you?"

He was being evasive, answering a question with a question. Haven stiffened. "You're not the police, are you? You have to tell me if you are."

He stared at her with surprise. "No, I don't. Or, well, they don't. Who told you that?"

"A friend."

"Well, they're wrong. The police can legally lie to you."

"Are you sure?"

"Yes."

"Does that mean you're one?"

He burst into laughter, so loud it seemed to bounce off the surrounding buildings, startling people walking past. "Most girls would be worried a guy is a serial killer or something."

"You're not, are you?"

"No," he said. "I'm not the police, either. I told you—I'm in construction."

Haven opened her mouth, considering conceding, when a phone rang in his pocket. He pulled it out, his smile falling as he silenced it.

"Well, you're in luck," he said. "Duty calls. It was nice to meet you . . ."

He paused, raising his eyebrows curiously. She realized she hadn't yet told him her name. "Hayden."

"Hayden," he echoed, smiling. "You can call me Gavin."

———

Ping, whack, ping, whack, ping, whack

Corrado lay in his bottom bunk with his arm draped over his eyes, listening to the sound of paddles striking Ping-Pong balls on the tier outside his small cell. Chatter accompanied their playing, the noise loud enough to make his head viciously pound. He squeezed his eyes shut tighter, trying to block out the commotion, but it only seemed to grow louder as time went on.

For the first time since arriving, he regretted requesting general population.

There was little to do at MCC, nothing to look at, and no one to talk to. Table tennis and card games seemed to be how most men passed the time, but neither activity interested Corrado. He occasionally went to the rec yard for fresh air, but he spent most of his days staring at the drab walls, blocking out the others as he counted the days. Three weeks down, God knows how many more to go.

Ping, whack, ping, whack, ping, whack

Corrado tried to take it in stride. After everything he had done over the years, a few months should be an easy punishment. The way he calculated it, it was less than a day for everyone he had hurt. A measly few hours of incarceration for everyone he killed. He would take his few months and then go right back to his life.

Today, however, he found being there insufferable. The pinging of the balls, the babble of the inmates, and the squeals of the pigs as they marched along the tiers, barking orders and throwing their weight around—it was all too much to take.

Sighing, he hauled himself out of the bed. His cellmate looked up from his book on the top bunk and eyed Corrado cautiously as he stood. They hadn't shared more than a handful of short conversations in three weeks.

"You all right, man?" he asked, his voice and eyes guarded.

"I will be in a minute."

Corrado walked out of the cell, no hesitation in his step as he made his way into the common area. A few of the inmates were off on their own, but the bulk of them were gathered around the Ping-Pong game. Corrado cut through the crowd, people stepping out of his way instinctively as he headed straight for the man at the end of the table. He was the loudest of the group, a large guy from the south side of Chicago doing a few years for drug trafficking. He clutched the paddle, laughing as he smacked the ball, oblivious to Corrado's approach.

Ping, whack, ping, whack, ping, whack

CRACK

The sickening crunch of Corrado's fist connecting with the guy's face echoed through the concrete room, bouncing off the metal doors. The guy hit the floor with a thud, stunned, as blood poured from his nose. The crowd was immediately silenced and took a step back, retreating, as whistles and lights went off on the tier.

Corrado stood in place and raised his hands in the air as a horde of correctional officers descended upon them. They ignored his peaceful surrender and grabbed him, violently shoving him against the nearest wall. His hands were forced behind his back, his wrists secured with handcuffs before shackles were attached to his ankles. In a matter of seconds he was led away, taken straight to solitary confinement.

"Dumb move, Moretti," an officer said as they placed him in the single windowless cell, brightly lit by a flickering fluorescent bulb. "You'll be lucky if you don't get an assault charge."

Corrado laughed dryly. The D.A. wouldn't waste his time. He had beat four trumped-up murder charges, seven assault charges, three counts of extortion, and a dozen weapons violations, give or take a few. A punch was nothing, no more than a speeding ticket.

The officer shook his head as he released Corrado from his restraints, annoyed by his refusal to react. "You're not as infallible as you think you are. If you were, you wouldn't be in prison right now."

"It's only temporary," Corrado said, rubbing his hand. His knuckles were already swelling from the force of the punch.

"That's probably true," the officer muttered. "I'll never understand."

"I'm not surprised," Corrado quipped. "Comprehension doesn't seem to be your strong suit."

The officer ignored the jab as he locked the cell and walked away. Finally alone, Corrado lay on the hard, thin mattress and once again draped his arm over his eyes. Silence surrounded him, blanketing him in peace as sleep took him away.

When he resurfaced, the pounding in his head had dulled. He sat up and glanced toward the door at the same time the slot in it opened, an officer's voice carrying through. "Mail call."

He slid in two envelopes that fell to the floor, both already opened. He wasn't surprised. His mail was routinely checked, confiscated for days and read countless times in an attempt to find some hidden message they would never find.

Not because there wasn't one . . . because they weren't smart enough to decipher their code.

"Heard it's your birthday," the officer said. "That true?"

"Yes."

The officer laughed. "Solitary confinement—hell of a birthday present."

Corrado stood and grabbed the mail when the slot closed. The first was a simple birthday card from his wife, plain blue with no sappy message inside. He eyed the second envelope curiously before pulling out the sheet of paper. It was short, the message scribbled in messy pen.

> Roses are red,
> Violets are blue,
> I went to work,
> How 'bout you?

> P.S.—I thought violets were purple, not blue. Color me surprised. Thinking I need some tutoring—the hands-on type.

He read it twice, surprised the message made it through security. The note wasn't signed, the return address sketchy, but he knew exactly who it had come from.

Corrado had no pen and paper, so he couldn't reply yet, but he knew exactly what he'd say:

> Flowers come in every color, but some aren't meant to be picked. Enjoy the view, but don't try to plant any of your seeds in my garden. I'd hate to see you piled high with fertilizer.

31

On the first day of spring, March 20, trucks and vans packed the streets surrounding the Dirksen Federal Building in downtown Chicago. The sun shone brightly, the afternoon warm as trees grew lush and flowers bloomed. The way it felt on the twelfth floor of the building, though, you wouldn't know things flourished outside.

Under the dim lighting of the courtroom, Corrado sat behind the long defendant's table, hands clasped in front of him, tie hanging sloppily around his neck. His wife hadn't been there that morning to fix it as he dressed in a room not far from where he sat. The air was frigid in temperature and feeling. Despite having lived in Chicago for decades, he still wasn't used to the cold.

He didn't shiver, though. He refused to appear weak.

UNITED STATES V. CORRADO MORETTI

DAY ONE

The courtroom was packed, not an empty seat anywhere to be found. Corrado had surveyed the spectators when he was ushered in, spotting Celia in the back with her nephew, Dominic. Besides them, he saw little in the way of friendly faces. No family, no friends, no *La Cosa Nostra* . . . victims and their relatives crammed the frozen room, sucking up all of the oxygen.

Corrado could feel their hostility ghosting across his skin.

He didn't care what they thought, though. The only opinions that mattered to him belonged to the twelve people stuffed into the secluded box along the side. Eight men and four women, housed in a dingy hotel for the duration of the trial, guarded twenty-four hours a day.

It was the first time Corrado had been given a sequestered jury. The judge was afraid he would bribe his way out of trouble or ultimately hurt someone to get his way. If it didn't annoy him so much, having to rely on a genuine outcome, he might have been flattered by their fear.

Sitting back in his chair, Corrado leaned toward his lawyer. "Doesn't the fact that they're locking the jury away with armed guards prejudice them against me?"

"Not any more prejudiced than they already were," he replied. "They came into this believing you're a monster. Our job is to humanize you."

"And how do you do that?"

"Watch and see."

Mr. Borza stood, straightening his tie as he approached the jury. "Ladies and gentlemen, during the next few weeks you're going to hear some terrible stories, some so horrific they'll turn your stomach. That's a guarantee. As the prosecution lays out its case, they're going to tell you about a violent man, a man without morals, a man without a conscience, who wreaks havoc on this great city day in and day out. But I'm here to tell you right now, if that man exists, I haven't met him, and I certainly wouldn't represent him."

The jury was attentive, hanging on to the lawyer's every word. Mr. Borza strolled along the carpet in front of them, looking each and every one in the eyes.

"Let me tell you about the real man on trial here," he said, motioning toward the defendant's table. "Corrado Moretti never went to college. He didn't even graduate high school, but that didn't stop him from following his dreams. He's a God-fearing man, a man who loves his family . . . especially his wife, Celia. They've been happily married for twenty-seven years."

It took everything in Corrado not to seek out his wife right then. He remained still, watching the jury, looking for signs of compassion.

He found none.

"The prosecution's case is based on half-truths from known liars who will get on that stand and tell you whatever the prosecution wants you to hear. They'll tell you these things, these fabrications, because the government cut them deals. You pat me on the back, I'll pat you. Why are they doing that? Because they have a personal vendetta against my client.

"Mr. Moretti built his business from the ground up, brick-by-brick, investing every penny he had into *Luna Rossa*. He's a small business owner, employing more than a dozen people and providing them with full benefits. He pays his taxes dutifully. He's living the American dream. Despite his lack of education, he made something out of himself. Does that sound like a man without morals? Does that sound like he lacks a conscience? In my opinion, it sounds like he's just like you and me."

Mr. Borza went on and on, twisting the facts, so by the time he finished he made Corrado seem like a bona fide boy scout. Corrado scanned the faces of the jurors as his lawyer took his seat, relaxing a smidgen when he finally saw it. There, in the eyes of a lone female—juror number six—a gleam of hope for humanity stared back at him. Naïve and foolish, maybe, but that woman wanted to believe the best in him.

It was all he needed: a foot in the proverbial door, the first step toward walking free.

DAY NINE

Wiretaps.

The sound of Corrado's voice resonated through the courtroom from a set of speakers in the front. Stacks of transcripts were piled high on the tables, completely untouched. His voice was clear and concise. They didn't need to read his words when they could plainly hear them.

"Do it," he barked on the tape. "When I wake up tomorrow, I better not hear about him still breathing, or you might not be by the time I go back to bed."

Corrado ran his hands down his face in frustration. How would his lawyer explain that one away?

Tape after tape, threat after threat. Little in the way of proof but a whole lot of damning insinuation.

They were all restless when the prosecution put on the last recording of the day. Corrado sat back in his chair, tensing when a familiar voice spoke through the speakers.

"It's done," Vincent said. "Happened tonight. Finally."

Corrado pinpointed the conversation immediately. He had been sitting at home when his brother-in-law called from Blackburn to say he had gotten Haven.

"About time," Corrado said. "How much did you pay?"

"A quarter mil, cash," he replied. "I've given more than that, though."

"I know," Corrado said. "You've paid a lot for that girl."

"Yeah." Vincent sighed loudly on the line. "We all have."

When those words hit him, Corrado shook his head. *Trafficking in persons for servitude.* Those words on his indictment made sense. Intentions hadn't mattered, and often never do.

DAY SEVENTEEN

Expert witnesses.

Corrado's attention wavered as the prosecutor questioned an accountant on the stand. They were going through his financial records one transaction at a time, trying to find a large sum of money they could prove was acquired illegally. Corrado was quite bored, knowing they would find nothing substantial. As far as he was concerned, a few dollars here and there didn't count.

"Objection!" his lawyer interrupted the line of questioning. "I fail to see why it's important to note how much Mr. Moretti spent for bathroom supplies in July."

"Overruled." The judge motioned for the prosecutor to continue.

More questions. More prying. More desperation. Corrado glanced at the jury, who appeared just as bored. Juror number six turned to him at that moment. He caught her eye, expecting her to look back away, but she didn't. She stared, studying him, a look of curiosity in her eyes.

"Objection," his lawyer said again. "I fail to see the relevance in *any* of this."

The judge sighed. "Overruled."

It went on for two excruciating hours before the prosecution finished. Mr. Borza stood then. "Based on your calculations, what's the total amount of money that went unreported at *Luna Rossa* last year?"

"Uh, $15,776.49."

Corrado cringed. More than a few dollars.

"Seems like a lot," Mr. Borza said, verbalizing his thoughts. "But we're talking about a club that made more than three million dollars last year, correct?"

"Yes."

"This unaccounted for money equals what, half of one percent?"

"Fractionally more than that, but yes."

"So more than ninety-nine percent of *Luna Rossa*'s revenue is right there in black and white. That half of one percent is the equivalent of blaming a man for losing a few pennies when he broke a dollar at the store. That's hardly what I'd call an elaborate money laundering scheme."

"Objection!" the prosecution declared. "He's trying to distort the math."

"Sustained. Move on, Mr. Borza."

The ruling didn't put off the lawyer. He had gotten his point across. "Could this half of one percent merely be a mathematical error?"

"It's possible."

"So there may not be any missing money at all."

"Objection!"

"Overruled."

"It's possible," the accountant said. "It's usually why taxes are audited during a series of years for consistency and accuracy, since mistakes happen."

Mr. Borza smiled as he sat back down. "Mistakes happen. I couldn't have said it better myself."

DAY TWENTY-TWO

Testimony.

Witness after witness took the stand, answering questions being fired at them. Former associates, a few *La Cosa Nostra*, testified to tales of mayhem, while shop owners and unlucky bystanders swore to what they knew. Not a single one of them would finger Corrado directly, but there was enough to loosely link him to the crimes.

"Mr. Gallo," Corrado's lawyer started, addressing a former street soldier on the stand, "you testified that you, along with three others, were involved in a string of robberies in March of ninety-eight. Is that correct?"

"Yes."

"And what role do you assert Corrado Moretti played in all of it?"

"He ordered us to do it."

"Personally?"

"Through text message."

"So there would be record of these messages, correct?"

"No, it was on a prepaid phone, a disposable."

"And the messages came from my client's number?"

"No, it came from a private number."

"Do you still have that disposable phone?"

"No, it was destroyed. You know, uh, disposed of."

"So, let me get this straight . . . you robbed these places because you received anonymous text messages telling you to, which you have no evidence of, and you expect us to just take your word that it came from Corrado Moretti?"

"It *was* him."

"What if I told you the three others you named in these robberies claim to not even know who Corrado Moretti is? They say it was a scheme the four of you cooked up on your own."

"I'd say they were lying."

"It's possible all three are lying," Mr. Borza said. "But isn't it more likely it's just you?"

———

A pin drop could be heard through the strained silence of the courtroom. The prosecutor stood beside his table, shifting through paperwork while everyone waited for him to speak. Nerves frazzled, the spectators were on the edge of their seats, eyes darting toward the big set of double doors every time there was a noise.

A month into the trial, the prosecution was down to the last name on their witness list.

Carmine held his breath, as did what seemed like half of Chicago crowded into the stifling room. He had avoided most of the proceedings—out of respect or selfishness, he wasn't sure—but today was one day he couldn't miss. He had to be there, had to see with his own eyes, face reality and learn the truth.

He needed to know if his father was still alive.

Had Vincent been located and taken into witness protection, nobody would know until he walked in, escorted by armed U.S. Marshals. But if he didn't show, well . . . Carmine didn't like to think about what that meant.

He glanced around, his eyes drifting to his uncle. Corrado seemed relaxed, borderline bored as he leaned back in his chair, his eyes focused on the restless jury. Had he been like that the whole trial, confident and calm, or did he know something the rest of them didn't?

Carmine shifted his attention to the other side of the room where his aunt sat with Dominic. Neither had seen him come in, and he appreciated that. The last thing he wanted was forced family time.

Mr. Markson cleared his throat. "Your honor, the prosecution . . ."

Carmine closed his eyes . . . *Calls Vincenzo DeMarco to the stand* . . .

". . . Rests its case. We have no more witnesses."

Carmine reopened his eyes as the silence was abruptly shattered by a wave of murmurs. The judge banged his gavel for silence as Carmine stood, slipping out of the courtroom before they could continue.

32

Gavin became a regular fixture outside the art building on the west side of Manhattan. It was rare that he wasn't standing there when Haven got out of her painting class, casually leaning against the wall as if there were nowhere else he needed to be.

Haven spoke to him on the days she saw him, and he would occasionally walk with her to the library on his way to the construction site a few blocks away, but he didn't push his luck by asking for anything more.

It was comfortable and easy, and she grew used to their strange arrangement after a while, enjoying their short conversations before they went their separate ways. It wasn't much, but it was something. It was a connection, a blossoming friendship she found herself looking forward to those three days a week he infiltrated her life.

Haven smiled to herself one Friday afternoon when they were strolling down the sidewalk, the crowd moving briskly around them, but they were in no hurry to get anywhere. Gavin filled the time by telling a joke he had heard at work, a vulgar one Haven didn't quite understand, but she laughed at what she figured were all the right places. "You know, you kind of remind me of someone I used to know."

"Really?" he asked, raising his eyebrows. "A boyfriend, maybe?"

"No, not at all. He was just a friend. He liked to tell jokes."

Gavin's expression fell. "Am I being friend-zoned already?"

Haven looked at him. "I don't know what that means."

He waved her off. "This friend of yours . . . was he anywhere near as handsome as me?"

She laughed. "Not quite, but few are."

"Shit, is that a compliment?" He stopped walking, dramatically blinking his eyes. "Are you *flirting* with me?"

Haven rolled her eyes and refused to respond, continuing to walk. He had no choice but to move again to catch up with her.

"Seriously, was that a compliment?" he asked. "I can't tell when you're being sarcastic."

"I'm never sarcastic."

"Oh." He paused. "Wait, was *that* sarcasm?"

Haven shook her head. "It was a compliment. I meant it."

"Wow, I'm shocked," he replied, grinning widely. "I honestly thought you were still entertaining the idea of a restraining order. Good to know I've worn you down enough that you like me a little bit."

She laughed. "I never said I *liked* you. I just said you were handsome. That says nothing about your personality."

"Now I know *that* was sarcasm," he declared.

"I wouldn't be so sure."

He clutched his chest. "I'm hurt."

Haven nudged him playfully with her elbow. "You'll get over it."

A sheet of notebook paper was taped to the glass of the locked art studio door that Friday, *class cancelled* scribbled on it with pencil. No explanation—just no class.

"Awesome!" Kelsey dramatically fist pumped in celebration. "No class!"

Haven frowned. She always looked forward to painting. "Wonder why?"

"Who cares?" Kelsey asked. "I have extra time to hit the computer lab and work on my design project now. Maybe I won't be stuck in the house all weekend after all."

"I guess that means I have time to . . ." Haven trailed off, unable to think of something to do. "go to the library."

Kelsey laughed. "You spend more time there than at home."

Haven shrugged. It was probably true.

After saying their good-byes, Kelsey headed to the lab the next floor up while Haven left the building. She strolled down the street, in no rush to get anywhere, and made the walk toward the library. Her mind wandered as she fell in with the bustling crowd, and before she realized it, she had already passed her destination. She looked around in confusion, catching sight of the closest street sign: Sixth Avenue.

A substantial construction site stood near the corner across the street, spanning about an acre and surrounded by tall buildings. The frame of a structure was built, metal beams stuck together like an elaborate maze. Dirty and chaotic, it looked a lot like she imagined a construction site would look.

Curious, Haven's feet carried her across the street for a closer look. Most of the workers were busy, operating equipment or scaling the structure, but a few guys in yellow hard hats stood around, chatting. One or two looked her way, someone even letting out a low whistle, but she ignored it as she walked through the lot. A trailer sat along the side, the low hum of an air conditioner buzzing from it. Something told her if Gavin was at the site, that was where he would be.

Haven felt out of place, her eyes locking on the ground as she headed straight for the trailer. She had come that far and figured it would be silly to leave without at least saying hello.

A thick man in scruffy jeans and a black tank top leaned against the corner of the trailer, tossing rocks at something in a nearby patch of dirt. Haven chanced a peek at him, her footsteps faltering when she heard a small squeal. Her eyes darted to the source of the sound, seeing a small white kitten. It could hardly walk, its fur matted with a bit of blood.

It squealed again as the man threw a rock at it, smacking it in the side.

"Stop that!" Haven said, the words flying from her mouth in horror. "Why are you doing that?"

The man looked at her with dark bloodshot eyes, no flicker of acknowledgment on his face. He turned away and grabbed another rock, striking the kitten again. It stumbled from the blow.

Haven's eyes burned with tears. "Don't do that anymore!"

"Mind your own business, sweetheart," the man grumbled. "Go on back to wherever you came from. You don't belong here."

He grabbed another rock, but Haven wasn't having it. She lunged for the cat, grabbing it as he threw the rock, smacking her with it instead. It stung as it struck her ankle, but she barely winced as she shielded the cat in her arms.

"What the hell are you doing?" the man spat, pushing away from the trailer. He took two steps toward her, his big stride closing the distance between them. Haven instinctively took a step away from the man.

Before she could say anything—or rather, run—the door of the trailer opened and laughter cut through the air. Two guys stepped out, one an old bald man in a black suit with a walking cane. He tipped his head in greeting to the other before heading to a waiting town car. The second man Haven recognized immediately, wearing freshly pressed khakis and a blue button-down shirt: Gavin.

He turned to them after the older man was gone, the smirk on his lips disappearing when he spotted Haven. His brow creased, his eyes darting between her and the worker. "What's going on here?"

"I'm wondering the same thing!" the man exclaimed. "I'm over here taking my afternoon break, you know, just hanging out, and this broad walks up and starts telling me what to do! Can you believe it?"

Gavin's expression darkened, his blue eyes clouding to a furious gray. Haven's heartbeat quickened, the cat meowing as she instinctively gripped it tighter.

The Gavin she knew was friendly, playful. She had never seen him angry before.

"Get back to work," he barked at the man.

"But—"

"But nothing. Go. Now."

The man hesitated for a fraction of a second before storming away. Gavin took a few brusque steps toward Haven, eliciting a small retreat from her, but he wasn't deterred in his approach. "What happened?"

"I, uh . . . the kitten was hurt, and he was throwing rocks at it, and I told him not to but he wouldn't stop, and the kitten yelped, so I couldn't just stand there. I had to help! He got mad, then you came out, and he told you what happened, and uh . . ."

"And here we are?" he guessed.

Haven nodded, avoiding his eyes. He reached toward her and she flinched, but he seemed not to notice as he grabbed the cat, taking it from her.

"It looks pretty messed up," he said, checking it out. "There's a shelter a few blocks over. I can drop it off there."

"And they'll fix her?" she asked.

"Maybe," he replied. "And it's a him."

"Oh." Her brow furrowed. "What do you mean maybe?"

"I mean they'll either fix it up or put it to sleep."

Haven recoiled as if he had struck her. "Why would they do that?"

"The city's overrun with stray animals, so I'm sure the shelter gets more than it can keep. Might not be worth saving."

Horrified, Haven ripped the kitten from his hands, taking it back. "They can't just kill it! That's not fair! It did nothing wrong!"

Gavin let out a sudden laugh of surprise as he held up his hands defensively. "Geez, all right, relax. There are other options."

"Like?"

"Like you can let it go and hope it can fend for itself."

Out of the question. "Or?"

"Or you can take it to the vet."

She glanced at the cat before looking back at him. "Do you know a good vet?"

"I might know of a place," he replied, eyeing her curiously. "Why are you here, anyway? I mean, don't get me wrong—it's a pleasant surprise, but still a surprise. I was actually about to head your way."

"My class got cancelled," she replied. "I was going to the library and kind of just ended up here instead."

Gavin stared at her with disbelief. "You just ended up here?"

"Yes. And since I was here I thought I would say hey, so . . . hey."

A smug smile formed on his lips. "You must've missed me."

"Why would you think that?"

"Because you didn't see me yesterday and you wouldn't see me today if you didn't have class. It's the weekend, so that means you'd have to wait until Monday to see me again. That's a long time."

She rolled her eyes at his cocky tone. "It was nothing like that."

"Admit it," he said. "You missed me."

"No."

"You like me."

"No."

"Not at all?"

"Well, maybe just a little," she admitted.

"I'll take it," he said. "It's better than nothing."

"But just as a friend," she clarified. "Not more."

Gavin shook his head as he took a step away. "Stay here and I'll get the address for the vet."

He disappeared back into the trailer as Haven strolled farther away, petting the kitten. It stared up at her, bright blue eyes alive with excitement, mismatched from its dull and lifeless exterior.

"Snowy," she whispered, the word popping in her mind. "I'll call you Snowy."

Gavin came back out, pausing on the steps of the trailer as he hollered for someone. The firmness was back in his voice, the hard edge once again etched in his expression. The man from earlier jogged over, and Haven watched as Gavin said something to him. He spoke too quietly for her to hear but the man's head dropped low, his shoulders slumping in defeat. He gave a slight nod before turning, and Haven tensed as he approached her.

"I'm sorry, ma'am," he muttered, refusing to meet her eyes. "I hope you can accept my apology. I ain't mean to hurt the cat or anything. I was just messing around. Send me the vet bills. Mr. Amaro can take it out of my pay."

Haven stammered with surprise, only able to get out an "okay."

Gavin walked over when the man scurried back to work. He handed her a scrap of paper with an address and phone number scribbled on it.

"Thanks," she replied. "What did you say to make him apologize?"

"I just told him who you were."

She tensed at those words. "Who am I?"

Gavin's eyes met hers. He stared for a moment before answering, his eyebrows raised as if that question surprised him. "A friend of mine, of course."

"Oh."

"Anyway, you want me to go with you?" he asked. "It's not far, just about a block back the way you came. We can walk."

She glanced at the address on the paper. "I don't want you to have to leave work."

"It's fine," he said. "I was about to leave anyway."

A few hours later, the two of them sat in flimsy blue plastic chairs in the busy waiting room of a walk-in emergency animal clinic.

Haven fidgeted anxiously, her backside starting to hurt from the hard seat.

A nurse eventually called Haven's name and she jumped up, not bothering to wait for Gavin as she made her way to the back.

"The kitten's going to be fine," the lady said. "We've cleaned him up and dressed the wound—just a small gash that should heal right up. He had a horrible case of fleas that we've taken care of, but there was nothing majorly wrong. You can take him home now."

Smiling with relief, Haven signed the heap of paperwork before taking the cat and rejoining Gavin. They left the clinic, the animal fast asleep in Haven's arms as they headed back out into the street. The sun had started to set, most of the day having faded away.

"So what are you going to do with the cat?" Gavin asked. "Keep it?"

She frowned. "I don't think I'm allowed to have pets."

"You can try to find it a home," Gavin suggested. "Put out an ad."

"But what if someone bad responds, like that guy you work with?"

Gavin sighed. "I don't know. I'm out of ideas short of me taking it home."

Haven's expression lit up. "Would you really?"

He blanched. "What?"

"Would you keep him?" she asked. "I know you'll be nice to him."

Gavin stammered, opening and closing his mouth a few times, before shrugging and letting out a deep sigh. "Fuck it, why not?"

Haven smiled, holding the kitten up and waving its paw at Gavin. "Snowy thanks you."

The clinic was near her art building, the students all gone for the weekend when they strolled past. "So it's kind of a long walk from the construction site to my school," Haven mused. "What in the world do you do up here all the time?"

"It's not that long of a walk," he said. "Ten, fifteen minutes at the most. I came up here that first day to hit up a deli nearby."

"And what about every other day?"

He shrugged. "I come for the company."

Despite herself, Haven blushed at that.

They chatted casually as they walked—about the cat, about school, even about the weather. It took nearly a half hour for them to reach Haven's neighborhood, although she usually made the walk in half that time.

"I'm sorry that took so long," Haven said, stopping in front of her brownstone when they arrived.

"I didn't mind," he replied, shrugging. "Didn't have much else to do."

"What about work? Didn't they expect you back?"

"I make my own hours, so it isn't a big deal. I come and go as I please."

She gazed at him curiously. He genuinely sounded like he didn't mind. "You know, you're really nice. Not many people would've done what you did."

"Did it make you like me just a little more?"

She laughed. "Maybe."

"I can tell," he said, smirking. "You actually let me walk you home."

Haven stared at him with surprise. It hadn't struck her until that moment. As many times as she had refused, she finally let him walk her home without him even having to ask.

Before Haven could respond, the front door of the brownstone flung open and Kelsey appeared, talking loudly into her cell phone. She looked at the two of them, her expression lighting up with surprise, before her attention went back to her call. Her gaze darted past them, scanning the street, before she started frantically waving. "You see me? Yeah, there. Find a parking spot."

She hung up and squealed. "Hey, guys! What are you up to?"

Haven held the cat up. "I found this, so Gavin went with me to the vet."

"Then I walked her home." Arrogance oozed from his voice.

Haven rolled her eyes at him as Kelsey cooed and petted the tiny animal. "I was just leaving, though."

Kelsey's attention switched from the cat to Gavin instantly. "Leaving? No way! I have some friends over . . . we were going to have a few drinks and hang out. You should totally join us. *Both* of you."

Haven shook her head, but Gavin's smug smile grew infinitely. "Really?"

"Yes, really," Kelsey said. "It'll be fun."

Kelsey's friends appeared then, a few Haven vaguely recognized, but none she really knew. They were sociable, while Haven preferred to keep to herself. They disappeared inside, gathering in the second floor apartment.

Raising his eyebrows, Gavin stared at her questioningly, awaiting a reaction. "Are you going to invite me inside?"

She shrugged slowly. "Kelsey already invited you."

"But I didn't come here for Kelsey, so I'm not going in unless *you* invite me."

Haven considered that, unsure of how to respond. It had been a long day and she really wanted to take a bath and maybe read a book, but when the music started upstairs, so loud it rattled the windows, Haven knew she wouldn't be getting any peace anyway.

"Fine." Go with the flow, she told herself. Live a little. "Let's go upstairs."

"What kind of invitation is that?"

"The only kind you're getting."

Gavin laughed, holding open the front door politely and pressing his hand gently against her back. Bypassing her apartment, she headed up the stairs, acutely aware of Gavin's eyes on her as he walked behind her. It made her skin prickle as her stomach churned from nerves.

Kelsey's apartment, identical to the one below it when stripped down to its core, looked like an entirely different world. Everything was brand-new and bright, expensive furniture filling every room while elaborate artwork hung on the walls. Haven gingerly took a seat in the first spot she came across, a tan leather chair with wide, plush arms. She kicked her shoes off and tucked her feet under her, protectively holding the sleeping kitten in her lap, while Gavin casually positioned himself on the arm of her chair.

It took only seconds before Kelsey thrust drinks at the two of them. Haven took the spiked lemonade with a polite smile while Gavin eyed the bottle of bright yellow alcohol with aversion. "Yeah, I can't drink this shit," he mumbled to himself.

"I'm sure she has other stuff," Haven said, pointing across the room. "The kitchen's over there. You can help yourself. Kelsey won't mind."

He stood up, looking down at her. "Are you going to drink it?"

"I guess," she said. "I might as well."

Gavin strolled away, stealthily handing the bottle back to Kelsey as he made his way to her kitchen. Haven watched him curiously, taking a moment to admire the way he seamlessly infused himself into a group. Poised and confident, he spoke to strangers as if they were friends.

Envy pecked at her, sudden and unexpected. Was it jealousy that he was sharing himself with others, or jealousy at the way he seemed to effortlessly fit in? She thought it was the latter, but the sheer possibility that she might yearn to keep him to herself filled her with uneasiness.

Gavin returned with a red plastic cup and retook his spot on the arm of her chair. He took a sip of his drink and smiled. "Better."

"What is it?" she asked curiously, peeking into his cup. "Beer?"

"Mountain Dew."

Haven took a sip of hers, puckering her lips. "You don't drink?"

"Yes." He smiled playfully. "I drink water, milk, and pop."

"But not alcohol?"

"I don't make a habit of it," he replied.

"I don't drink, either," she said, elaborating when his brow furrowed. "Well, not usually. I'm not old enough."

"Well, I am old enough, but I prefer to keep my wits about me."

Haven surveyed him as he sipped from his cup. His smooth skin showed no sign of age, his eyes bright and encouraging, his smile genuine. He had had a good life—that much was clear—but small scars on his hands told her he had fought for it.

Gavin looked at her as if he could sense her gaze. "What?"

"How old are you?" she asked.

"Twenty-six."

"Wow, that's—"

"Old?" he guessed.

She laughed. "No, I was going to say that's kind of young to be a manager."

Gavin's brow furrowed. "Manager?"

"At the construction site. You work in that little office. You said you supervised things, right?"

His face lit up with understanding. "Ah, yeah. Well, what I do is less about your résumé and more about your references . . . if that makes sense."

Haven nodded. "It does." It was precisely how she had gotten where she was, how she had been admitted into school and settled into New York. Corrado had pulled strings, bypassing policies to manipulate the system to his benefit.

Haven nursed her drink as she mused over that. Despite the fact that she sipped slowly, she could feel the alcohol taking affect after only a few minutes, relaxing her back into the seat as her eyelids drooped a bit. Buzzing, her head swam as her body tingled, warming slightly under Gavin's intense gaze. He remained perched on the arm of the chair, his attention unwavering.

She excused herself when her drink was empty and grabbed another from the refrigerator, taking a moment to clear her head before returning back to the others. They were playing a game, their laughter bouncing through the apartment and mixing with the music. She sat down again and had just opened her bottle when Kelsey's voice rang out above the others. "Play with us!"

Haven looked up, her eyes connecting with her friend's. "Play what?"

"Never have I ever," Kelsey said. "Come on, it's easy. We take turns saying things we haven't done, and everyone who has done it has to take a drink."

The blood rushed to Haven's cheeks as everyone looked at her. She peeked at Gavin, hoping to divert the attention away from herself. He shrugged. "Sure, why not."

Everyone migrated to the small living room, a dozen of them gathering around, and the music was turned down so they could hear the declarations called out one by one. Never have I ever had sex in the house with a parent home. Never have I ever been high. Never have I ever had a fake ID. Never have I ever gotten drunk at a school dance. Never have I ever driven a car without a license. The others laughed, trading playful jabs and reminiscing about shared experiences, while Haven quietly took sip after sip.

She found herself drinking more than she had expected to, given how sheltered a life she had lived. She realized, as the alcohol gradually seeped into her bloodstream, intoxication taking over her mind and loosening her hold on her emotions, exactly how many experiences Carmine had unknowingly exposed her to. Their lives had been anything but normal, their love anything but average, but he had managed to show her the same world everyone else knew, the world she had always yearned to be a part of, the one she thought she had only just stepped into.

The game grew more intense as it went on, the statements cruder. Haven didn't drink so much then, but she was already past the point of no return. Gavin played along, steadily sipping his soda to things that made Haven even blush to imagine. He chuckled at her reactions, smiling guiltily at the questions in her eyes.

"Never have I ever been in handcuffs," someone called out.

Bottle halfway to her lips, Haven hesitated as she thought of Dr. DeMarco and the day he had bound her to her bed as punishment. She took a quick drink and Gavin cocked an eyebrow at her as he took his own sip. "Don't ask," she muttered, shaking her head. He didn't want to know.

A few more were thrown out, raunchy ones that gave her a quick reprieve from the alcohol, before someone shouted, "Never have I ever seen a dead body!"

The room erupted in laughter, others rolling their eyes at the absurdity, but Haven blanched as visions flashed through her mind of the death, and chaos, and destruction she'd seen. She saw Number 33, the lifeless blue eyes that still haunted her, the blood pooling around the young girl's blonde hair.

Closing her eyes, she took a long pull from her bottle, downing the rest of her drink as she tried to clear the memory away. And maybe she had imagined it, or maybe it was purely coincidence, but when she reopened her eyes, Haven noticed that Gavin, too, had taken a sip from his cup.

The game came to a stopping point, people dispersing for more alcohol as the music was turned up again. Gavin let out a long sigh, glancing at his watch as he stood. "It's getting late."

Haven glanced around for a clock, but her vision was too blurry to make out the numbers. She climbed to her feet, still holding the sleeping cat, and swayed a bit. Gavin grasped her elbow to steady her, taking both the empty bottle and the kitten.

"We should get you home," he said quietly. "You're drunk."

Despite Kelsey's objections, Gavin led Haven from the apartment. He helped her down the stairs, pausing in the foyer outside of her apartment door as she fumbled with her keys. "Thanks again for tonight. I'll see you Monday."

She turned away, but he reached out to stop her. "See me sooner."

"What?"

"Go out with me."

The color drained from her face as those words washed through her. "What?"

"Tomorrow. Go out with me."

"I can't," she said, shaking her head. "I have plans."

At the library, she thought, but she refrained from saying it out loud.

"Then the next day," he said. "Go out with me on Sunday."

33

Haven fidgeted, peeking through the thick white curtains that hung in her living room. It was early afternoon on Sunday, and the Manhattan neighborhood was as hectic as ever. Tourists wandered the streets, mingling with the locals and the busy street vendors. Usually watching the flurry of activity put Haven at ease, but today every movement just made her more edgy.

"Relax," Kelsey said, plopping down on Haven's couch with the remote control. "You're stressing for no reason."

Haven shook her head. "He'll be here soon."

"So? It's a Sunday. It's not like it's a real date."

Not a real date. Haven tried to tell herself that, but it had yet to work. It certainly felt real to her.

"What is it then?" she asked.

"It's just two people getting together to do whatever it is you people do," she said. "Personally, unless it involves sex or bacon, I see no reason to do *anything* on Sundays."

"Well, we won't be doing that," Haven muttered.

"No bacon? He isn't vegan, is he? I don't trust a guy that won't chow down on a steak."

Haven felt the blood rush to her cheeks. "I meant the sex."

She could hardly get the word past her lips.

Kelsey laughed. "What a shame. I had hope for you."

Shaking her head, Haven peered back out the window. She saw him right away, halfway down the block, walking through the crowd. He was dressed impeccably, wearing black slacks and a white shirt. His dress shoes shone under the afternoon sunlight, a dark pinstriped tie hanging loosely around his neck. He walked with confidence, comfortable in his skin.

Watching him made her dizzy.

"I don't get why you're freaking out over this," Kelsey continued. "You see this boy all the time."

It was different, but Haven knew her friend wouldn't understand. Kelsey dated all the time, meeting new guys every week, but that wasn't Haven. She had no interest in dating at all. The afternoon walks after her painting class and the friendly banter she shared with Gavin were innocent. But this . . . this was planned. This was contrived. And to her, that was the difference between being friends and something more.

That thought alone—the thought of someone wanting something more with her—made her stomach clench with severe angst.

She dropped the curtain back into place, smoothing her clothes when Gavin knocked. She felt underdressed in her jeans and pink blouse. *What did people wear on a possibly-but-maybe-not real date?*

"Have fun," Kelsey said, a mischievous glint in her eyes. "Don't do anything I wouldn't do."

"Don't worry," Haven mumbled. "I won't do half of what you would."

Haven opened the door, smiling sheepishly when she came face-to-face with Gavin. "Hi."

"Hey there," he said. "You ready?"

"Uh, yes." She took a tentative step outside. "I look okay, though, don't I?"

His eyes quickly raked down her body at that question. Her skin prickled at the attention. "Yeah. Why?"

"I don't know," she said. "I just saw you were dressed up and . . ."

"Oh, yeah, I guess I'm a little overdressed," he said, looking down at himself as he rocked on his heels. "You look fine for what we're doing."

Haven shut the door, taking another step toward him. "What are we doing?"

He shoved his hands in his pockets as he stepped off the porch, motioning for her to follow him. "I thought we'd take a walk or something."

"But that's what we do every day."

"True." He laughed. "It works for us, right? We can just see where we end up. I mean, unless you'd rather—"

"Oh no." She cut him off, her anxiety lessening. "Walking is great."

Maybe it wasn't a date.

The two of them set off through the streets. Gavin struck up conversation, their usual friendly banter returning as he led her down to the subway on Twenty-third Street.

Haven froze on the platform after he grabbed their passes, her eyes scanning the others waiting. A white tile wall loomed behind her, while trash littered the grimy concrete ground. Bells and whistles sounded, a crackling loudspeaker drowning out the chatter of the crowd. People pushed, others yelled, as the whoosh of trains rushing past stirred up the musty odor of dirt and rank urine. Electricity buzzed and lights flashed as doors clattered, noisily opening and closing before the trains sped away.

It was contradictory—loud and chaotic, yet orderly at the same time, like an assembly line in an overworked factory. It felt robotic, almost inhuman, as people packed the vessels, methodically moving on and off like clockwork. It was an entirely different world underground, one Haven never realized existed beneath her feet.

Haven's wide eyes scanned the scene, taking it all in with stunned silence. Gavin noticed her expression, scrunching his nose. "I know, it's disgusting down here."

"No, it's, uh . . . I've just never taken the subway before."

"Never?"

She shook her head. "Never."

"How can you live in New York and not take the subway?" he asked. "How do you get to the other side of the city?"

"I don't. I've never been."

He stared at her. "Never?"

"Never."

"Madison Square Garden?"

She shook her head.

"Times Square?"

"No."

"Broadway?"

"Nope."

A train pulled up to the platform, the silver doors creaking open. People moved toward it and Gavin pressed his hand to Haven's back, guiding her into a graffiti-ridden car. He muscled his way through the crowd, acting as a shield between her and the others. She slid into the last empty spot on a hard plastic bench, her small frame squeezed between a teenage boy humming and an overweight bald man with body odor, slumped over and snoring.

Gavin stood in front of Haven, leaning against a metal pole as the doors closed. They jolted as they took off, shoving her into the sleeping man, but he hardly stirred. The floor beneath her feet vibrated as they sped along the old tracks, metal grinding as the lights inside the cramped car flickered.

Haven's heart thumped wildly in her chest, a mixture of exhilaration and alarm, and blush stained her cheeks when she noticed Gavin's eyes fixed squarely on her, watching with curiosity. She looked away from him, her gaze timidly dipping to the floor. He stood so close their knees almost bumped, the tips of their shoes touching—his: shiny, new, and black; hers: old, scuffed, and dirty.

She slid her foot back impulsively, away from his, before chancing a peek at him again. He, too, stared at their shoes, his eyes darting back to hers as if he could sense her gaze. His curious expression held questions, but he asked none of them.

After a few minutes, the air brakes whistled loudly like fireworks about to explode. Haven clung to the seat, careful not to bump anyone as the train came to a screeching halt. The doors opened and Gavin led her onto another platform, COLUMBUS CIRCLE written in mosaic tile along a wall.

"Where are we?" Haven asked as he led her through the crowd. The fact that she was in a part of the city she had never been to before both unnerved her and excited her.

"You'll see in a minute," he said.

She followed him out of the subway station and onto the street above. The moment she stepped out, something inside her twisted. She saw it then, just as he had said she would. Trees spanned as far as her eyes could see, a forest tucked into the heart of the bustling city.

"Central Park," Gavin said. "Ever been?"

"Not yet," she whispered. "I've always wanted to, though."

"Well, come on, then." Gavin motioned with his head, a smirk highlighting his face. "Nothing stopping you now."

Nothing stopping you now.

Haven followed Gavin across the street, passing the massive statue and into the park. The two of them strolled side by side in peaceful silence as Haven admired the trees towering over them like oversize green umbrellas. Sunlight spilled through the branches in spots, patches of light scattered along the path of cool shade, warmth forcing its way into the shadows. Haven reveled in it, stepping into the glow when they came upon it and glancing up into the sky with a smile on her lips.

Heaven, she thought. It felt like Heaven streaming down on her.

"So what do you want to do?" Gavin asked.

Haven's brow furrowed. "Aren't we doing it?"

"Well, we can just walk around if you want, but there's more to do here."

"Really? I thought it was just, you know . . ." She motioned all around them. ". . . trees."

He laughed. "Not at all. Come on, I'll show you."

Statues, bridges, trails, wildlife . . . hours passed as Haven took it all in. They watched a puppet show and she swung on the playground swings before exploring the zoo and feeding the ducks on the lake. Gavin taught her how to play checkers and blatantly let her win, even buying her ice cream when they passed a vendor. There was music and games, laughter and excitement. She hummed along to the musical tower clock as they watched people toss a Frisbee and plant new trees.

Everywhere she looked there was something else, something new, something more, and little by little a part of her guard crumbled. The hurt she carried with her took a hit, hope and happiness resonating inside her again. The strong-willed girl, restrained and suspicious, didn't even notice as her vulnerability showed, bits of the real Haven Antonelli shining through for once.

"Let's get some food," Gavin suggested. It was growing late, already close to dusk. "We haven't eaten all day."

"I had ice cream, remember?"

He laughed. "That doesn't count. I know a nice place. We can grab some dinner and get you home, since you have school in the morning."

"And you have work," she said. "Do you have to get up super early?"

"No, I get up when I get up," he said. "I make my own hours. Remember?"

"That's right. Is your dad in construction, too?"

"Sort of," he said, frowning as he looked at his watch. "My father's got his hands in a bit of everything."

They headed out of Central Park, catching the subway back to Twenty-third Street. Gavin sat beside her on the bench this time because there were far fewer riders at that hour than in the afternoon. They got off at their destination, walking about a block to a small restaurant. Long windows overtook the front of the brick building, and Haven could see quite a few tables inside.

They were seated along the side of the dining room at a table with two wooden chairs. Gavin ordered vegetable curry with spicy noodles without looking at the menu, while Haven picked a cheeseburger with fries. They were both quiet as they waited, sipping their drinks and resting their feet from walking so much.

It took ten minutes, maybe fifteen, before their food arrived. Within a matter of seconds, Gavin cleared his throat. "Can I ask you something?"

"Sure," she said, popping a fry into her mouth.

"What's your deal?"

She stopped chewing. "What?"

"It's just that, you know, you're not like the usual people I deal with. There's something different about you."

And just like that, Haven's guard crept right back up, the wall of disconnect rebuilding. Different wasn't blending in. Different wasn't staying out of the limelight. Different wasn't a part of the plan. "How am I different?"

He shrugged. "You live in New York but you haven't seen much. You've gone nowhere and done nothing."

Haven had no idea how to respond. She swallowed harshly, her appetite gone. "I was born in a really small town and never got to go anywhere. There wasn't really anywhere to go, anyway, even if I could. I only had my mama growing up, and she couldn't take me places. My father . . . I never really had one of those, and then I lost my mama, and well . . . here I am, I guess."

She stumbled over her words, cringing at her explanation. While true, technically, it was a lie by omission. A half-truth. It was all, she realized, she could ever give him.

"You have other family, right? Aunts? Uncles? Cousins?"

The question spurred an image in Haven's mind of her last Christmas in Durante. Dominic. Tess. Dia. Celia and Corrado. Dr. DeMarco. *Carmine*. While technically not her relatives, they were the only other family she had ever known. "Yes, but I don't talk to them much."

"Why not?"

"I don't know." That time, it was one hundred percent truth. "They all live far away."

"So why are you here then?"

Haven started to reply, looking up from her plate, but her words trailed off when her gaze drifted past Gavin. Her eyes were drawn to the back of the restaurant, out of the glass wall and onto the patio, where a row of potted palm trees aligned the railing. "Palm trees."

"Palm trees?" he asked, Haven's attention returned to him when he spoke. "That's why you came here?"

"No, well, uh . . ." She let out a sudden laugh, tears prickling her eyes. "I didn't think there were any in New York."

He glanced over his shoulder. "Ah, yeah, they imported them. You know, for ambiance. A bit tacky, but whatever."

Gavin pried no more after that, but the damage had been done. Haven was distracted, her thoughts lodged in the distant past as her eyes continually drifted back to the patio, her food remaining untouched. She missed them all, more than she had wanted to admit, but she missed *him* most of all.

She tried not to dwell on Carmine, but sometimes it was unavoidable. Sometimes something small rubbed against the wound, reopening it, reminding her of what she tried to forget—not him, never him, but the ending. The devastation. The good-bye.

Or lack of one, really. The lack of closure. Without it, the wound could never properly heal. It would linger forever, fueled by the ideology of what could have been.

What could have been? It could have been Carmine there with her, exploring Central Park, traveling around New York. It could have been Carmine sitting across from her, not asking questions because he already knew the truth. He knew her past.

He knew where she came from. He understood what she had gone through.

But it wasn't him, and as she sat there, she allowed herself to feel that void again.

Gavin paid when they finished. They left the restaurant, neither speaking on the walk to her apartment. He reached over and took her hand halfway there, his fingers loosely linking with hers. She didn't pull away, didn't fight it. Her emotions were all over the place, up and down, a roller coaster of twisted thoughts and confusion.

"Thanks for today," Gavin said, pausing in front of the brownstone.

"No, thank *you*. It was nice."

"Nice." He repeated the word, eyeing her peculiarly. "Nothing more?"

"Don't get me wrong, I had a wonderful time, and I do like you."

"But?"

"But I just . . ."

"Nothing more," he repeated.

"Right." She sighed. "It's nothing you did. It's just me, I guess."

He let out a sudden, abrupt laugh that startled her. "Are you giving me the 'it's not you, it's me' line?"

"No. Well, yes. It's true, though. You're really nice, and you have a great personality, but—"

"That's what they say about ugly people," he deadpanned.

She rolled her eyes. "No, it isn't. It's true. And you're not ugly. You're handsome." She felt the blush rise to her cheeks at the admission. "Very handsome."

"So what is it?"

She glanced down at their still connected hands. "There's no spark. No electricity. No lightning."

Something flickered in his eyes then, his face softening as he let go of her hand. "Ah."

"I'm really sorry," she said.

"Don't be," he said. "No harm done."

"Are you sure?"

He smiled genuinely. "Absolutely."

"I did have fun, though," she said. "I'm glad I went."

"Me, too," he said, taking a step back as he shoved his hands in his pocket. "I should be going. Have a good one."

He walked away without another word, jogging across the street and disappearing into the darkness.

————

Monday came. Haven stepped out of her art building at precisely one o'clock and looked up to see Gavin leaning against the wall. They shared warm smiles and he strolled beside her to the library like usual, conversation flowing easy.

Wednesday he was there again, as he was on Friday. But the following week, when she walked out of her painting class, the sidewalk was vacant. For the first time in weeks . . . months . . . Gavin wasn't there.

She waited for a few minutes, lingering along the side of the building, before making the journey alone.

Days passed, then weeks, with no sign of Gavin. What started as confusion quickly grew into frustration before finally morphing into concern. Had something happened to him? Was he okay?

One Friday afternoon, instead of heading to the library, she made the trek to the construction site. She stopped near the corner when she reached it, remaining on the old cracked sidewalk, her eyes scanning the property. They had made little progress from what she could tell, a few more levels of metal beams erected, but it was still no more than a fractured shell. Workers swarmed the grounds, a sea of yellow hard hats in the distance, bobbing and moving like rubber ducks in the water.

Her attention shifted to the trailer as the door flew open and Gavin appeared in the doorway. A group of guys greeted him when he stepped outside. He joined them, sipping on a bottle of water as he sat on the trailer steps, laughing.

Relief washed through her instantly before a tinge of hurt bubbled up. He appeared to be more than okay. Happy, even.

Haven stood there for a minute before turning away. She knew it then, could feel it in her gut, the concern and frustration fading right back to utter confusion. Their friendship was no more, tossed away haphazardly like it no longer meant anything . . . if it ever even did.

34

Intuition.

It was something Haven relied on since she was a child, living on the isolated ranch in the long-forgotten town of Blackburn. It had kept her out of trouble, warning her when something was not quite right. It was a sensation along her skin, a twisting in her gut that set her on edge. Whether it was coyotes prowling in the night or monsters lurking in the shadows, she had always sensed when something—or someone—was there who shouldn't be.

She could remember only a handful of times when her intuition failed her. The afternoon in Dr. DeMarco's bedroom had been once, when he had cornered her after she touched his gun. The warning signs had gone up too late. He had caught her red-handed, vulnerable and alone.

It had happened another time, too, years earlier when she had been a small girl. Trudging along after her mama in the greenhouse along the side of the property, boredom nagged at her as Miranda was busy at work. She was at that age where she still didn't understand the reality of her existence, the dreamer inside of her still alive, naïve and innocent.

"Can I go see Chloe?" she had asked, tugging on the back of her mama's shirt to get her attention. The cool air from an air conditioner blew on them from behind, stirring her filthy white summer dress.

"I don't think that's a good idea," her mama said, not taking her eyes off the rows of plants. "You should stay with me."

"I don't like it in here," she said, scrunching up her nose. "It smells funny."

"It doesn't smell funny."

"Yes, it does. It's cold, too. See!" She held out her arm to show her the chill bumps covering her tanned skin, even though her mama wasn't looking. "And it's too bright. My eyes hurt."

"You're just full of complaints today."

"But it's all true!" Haven said. "Can I go? I promise I'll be good!"

"I know you'll be good. I just . . . I don't know."

"Please? Chloe's my best friend!"

She frowned. "Fine."

Haven ran from the greenhouse, hearing her mama call after her to be careful, but she was too excited to respond. She hadn't seen Chloe in more than five sunsets and missed her, but her mama said it was too dangerous for them to visit a lot.

Haven looked around when she got outside, making sure no one was there, before running across the yard as fast as her legs would go. She slowed when she got to the building on the other side of the house, right beside the stables that she and her mama stayed in. The building was gray, like a big metal house, and she quietly tiptoed to the back, where a bunch of cages were lined up against it.

"Chloe!" she called, seeing her right away in the first cage. She jumped up as soon as Haven said her name, looking as excited as she felt inside. "I missed you!"

She started crying out and Haven ran over to her, shushing her. "You have to be quiet before they hear!"

Haven got down on her knees, reaching her hand through the links in the cage. "Mama's working in the greenhouse again," she told her. "Master's crop is sick and he told Mama she better fix it, but I don't think she knows how. She asked me if it looked like she had a green thumb, but when I tried to look at her thumb she told me I was being silly. So I don't know if she does."

Chloe just stared at her. Haven guessed she didn't know, either.

"Oh and someone came here yesterday! I don't know who, because Mama made me stay away. She said it was for my own good, but what if it was my friend?"

Chloe yelped. "My other friend," Haven said quickly. "You're still my bestest friend, but I have another friend that lives out in the world. Mama says the world is big. Did you know that? She says there are bunches and bunches of people out there, and there are so many houses! Like, bajillions of them!"

She held her arms out wide to show her how many. Chloe got excited, jumping up and down and making noise. She quickly dropped her arms, putting her finger against her lips. "Shhhh, quiet! If someone hears you . . ."

"Too late."

It felt like all the blood in Haven's body froze. She jumped up and turned around, wanting to hide, but Frankie was there. He had her cornered.

She stood like a statue, stubbornly, childishly hoping she would disappear and he wouldn't see her anymore. He would go away and forget she existed again. She tried to count in her head, like her mama taught her to do when she was scared, but she got stuck after six, and he was looking at her too hard.

Haven took a big step to the side, thinking she could escape, but it didn't work. His eyes widened as he shook his head. "Don't run, girl."

She didn't run. She stood like a statue again.

He walked over and bent down, reaching his hand in the cage, snapping his finger. Chloe came right to him, whining for attention as he rubbed her head.

"Do you like my beagle?" he asked, looking at Haven.

She didn't know what a beagle was but she nodded.

"She's a good girl, makes a good hunting dog." He patted Chloe on top of the head once more before standing back up. "Do you have a name for her?"

She nodded again.

"Will you tell me it?"

Another nod. She didn't know what else to do.

He laughed at her muteness, and Haven squeezed her eyes shut tight when his hand came toward her. She braced herself for the hit, for the fingers digging in her flesh, the scratches and bruises, but none of it came. Instead, he patted her on the head like he had done Chloe. His hand was heavy, but it didn't hurt.

"You ought to be more careful, kid," he said, still laughing to himself. "It's never good when the likes of me can sneak up on somebody like you."

It was then, as Frankie sauntered away, that Haven felt the telltale signs of her intuition striking, warning her when it was already too late.

And years later, as she sat in a booth in the back of a small diner, sipping a cup of black coffee as Kelsey stabbed at a plate of scrambled eggs, she felt it stirring yet again. It started with a prickle, a tickle across her taut skin, before the tiny hairs at the nape of her neck stood on end. She ignored it at first, trying to pay attention to Kelsey, but the sensation just grew stronger and stronger.

"Are you even listening to me?" Kelsey asked, pointing her fork at Haven.

"Sure," Haven said, absently rubbing her neck. "What did you say again?"

"Let's take a road trip."

Brow furrowed, Haven stared at her friend. "What?"

"Let's take a road trip," Kelsey repeated for what was likely the third time. "We don't have anything else to do this summer, right?"

"Uh, well . . ." Haven hesitated. *Road trip?* "I kind of thought I'd just stay around here this summer and take a few extra classes. You know, get ahead."

Kelsey dramatically rolled her eyes. "Oh, come on. School will be here when we get back. It's been a long year, and we deserve a break."

"I don't know . . ."

"Well, think about it." Kelsey threw her fork down and stood up, tossing some cash down on the table. "We can leave after the Novak Gala."

"Okay," Haven said, drinking the rest of her coffee before setting the cup aside. "I'll think about it."

She had no intention of thinking about it, no intention of leaving New York.

The two of them left the diner, Kelsey once again babbling as they walked side by side toward the school. Haven was tense, her eyes darting around as they passed through crowds, surveying faces, analyzing looks. She kept peering over her shoulder, but she wasn't sure why.

What she was sure of, though, was the twisting in her gut, her intuition telling her that someone—or something—was there that shouldn't be.

———

"Explain it to me again."

Haven ignored Kelsey, acting as if her friend hadn't spoken as she studied the canvas in front of her. The fresh paint glistened under the fluorescent lights of the art studio, the vast array of colors weaving together like a tangled rainbow.

Abstract art—Haven was still trying to get the hang of it.

"Does this look okay?" she asked anxiously.

"It looks fine," Kelsey said. "Now explain it to me again."

Haven sighed. "We went out, it was nice, but it didn't work."

"And that's it?"

"That's it," Haven confirmed, still staring at the canvas. "Are you sure this is okay? Does it make sense?"

"It's abstract. It's not supposed to make sense." Kelsey snorted. "I don't get why you and Gavin can't be friends. So there's no spark, but you were totally friends before, right? What changed?"

Haven sighed. She didn't want to talk about it anymore. They had been talking about it for weeks. "I guess it was all or nothing with him."

"Nonsense," Kelsey argued. "He's not that kind of man."

Haven rolled her eyes. "You hardly knew him."

"But you did."

Silence permeated the studio. Did she know him? He worked at the construction site. Family business, he had said, but Haven knew nothing about his family. In fact, she knew little more than his name: Gavin something-or-other. She had heard his last name before, but she couldn't recall it.

"It doesn't matter," Haven said finally. "It wasn't meant to happen. People come into our lives for a reason, so I have to believe there was a point to it somewhere, but it wasn't for us to be friends, I guess."

Setting down her paintbrush, Haven stepped back from the canvas. The spring Novak Gala was fast approaching, their submissions due by the end of the week, and Haven was struggling to create something she felt worthy of turning in.

"I'm going to miss seeing his face around," Kelsey said. "Talk about good looking!"

Haven laughed. "If you like him so much, go ask him out."

Eyes wide, Kelsey fervently shook her head. "No way. I couldn't do that."

"Why not?"

"Because of you, duh," she said. "It's breaking the friendship code."

"Don't be silly. He's a really great guy. Funny. Nice. You could definitely do worse. Actually, you *have* done worse."

"You really liked him." A statement, not a question.

"Yes."

"Then why? Really?"

Haven half shrugged, half shook her head. "There was nothing there."

Kelsey's expression softened. "Your ex."

Carmine. "What about him?"

"That's why you felt no spark with Gavin. You had it with someone else."

Haven thought that over, remembering the chemistry she had felt with Carmine. There had been electricity, so much he made her glow. The thought of never having that again, having to live her life with nothing but the memory of the way she had felt, troubled her. "Do you think it's possible to feel it more than once?"

"Absolutely," Kelsey said. "I feel it every time a guy so much as looks at me these days."

Haven laughed.

"Or . . ." Kelsey took a few steps toward her, scanning the colorful painting. "Or maybe I've never really felt it at all, and you're just one of the lucky ones."

———

"Corrado Moretti is notorious. They call him the Kevlar Killer on the streets, insinuating he's bulletproof, untouchable, and maybe out there he is, but not in here. Here we seek the truth. Here we get justice. And justice, today, would be a guilty verdict. The defendant is a murderer, a liar, and a thief. Nobody is safe with him roaming free. We have proven he belongs to an organization that prides itself on killing, an organization that advances people for hurting others. What kind of organization does that? An immoral one. An illegal one. A dangerous one."

The prosecutor babbled on and on as Corrado sat still in the hard chair, waiting. The eight-week trial was finally coming to an end with closing statements. It would soon be over and time to move on.

Or so he hoped.

When it was their turn, Mr. Borza stood and let out a bitter laugh. "The Kevlar Killer. It should be noted the media invented that nickname to sell papers. Sensationalized, to make money off an innocent man. The only reputation my client really has is for being a savvy businessman, a family man. His criminal record is clean. The government spent millions of dollars and thousands of man hours digging into every aspect of his life for *years*, trying to find something big, something scandalous, and the most they got was a bunch of heresy from convicted criminals looking for a way out of jail and a potentially unpaid tax bill, for which—if it makes them feel better—Mr. Moretti will write a check today. That's it."

Corrado tuned his lawyer out as he glanced around the courtroom, still banking on juror number six to come through for him. Mr. Borza kept it short and sweet, and the judge instructed the jury, sending them to the back to deliberate.

"How long do you expect it to take?" Corrado asked after court was in recess.

"There's no way to tell," he replied. "If they come back today, I'd say it's good news. But honestly, Mr. Moretti? If they're out more than forty-eight hours, I'd start praying for a hung jury."

———

Forty-eight hours came and went with nothing. Three days passed, then four. Corrado remained locked away at MCC, outfitted once again in an oversize orange jumpsuit. Warm weather had somehow crept up on them, the prison sweltering as the faulty air conditioner kept breaking down. The stench of stale sweat hung in the sticky air, clinging to everything its vileness could touch.

Corrado's patience dwindled. Every time footsteps approached his tiny cell, he stood at attention, waiting for them to deliver some news.

None came.

After a week, the jury sent a note claiming they were deadlocked and couldn't agree, but the judge sent them back to deliberations, ordering them to give it a few more days. While a hung jury was certainly better than a guilty verdict, he wasn't as excited at the prospect as his lawyer. A mistrial meant another trial. Another jury. More time away from his life . . . his *wife*.

Twenty-four hours later, Corrado was lying on the bunk in his cell when heavy footsteps slowly approached the door. He got up and eyed the door, hoping against hope it was finally over.

"Mail call," the guy hollered, opening the slot in the door and dropping in an envelope. Corrado snatched it off the floor. Another false alarm.

Sighing, he eyed the ripped open envelope with the sketchy address, surprised yet again that it passed security. He pulled out the greeting card, eyeing the photo on the front. Corrado knew little to nothing about art, but even he could recognize the painting *The Scream.*

Hope your day is a scream the card read, sloppy handwriting under the typed message: *I scream, you scream, we all scream . . . until somebody hears.*

Corrado stared at the message, reading it again and again. He was so busy deciphering the short message that someone managed to sneak up on him.

"Moretti."

Corrado looked over, eyeing the correctional officer. "What?"

"Show time." He smirked. "The jury came back with a verdict."

———

Haven darted across the busy New York street, long wavy hair flowing behind her as her feet zealously carried her down the block. Despite her best effort, she repeatedly knocked into others, elbows jabbing and shoulders bumping as she flew past.

"Sorry," she muttered, breathing heavily as she ran along the sidewalk, heading straight for her brownstone apartment. The white envelope crumpled in her hand as she fisted it, making sure not to lose her grip.

Once she made it home, she bolted inside, no hesitation in her steps as she bypassed her door. She frantically took the stairs two at a time, heading straight for Kelsey's apartment on the second floor.

She didn't bother to knock in her haste. Grabbing the knob, she shoved open Kelsey's front door. "Kelsey, you won't belie—Oh, God!"

Startled yelps echoed through the living room. Haven shielded her eyes and quickly swung around as Kelsey and a male friend fumbled for their clothes.

"I'm so sorry!" Haven's cheeks turned scarlet and warm from embarrassment. "I didn't realize, well, you know . . ."

"It's okay," Kelsey said. "We're dressed now."

Slowly, Haven turned back around, tentatively peeking through her hands at them. "I should've knocked."

"You think?" Kelsey stood as she motioned toward the guy. "You remember Fred, right? The architect?"

Haven eyed the tall man peculiarly, taking in his short blond hair and blue eyes. She didn't remember him at all, but Haven politely smiled and nodded anyway. "Sure. It's nice to see you again, Fred."

"You, too," he said. "Well, I should be going."

He kissed Kelsey's cheek before strolling past and disappearing downstairs. Haven stood there for a moment, watching her friend as she stared at the now empty doorway. "He's hot, right?" Kelsey asked. "I think he might actually be the one."

Haven's eyes widened. "Did you feel it? The spark?"

"Oh, I felt it all right." Kelsey laughed, turning her attention to Haven. "Anyway, what's up? Why the speedy entrance?"

All thoughts of the awkward incident evaporated as Haven's face lit up with excitement. She held up the crinkled white envelope, waving it frantically at her friend. "I did it! I got in!"

Kelsey's brow furrowed. "Got in where?"

"The Novak Gala," Haven declared. "Miss Michaels pulled me aside in the hallway. I came in thirteenth! They're going to display my painting!"

Kelsey let out a sudden shriek. "No way! That's amazing!"

The two of them jumped around and squealed, hugging as they

celebrated the news. Tears sprung to Haven's eyes, overwhelming elation running through her veins. She had done it. Out of three thousand entries, she had made the cut.

"This is so crazy," Kelsey said, pulling away. "We have so much to do now! We need to get you a dress and shoes. You'll need hair and makeup."

She blanched. A dress? High heels? A *makeover*?

"Oh, oh oh! And a date! We have to get you a date!"

Haven blinked rapidly. "A date?"

"Yes! You get to bring guests, right? You can't go alone!"

Reaching into the envelope, Haven pulled out the letter and unfolded it, eyeing the three wrinkly tickets tucked inside. She put hers back into the envelope and held the other two out to her friend. "I want you to come with me."

"Me? But—"

"Take them," Haven insisted. "You've been so great to me. You took me home on Christmas and introduced me to your family."

"I should be making that up to you, not the other way around."

Haven laughed. "Come with me. And if Fred's the one, bring him, too."

Kelsey hesitated before taking the two tickets. "You're sure?"

"Positive." Smiling, Haven took a step back toward the door. "Invite whoever you want. My thanks to you for being such a great friend."

Haven started out of the apartment, hearing Kelsey yell after her as she descended the stairs. "Fine, but you're still getting a dress! Don't think you're getting out of that one!"

"As to count one, participating in the conduct of the affairs of an enterprise through a pattern of racketeering activity, we the jury find the defendant, Corrado Alphonse Moretti . . ." There was a pause, one that seemed to stretch for eternity, before the fateful words were read. ". . . Not guilty."

The packed courtroom erupted in noise, a few elated cheers mixing with the horrified shouts of disbelief from onlookers. Cameras flashed from the media, recording the moment, as the judge feverishly banged his gavel for silence.

Count after count was read, all of them with the same result: not guilty, not guilty, not guilty. Corrado remained still as he stood at the defendant's table, the only one in the room not reacting emotionally. He felt it, though, churning in the pit of his heavy stomach, evident in the cold sweat formed along his back. It was the only time he had ever been unsure of a verdict before it was read. For the first time in his life, he had had a moment where he actually wondered if it could be the end for him.

And that moment to Corrado, as he contemplated his uncertain future, was worse than facing death. Death he could accept . . . being a caged animal he couldn't. He would never let it show, though. He exuded nothing but total confidence, bordering on callous conceit.

When the jury finished, the judge ruled for Corrado's immediate release. Corrado stood after the final bang of the gavel, ignoring the incessant shouting and name-calling from the gallery as he shook Mr. Borza's hand. He turned then, seeking out his wife in the crowd, and found her in the back, standing all alone and smiling.

Corrado's chest swelled. It felt like forever since he had seen her look happy.

"Congratulations," Mr. Markson said, his voice laced with bitterness. "I'm curious how you did it this time. Intimidation? Extortion? Plain ole bribery?"

Corrado shook his head. "I did none of those things."

"Murder, then?" The prosecutor raised his eyebrow in challenge. "Did you kill your own family, Mr. Moretti? Is that what happened to Vincent DeMarco?"

Corrado stared at the man, keeping his expression blank. If he only knew the depth of that question . . .

"The jury just saw through you," he responded coolly. "You had no case. You should work on that, you know. You don't seem to be very good at your job."

The prosecutor's posture stiffened. "I am good at my job. The problem is people like you have absolutely no respect for it. You have no respect for the law. But you'll get what's coming to you someday."

"I look forward to it."

The prosecutor stormed away as Corrado addressed his lawyer. "Juror number six . . . I want you to find out who she is."

Mr. Borza blanched. "Why?"

"I think I owe my freedom to her."

Corrado turned to the crowd of spectators, watching his wife make her way toward him. He opened his arms, pulling her to him in a tight embrace. Her body shook with happy cries as he kissed the top of her head.

"Six months away from you was far too long, *bellissima*," he whispered. "I promise it'll never happen again."

35

The gallery was packed, hardly a foot of space between the people inside. Haven stood outside the building, gazing through the sheet of thick glass that separated her from the Novak Gala. Every time the door opened, she could hear the soft melody of classical music filter out into the street, fading away into the darkness as soon as the door closed again. She could see the patrons smiling and laughing, socializing as they admired the artwork, comfortable in their surroundings, while Haven was anything but.

Nervous, she tugged at her dress, feeling ridiculously out of place and awkward in a pair of high heels. Her heart hammered in her chest, pounding so hard she could feel it clogging her throat, the only thing, she feared, keeping her from throwing up. She regretted telling Kelsey she would meet her there, afraid with every step she took that she would fall flat on her face.

Taking a deep breath to steady herself, she opened the gallery door, stepping inside and holding out her ticket to the man working. He took it with a smile, nothing but warmth in his eyes as he gazed at her, no sign he felt she didn't belong.

"Welcome, ma'am," he said politely, motioning toward a guest book to the right. "Please sign in and enjoy yourself."

She nodded, stepping to the side and grabbing the pen before she scribbled on the first blank line: Hayden Antoinette. She gazed at it for a moment, her smile fading a bit, but pushed the sadness away. She knew who she truly was, even if nobody else did.

The lighting was warm and the atmosphere welcoming. Haven strolled through the crowd, mostly keeping her head down, her eyes flickering periodically to the paintings on the wall. It wasn't until she came to the back of the gallery that she spotted hers, the familiarity stalling her footsteps immediately. She stared at it with wide eyes, her initials scribbled in the corner of the canvas.

It was surreal. In that moment, Haven had to pinch herself.

I had a dream, Carmine had said on their last night together. *You made a painting—some abstract shit, I don't know—but it was so good they hung it in a museum and raved about how talented you were. It was like you were the next fucking Picasso,* tesoro.

"It's quite a spectacular piece of work, isn't it?" a man asked, pausing beside her as he gazed up at it. He squinted his eyes, studying it, analyzing the dark background tinged with white and tan, musical notes distorted by splatters of red. "It looks like a concert to me. Maybe the artist is also a musician."

Haven smiled. He couldn't be further from the truth. "Maybe."

He walked away and Haven stood there, listening as a few others offered their unsolicited analysis, every one of them missing the mark. She was about to walk away, to stroll through the gallery and check out the other works, when a throat cleared behind her. "I take it this is yours."

She spun around so fast at the sound of the familiar voice that she nearly lost her footing, staggering. Her eyes met a pair of blue ones. "Gavin? What are you doing here?"

He shrugged, stepping forward. "Kelsey invited me."

"Oh." It took a second for those words to sink in. "Oh! So you and her . . . I mean, you guys . . . ?" She paused, brow furrowed. "What happened to Fred?"

"It's nothing like that," he said, shaking his head. "I'm not interested in her."

"You're not?" Guys were always interested in Kelsey.

"Nope."

"Why not?"

"I don't know. I guess my interests are elsewhere."

"Where?" she asked. He cocked an eyebrow at her playfully, and a warm blush rose to her cheeks. "Oh."

Gavin laughed, turning from her to the painting. "It's nice."

"Thank you," she said, relaxing a bit as she gazed at it too. "What do you see?"

He was quiet, studying it, before a smirk lifted the corner of his lips. "Spark."

Nailed it right away.

The Gala carried on as Haven was showered with praise. She basked in it, sipping seltzer water and hanging out with Gavin, laughing and chatting the night away. Kelsey appeared at some point, briefly stopping her to say hello, but Haven barely noticed amidst the chaos. It was more than she had expected, receiving so much acclaim over something she had poured her soul into, and by the time the evening started winding down she felt as if she were floating on air.

It was toward the end of the evening when Gavin's phone rang, interrupting the tranquility. He pulled it out, silencing it. "I have to get going. Work stuff."

She frowned. "Thank you for coming."

"My pleasure," he said genuinely. "It was nice seeing you again."

"You, too."

Smiling, he reached over and caressed her flushed cheek. "See you around, Haven."

Before she could come up with any words, he walked away. It wasn't until after he passed through the door that what he had said struck her. It sounded so natural coming from his lips, so casual, that she was lucky to have caught it at all.

Haven.

Coldness washed through her so fast she visibly trembled. Her eyes remained glued to the exit he had disappeared through as her mind frantically worked. Could she be mistaken? Had she misheard? Maybe he misspoke and didn't really know at all. She had never told him—she was certain of that—so she couldn't imagine where he would have heard her real name.

Trying to squelch her panic, she walked over to the guest book and flipped back through it, reading the countless names until she came to his: *Gavin Amaro.*

Her stomach dropped.

She bolted straight for the door. Bursting out to the sidewalk, she took a deep breath of the fresh night air, her heart beating like wildfire in her chest.

She felt it then, the current running across her skin, jolting her spine and warning her. *Intuition.* Terror coated her like ice as she let out a shaky exhale, swinging around abruptly to face whoever was there.

And in an instant, she nearly lost her balance in her high heels as she stared at a startlingly familiar face, so close she could reach out and touch it. She didn't, though. She couldn't move. She just stood there, completely still, as she whispered his name. "Dr. De-Marco?"

———

"Hello there."

Vincent's greeting hung in the warm air around them, lost somewhere between his lips and her ears. She gaped at him, her face a sheet of white like she had seen a ghost, as she stood in the middle of the sidewalk, wobbling in a pair of high heels. "Dr. DeMarco?"

He let out an awkward chuckle when she said his name for the second time. "Yes."

She shook her head in disbelief, cautiously surveying their surroundings as she took a step toward him. "Is something wrong? Did something happen?"

"No," he said, anxiously rubbing the back of his stiff neck as someone stepped out of the gallery behind her. He averted his gaze, turning slightly so he was angled away until they disappeared down the street.

Paranoid, maybe, but he had good reason to be.

"Are you okay?" she asked, taking yet another step toward him. "You seem . . ."

"Sketchy?" he guessed when she trailed off.

"More like nervous," she replied.

Nervous. That was putting it mildly.

"I'm okay," he assured her, giving her a smile, hoping it would ease her concerns. "Do you think we can go somewhere to talk?"

"Uh, sure." Haven glanced briefly behind her at the art gallery before starting toward him. She only made it a few steps before kicking off her shoes and carrying them. She nodded at him, smiling sheepishly, as they started down the street. They walked in silence, her eyes darting to him periodically as if still in disbelief, while he kept his head down, monitoring their surroundings.

It only took a few minutes for them to reach their destination. Haven pulled out a set of keys and unlocked the front door of an apartment. Vincent ducked around her, not waiting for an invitation, and exhaled with relief once he was safely away from the public street.

"This is your place?" he asked, glancing around the one-bedroom apartment he'd stepped into. *This is the place Corrado set her up in?* "It's kind of small, isn't it?"

"Not really. I mean, it's bigger than the horse stall I grew up in."

Touché.

"So was there something you wanted to talk about?" she asked, nervously sitting in a chair in the living room. "Why are you here?"

Vincent strolled over, taking a seat in the center of her couch. "I was actually hoping you would tell me about your kidnapping."

As if by some miracle, Haven managed to turn even paler. "My kidnapping?"

"Yes," he replied. "You don't have to, of course, but I just wondered if you could tell me who you remembered seeing there."

She hesitated, her forehead scrunching up in concentration.

"You already know. I mean, they were there when . . . well, when you came for me."

"Yes, I know, but I'd like to hear it from you," he said. "I'd like to know what you remember."

She let out a deep sigh as her gaze drifted to her hands in her lap. He could tell she didn't want to talk about it and nearly felt ashamed for bringing it up to her, but it was important he heard it from her. Very important. "Nunzio was there. That guy Ivan was in charge. There were some other men, but I don't know their names. Mostly Russians. And the girls . . . the nurse showed up, and then there was the other one."

"What other one?"

Haven hesitated. "I don't remember her name."

"Okay," Vincent said. "And that's it?"

"Uh, yeah, I guess."

"You guess?" Vincent rested his elbows on his thighs, leaning forward to look at her pointedly. "Who else was there?"

"Just people who don't exist anymore," she whispered. "If they ever did."

Vincent quietly processed that, the meaning sinking in as he thought back to the images he had seen in Haven's notebook. The memory stung. "Maura."

"Yes," Haven whispered. "And my mama. And Number 33."

His eyes met hers, curiosity brewing inside of him. "Number 33?"

"A girl I saw at one of those places . . . she was for sale. She was number 33."

Vincent frowned when it struck him what she meant. "An auction?"

"Yes. Frankie took me as a kid."

Sickness stirred Vincent's stomach. He never knew. "Why?"

"He said it was to teach me a lesson," she replied. "The girl tried to escape, so well . . . Frankie killed her. He said it was what happened when people like me forget their place. It's why, when you said you were going to remind me of my place that day, I thought . . ."

Vincent closed his eyes when she trailed off. He could still remember the look on her face when she came around that afternoon, waking up handcuffed to the post of her bed. *"Please,"* she had whispered. *"I don't want to die."*

Before Vincent could come up with words, Haven spoke again. "I know they weren't really there, but I saw them in the warehouse. They talked to me. They gave me the strength to hold on."

"Was there anyone else?" Vincent asked. "Maybe someone less desirable, like a . . . monster?"

Haven remained still, staring at him, before softly whispering, "Carlo."

Vincent was stunned. "You know his name."

"I heard Frankie say it the day of the auction," she replied. "He wanted my master to sell me to him. Terrified me. I thought he'd do it."

"Thank God he didn't."

"Yeah, but he still taunted me over the years. I'd see him when he came to Blackburn. He'd stand there and stare at me. Just stare. He always hurt my mama. He always . . ." She paused, angry tears glistening from her eyes. "He did things to her, but never me. He just watched me all the time, like he was waiting for when the time was right."

"And you saw him when you were in the warehouse?"

She nodded, wiping her eyes as a tear fell down her cheek. "I imagined him, I guess. Standing over me, just staring as usual, like the time still wasn't right. He looked older, but it was definitely him. I'd never forget that face."

Haven let out a bitter laugh while Vincent remained stoic. He hadn't wanted to believe it, but something about her words made him wonder if she hadn't imagined it at all.

"Thank you," Vincent said. "I just needed to hear you confirm it."

"You're welcome." Haven eyed him peculiarly. "Are you sure you're okay, Dr. DeMarco? Won't the people who monitor you track me here now?"

"I don't have my ankle monitor on anymore."

Her eyes widened. "Is your trial over?"

He stared at her, realizing at that moment how cut off she was from everything. He had been following her for weeks, gathering the courage to approach her, unsure how she would react to a wanted man showing up at her doorstep . . . a man most people suspected to be dead. But she didn't even know. She knew nothing.

Standing, Vincent stretched his aching back. "It's not over yet, but it will be soon. Nothing to worry about."

"Okay."

"Anyway, I should be going. I've taken up enough of your time."

Haven walked him to the door, the two of them silently hesitating in the foyer. There was so much Vincent still felt he needed to say, the words stuck on the tip of his tongue. He nearly managed to force them out, overpowering his lingering pride and overabundance of shame, when the front door to the brownstone thrust open behind them. A female's laughter carried through the downstairs.

Vincent immediately dropped his head, his eyes darting to the girl. She looked at him with surprise, and familiarity struck Vincent as he vaguely recognized her.

Senator Brolin's daughter.

"Oh, wow," she said, a grin lighting up her face. "Another one?"

Vincent didn't stick around to find out what she meant by that.

36

The first weekend in June, Carmine received a call from Salvatore about a celebration for Corrado's exoneration. He begrudgingly got dressed that Saturday night and drove to Salvatore's house at dusk, parking his car toward the back before hesitantly making his way to the front door. He pressed the doorbell and Abby appeared, seemingly relieved when she saw Carmine there.

"Hey," he said when she ushered him inside. "How are you?"

She smiled softly, her voice barely a whisper. "Fine. You, sir?"

"I'm *here* with these motherfuckers, so I'm obviously not doing *that* good."

"I'm glad you're here," she said shyly, offering to take his coat. "You talk to me like I'm a person."

"You are a person, Abby. They're just too nasty to see it."

She stared at him, surprised by his candid response, before slinking away to do her work. Carmine headed for the den when someone called his name, and he turned, his blood running cold the second his eyes came into contact with Carlo's. The man smirked as he strolled toward Carmine. "You're lucky your godfather didn't overhear that exchange. Something tells me he wouldn't be amused."

Carmine stared back as he fought to control his temper at the man's smug expression. "There's nothing wrong with saying hello."

"You said much more than hello, boy."

Carlo looked as though he was going to say something else when Corrado walked over and interrupted. "Carlo, Carmine. Is there a problem?"

"I was just reminding young DeMarco that he should be mindful of what he says and who he talks to," Carlo said. "If he isn't careful, someone might get the wrong impression."

"I didn't—"

He was about to say he hadn't done anything wrong when Corrado cut him off. "Carmine's sarcastic mouth is notorious. I think at this point people would get the wrong impression if he didn't have a snide remark here or there."

Carmine looked at Corrado with shock, not expecting his defense.

Carlo laughed bitterly. "Just because it's expected doesn't mean it's acceptable. He needs to learn respect. He was talking to that slave and—"

"Respect?" Corrado snapped. "And I suppose you think *you* could teach it to him after speaking like that in his presence? You're well aware of his mother's background, and you want to speak about *respect*? Maybe you need to learn some yourself."

"I've earned my place here—I've put my time in," Carlo said, anger clouding his face. "I've proven myself and he hasn't. He needs to mind his superiors."

"So do you," Corrado said pointedly. "Or have you forgotten *I'm* your superior? You know protocol, or have you forgotten that as well? Carmine's my soldier—if you have an issue with him, you air your grievance with me."

Carlo narrowed his eyes. Corrado had struck a nerve. "All I'm saying is maybe he shouldn't mouth off so much."

"I heard you the first time, but I don't see why you'd want to create a scene over it," Corrado said. "It's not that serious. So he's mouthy? It's not like he murdered your family, Carlo."

Carmine froze when those bitter words came from his uncle's lips. Carlo looked like a deer caught in headlights as Corrado stared at him with an eyebrow cocked, waiting a response that never came.

"Gentlemen," Salvatore said, pausing between them, his expression stone cold serious. "Perhaps we should have a sit-down later to clear the air, but for now we celebrate. Go enjoy yourselves, have a drink, get to know one of the beautiful ladies here."

Corrado nodded obediently. "Yes, sir."

Carlo echoed his words and walked off when Salvatore excused himself, the situation diffused for the time being.

"I don't know what you said, but he was right," Corrado said once they were alone. "You *do* need to learn to watch your mouth."

"I know."

"You should've worn a suit, too," he said. "You look like a slob."

Carmine glanced down at himself. He had on a long-sleeved button-up shirt and slacks—he had just nixed the tie. It wasn't as if he had strolled in wearing faded jeans and a hoodie.

He wished he had, though. That way if he was forced to be miserable, at least he would be comfortable.

He spent the next two hours making small talk with other made men and associates, getting to know the families of the ones brazen enough to bring them around such a heartless crowd. Carmine pretended to care, smiling and entertaining curious questions about his father's whereabouts (No, I haven't heard from him. I'm sure he's just lying low.); playing the part of *Principe*, grandson of Antonio (Yes, my grandfather was a God among men, I hope to be just like him someday.). But in his mind he was counting down the time until he could leave (Two more fucking hours. You're already halfway there.).

For a group that prided themselves on silence and honor, they gossiped more than a group of catty high school bitches. It wasn't Carmine's first mandatory gathering, but it was certainly the most uncomfortable one. His father was on the lam and everyone was well aware that the expiration date on Vincent DeMarco's life had already passed.

Carmine drank heavily as the time slipped away, painfully aware as Corrado watched him from across the room. He had warned him before never to drink at these things, but he couldn't help it. The alcohol seeping into his bloodstream was the only thing keeping him from jumping out of his own skin.

The crowd thinned eventually, associates and soldiers clearing out while the ones at the top of the chain of command gathered in the den. Carmine took the shift in atmosphere as his cue that the night was finally over. At a little after nine, he strolled over to Corrado, his body relaxing naturally as relief set in. "I'm leaving."

"Good," Corrado said. "Go home. Sober up."

Carmine turned and mock saluted his uncle behind his back as Corrado went into the den. Carmine started for the door, but Salvatore's shrill voice stopped him halfway there. "Where do you think you're going, *Principe*?"

He glanced at him apprehensively. "Home, sir."

"Nonsense." Salvatore motioned in the direction of the den. "Join us."

Carmine sighed, not wanting to be there any longer. "I'd really rather just—"

"It wasn't a request," Sal said, cutting him off as he walked away.

Carmine cursed under his breath, catching a look of alarm on Corrado's face the moment he stepped in the den. "I thought you were leaving."

"Ah, he was, but I requested he stick around," Salvatore chimed in, taking his usual seat. He motioned toward an empty chair beside him and Carmine slid into it, running his hand nervously through his hair. There were a dozen men in the room besides him, but he was the only low-ranked soldier present. These gatherings were always invitation only, and Carmine had appreciated the fact that he had never been invited to stay for one until that moment.

The men talked for a while about things that didn't matter, like baseball teams and brands of liquor, while Carmine sat quietly, drinking more to calm the flare of his nerves. He wasn't sure how long they had been sitting there when they finally delved into business—who owed money, who wasn't producing enough, who had potential, and who they frankly were sick of dealing with. The ones in the last category were immediately written off, no questions asked, no objections. There was no regard for their families or their obligations. Intentions didn't matter—they had been judged without having a chance to defend themselves.

It made Carmine sick to know that someday it could be him, sentenced to die callously, his murder plotted casually like they were deciding something as petty as preferable brands of alcohol.

"Dismember him," someone said. "Take him apart piece by piece, and then incinerate the leftovers."

"Too messy," someone else chimed in. "Slip something in his food. Make it look like a heart attack. Clean and easy."

"That's cowardly! You're better off putting a bomb in their car."

"Oh, bullshit! And a bomb isn't cowardly?"

"No. It'll send everyone a message when the whole street blows up."

"Yeah, it'll send them a message, all right . . . it'll probably send some of his neighbors to the hospital, too. They didn't do shit to us."

"So? Like bystanders haven't been hurt before?"

"Yeah, but they got kids. We don't fucking hurt kids, not if we can help it."

"Just make him go missing," someone suggested. "It's not cowardly—it's smart. The fact is he's nobody. No reason for a scene. Just *poof*, be gone."

Somebody scoffed. "It's all cowardly unless you make it personal. Ain't that right, Carlo? That's what you always say."

Carmine's eyes shot across the room to where the scarred man sat in the corner, quietly sipping from a glass of scotch. Carlo tipped his head at the man in confirmation. "Always look them in the eye so they know it's you, so you can see their fear. You want them to associate your face with death . . . that's how you know you're doing it right. Then when they understand, you do it quick—blow their head off, shut them up with a gun in the mouth when they try to scream for help. There's nothing better. Always been my signature move."

Those words hit Carmine hard and sharp, striking at his insides ferociously when flashes of the night in the alley ran through his mind. The sound of his mother's terrified screams, the fear in her eyes as she somehow knew she was going to die. "Shut her up!" a man yelled. "Do it quick!" Then there was nothing but the loud bang of the gunshot as the man shoved the pistol in her mouth and pulled the trigger, forever silencing her.

Carmine was on his feet before he even knew what he was doing, the liquor splashing from the glass he clutched and splattering on the floor. His sudden movement startled the others, conversation instantly ceasing as men jumped to their feet, trained to sense danger. Guns were drawn and a chorus of clicks echoed through the room as safeties were released, the weapons pointed at Carmine's head.

Tunnel vision fixed Carmine's gaze on Carlo. He remained in his chair, slouching casually as he swirled the scotch around in his glass, staring right back. His face was a mask of indifference, but his eyes told a much different story. There was a challenge in them. He dared Carmine to say something to him.

Seconds passed—long, infinite seconds of tension and inner turmoil—before Salvatore broke up the sudden standoff. "Gentlemen, this is unnecessary. We're all family here."

The men lowered their weapons at once, concealing them again as they retook their seats. Low grumbling vibrated the room, their words indiscernible, but hostility infused the air, smothering Carmine. They would have shot him easily, the simple flick of a finger stealing his life.

He felt like he was going to throw up as that sunk in.

"Carlo, Carmine," Sal said, looking between the two of them. "Outside now."

Sal walked out but Carmine remained rooted to his spot for a moment, his eyes following Carlo as he sauntered from the room behind the boss. Carmine hesitantly followed them, knowing he had no choice, and the three took seats on some tan chairs on the outside patio beside the inground pool. Sal called for Abby to bring them drinks before dismissing her with a wave of the hand, ordering her to remain in her room for the rest of the evening.

It didn't escape Carmine's notice that Carlo's eyes followed the girl as she scampered away, his gaze that of a predator stalking its prey.

Fucking sick.

When she was gone, Salvatore raised his eyebrows curiously. "How are things, *Principe?*"

The question rubbed Carmine the wrong way. *Just fucking peachy, thanks for asking.* "Fine."

"Fine," Salvatore echoed, glancing between the men briefly before settling back on Carmine. "And what's going on between the two of you?"

"Nothing."

"Nothing? I can feel the tension rolling off of you. You're hiding something. What happened earlier to cause the argument in my parlor?"

Carmine said nothing. Regardless if he remained silent or told his side of it, he knew he would be on the losing end.

Salvatore realized he wasn't going to get an answer from him and turned to Carlo. "Maybe you'll be more forthcoming."

"I was just put off by young DeMarco's attitude," Carlo said. "I've never heard someone speak so vulgar and disrespectfully."

Salvatore turned back to Carmine curiously, but before he could speak, unexpected laughter rang out beside them. The sound of it nearly made Carmine's heart stop. He quickly looked in the direction it had come from, in utter disbelief as his eyes fell upon his father. Vincent DeMarco stood about twenty feet away at the corner of the house, dressed from head to toe in all black. He wore a new Italian suit, which was covered by a long trench coat, sweeping at his ankles and exposing a pair of black dress shoes that shone under the moonlight. His dark hair was slicked back, his face freshly shaved.

"Now Carlo, you know that's not true," Vincent said, taking a few steps toward them. "You act like this organization is filled with saints. My son's hardly the first to have a smart mouth."

"Ah, Vincent," Salvatore said, confusion evident in his voice. His shoulders were tense, his expression hard as if chiseled in stone. It didn't happen often, but the Boss had been caught off guard. "I was wondering if I'd ever see you again."

None of them knew how to react. Carmine just stared at his father as Carlo placed his hand on his gun under the table.

"You had to have known we'd see each other again, Sal. It would be rude of me to take permanent leave and not say good-bye to you."

"True." Salvatore eyed him cautiously, desperate for the upper hand. "Come, have a seat. We'll chat."

Vincent lingered, slowly shaking his head. "I'm fine where I am."

Sal subtly shifted in his seat to get a better view. "You know, you've been gone for a while now. I was worried something happened to you."

"I'm sure you were."

"I was, honestly," Sal said. "Especially when you skipped out on the trial. I was deeply concerned what that meant for your future."

"Ah, yes, *that*. I figured there was no use going through the charade."

"Can't say I'm surprised, Vincent. Disappointed, yes, but not surprised."

"Well, you always did know me well," he said. "It's a pity I never really knew you, though. I thought I did, but I was wrong."

Sal laughed, a tinge of nervousness to his forced chuckle. "What you see is what you get with me."

"I wish that were true," Vincent said. "I always thought you were a man of your word, a man who saw the world as black and white. I never realized how much you skirted in the gray area to suit your needs."

"What makes you think such a ridiculous thing?"

"Haven Antonelli."

A gasp involuntarily flew from Carmine's lips at the sound of her name. Salvatore's gaze flickered to him, anger in his eyes, before his attention shifted right back to Vincent. "What does that girl have to do with this?"

"Everything," Vincent said. "Don't act like you don't know what I'm talking about."

Salvatore stared at Vincent with disbelief, but whether he was truly dumbfounded or just shocked at being called out wasn't clear. Carmine's heart beat rapidly as his eyes darted between the silent men. All of them were on edge, shoulders squared, poised for a fight.

"Go inside, son," Vincent said. "I'd like to speak to your godfather alone."

Pushing his chair back, Carmine started to stand when Salvatore slammed his fists down on the table in front of them. "Stay where you are!"

Carmine knew he couldn't disregard a direct order from the Boss. Glancing at his father, he shot him an apologetic look as he forced himself back into the chair.

Panic flared in Vincent's expression, and Carmine knew it then. Whatever was about to happen was *not* going to be good.

"I still fail to see what the Antonelli child has to do with anything," Salvatore said, turning his attention back to Vincent. "Enlighten me."

"Are you aware she's an artist?"

"I couldn't care less what she is," Sal said. "She's *nothing* to me."

"Of course you know she's an artist," Vincent continued, ignoring his hostility. "In fact, you know a lot about her, more than you'd ever admit, including the fact that she's not *nothing* to you."

"You don't know what you're talking about," Sal said. "She'll never be anything more than a slave in my eyes, a worthless piece of flesh you idiots waste your life on. She's irrelevant in my world. She shouldn't even exist!"

Carmine flinched as irritation flashed across his father's face.

"You know, it didn't make sense at the time," Vincent said. "I never understood why Frankie refused to give her up, why he wouldn't let her go when he wanted nothing to do with the girl. She was a burden, another mouth to feed, so why not take the cash to be rid of her?"

"She was his granddaughter," Salvatore said pointedly. "You know that."

"That didn't matter to him," Vincent retorted. "His son getting a slave pregnant would've been a disgrace in his eyes, tainting his bloodline—he would've wanted to be rid of the child. So why did he not only keep her but kill over her, too?"

"He didn't want anyone to find out."

"Yeah, that's what you told me." Vincent shook his head. "I believed it for years because I didn't think you'd lie to me and you told me you were *sure*. I slaughtered him and his wife, and then I put my gun to that girl's head as she slept and pulled the trigger, because you swore she was the reason my wife died. And that's exactly what you wanted, wasn't it? You used my grief to solve your problem, and it almost worked. If my gun hadn't jammed, I would've killed everything there that breathed."

"I didn't tell you to kill *any* of them."

"You didn't have to! You knew *exactly* what I would do with the information you fed me, and you gave me just enough time to do it before calling me in."

"I would've *never* ordered a hit on a child!"

"Because you can't! The men wouldn't have trusted you anymore if they even *suspected* you had anything to do with it. There would've been a mutiny! But you knew how to push my buttons, how to get *me* to react. You wanted them all dead and you used me so you could keep your hands clean."

"That's ridiculous," Salvatore said. "Why would I want them dead?"

"Evidence," Vincent said. "Never leave anything behind if it can be linked to you. It's simple, something *all* of us know. The moment you realized your mistake, you wanted it disposed of."

"What evidence?"

"The girl's bloodline."

Panic swept across Salvatore's face. Carmine stared at him in shock, realizing he wasn't surprised . . . he *did* know. Confusion rocked Carmine's brain, the knowledge nearly crippling him. The entire time, through it all, Salvatore *knew* they were related.

"You're crazy."

"Maybe so, but I'm still *right*," Vincent said. "All it took was a simple prick of a finger and a lifetime of secrets came spilling out in the blood."

"I don't know what you're talking about."

"I once believed that. I thought you were as much a victim as her, but that changed when she was kidnapped. You wouldn't get involved because you knew why they took her and you wanted nothing to do with it! You were afraid they'd expose you and you thought . . . you *hoped* . . . they'd get rid of her. But they didn't.

"You were power hungry and had your own family murdered. You used to talk about how much family meant, and I actually pitied you because you didn't have anyone left! And the whole time it was your own fault!"

"How dare you accuse me of that!" Salvatore spat. "I'll kill you for this!"

The moment he spoke those words, Vincent reached into his coat and pulled out a gun, aiming it at Salvatore. Carmine jumped up, as did Carlo, knocking chairs over in haste, one flying into the shallow end of the pool. Salvatore sat still, unmoving, barely blinking. Carmine was frozen with fear as Carlo pulled his gun, aiming at Vincent.

"You had no idea thirty years later DNA testing would exist," he continued, keeping his eyes and gun trained on Salvatore. "That's the real reason he wouldn't sell me the girl . . . he was trying to protect you, and maybe even protect her in the process. When it got back to you that Maura was asking questions, you panicked, and that's when you set the plan in motion. You put the hit out on my wife to cover your tracks, and I never wanted to believe it. *Never* did I want to believe you'd do that to me, that you'd do that to my children.

"Haven drew pictures after her kidnapping—like I said, she's an artist—and she drew one of Carlo. I denied it to myself, I denied it to my son, but there came a point where I couldn't deny it anymore. Your man—your best friend—had been there for it all!"

Tears slid down Vincent's cheeks. Carlo yelled, denying it all, while Salvatore glanced around with fear. Carmine stared at his godfather with disgust.

"Carmine," Sal said firmly, and he knew instantly what he wanted. He expected Carmine to follow his orders, to do what he had told him to do.

"Don't talk to my son!" Vincent snapped. "You've hurt him enough! Tell me, when you had my wife killed, did you want *him* dead, too?"

"Of course not! He's my godson!"

"But you don't deny you wanted my wife dead? You don't deny you had your sister murdered? You don't deny you were in bed with the Russians? God, how sick does a man have to be to make his own family slaves?"

"She was supposed to have a good life!" Salvatore spat, losing control of his temper as he reached for his gun. Carmine cursed and backed up a few steps, nearly tripping over a chair. "Frankie begged me to let him have her, the fool! He begged me to let the child live! He's the one who failed! He treated her like crap! He let his son have his way with her! She would've been better off dead!"

"Is that why you never went to Blackburn, why you always sent us?" Vincent asked, no hesitation in his voice. "You couldn't look at her, knowing what you'd done?"

"You're wrong!"

"And is that why you were so insistent on seeing Haven when you visited? Why you were elated Carmine fell in love with her, why you wanted *him* to vouch for her? You'd finally be family again!"

"Shut up!"

"You thought it was redemption! They were possessions to you! And you had the *nerve* to ask me if she'd been worth it, if she was worth all the pain I went through, if she was worth everything I lost, and *you'd* been the one to do it to me! Did you enjoy that? Did you get off having so much power over everyone?"

"You're delusional!"

"And you're disturbed! You're a traitor!"

"How dare you accuse *me* of that! You, who has been feeding information to the Feds? Tell me, Vincent, how does it feel to be a rat? How does it feel to break the oath you swore? How does it feel knowing you're going to die for it?"

Vincent stood frozen for a second before a sinister smirk turned the corner of his lips. "You first."

The bang of a gunshot ripped through the night air and Carmine recoiled, realizing his father had pulled the trigger. He covered himself defensively as Salvatore stumbled backward, the bullet ripping through his shoulder, and dropped his gun as his arm went limp. Flipping the patio table over, Salvatore ducked behind it as Carlo returned fire. Vincent shot again, hitting Carlo's thigh with a bullet, making his leg buckle, but he managed to stay upright and shoot back.

A bullet from Vincent's gun hit the table Salvatore hid behind, ricocheting off of it and flying in Carmine's direction. He ducked as soon as he heard it hit and it whizzed past his head, barely missing grazing his temple. "Fuck!"

"Carmine!" Salvatore yelled, barely audible above the sudden rampant gunfire. "Kill him!"

Carmine didn't know what to do. He slowly pulled his gun out, his thoughts frantic as he fought off dizziness. Kill or be killed. He knew how it went. If he didn't kill his father, Sal would kill him next.

Before he could consider aiming at *anything,* another gunshot ripped past him. Carlo stumbled backward, blood pouring through his button-down shirt. He tripped and fell, his body trembling as he clutched his stomach. Awful cries escaped his throat as Vincent closed the distance between them, firing off more shots in anger. Two rounds went through Carlo's arms, disabling him, and another bullet ripped through his kneecap as he tried to drag himself away.

Salvatore jumped up and grabbed his gun again before ducking out of the way. Vincent was clearly on a mission, his expression grave as he crouched down and grabbed Carlo by the collar. He shoved the muzzle of his gun in Carlo's gaping mouth and pulled the trigger without hesitation. Blood splattered, the back of Carlo's head exploding, and Carmine couldn't stop the scream that reverberated from his chest as violent flashes of his mother overwhelmed him.

Vincent looked at Carmine with concern, his eyes scanning him quickly, assessing for wounds. "Get out of here, son," he demanded before turning to Salvatore, who had taken shelter by the back door. He stood but didn't have enough time to aim before Salvatore shot at him, a bullet hitting Vincent straight in the chest. He grunted and staggered but stayed on his feet to fire back.

"Carmine, it's an order!" Salvatore yelled, continuing to shoot, but his aim was off. "Do it now, or I'll kill you!"

"Don't threaten my son!"

Salvatore's words gave Vincent his strength back. There was a commotion as he steadied himself, the back door of the house bursting open and guys running outside. Corrado followed behind them but froze, taking in the scene as Carmine released the safety from his gun.

Corrado noticed the movement. Raising his gun, he aimed at Carmine.

"What the fu—" he started, unable to get the entire thing out before his uncle pulled the trigger. The bullet grazed the back of his right hand and he cried out, dropping the weapon and grabbing the searing wound. It felt like it was on fire, throbbing painfully as blood dripped onto the patio.

Corrado sprinted toward Carmine and tackled him, shoving him onto his stomach on the ground, his low voice demanding. "Don't move."

Standing, Corrado haphazardly fired across the yard, the bullets deliberately flying past the target. Vincent turned and fired a wayward shot toward Corrado, his aim just as bad, before ducking for cover around the back of the house.

Salvatore and the others shielded themselves near the back door, as Corrado and Carmine hunkered down to the side with a clear line of sight. The gunshots slowed to a trickle as they reloaded, the rest of the men filtering out to come to Salvatore's aid.

Carmine watched his father drop his pistol, clutching his heaving chest as he staggered a few steps. Vincent shrugged off his coat then, revealing a small Uzi hanging by a strap around his shoulder. The blood rushing through Carmine made him light-headed, his vision blurring as tears flowed down his cheeks.

Vincent bowed his head and made the sign of the cross, his mouth moving furiously as he spoke to himself. Praying, he realized. His father was praying.

"No!" Carmine screamed the word as realization dawned—it was a fucking kamikaze mission.

Vincent turned, his eyes falling on him briefly before he stepped into the wide-open yard. Corrado dropped to the ground instantly, roughly grabbing Carmine as he tried to get to his feet. He pinned him down with his body as the loud spray of bullets ripped through the night. It was deafening. Carmine's head thumped ferociously with every loud bang as the frantic explosion of gunfire lit up the yard.

Carmine screamed, begging his father not to go through with it, but it was too late. There was no turning back. He had made his bed and he was prepared to lie in it . . . he was *ready* to lie in it.

But Carmine wasn't fucking ready. He never would be.

He tried to push Corrado away but his uncle wouldn't budge, shielding him as the spray of bullets flew all around them. Two guys dropped nearby, their bodies convulsing, and others ducked for cover to fire back. In the midst of the chaos, Carmine lost track of who was where, bodies dropping and people running, painful screams mixing with the gunfire.

A shot ripped through Vincent's stomach and he stumbled, his finger leaving the trigger briefly as he lost his grip, giving the others enough time to recover. They fired in succession, a bullet tearing through Vincent's shoulder as another one struck his calf. He dropped to his knees, swaying as he tried to stabilize himself. Vincent pulled the trigger again, more people hit with the wild spray of bullets.

The gunfire stopped abruptly as the cartridge was spent. Vincent shrugged the weapon off his shoulder, letting it drop to the ground. He sat back, his head dropping and body shaking as he stared at the trampled grass. Someone stood up near the house and Carmine panicked because his father was unarmed, but Corrado reacted instinctively. He fired off a shot, the bullet hitting the man straight in the temple.

Carmine yelled for his father but Corrado shoved him farther into the ground, busting his face on the concrete to silence him. He cursed, blood seeping from his nose, as sirens blared in the distance. Someone yelled, "Police!" as others fled, scrambling to disappear into the night.

Corrado finally let go of him when the crowd dispersed. Carmine pushed away from the ground and glanced across the yard as his father crawled toward the side of the house. Corrado started toward him as Vincent stopped at the corner, sitting back on his knees as he grabbed his discarded pistol.

"Vincent!" Corrado yelled, panic in his voice.

Vincent glanced in their direction, the breath leaving Carmine when he saw his father's face. The color had drained away, his skin the ashy pale hue of death, his eyes dull and lifeless.

Vincent said something quietly, not loud enough for Carmine to hear, but whatever it was made Corrado's footsteps falter. The sirens grew louder and Corrado shook his head, stiffly, angrily, but Vincent nodded with determination.

"Get out of here, Carmine!" Corrado yelled.

Carmine started across the yard toward them, ignoring his uncle, but nearly buckled from fright when his father raised his gun and pointed it below his chin. "No! Dad, no!"

Vincent's eyes drifted closed, his finger shaking violently on the trigger.

Corrado bowed his head with a long sigh, his voice quiet. *"Perdonami."*

Forgive me.

Without hesitation, Corrado raised his gun and squeezed the trigger. A hoarse scream vibrated Carmine's chest, painfully clawing its way from his throat, as the final bullet tore through his father's skull. Vincent dropped backward, his body limp on the grass. Carmine collapsed at the same moment, unable to move any farther as sobs rocked his body.

Corrado walked past him and approached the pool. He grabbed Carmine's gun and took his own, wiping them off with his shirt before dropping them into the deep chlorinated water. His eyes scanned the property then, surveying the carnage. Bodies were scattered everywhere, puddles of blood all around.

The sirens wailed louder, lights flashing as police raided the property. Corrado raised his hands in the air and dropped to the ground before they had to tell him, and Carmine rolled onto his stomach to assume the same position.

Carmine was in a complete daze as they were handcuffed. Corrado lay beside him in the grass, muttered to himself in Italian. It took a minute for Carmine to register that he was praying, and Carmine lost control of himself at the sound. A loud sob escaped as they placed a sheet over his father's lifeless body, blood soaking through and turning the crisp white to a vibrant red.

Carmine tried to silence his cries when they pulled Corrado from the ground to lead him away, but it was senseless. He was distraught.

"Seven deceased, including Dr. DeMarco," an officer said. "Still waiting on confirmation of the other six."

"Get a move on it," a second man responded, his voice vaguely familiar. "Anyone inside?"

"Just the trafficking victim DeMarco said would be here," the man said. "The girl wouldn't speak to anyone, though, so we don't know who she is."

"Give her some time. She'll come around once she realizes she's safe."

Footsteps approached, the familiar voice calling Carmine's name. He glanced up, coming face-to-face with Special Agent Cerone. He crouched down and unlocked Carmine's handcuffs, sighing as he grabbed his hand and eyed the wound. "Get the medic to come look at his injury, please."

"Yes, sir."

He stared at Carmine for a moment as he sat up. "We'll have to take you in for questioning, but you'll be out by morning as long as you cooperate. Do you want to make a statement now?"

He wiped his face, trying to get rid of the tears, and groaned when it did nothing but smear blood on his cheek. "Abby," he said quietly. His throat burned from screaming, the word barely audible.

"Abby?"

"The girl inside," Carmine said. "Her name is Abby."

37

The interrogation room at the Cook County police station smelled like someone had attempted to clean up week-old piss. Corrado grimaced as he took a deep breath, the harsh stench of ammonia and bleach burning his lungs. Gazing across the metal table in front of him, he eyed the federal agent with distaste.

Agent Cerone started to speak, but Corrado cut him off before he could get started. "I wasn't there. I was home, I was alone, I was asleep, and nobody saw me."

The agent gaped at him. "*I* saw you tonight, Mr. Moretti."

Corrado raised his eyebrows. "Did you?"

"Yes."

"Are you certain?"

"You were even arrested at the scene."

"Was I?"

"Is there something wrong with your memory?"

"Maybe," Corrado said. "I suppose I don't recall a thing from tonight, then."

Corrado forced a look of indifference on his face as Agent Cerone stared at him with disbelief. The agent pulled himself together quickly, gritting his teeth as he flipped through pages of notes. He had hundreds of documents, but nothing to prepare him for facing Corrado. "You know, Vincent DeMarco was a good man."

"Was?" Corrado asked. "Did something happen to him?"

The agent shook his head exasperatedly. "You're really going to play ignorant, aren't you?"

Corrado merely shrugged.

"As I was saying, he was a good man. I judged him wrong. He wasn't callous or selfish. He cared about his family, would do anything for them. And I got to thinking . . . maybe you're the same way. Maybe I was wrong about you, too."

The corner of Corrado's lips turned slightly with amusement. "I doubt it."

The agent stared at him for a moment before genuinely laughing. Corrado was much too street smart for the psychological tactics to work on him. He had been through it all before and knew their tricks. "Yeah, you're probably right. Out of curiosity, would you be willing to take a lie detector test?"

"I'm afraid not," he said. "It goes against my religion."

His brow furrowed. "How?"

"Only God can judge me. I certainly don't trust a machine to do it."

"You only have to worry if you're untruthful. Do you plan to lie?"

"No, I prefer to sit, thank you."

The agent sighed. "When did you get to be so sarcastic?"

"I'm not sure what you mean," Corrado said. "I don't even know why I'm here."

"I see I'm wasting my time," Agent Cerone said. "Anything you want to say before we end this?"

"Just that I'd like to speak to my lawyer."

Agent Cerone gathered his things, not the least bit surprised. "Of course. Hang tight. It'll take a while to get you released, but we should have you out in plenty of time for the funeral."

"Whose funeral?"

"Vincent's."

"Vincent's dead?"

The agent shook his head. "At least you're consistent. But yes, he is. They should be alerting the next of kin any moment."

As Agent Cerone stood to leave, Corrado's expression fell. He was much too weary to keep up the charade. He sat still in the seat and stared at the far wall as his stomach twisted again . . . this time with something much closer to anxiety. He hardly noticed the stench anymore, his grief strong enough to overpower it.

"Wait," he said, stalling the agent's footsteps.

"Yes, Mr. Moretti?"

"I need to make a call."

The agent sighed. "Your lawyer's already next door with Carmine DeMarco. I'll send him over as soon as we're done there."

"I don't need to call my lawyer," he said. "I need to call my wife."

"Your wife can't help you right now."

Corrado glared at the man. "She's going to think it's me."

"What?"

"You said they're going to be making the notification soon. As soon as they show up at my door, she's going to think it's me."

A debate played out on the man's face momentarily, his lips twitching into a frown. "Her brother, her husband . . . it'll hurt either way. They'll explain it to her."

"I made her a promise that I'd never leave her again," he said. "I don't want her to think I broke it, even if it's only for a minute."

The agent's brow furrowed. "How could you promise her that? Living the life you live, you're bound to break it someday."

"I won't," he said. "There's nothing I won't do to keep my vows."

"Even if it means killing?"

Corrado just stared at the man, and he stared right back. The agent broke first, though, a deep sigh reverberating his chest as he looked away. Frowning, he released Corrado from the interrogation room and led him to a small cubicle, where he picked up a black phone and handed it to him. "You have five minutes."

Corrado dialed his house number, listening as it rang and rang. He was on the verge of giving up when he heard Celia's voice on the line. Although she spoke hesitantly, he could detect no distress. Worried, but not heartbroken. She hadn't been told yet. "Hello?"

"I didn't think you were going to answer."

Celia let out a deep sigh. "Corrado, why does the caller ID say the Cook County Police Station?"

"It's a long story."

"Does it end with you getting arrested again?"

"No." He glanced down at himself, eyeing the handcuffs secured to his wrists. "Not technically."

"Do you need me to get you out?" she asked. "I don't think I can come up with bail money until morning, although we might have—"

"Celia, stop. I'm not calling about me. I can take care of myself."

"Carmine!" she gasped. "Oh God, what did he do? Is he okay?"

"He's . . ." Corrado shook his head. "Carmine will be fine. This isn't about him. It's about his father."

There was nothing but silence on the line for a moment. Had he not detected her steady breathing, he might have suspected she hung up.

"Celia, Vincent is—"

"No." She cut him off. "Don't say what I think you're going to say. Don't . . . just don't say it, Corrado."

"I'm sorry, *Bellissima*."

Before she could react, before he could say another word, the federal agent reached over and pressed the button on the phone, effectively ending the call.

"You have a lot of nerve," Corrado seethed, his voice a low hiss escaping from between his angrily clenched teeth.

"You wanted to tell her and you did," the agent said. "I didn't have to give you that much."

Disoriented, Carmine's surroundings twisted and distorted as the interrogation room spun, the dark gray walls slowly closing in around him. Even though frigid air blew out of the vent above him, chilling his taut skin, his body felt like it was engulfed in fire. Teeth chattering, his flushed skin poured sweat, making his torn and bloody shirt stick to him uncomfortably.

Carmine tried to sort through everything that had happened, but he couldn't think straight. It was all just too much. Agent Cerone and another man, whose name Carmine couldn't remember hearing, sat across from him, while Mr. Borza sat to his right. The lawyer urged Carmine to cooperate, but the flickering fluorescent lights made it impossible for him to concentrate.

"Who fired the first shot?"

"I don't remember. It happened too fast."

"How many people were shooting?"

"I didn't know. A few."

"Did *you* fire a gun?"

"No."

"Did Corrado Moretti?"

"Uh, I can't say. I told you, it all happened too fast."

"Well, what did you do when the shooting started?"

"Nothing."

"Nothing?"

"That's right. Nothing."

"And you didn't see what happened?"

"No."

"Did you hear anything?"

"Gunshots."

"How many?"

"A lot. I didn't count them."

"Who was involved in the shooting?"

"I don't know."

"So it *could've* been Corrado?"

"It fucking could've been Jimmy Hoffa."

"I'd rather you keep the sarcasm to a minimum. This is a serious situation."

"I'm not being sarcastic. I told you I didn't see. I don't know who shot first, who shot who, who's dead, and who's still alive. All I know is what I did."

"And what's that?"

"Nothing. I didn't do a goddamn thing."

Round in circles they went, the same vague answers being given for the same questions. He saw nothing, he did nothing, and he couldn't recall a thing.

It was the truth . . . partially.

He didn't know what they expected from him. All he could recall were his father's last moments, the brutal image haunting Carmine like someone had taken a blowtorch and burned it in his brain.

Gone . . . his father was *gone*.

As Carmine's chest constricted, a memory came to his mind. It happened a few weeks before his mother had been murdered when his parents had taken them to Six Flags. He and Dominic had climbed into one of those spinning cups and spun it so furiously that by the time the ride was over, he couldn't make sense of which way was up. His legs buckled as he climbed off the ride, his stomach churning ruthlessly. Collapsing, he threw up right there in the middle of the busy amusement park.

Today, in that room, he felt a lot like he did back then—dazed and disoriented, betrayed and confused.

Vincent had pulled him to his feet that day, kneeling in front of him. Carmine's face turned bright red as tears of embarrassment welled in his eyes. He kept his gaze fixed on the cement, not wanting anyone to see him cry—especially not his father.

"Are you okay?" Vincent had asked. Carmine hesitated but slowly lifted his eyes, nodding as he took in his serious expression. "Everyone falls sometimes, son, even me, but the trick is to get right back up. They'll always target the ones who appear vulnerable, so you need to be strong. Fake it until you make it."

Carmine hadn't known it at the time, but his father was giving him his first piece of advice on how to survive the lifestyle, and it was a lesson that sunk in as he sat in that cold, tense interrogation room. Unshed tears burned his eyes as he fought to hold them in, not wanting to buckle under the weight of his grief. He needed to be strong; he needed to keep his composure.

He couldn't let those motherfuckers see him break.

The sound of Carmine's name being called pulled him back to reality. Agent Cerone and the other man stared at him, throwing out the same questions. His ears still rung from the incessant gunfire, the buzzing noise in the air driving Carmine to the brink. He clenched his hands into fists, wanting it all to stop, and cringed as searing pain shot up his right arm. He looked at his hand, seeing the blood seeping through the white bandage. His vision went white and flashes of random memory struck him. He tugged at his collar, the air so thick he felt like he was suffocating.

Blood . . . *there was so much fucking blood*.

Squeezing his eyes shut, he forced himself to think about something else, conjuring up an image of Haven. She was free, he reminded himself. She was following her dreams. As long as she was out there, as long as she had her life, all of it was worth it. The ache in his chest was worth it, the throbbing in his hand was worth it, and being in that room was worth it. All of the blood, sweat, and tears he had shed were worth it, because s*he* was worth it.

He missed her.

God, how I fucking miss my hummingbird.

Carmine was so wrapped up in the moment that he forgot where he was until someone shook him. He jumped, clutching his chest with his injured hand and wincing as he opened his eyes. Agent Cerone stood beside him and grasped his shoulder, raising his eyebrows questioningly. "Can I get something for you? A glass of water, maybe?"

"You can get me out of here," he snapped. "How long do you plan on keeping me? I didn't fucking *do* anything!"

"We just need to ask you a few more questions."

"There's nothing else I can tell you," he said, shaking his head.

"Who's your *hummingbird*?" he asked as he sat down again.

Carmine's eyes widened. "What?"

"Just a moment ago you said you missed your hummingbird."

He stared at him in shock, realizing he had said that out loud, and wondered what else he might have unknowingly said.

"I fail to see what this has to do with the incident tonight," Mr. Borza chimed in. "I would appreciate it if we could stay on topic."

"Fair enough." Agent Cerone's eyes lingered on Carmine for a moment longer. "How well do you know Salvatore Capozzi?"

"He's my godfather," he muttered, the agent's expression instantly lighting up at the word. Carmine shook his head as he clarified. "I was baptized as an infant and my parents named him my godfather."

"Oh, so he's like a parent to you?"

"He was."

"Was?" Cerone asked curiously. "Are you saying he isn't anymore?"

"He's fucking dead, isn't he?" he spat.

"Oh, uh, no."

Carmine stared at him, hoping he had heard him wrong. "No?"

"No," he repeated, the confirmation sending Carmine's heart racing. If Salvatore wasn't dead, he was in danger—*a lot* of fucking danger. Not only had he witnessed everything and knew his darkest secrets, the things he would kill *anyone* to keep from being exposed, but he had also disobeyed an order. There was no way Sal would just forgive and forget. He had too much to lose to give Carmine a pass. "As far as we can tell he fled the scene. We have reason to believe he's injured, but there's no evidence he didn't survive the attack."

Carmine absorbed that information, trying to keep his expression blank although he was panicking inside.

"How long ago did you initiate?" the other officer asked casually, changing the subject.

Carmine glanced at him, surprised at his nonchalance. "Initiate what?"

"*La Cosa Nostra.*"

He scoffed. "You're joking, right?"

"Do I *look* like I'm joking?" he asked, raising his voice. "We know you're involved, so there's no sense denying it."

"You must've watched *Scarface* one too many times," he muttered. "That shit's not real. It doesn't exist."

He sighed exasperatedly, giving Carmine an annoyed look. "We *know* it exists. We're not stupid."

"Neither am I," Carmine snapped. "Take your bullshit questions about the Mafia elsewhere, because I have nothing to say about it. Period. End of motherfucking story."

A tense silence fell over the room before Agent Cerone cleared his throat. "I saw her, you know."

"Who?" Carmine asked, the shift in topic catching him off guard.

"Haven," he clarified, his lips twitching as he fought back a smile.

"How . . . ?" His confusion deepened. *How the fuck?* "You're lying."

"I'm not," he said. "I've been thinking about looking her up again."

"Leave her the fuck alone," Carmine spat, standing and shoving his chair back in haste. "I swear to God if you—"

Before he could finish, Mr. Borza grabbed his arm and pulled him back into his seat. "Threatening my client's loved ones isn't going to help you."

"I wasn't threatening anyone. I was simply saying—"

"We're *all* well aware of what you were saying," Mr. Borza said, "and it was nothing but a thinly veiled threat. You claim to want his cooperation, but yet you bring up Miss Antonelli in an attempt to upset him further."

"I did *no* such thing," Agent Cerone said. "As far as I'm concerned, he doesn't care about her. In fact, last we spoke, he denied even *knowing* her."

"Then why bring her up at all?" Mr. Borza countered. "I requested once that you stay on topic and it's clear you have no intention of doing so. Mr. DeMarco agreed to answer your questions, but he's under no obligation. Given the fact that mere hours ago he witnessed his father's murder, I'd say he's been quite forthcoming."

"He's given us *nothing*," the other officer said, still glaring at Carmine.

"That's because he has nothing to give," Mr. Borza retorted. "You can't get from him what he doesn't know. Because of that, I'm going to have to say this conversation is over. Either charge him with something or let him go."

"We don't have to do *either*," the officer said smugly, crossing his arms over his chest. "We have every right to detain him."

"True, but you won't. Not only is my client injured, but he's also traumatized. The media would have a field day if you detained him . . . as if you don't already have enough damage control to do. You don't need to add harassing an innocent man to it."

"*Harassing? Innocent?* He's one of them!"

"*Him?*" Mr. Borza asked, glancing at Carmine. "You honestly believe the public is going to look at this boy and think *'criminal'*?"

Agent Cerone sighed. "You're right."

The officer looked at him with disbelief. "You're going to let him walk?"

"I gave my word," Agent Cerone said quietly, pushing his chair back and glancing at his watch. "Sit tight while I secure your release. I told you I'd have you out by morning and it looks like I was right, considering the sun will be up soon."

38

Kelsey and Haven sat at the diner near their brownstone in a booth by the door. It was Sunday morning on their first weekend of summer vacation. There were a few other patrons in the diner, an elderly couple a few seats away and a family in the back, as well as two men drinking coffee at the bar.

A lady in a white top and khakis with a black apron tied around her waist plopped two plastic menus down on the table. "What can I get you ladies to drink?"

"Coffee," Kelsey said. "Two creams, a dash of skim milk, and three packets of Splenda. Oh, and two ice cubes."

"I'll take coffee, too," Haven said. "Just black, please. You know, normal."

She returned with their drinks as Haven opened the menu and scanned it. Kelsey rattled off a list, emphasizing her need for extra bacon, whereas Haven asked for a stack of pancakes. As hungry as she was, nothing sounded appetizing.

"I'll have it to you in a jiffy," she responded, taking the menus and walking off. Haven sighed and picked up her coffee, taking a sip of the hot bitter liquid as she gazed out of the window. She heard one of the men ask the waitress to turn on the television and a few seconds later the diner was filled with the sound of the news.

The reports were mainly politics, with local scandals dominating the headlines. She had spent some time learning about political parties in New York. Kelsey's dad was running for office again and Haven often asked her about it, but she always blew off the questions and claimed none of it mattered. She said she wouldn't bother voting if her father's job didn't rely on it, insisting nothing would ever change no matter who got into office.

Haven never contradicted her, but she didn't agree at all. Abraham Lincoln and the Thirty-eighth Congress passed the Thirteenth amendment that abolished slavery. Woodrow Wilson and the Sixty-sixth Congress passed the Nineteenth amendment to give women the right to vote. To Haven, it mattered.

The men started debating issues, the two opposite on everything. She sipped her coffee as their bickering grew louder, a debate about gun control, and Haven froze, spilling her coffee when she caught a glimpse of the television. Her stomach lurched at the sight of the familiar man, her eyes quickly scanning the caption on the bottom of the screen: *D.O.J. Special Agent Donald Cerone.*

The coffee scorched her skin and she gritted her teeth from the searing pain as her coffee cup clattered to the table, slipping from her hand. The diner grew quiet as people turned to the commotion at her booth, but Haven ignored them, her attention focused squarely on the television. She had a hard time catching the words, the throbbing in her hand distracting, as she felt like she was sinking under water.

". . . Issued a statement about the incident in Chicago . . . embarrassment for the department . . . massacre at alleged Mob boss Salvatore Capozzi's home . . . single deadliest incident in the history of the Outfit . . . debate on how witnesses are to be properly handled . . ."

It hit Haven like a ton of bricks when a picture of Dr. DeMarco flashed on the screen. "Alleged mobster had been on the run . . ."

"Oh God," she gasped as they showed a clip of a large mansion, dozens of police cars parked in front of yellow tape.

"A federal witness . . . provided information that triggered the raid . . . opened fire before police arrived . . . unsure of the main target . . . warrant issued for Capozzi . . . believed to be injured in the gunfire . . ." They showed a picture of Salvatore with a number on the bottom to call. Haven shuddered, tears welling in her eyes. ". . . Seven dead at the scene . . . several taken into custody . . ."

Haven gasped as a picture of Carlo flashed on the screen, followed by footage of several others. Victims, they said, dead when police arrived. She stared in shock . . . Carlo was dead? She was so stunned she almost didn't catch the next words.

"DeMarco's funeral is scheduled for tomorrow . . ."

Funeral.

One of the men in the diner sighed exasperatedly. "Perfect example of why we need gun control."

"No way," the other man said. "They do us *all* a favor by killing each other."

A loud sob escaped Haven's throat when it hit her and she quickly brought her hands up to cover her mouth. She trembled, shaking her head furiously. *Funeral?* Dr. DeMarco was *dead?*

"Hayden?" Kelsey's voice rang out. "Are you okay?"

Haven tried to respond, but as soon as she uncovered her mouth another sob echoed through the diner. She jumped up from the booth and nearly fell, her legs barely able to withstand her weight. She pushed past her friend as she ran for the door and bolted down the street to her apartment. Kelsey yelled after Haven but she didn't turn around, fumbling for the keys and rushing inside. Leaning back against the door, she closed her eyes and tried to get a grip on herself. The words of the news report continually ran through her mind, although she couldn't make sense of it. How could he be dead? What *happened?*

After her breathing was under control, she opened her eyes again and wiped the tears from her cheeks. Grabbing the small black cell phone, she dialed the Chicago number and listened as it rang. "Corrado Moretti. Leave a message."

Haven pushed back the nerves that always accompanied the call. The words escaped her lips, the burn in her chest dulling as another sensation settled in. Through the shock, through the horror and fear, she felt the *resolve*.

"I'm coming to Chicago."

———

Haven left her apartment under the cloak of darkness, taking only a small bag of clothes. She locked up before making her way down the block to the nearest parking garage, taking the elevator up to the third tier. She spotted the black Mazda parked precisely where she had left it almost a year before. The thick layer of dirt and dust covering the paint concealed the scratches still adorning the top.

It took nearly every penny she had in her pocket to pay the parking fees and fill up the gas tank for her trip.

Her heart ached as she drove out of the city, thoughts of Dr. DeMarco infiltrating her mind. Unlike so many times before, when the incident where he had punished her would spring to mind, all she could think about were the good moments: the time he had given her the picture of her mother, the holidays, the sound of his laughter, and the look of pride on his face when Dominic graduated. She thought about the food he had given her and how he had handed over his keys so she could learn to drive. He hadn't even been angry when it was returned with a scratch.

It seemed as if more than a year's worth of memories flooded Haven, and with them came the tears. Dominic's words ran through her mind, ones he had spoken down by the river in Durante.

"I already lost my mom to this life," he'd said. *"I don't want to lose him, too."*

Dominic had made Haven see that it was okay to want more in life. He had helped her face her worst fear. It was only fair she would be there to help him face his.

39

Haven sat in the car along the curb, her stomach churning as she stared at the blue door of the old house. She had only seen it once before, sitting on the bottom step with Carmine by her side. More than a year had somehow passed since that day . . . more than a year since she had laid eyes on him. She wondered if he would be happy to see her, or if he would be angry she came.

So many scenarios flooded her mind as she got out of the car and made her way across the street. She tried to push back her anxiety as she stepped on the porch, but before she could even knock her name was called from down the street. Her vision blurred, her heart rate skyrocketing as she turned around, watching Corrado's leisurely approach. "Sir."

"I'm glad to see you're well." He eyed her intently, a serious expression hardening his face. Haven immediately grew paranoid, wondering if it was wrong for her to be there.

Panic crept through her at the prospect that she could be in danger. "I didn't know if I should come."

"It was nice of you to show up," he said as he stepped closer. "I apologize for not calling. By the time I had a chance, you'd informed me of your intention to come, so I assumed someone else told you."

"I saw it on the news," she said quietly. "They said there was a massacre."

Corrado scoffed at the word. "It was hardly a *massacre*. If it was, no one would've survived, but Carmine and I walked away."

"Carmine?" she gasped, horrified. "He was there?"

"Yes," Corrado said. "And as you can probably guess, he isn't taking it very well. After Maura's murder, he didn't speak to anybody for a long time. It seems he's dealing with his father's death the same way."

"Oh God." The burn flared in her chest as her eyes filled with tears. "He saw them *both* die."

"He did."

"Is he, uh . . . ?" She motioned toward the door behind her. "Is he home?"

Corrado shook his head. "He's already gone to the service with my wife."

"Oh."

"You're welcome to join me," Corrado said. "I'm waiting on the car service to pick me up. Plenty of time to meet them at the cemetery."

Haven looked down at herself, eyeing her wrinkled shirt and dirty jeans. She had had them on since yesterday morning, having not taken the time to change before leaving. "I don't really have anything with me to wear."

"God doesn't care what you wear, Haven," Corrado said. "It wouldn't matter to Vincent, either. But if it would make you feel better, I'm sure there's something in my wife's closet that would suffice."

"Oh no, I couldn't." Haven furiously shook her head. "I couldn't impose like that."

Corrado let out a sharp bark of laughter. "As much as I've already done, a change of clothes is hardly an imposition."

That silenced her immediately.

"Come," he insisted. "No excuses."

Haven quietly followed him to his house and upstairs to the bedroom he shared with Celia. She glanced through the closet, pulling out a plain black dress she found in the back. It was slightly too big but fit better than she expected.

She borrowed a pair of shoes, too, some simple black heels that pinched her toes, a size too small but good enough for the moment. She did little else to prepare, in and out in less than twenty minutes.

Corrado waited downstairs for her, peering out the front door at the black town car parked along the curb. They climbed into it, and Haven shifted anxiously around on the leather seat.

"I've tried," Corrado said quietly a few minutes into the drive. "I've done everything within my power for Carmine, but it seems to be beyond my reach. He's too stubborn and reckless. The way he's going, he's doomed."

Doomed. That word rippled through her, a cold chill striking her bones. "You've given up on him?"

"It doesn't matter . . . not when he's already given up on himself."

Before Haven could respond, Corrado's cell phone rang. He pulled it out, letting out a long exhaustive sigh as he answered the call. "Moretti speaking . . . Yeah, it's all settled. I'm certain it'll go according to plan."

He hung up quickly, slipping his phone back away as his attention once more turned to her. "Is this visit temporary, or do you need to retrieve your things from New York?"

She blanched. "Well, I . . . I don't know."

He turned away from her, his eyes focusing straight ahead. "Let me know when you figure it out."

———

The long, gold-toned casket stood out strikingly on the grassy knoll, a makeshift memorial of colorful flowers surrounding it on all sides. A crowd of mourners gathered, dozens of people dressed in their most expensive black clothing, their heads bowed and gazes cast away, as if avoiding having to face reality. Sorrow and misery wafted around them, the atmosphere stifling with pain lingering in the air.

Haven paused a few yards away from the service, her knees weak. Dr. DeMarco's cold body lay in that box, his heart no longer beating and the life expelled from him. He was gone, never again to open his eyes and see another day.

The air seemed to be forced from Haven's lungs at the thought, dizziness blurring her vision. She took a few steps to the side to lean against a tall maple tree in order to catch her breath as Corrado continued on, infiltrating the crowd. She scanned them as she composed herself, catching brief glimpses of Celia and Dominic, but the others were shielded from view.

She wanted to go closer, desperate to see Carmine, but her feet wouldn't move no matter how hard she tried to make them.

"Vincenzo was a loyal man," the priest declared, clutching a Bible to his chest as he stood behind the casket. "He was a husband and a father; a son and a brother. He wasn't a perfect man, he made mistakes, but *no* man is perfect. We all sin; we all fall victim to temptation. Vincenzo was no different.

"Greed, lust, gluttony, sloth, wrath, envy, pride—the seven cardinal sins. He struggled with them, trying to balance the good and evil in his life, and many times he failed. But just because he succumbed to evil doesn't mean he *was* evil. Vincenzo visited me often before his life came to an end. He expressed remorse for all of the hurt he had caused, and because of that I am certain of one thing—despite his flaws, Vincenzo Roman DeMarco was a true Man of Honor."

Sobs rang out from the crowd, but Haven couldn't decipher who they came from. When the priest finished a few minutes later, mourners took turns placing long-stemmed red roses on top of the casket, one by one saying their final good-byes to the man inside. Haven caught a glimpse of Tess and Dia, but the family stood in the front and remained mostly blocked.

Haven picked at her nails nervously as the crowd dispersed, chipping away at the pale pink polish when Carmine finally came into view. He wore a black suit, his hair slicked back and head bowed as he stared into the massive hole in the ground. People spoke to him as they passed, but he didn't acknowledge them. He just stood still, a cold marble statue, unmoving and unwavering, looming in the pathway as everyone moved around him.

She watched Celia rub Carmine's back before she and Corrado walked away. Corrado steered her in Haven's direction, her footsteps faltering as a look of surprise passed over her face. She smiled warmly as she approached, pulling her into a hug. "You look great, kiddo. It's been *way* too long."

"Thank you," Haven said quietly as she let go, seeing Celia's face was flushed, her makeup was smudged from crying. "I'm so sorry for your loss, Celia."

"Me, too, sweetie," she whispered, glancing back over at Carmine, frowning, before looking at Haven again. "Go on," she said, motioning toward him. "Make sure he gets home safely, okay?"

Corrado put his arm over Celia's shoulder, nodding at Haven in approval before leading her away. Haven remained in place for a moment as she stared at Carmine, wondering if she even knew the person in front of her anymore. He seemed so different, from his stance to the way he was dressed, all of it foreign. His slumped shoulders screamed with defeat, as he stood seemingly oblivious to anything in the world around him.

Haven took a few steps in his direction but stopped again when he broke his stance, grabbing a rose from the closest display and slowly approaching an adjacent grave. He crouched down in front of the headstone and laid the rose on the ground before running his fingers along the words engraved on the worn white marble.

Haven started his way again, her curiosity fueling her, but stopped after a few steps when realization struck. He had once told her his mother was in Hillside.

Her heart pounded rapidly as she suddenly felt like she was invading his privacy. The memory of him sitting in front of his piano, slumped down and crying on the anniversary of her death came to mind. Pain ripped through her chest.

She immediately took a step back.

Carmine must have sensed her movement, because his body stiffened at that moment, his shoulders squared and head held high as if on alert. Something in the atmosphere shifted—the afternoon sun disappeared behind a thick cloud, encasing the cemetery in gloomy shade. A cool breeze blew through, ruffling Haven's dress and causing a shiver to run the length of her spine.

It felt like it happened in slow motion as Carmine turned in her direction, their eyes locking across the way. She finally saw his face, taking in the deep frown on his lips and dark bags under his bloodshot eyes. His blank expression changed as he stared at her, distinctive emotions flashing across his face that matched the ones surging inside of her. Shock, disbelief, confusion, desperation, fear, longing, hope, sorrow, grief . . . all of it hit Haven at once as she stared at the broken boy she had once given her heart to—a heart she had never quite got back.

She loved him, just as much as she ever had, and when she saw that same feeling reflected back at her, it all came together. Because despite everything that was different, despite everything that felt unfamiliar, despite the pain and heartbreak, the love was still there.

Finally, something felt *right* again.

He hesitantly took a step toward her, his movement causing Haven to break into a run. She kicked her shoes off in the grass as she sprinted in his direction, shaking and crying as she rammed right into him. He braced himself in an attempt to keep his footing and wrapped his arms around her, staggering a few steps from the force of the collision. His body violently shook as a strangled sob tore from his chest.

Neither spoke, the lump in Haven's throat making it impossible for anything to escape but cries. She closed her eyes as he held her, reveling in his familiar scent and body warmth. Despite how vulnerable she knew he was, how shaky the ground was beneath his feet, she felt secure in his arms, like all of her wandering had come down to that moment, in that place, where she finally felt like she was home again.

He was her home. He always had been.

She wasn't sure how long they stood between his parents' graves, clinging to each other, all of their hurt, and pain, and heartache expelled through each shuddering breath, each salty tear staining their cheeks. It could have been minutes or hours, but it felt as if time had stopped for them once again.

"La mia bella ragazza," he whispered, his voice cracking.

The words sent a pang of longing through her body, and she closed her eyes as the electricity of his touch coursed through her veins. "Oh, Carmine."

He pulled back to look at Haven, his face wet with tears and hair a disheveled mess. She reached up to run her hand through it, cringing as her fingers got tangled in a stiff nest of hair product. "Your hair."

A sad smile lifted the corner of his mouth, and although he didn't respond, she knew he understood. He reached out and wiped the tears from her cheeks, her eyes fluttering closed from his touch. He ran his fingertips down her jaw, his hand gently exploring her face, before he tucked a wayward strand of hair behind her ear.

Wiping his tears, Haven explored his face much like he had hers, eyeing the small mark on his cheek peculiarly as she ran her pointer finger across it. She had never seen it before. "You have a scar."

"You're beautiful." He cracked a smile as the blush rose into her cheeks. "You still blush, too."

"You still make me," she whispered, surveying him. "You're wearing a suit."

Glancing down at himself, he grimaced. "I still hate them, but it's a funeral." His voice cracked on the word and he turned away, taking a deep, calculated breath. He gazed past her at something. "You wore high heels."

"I still hate them, but it's a funeral," she said, repeating his words. "You're not wearing Nike's."

"I wish I was," he muttered. "These fucking shoes hurt my feet."

She stifled a laugh. "You still say that word."

"What word?" He raised his eyebrows when she didn't respond. "I guess you still don't use it."

Haven shrugged.

They stood there for a while longer trading observations. It might have been trivial, given the weight of the circumstances, but it was their way of reconnecting. They memorized each other again, becoming acquainted with the things that had changed in their absence as the comfort and familiarity settled back in. Countless times she wondered what she would say if she ever saw Carmine again, musing about what he might possibly say in response, but she never considered that it would be so seamless for them.

They had both changed, and it was obvious, as she stared into his deep green eyes, that there was a darkness lurking inside of him, but it hadn't consumed him. Carmine's spirit might have been broken, but his soul remained intact. It was like meeting him for the first time all over again, but knowing in her heart exactly who he was from the beginning.

He was Carmine Marcello DeMarco . . . and even broken, he was beautiful.

"I can't believe you're here," he said, pulling Haven into his arms again. He buried his face in her hair and inhaled deeply. "This has to be a fucking dream."

"It's not a dream," she said. "I'm really here."

"For how long?"

She hesitated. Carmine's phone rang then, tension sweeping over them as he motioned for her to stay where she was. She eyed him warily as he stepped away, bringing his phone to his ear and speaking quietly to ensure she couldn't overhear.

A sinking feeling settled into the pit of her stomach. She knew the *easy* couldn't last, that the seamless would have snags. He was a part of that life, and there were things about him she couldn't be involved in—things she could never know. Carmine harbored secrets that would never be spilled.

Not wanting to appear to be eavesdropping, Haven took a step away and quietly gazed at the headstone that marked his mother's grave.

Maura DeMarco
April 1965–October 1996
"Ama, ridi, sogna—e vai dormire"

She had only been thirty-one, too young to be ripped from the world. Dr. DeMarco had lived more than a decade without his wife. Haven couldn't begin to imagine how he had felt waking every morning to face the realization that he would never have it back, he would never feel the spark again.

"Sorry about that," Carmine said, interrupting her thoughts. "It was—"

"I don't need to know," Haven cut him off, but she heard him mutter Corrado's name regardless.

An awkward silence lingered before Carmine sighed. "*Ama, ridi, sogna—e vai dormire,*" he said, reading the line chiseled into the stone. "It means 'Love, laugh, dream, and go to sleep'."

Haven smiled softly. "I like that."

"Me, too," he mumbled, a sad smile tugging his lips. "That's what she did."

"She was an amazing woman."

"She was. Too bad I couldn't take after her more. Instead, I'm like *him.*" Tears brimmed his eyes, sudden anger flowing out with those words. "Vincent DeMarco's son, so that makes me the fucking enemy. As much as I hate it, it's true. I'm one of them."

"You aren't."

"I *am.* You don't even fucking know." He shook his head. "You wouldn't be able to look at me if you knew."

"You only did what you had to do."

"You don't even know *what* I've done," he said. "What I've stood by and watched without saying a goddamn word. I've watched people die and kept my mouth shut like they didn't matter, like they didn't fucking count. What kinda person does that?"

"Me," Haven said quietly. "Did you forget about Frankie killing that girl? Number 33—that's all I know about her, a number written on a piece of paper someone stuck to her. She's dead and I don't even know her name. I never did anything to help her."

He shook his head. "That's different."

"How?"

"He would've fucking killed *you*."

"Are you saying they won't kill you if you don't go along with it?"

"It's still not the same," he said, the aggravation clear in his voice. "You were born into it, but I chose this life. I chose to be this fucking person."

"For me," she said. "If nothing else, that makes you good."

"*Good,*" he sneered. "They talked today about how good my father was, about all the people he helped, but what about the bad? He helps a few people and suddenly all the ones he hurt are forgotten? What about what he did to *you*? What about what he did to *me*? He opened fire on a house and I had to see that shit! Then he . . . then he fucking tried to . . ."

He shook as he fought for control, on the verge of hyperventilating. Haven rubbed his back, her tears steadily falling. He hurt, and she had no idea how to make it any better.

"He's gone," Carmine said after a moment. "He went out in a blaze of glory, and I can't help but hate him for it because now he's gone, too! And the worst part is that I wasn't surprised, because he did exactly what I would've done. I would've killed every single one of those motherfuckers. I'm just like my goddamn father."

Haven grabbed his arm to calm him down, his moods shifting so quickly she had a hard time keeping up. He shrugged away from her, reaching into his pocket and pulling out a silver metal flask.

Bringing it to his lips, he closed his eyes and shuddered as he took a drink. "I owe you a lot of apologies, but sorry doesn't seem good enough."

"Your intentions were always good," Haven said, not liking his self-loathing. Based on his demeanor, he had been beating himself up for a while.

"How's that saying go—the road to hell is paved with good intentions? Makes sense, I guess, since I'm heading that way."

She winced. "Don't say that, Carmine."

"Sorry, you're right," he said quickly, taking another drink from his flask. "I shouldn't be saying this shit to you. I just . . . I'm sorry. I'm glad you're here. You didn't have to come. You don't owe my family anything, but it's good to see you."

His words lacked the emotion he had had just minutes before. "It's good to see you, too. I've missed you."

"Yeah?" He glanced at Haven. "I've missed you, too. You look good, *tesoro*."

Her heart started acting erratically, a fluttering in her stomach as the word *tesoro* escaped his lips. He tried to run his hand through his hair but cringed, a white bandage covering it. "What happened to your hand?"

He shoved it back in his pocket as if to hide the injury. "Corrado shot me."

"He *shot* you? Why?"

"You'd have to ask him." He grew quiet again and Haven knew he was holding back. "That's where the scar on my face came from, too. Someone shot at me. Wasn't Corrado that time, though . . . some Irish fucker."

Haven stared at him as that sank in. "That's scary."

"That's *life*," he said, shrugging as if it weren't a big deal. "That's my life now, anyway. Thank God it's not yours."

Silence lingered between them as he took sips from his flask, his eyes looking everywhere but at her. She could see the sadness, the yearning for something he felt he couldn't have. It made her chest ache.

"A guy named Gavin asked me out a few months ago," she blurted out.

Carmine froze with the flask to his lips, cringing at her words. Tension rolled from him in waves. "Did you go out with him?"

"Once, but it could never work."

"Why's that?"

"Because he could never know me," she said quietly. "I had friends, but they didn't know me, either. No one did. They don't know where I came from or what I went through. They only know the cover story, the girl I pretend to be . . . the girl everyone *wants* me to be . . . the girl I still sometimes wish I could be. They think the world I came from only exists in movies."

"That's the point," he said. "You can be whoever you want to be."

She sighed. "Don't you get it, Carmine? I am that girl. I always will be, and believe it or not, I like her. I like being her. I like *me*."

"I like you, too," he said, "but you deserve more than this life, Haven."

"Well, so do you."

He groaned. "I chose this shit."

"Then why couldn't I?" she asked. "Why did you choose for me?"

"Because I'd be goddamned if I was going to let you throw everything away for someone like me. You're better than my kind."

Haven shook her head with disbelief. "Your *kind*? How can you say that? You, the boy who told me over and over again that I'd overcome my label . . . how can you label yourself? You wanted me to go out there and explore my options. I did that, Carmine, and I loved it, but I was lonely. Do you know what it's like to stand in a crowded room and still feel like you're the only one there? Do you? Because that was how it felt to me."

"I couldn't be something you settled for, Haven."

"You think being with you would be settling? I'll always be a part of your world. I'll always have someone keeping tabs on me, making sure I don't break my silence. My house got broken into and I couldn't even call the police, I had to call your uncle! How do I explain *that* to people? It's not normal—*I'm* not normal! Being out there in the world alone, spending my life pretending to be someone I'm not . . . *that's* settling, Carmine. Does it even matter what *I* want?"

Carmine sighed exasperatedly, taking another drink. "Of course it matters."

"Then why'd you do it?"

He stared at her, his eyes boring into hers intensely. "What do you do when the thing you want most suddenly feels like it's just beyond your fingertips?"

The question caught Haven off guard. "What?"

"You wrote that in your journal," he said. "I couldn't hold you back."

A bitter laugh of disbelief erupted from her chest. "That's why you did it? Are you kidding me? The answer to that question isn't to give up, Carmine. You don't just quit. You keep trying. You keep *reaching*. All I ever wanted was someone to see me, to love me, to *understand* me. I didn't have to hide from you; I didn't have to pretend to be someone I wasn't. You know me, the person no one else will ever know. I wanted to be with you, I thought we'd be together, and then you left! You walked out on me as I slept!"

Haven shook as all of the hurt came pouring out in her words, everything she had kept bottled in for the past eighteen months erupting in a cloud of anger.

"I wanted what was best for you," he said. "I wanted you to have a chance."

"A chance?" she asked. "You asked me for a chance once. Do you remember that? I gave it to you, and I don't regret that for a second. I'll never regret it. If you didn't love me, that's one thing, but—"

"Of course I loved you!" His eyes filled with tears. "I didn't want to get you killed!"

"You're not your father, Carmine, and I'm *not* your mother."

"I know that," he spat.

"Do you? You're so busy trying to stop history from repeating itself that you're completely ignoring what's right in front of you!"

He wiped his eyes. "And what's that?"

"Fate," she said. "You came into my life because you were meant to be in my life. It wasn't an *accident*! So don't push me away, because I fucking *love* you, Carmine DeMarco, and you're just hurting yourself doing it!"

Frantic, Haven wrapped her arms around her chest, trying to hold herself together. Carmine stared at her in a daze, but the moment a sob escaped from her throat he snapped back to reality. He wrapped his arms around her tightly. "Oh, *tesoro*," he whispered into her hair. "I fucking love you, too."

They clung to each other again until Carmine's phone shattered yet another moment. He groaned as he reached for it and glanced at the screen.

"Sir?" His voice was even as he answered, his eyes refusing to leave Haven's face. "Yes, sir. Thirty minutes. I got it."

He hung up, giving Haven a curious look.

"You have to go?" she guessed.

He nodded. "You, too. We're expected at the gathering."

"Was that Corrado?" she asked, surprised when he nodded. "It sounded serious, like, you know . . . *work*."

He smiled sadly. "Corrado is work to me. He's my boss first and family second. I can't tell him to fuck off anymore. I'd hate for him to shoot me again."

Haven glanced at his hand instinctively. "I still can't believe he did that."

"Yeah, well, *I* can. He's threatened to kill me more times than I can count, so it was only a matter of time." Haven looked at him with horror and he chuckled nervously. "I deserved it. I've fucked up a lot."

"How? I mean, if you can . . ."

"Maybe later." He glanced at his watch. "We'd be here all night if I tried to explain, and we're down to twenty-eight minutes now."

He glanced around briefly, his eyes darting between his parents' graves as he pressed his hand against Haven's back to lead her away. "I guess I was wrong."

"About?"

"Probably most of it, really, but I was referring to you not saying *fuck*," he said, shaking his head. "I can't believe you cursed at me."

———————

Neither spoke during the drive. So much time had passed that Haven knew it would be impossible for them to just pick up where they had left off, unrealistic to expect to have back exactly what they had once shared. It was still there, though, buried beneath the surface. It would take time to unearth it and nurse it back to health.

If he was willing to try, that was.

They made their way into the Morettis' house when they arrived. Carmine was on edge, his hands shoved into his pockets and body tense. He kept his head down, retreating further into himself with each step. He walked inside without knocking, stopping in the foyer. She stepped in behind him and saw Corrado standing by the bottom of the stairs.

He glanced at his watch. "Thirty-nine minutes."

Late.

An animated voice carried through the hallway as they headed toward the living room. Haven smiled at the familiarity, recognizing Dominic. Carmine paused in the doorway and she stopped behind him, glancing past him nervously. The large room was packed with people and she spotted Dia right away, sitting on the couch. Tess was beside her but mostly blocked from view by Dominic, who stood directly in front of her. Celia sat in a chair near the door beside an older woman.

There were at least two dozen others, people Haven didn't recognize, but each of them listened intently as Dominic spoke. He told a story about a fishing trip they went on when they were children, about how Carmine had dumped out all of the worms they had caught the night before.

Gazing at Carmine, Haven saw no flicker of emotion in his face, no recognition as Dominic recounted the story. He stood tensely right inside the doorway, his hands still shoved in his pockets with his head down. Haven realized then, looking at him, that he knew exactly how she had felt on her own. He knew what it felt like to stand in a crowded room, surrounded by people, yet feel utterly alone.

Haven slid her arms under his from behind, shoving her hands in his pockets with his. She laced their fingers together as she laid her head against his back. Carmine didn't move or speak, but his body relaxed from the contact.

Stories were shared, one after another, until the room grew quiet, a somber feeling taking over as no one seemed to know what else to say. Haven pulled away from Carmine and felt him tense again as she cleared her throat. "I think I have something to share."

"Twinkle Toes!" Dominic bounded across the room the second he noticed her and pulled her into a hug. "I'm glad you're here!"

"Put her down, Dominic," Tess said sternly.

Dominic put Haven back on her feet, smiling sheepishly. Dia and Tess both said hello to her before Celia chimed in. "Go on, Haven. I'd love to hear what you have to say about Vincent."

Not everyone seemed as confident as Celia about hearing Haven speak. Corrado watched her apprehensively and she noticed a few others were, too, all of them likely aware of what Dr. DeMarco had done to her.

"About a year and a half ago, when I was living in Charlotte, I wasn't doing so well. I guess you could say I was, uh . . . *homesick*."

She glanced at Dia, who smiled knowingly. "I wanted nothing more than to run back to what was familiar to me, and Dr. De—err, Vincent knew that. I hit bottom one night and did something stupid out of desperation, and he came to talk to me. He said he knew I was scared but that I needed to give life a chance. He told me to show those who had doubted me that they were wrong, that I was strong enough to make it, and after I did, if I was still *homesick*, he'd help me find my way home. He promised when I was ready he'd help me, even if it was the last thing he did."

She took a deep breath and glanced at Carmine, their eyes connecting. "He probably thought he'd have to break his promise, but he didn't, because he did exactly what he said he would. Now that I'm ready, he helped me find my way home. I just wish it hadn't really been the last thing he did."

A tear slid down her cheek as she stared into swirling deep green eyes that seemed to beckon to her. He opened his mouth like he was going to speak, but no sound escaped as he moved his lips. It didn't matter, though, because she knew what he was trying to say.

Welcome home.

The woman sitting beside Celia spoke up then, her voice laced with cynicism. "Who is this girl? How'd she know Vincenzo?"

"This is Carmine's, uh . . ." Celia trailed off. "Well, Mom, this is Haven Antonelli. She's—"

"Antonelli? You mean that little slave girl?"

People cringed and gasped, shaking their heads and muttering under their breath from secondhand embarrassment, but Haven just nodded. "That's me."

"I'll be damned." The woman surveyed her. "I guess we can't really call you that, though, can we? No, Federica's grandbaby isn't a slave. She's family."

Dozens of eyes shot straight to the woman at those words, a deathly silence falling over the room.

"What did you say, Gia?" Corrado asked, blinking with shock.

"I said she's Federica's grandbaby," Gia replied. "What, you didn't know?"

"No, I knew, but how did *you*?"

Gia waved him off. "Antonio told me ages ago. He was planning to kill that *Salamander* when he found out, but he never got the chance. God got to my husband first, I guess."

Corrado gaped at her. "Why didn't you ever say anything?"

"You never asked," Gia said, shrugging. "Besides, you all think I'm crazy, anyway. Would you have believed me?"

A minute of tense silence passed before Corrado shook his head. "No, I probably wouldn't have."

40

I *fucking love you.*"

The words still echoed in Carmine's head an hour later. Could it be that easy? He wanted to believe it, wanted to give in, but he was still conflicted. He couldn't be positive he could keep her safe or be the man she deserved. He struggled to function on his own, and the last thing he wanted to do was drag her down with him. He would never forgive himself if he got her hurt.

Carmine glanced away from Haven, sighing as he considered that, and noticed Corrado watching him with a peculiar look on his face. His penetrating stare burned through him, painful and raw, a bit of pity lingering behind the obvious judgment. Carmine stared back, their eyes connecting for only a few seconds, but it felt as if an eternity passed under the scrutiny of his gaze.

A phone rang then and Carmine breathed a sigh of relief when his uncle looked away. Corrado pulled out the phone, silencing the ringing before casually slipping it back into his pocket. He sat unmoving for a moment, his expression vacant and shoulders relaxed, but Carmine could tell from the way he flexed his fingers at his side that he was stressed.

And Corrado on edge was never good for anybody.

He draped his arm over Celia's shoulder and pulled her closer, whispering something in her ear. She tensed as she listened, glancing past him to where Carmine stood by the door. When he saw her worry, every ounce of relief he had felt a moment before washed away. Something was going on, and based on Celia's expression, whatever Corrado had planned most likely concerned him.

Carmine wasn't surprised. As long as Salvatore was still out there, somewhere, his life was at risk. Glancing at Haven again, his paranoia flared. They had fought to keep her out of the line of fire, and she had unknowingly walked right onto the battlefield.

He stood there for another minute, his unease growing until it all got to be too much. He slipped out of the room quietly, desperate for a drink, hoping it would help him clear the convoluted thoughts from his head. He ducked outside, surveying the streets quickly for any sign of trouble, but someone called his name before he could get more than a few steps away. Carmine froze at the sound of the voice and glanced behind him, seeing Corrado following.

"You're leaving without saying anything? Where are you going?"

Carmine sighed as his uncle paused beside him on the sidewalk. "Home."

"Home?" Corrado shook his head. "As many times as I speak to you about your behavior, you'd think it would sink in by now! You have absolutely no respect for your family. You treat them as if they're disposable to you. Do you even care what they're going through right now? Your father's dead!"

Carmine scoffed defensively, words flying from his mouth as he lost his temper. "Yeah, because of you."

Corrado's eyes darkened. He grabbed Carmine before he could utter another word and slammed him back against the brick house. Clutching his throat tightly, Corrado pinned him there, cutting off the flow of air. Carmine desperately grasped at his large hands, trying to pry them off as he struggled to breathe, but Corrado's grip was too strong.

"If you know what's good for you, you won't *ever* speak to me like that again," Corrado said, his voice low and laced with venom. "Your family is in enough pain right now. Don't make me give them another reason to grieve."

He let go and took a few steps back as Carmine bent over,

gasping for air. "What the fuck?" he spat, his eyes burning with tears. Corrado stepped forward again and Carmine flew upright immediately, holding his hands up defensively. "Christ, I didn't mean it! I, uh . . . I'm sorry, okay?"

"No, it's *not* okay," Corrado replied. "This entire time I've been cutting you slack because you can't get over whatever you shared with Haven, and now that she's here, *this* is how you act? What's wrong with you?"

"What's wrong is she shouldn't be here," he gasped, still trying to catch his breath. "She's going to get hurt. They're *all* going to get hurt."

"You're avoiding them to keep them safe?" Corrado laughed bitterly. "Well, that's . . . *honorable,* I suppose, but it's also insulting. Do you honestly believe I won't protect them? That I *can't?* They're *my* responsibility. Keeping them safe is *my* job. If I didn't know Haven would be perfectly fine in your presence, she wouldn't be here right now. If I thought you posed some danger to my wife, I wouldn't let you within a hundred feet of her."

Corrado paused as his phone rang again, to silence it once more. "Do you understand what I'm telling you?" he asked, continuing as if it never interrupted. "The odds of Haven dying in an accident are far greater than the odds of her being killed because of someone as trivial as you. Because that's exactly what you are— insignificant. Do you get that? You're *nothing.*"

He paused once more as his phone rang again, anger clouding his face at the sound, but this time he didn't even bother to look at who was calling. "I have things to take care of. Go be with people who actually care about you. Don't waste the chance. You never know when you might only have a few hours left to enjoy them."

A chill ran the length of Carmine's spine at his words. He stood there for a moment after Corrado left, trying to calm down, and bummed a cigarette from the first person that happened to stroll by. The smoke burned his lungs as he inhaled, the nicotine instantly soothing his frazzled nerves. He took a few quick puffs of the cheap generic menthol before tossing it onto the sidewalk and stamping it out.

The house was still noisy when he reentered, but the crowd from the living room had disbursed. He wandered through the downstairs and found Celia in the kitchen, surprise flickering across her face when she spotted him. "Hey, kiddo."

"Hey," he mumbled, grabbing a bottle of water from the fridge. He desperately wanted a *real* drink, something hard and straight from a glass bottle, but he knew better than to pull out the alcohol there. "Is, uh . . . I mean, where . . . ?"

"She's out back," Celia said, knowing what he wanted without Carmine even getting it out.

"Thanks." He headed for the back door, spotting them lounging on the old wicker lawn furniture as soon as he stepped outside. He strolled in their direction, suddenly nervous again, but it all faded away when Haven looked at him. A radiant smile lit up her face as her eyes sparkled. His heart nearly stilled at the sight.

It took everything Carmine had in him not to fall to his knees right then and there and beg her to *always* look at him that way. He wanted to plead with her to never stop loving him, for her to forgive him for everything he ever did wrong, even the shit she didn't know about and never would. He wanted her to grant him absolution, to be his saving grace, to swear he was worthy of being saved. He never wanted her to be ashamed, and he sure as hell never wanted to see disappointment in her eyes. He wanted her to be proud, and at that moment, he wanted to swear he would do *anything* she ever asked of him to make it so.

But instead, he choked back the flood of emotion and kept his mouth shut as he grabbed a chair from the patio and joined them out on the lawn. He sat beside Dominic and directly across from Haven, his eyes fixated solely on her.

"Hey, bro," Dominic said, slapping Carmine on the back. "Back already?"

He shrugged. "I never left. I just went out for some air."

"Yeah, I'm sure you went out for *air*," Tess said sarcastically. "You smell like smoke. Go sit downwind from me. It reeks."

"The wind isn't even blowing, Tess," he said. "Shut the fuck up."

Haven's soft voice captured his attention, an inquisitive look on her face. "You smoke?"

"Every now and then I'll have one, but I don't make a habit of it."

"Speaking of habits . . ." Dominic motioned toward the bottle in Carmine's hand. "Is that really water, bro? It's not usually your beverage of choice."

Carmine narrowed his eyes. "Yes, it's water. Is it *that* hard to believe?"

"Well, yeah. The only clear liquid you've had to drink in a year is vodka."

"Bullshit. You can't say that when you haven't even seen me much."

"That's because you've been drunk the entire time," Tess chimed in, laughing humorlessly. "You probably wouldn't even remember seeing us."

"I don't drink *that* much," he retorted, knowing it was a lie the moment the words came out. He'd drunk himself unconscious more times than he could count. There were definite blank spots in his memory, entire days he couldn't remember.

"Did you drink at all today?" Dia asked from her seat beside Haven.

"Yeah, where's your flask?" Dominic asked. "Do you have it with you?"

Carmine dropped his gaze. The subject made him want a drink even worse than he already had. He started rubbing his neck absentmindedly, his anxiety growing. "What is this, an intervention?"

"Maybe," Dominic replied.

"Well, you're wasting your breath, because I don't need it."

"We disagree," Dia said. "You always drank, but it's worse now."

"Leave it the fuck alone, Dia."

She started to argue but Tess cut her off. "Let's just drop it. So, yeah, he drinks. Whatever. At least he's not messing around with Molly anymore."

A tense silence instantly strangled them. Carmine slowly raised his eyes to glare at Tess, anger surging through him. She saw his hostile expression and blanched, starting to stammer about not meaning it how it sounded, but he stopped her. "Just . . . shut the fuck up, Tess. Talk about something else, whatever you all were talking about before I interrupted."

"We were reminiscing," Dominic said, casting Carmine a worried look as he quickly changed the subject. "Sharing some of our favorite memories of Dad."

"Well, then, continue," he responded, opening his bottle of water to take a drink. It was cold and went down smooth, none of the burn or warmth he craved.

The atmosphere grew a bit lighter as they shared stories and traded playful jabs. Haven seemed at ease as she smiled and laughed, but she didn't contribute much to the conversation. He yearned to hear her voice and listen to her stories, to know what she had done off on her own. He wanted to know *everything*, a twinge of jealousy brewing deep within him when he thought about how much he must have missed. She had an entire life he knew nothing about.

He didn't like that shit one bit.

Celia joined them when the other guests started leaving, sharing a few more stories of her own. Every now and then Haven would peek at Carmine and her cheeks would turn pink, hints of the timid girl he remembered shining through. The sight of it gave Carmine hope, something he hadn't felt since walking out that door in Durante.

Maybe they had a chance. Maybe she could forgive him someday.

"Tess, babe, we need to get going," Dominic said eventually, the two of them standing. Dominic glanced around at everyone, his eyes locking with Carmine's momentarily. "It's been nice hanging out again. We need to get together more often, not just when, you know . . . something happens."

Everyone murmured in agreement.

They said their good-byes, making Haven promise to stay in touch, before heading out. Dia departed right afterward, scurrying away to leave Haven and Carmine alone. They sat quietly, gazing at each other, the air between them growing thick with unspoken questions.

"Do you, uh . . ." he started, unsure of what to say. "Fuck, I don't know. Do you wanna get coffee or something? Is that what people do?"

She laughed. "I don't know about other people, but it sounds nice to me."

Carmine's nerves flared again, queasiness stirring in the pit of his stomach. He was afraid he would say something wrong and ruin any chance he had at fixing things.

He held his hand out to her but she simply gazed at it, the apprehensive look on her face making him second-guess himself. He dropped his hand, shoving it in his pocket when she didn't take it. "You don't have to. I just thought, well . . . Christ, why is this so fucking awkward?"

"I don't know," she said as she stood. "I mean, it's just us, right? And it's not that I don't want to hold your hand, but you're injured and I don't want to hurt you."

"Oh." He pulled his hand back out to look at it. "You aren't gonna hurt me."

She bit her bottom lip nervously as she offered her hand to Carmine this time. He took it with a smile, lacing their fingers together and squeezing gently. Pain shot through his wrist and he winced, his hand clearly *not* fine despite what he had said.

"How bad is it?" Haven asked. "Honestly."

"I don't know," he muttered, letting go of her and unwrapping the white bandage. "The medic said it wasn't serious, but I didn't go to the hospital."

Haven surveyed his hand. The back of it was red and she pressed her fingers to the skin, sighing when he grimaced. "It's infected."

"How do you know?"

"Seriously?" She raised her eyebrows at Carmine like it was a stupid question. "We got hurt a lot in Blackburn and weren't allowed to see doctors, so we learned to watch for the signs. I've seen people die from wounds less severe than this."

"Oh," he said, looking at his hand. "Can't I just soak it in peroxide? Get some Neosporin?"

"So stubborn," she muttered, lacing their fingers together once more. "It's better to get antibiotics, so go to the doctor. Please?"

He sighed, resigned and partly annoyed that she knew how to get to him. All it took was a fucking *please*. "I'll make an appointment tomorrow, but right now I have a, uh . . . whatever this is. A date, I guess."

A small smile curved Haven's lips at those words.

They headed around the side of the house to avoid seeing anyone as they left, because Carmine wasn't in the mood for their pity disguised as sympathy. He was on edge as they walked down the street, keeping his head down but acutely aware of everything going on around them. It didn't matter what Corrado had said—he couldn't stop his paranoia. Salvatore was still out there, somewhere, and until he was sure that was dealt with, there was no way he would be able to relax.

Carmine let go of her when they reached his house and unlocked the front door. She stepped inside, her eyes darting around curiously. It didn't escape Carmine's notice that she cringed at the utter mess.

"Uh, kitchen, dining room, living room, bathroom and laundry room or whatever," he said, pointing out the areas on the first floor. "The room down the hall across from the living room used to be my father's office when I was a kid but right now it's just full of boxes. I never bothered to unpack everything."

"You've been here over a year and you still haven't unpacked?"

"No."

"Have you cleaned at all in that time?"

He blinked a few times, gazing at her, but didn't bother answering that question. "Make yourself at home. I'll be right back."

Carmine left her alone in the hallway as he headed upstairs and kicked off his shoes, tossing them into the closet before stripping out of his clothes. He put on a pair of jeans and a green long-sleeved t-shirt, slipping his Nike's on before going into the bathroom. He wet his hair and attempted to run his fingers through it, the act making his hand viciously throb. He rooted through the cabinets and found a bottle of peroxide, the wound scorching as he poured it on his hand.

He headed back downstairs and found Haven in the living room, staring at the covered piano. She glanced back at him questioningly. "Carmine, who's Molly?"

He froze, caught off guard.

"It's okay if she was, uh, you know . . . it's not a big deal." She grimaced, her reaction at odds with her words. "I just wondered if you and her . . ."

"Molly's not a person," he said, shaking his head. "Molly's a drug. I wanted to feel better and got hooked on it. It probably would've killed me . . . well, fuck, it almost *did* kill me, but I'd definitely be dead by now if Corrado hadn't intervened."

"He got you off of it?"

"You can say that."

She stared at Carmine as she took in his words. "Did it work?"

His brow furrowed. "I told you I stopped."

"I mean Molly," she clarified. "Did it make you feel better?"

He sighed as he considered the question. "It did for a while, but it wasn't real. No matter how high I got, I never found what I was looking for. And it ended up taking from me more than it gave."

He pulled her into a hug and she gazed up at him, her eyes

sparkling. The air around them grew thick with emotion as she wrapped her arms around his waist. His heart raced, blood rushing furiously through his veins as his body tingled from her embrace. He moved forward a bit, hesitantly, gauging her reaction, and her eyes seemed to instinctively dart to his mouth. He took that as a sign and hoped like hell it wasn't a mistake when he leaned down, aiming for her mouth.

At the last second, panic overtook Haven's face. She pulled back, turning her head so his lips brushed against her flushed cheek. He silently cursed himself as he let go of her. *Too soon.*

"I, uh . . ." She picked at her fingernails, moving away from him. "I'm sorry."

"Don't be." He glanced at his watch with a sigh. It was already a little after seven in the evening. "How about that coffee?"

She nodded, reaching into her pocket and pulling out her keys. She tossed them at Carmine with no warning, and he barely got a grasp on them before they hit the floor. He eyed them peculiarly, spotting the familiar key. "No fucking way."

"It's parked out front," she said. "Thought maybe you'd like to drive."

Carmine cruised through the streets of east Chicago, lounged back in the driver's seat of the black Mazda. The dark interior smelled just as fresh as it had the last time he had driven it, the plush leather seat somehow still formed to his shape. North Carolina radio stations were programmed for the buttons of the stereo, the dial turned to his favorite—97.1 FM. A black tree-shaped air freshener hung from the rearview mirror, and he suspected it was the same one he had put there back in Durante.

"Did you even drive this thing?" he asked, looking at the mileage . . . a few hundred miles more than he remembered it being.

"Sure," she said. "I drove it here last night."

Carmine shook his head, turning his focus back to the street.

He pulled into the parking lot of the first coffee shop they saw, politely opening Haven's door for her. She smiled sweetly and took his hand as they headed inside. Customers packed the small building, standing in groups and huddling around the tables.

"What do you like?" Haven asked as they got in line.

Carmine laughed dryly. "I can't say I *like* anything. I don't drink coffee."

"Then why'd you ask me out for it?"

"I figured I had a better chance of you saying yes to something as simple as a drink than a whole meal," he said, gazing at the menu board. "Christ, who pays five dollars for a drink that doesn't have alcohol in it? For that price it better come with a complimentary blow job or something."

"Carmine," she gasped, his rant drawing the attention of people around them. He muttered an apology to her and noticed a man a few feet away glaring at them. He narrowed his eyes at him as he mouthed *"Problem?"* and the man looked away quickly. Carmine smirked, looking back at the menu as Haven spoke again. "Do you see anything you think you *might* like?"

"I don't know what any of this is," he said. "The Italian I can read, but that doesn't tell me a damn thing about how it tastes. What do you drink?"

"Black coffee."

"Seriously? All of this fancy caramel chai frappe cappu-fuck-ing-ccino venti latte bullshit and you get plain coffee?" She nodded and he chuckled, pulling her hand up and pressing a kiss on the back of it. "That's the Haven *I* remember, the one who likes the simple shit."

The barista asked Carmine for their order and he muttered, "Two regular black coffees," his expression daring her to try to correct his lingo. She simply nodded as she rang it up, and he groaned when he saw the price.

"I have some cash on me," Haven said, reaching into her pocket. "I think."

"Don't even dare," he said, shooting her an incredulous look. "I'd rob the place before I let you pay."

She removed her hand as he grabbed his wallet, pulling out a twenty-dollar bill. The woman gave Carmine his change, eyeing him warily, and he slipped a ten into the tip jar on the counter.

"That was generous," Haven commented.

"Yeah, well, I kinda just threatened to rob the place, so I figured I probably shouldn't stiff them on top of it."

"You wouldn't actually rob the place, though," she said confidently.

"No, I wouldn't," he replied. "As long as I wasn't ordered to, anyway."

Carmine grabbed their drinks, leading her to a table in the corner away from everyone else. They sat and Carmine took a sip from his steaming cup, gagging from the taste. "This shit is bitter."

She took a drink of hers. "Tastes fine to me."

He dumped in as much sugar as he could fit, adding some creamer to make it a bit more tolerable, but he still had no desire to drink it. They chatted as Haven sipped her coffee, and he listened intently as she told him about her life in New York. She talked about going to school and creating art, about the people she had met and the friends she had made, before she explained about hearing the details of his father's death on the news.

"This wasn't the first time I wanted to come. When I was in Charlotte, I ran out in the middle of the night and took a cab to the bus station." She laughed humorlessly at the memory. "I was out of my mind, hadn't slept in a while. Your father stopped me. That's what I was talking about at Celia's."

Carmine gaped at her. "You could've been arrested for suspicious behavior. The cops don't fuck around, you know. Everyone's worried about terrorism."

She laughed it off. "I don't look like a terrorist."

"Well, neither do I, but looks don't mean shit."

"But you aren't a terrorist," she refuted. "So that proves my point."

"No, it doesn't," he said. "It doesn't prove shit. I terrorize people."

"That's not the same," she said, narrowing her eyes as annoyance flashed across her face. "You're being too hard on yourself."

"No, you're just being too easy on me," he said. "You don't even know . . ."

"Then tell me," she said seriously.

"I can't."

"You can't tell me anything?" she asked, cocking an eyebrow in challenge. "Or is it just that you don't want to tell me because you don't want me to know?"

"It's because *you* don't want to know. Trust me."

"If you think I'm going to run out that door because of something you tell me, you're wrong," she said. "If you *can't* tell me, I understand, but don't hide things from me just because you believe it's better if I don't know them."

"No good can come from you knowing," he said. "You'll look at me and you won't see *me* anymore. You'll see *them*. You'll see the people I've hurt and the things I've done, so excuse me if I sorta fucking like you seeing *just* me."

She opened her mouth to respond but hesitated briefly, leaning her elbows on the table and moving closer to Carmine. "Have you had to, uh . . . ?"

"Kill?" he asked, finishing her question. She glanced around anxiously to make sure no one was listening before nodding. He could see the curiosity in her eyes, but he could also see the apprehension. That was something he never wanted from her. "Would it make a difference?"

"No," she said. "If you did, I know it's because you had to."

"Then why are you asking?"

"I just want to know."

"No."

She looked at Carmine cautiously. "You aren't going to tell me?"

He sighed. "That's the answer, Haven. No."

"Oh." She was quiet for a moment, appearing deep in thought. "Is that what you see when you look in the mirror? The people you've hurt?"

"It's hard to see the good when there's so much damn bad."

"I see the good." She smiled softly as she gazed at Carmine. "It might help you to talk to someone, though. You shouldn't keep it all bottled in."

"I'm still not going to tell you that shit," he replied, shaking his head.

"I know," she said. "I meant, like, a professional."

His brow furrowed. "Are you suggesting I go to a shrink?"

She shrugged. "Why not? I know there are some things you can't tell them, but that doesn't mean they can't help at all. I saw a movie where a mobster guy went to a psychiatrist, and so did that other one in that TV show. He was the boss, too."

Carmine smirked when it struck him what she had said. He tried to contain his amusement, but his laughter escaped when a blush overtook Haven's face. "Aw, don't be embarrassed," he said, reaching across the table and cupping her cheek. It was warm against his palm and she leaned into his touch, smiling sheepishly. "It's sweet of you to worry, but this isn't like TV, *tesoro*. We can't do that shit in real life."

He stroked her cheek softly as she whispered, "I wish you could."

"Me, too."

————

The sun had set by the time they left the coffee shop, darkness surrounding everything. He held her hand as they strolled through the parking lot toward the car, the atmosphere between them light once again. It felt like a weight had been lifted from his chest, his world just a tad brighter since she had walked back into it.

The carefree feeling didn't last, though—not that he had actually expected it to. They made it back to his house and he asked if she wanted to watch a movie, but they barely made it through the opening credits before his phone rang.

He pulled it out hesitantly, tensing. *Corrado.* "Sir?"

"Be in front of my house in five minutes."

"Yes, sir," he grumbled, but responding was pointless because Corrado had already hung up. He slipped the phone back in his pocket and looked at Haven, running his hand through his hair anxiously.

"You have to go," she said quietly, a tinge of sadness in her voice, but she forced a smile. "I understand."

She started to stand but he grabbed her arm to stop her. "Don't leave."

She looked at Carmine with confusion. "What?"

"I just . . . fuck. Just stay, okay?"

"I don't know," she said. "It's late. I should find a hotel."

He groaned loudly, the noise sounding like a growl. "Look, I'm not telling you what to do. If you want to go, *tesoro,* by all means go, but I'd rather you stay."

"I, uh . . ." she started, but she trailed off when his phone rang again.

Five minutes had already passed.

Carmine cursed, answering it quickly. "I'm coming, sir."

"*Now,*" Corrado barked before hanging up.

Carmine stood, eyeing Haven carefully. "Just . . . wait for me, okay?"

She didn't say a word but she also made no move to leave, so he wasn't sure what she was thinking. He didn't have time to stick around and figure it out, though, so he gave her one last look before grabbing his gun and bolting for the door. He stepped outside as a memory hit him, the last time he had said those words to her running through his mind.

She had refused to wait for him that day.

He glanced behind him at the house as he headed down the street, hoping like hell she would wait this time.

41

Carmine's phone was ringing again by the time he reached Corrado's, but he didn't bother answering it since he was so close. Corrado's car was parked along the curb, the headlights blacked out but engine running. Carmine climbed in the passenger side and gave his uncle a cautious glance, seeing the look of impatience on his face, and tensed in anticipation of him snapping. Corrado closed his phone and Carmine's instantly stopped ringing, but he didn't say a word.

Corrado pulled away and sped down the street, waiting until he was a block away before flipping on his headlights. Carmine surveyed his uncle, noticing he wore his black leather gloves, and instantly knew something serious was happening.

"I hope you had a nice time with Haven tonight," Corrado said, shattering the tense silence.

"Uh, yeah, I did," Carmine replied. "Thank you for everything you did for her. She told me about it all."

"No reason to thank me," he said coolly. "I was only doing the job that was given to me, Carmine. That's what we do. Personal feelings are irrelevant. We follow orders and one thing you should know about me by now—one thing I hope you respect me for—is the fact that I don't fail when I take on a task. *Ever*."

Carmine nodded. "Yes, sir."

"Good. And I didn't want to interrupt your evening, but it's time."

Carmine eyed him warily, wondering what *time* it was, but Corrado didn't elaborate and Carmine knew better than to question him.

A bad feeling seeped into Carmine's bones as Corrado drove without saying another word toward a rough area in the south side of Chicago. It was fairly deserted except for the occasional scraggly passersby, the street aligned on both sides with condemned buildings covered in graffiti. It was gang territory, the part of town where they battled for control of corners no one really *wanted* in the first place. They killed one another for the fuck of it, for the right to rule the forsaken streets.

The fact that they were there, moving deeper into the midst of gangland territory, didn't sit well with Carmine. He reached under his shirt and felt his gun secured in his waistband, his thumb flicking the safety off just in case.

"Do the thugs in this neighborhood scare you?" Corrado asked, noticing his movement.

"No," he replied. "I just know anyone who comes to this side of town is up to no good."

"True," Corrado responded, pausing before adding, "It'll be over quick."

His cryptic words sent Carmine's heart pounding furiously. They neared the end of the main street and took a left onto another narrow road, stopping halfway down. Corrado cut the engine and opened his door, hesitating as he glanced at Carmine. "Leave your gun in the car. You seem to have an itchy trigger finger tonight."

"Excuse me?" Something was off, Carmine could sense it, and being unprotected was as good as asking to be killed.

"You heard what I said," Corrado said. "Don't question me."

Carmine grabbed the gun and shoved it in the glove box. He had to do it. Corrado would have taken it.

Carmine followed Corrado across the street to a run-down house. It looked like it hadn't been inhabited in decades, the shutters barely hanging by their hinges and old wooden boards nailed up along the windowpanes, the glass long gone. They stepped on the porch and Corrado knocked twice on the large door. Before he could knock a third time, it opened. Corrado walked in and Carmine followed him cautiously, his eyes falling upon an Italian man right inside. He was about Corrado's age and familiar, definitely a friend in the organization. He held a gun defensively, but he seemed to relax a bit when Corrado nodded at him.

Their silent exchange made Carmine feel queasy, the bad feeling nearly overpowering him.

He tried to sort through his thoughts to make sense of what was happening, briefly considering bolting back out the door while he still had the chance. He wondered how far he could get while unarmed, but such a train of thought was senseless. He would be caught before he even made it off the porch. He needed to stay calm, to play cool, and not let them see his fear, even if that was exactly what he felt.

He was fucking *terrified*.

Corrado grabbed his arm as he shut the front door, shoving Carmine toward the staircase that the man started up. No one said a word, no instructions given as Carmine begrudgingly climbed the creaky steps with Corrado on his trail. He felt like cattle being herded to the slaughterhouse as he followed the man down a long hallway.

They approached a room, and Carmine froze in horror as soon as he stepped in the doorway. Vision blurring, his knees went weak as fear slammed into him. He nearly collapsed but Corrado grabbed him, keeping him on his feet as he pushed him farther into the room.

The pieces of the puzzle clicked together in an instant. He should have sensed it earlier, should have known what was happening. The signs were all there. The look on Celia's face . . . Corrado's cryptic words . . . "You never know when you might only have a few hours left." "I didn't want to interrupt your evening, but it's time . . . " "It'll be over quick."

The moment he told Carmine to leave the gun in the car, he should have known what he would find in the house: his demise.

As his green eyes met the pair of dark, cold muddy ones across the room, it made sense. Corrado told him not to worry about retaliation because the entire time he had planned to take him straight to Salvatore.

The Boss stood in the corner of the empty room, near a shattered window with a single board nailed over it. Moonlight filtered inside, giving Carmine barely enough light to see. Salvatore appeared disheveled, his right arm bandaged sloppily in a blue sling. He took a few steps in their direction, his movements rigid like he could no longer bend his left knee.

"About time," his raspy voice called, his eyes trained on Carmine as the other man strolled to the window to gaze out.

"I apologize for being late, but you know how he can be," Corrado said behind Carmine, blocking the only exit.

"Yes, I know *exactly* how he can be." Salvatore's voice seethed with anger. "He doesn't listen. You tell him to do something and he ignores it. He seems to think he knows better than everyone else, like he's above us all and doesn't have to fall in line."

"Well, he certainly *is* his father's son," Corrado said.

Carmine sensed something in his uncle's voice, amusement with a hint of sarcasm. He started to turn around to look at him, to get a read on his mood, but Corrado grabbed the back of his neck roughly, keeping him in position.

Rage flashed in Salvatore's expression at the mention of Vincent. He angrily spit on the floor with disgust, like just the thought of him made him sick.

Carmine shook, his eyes darting around the room. The sins of the father were about to be paid for by the son. His brain worked a million miles a minute as he tried to think of some way out. He was unarmed and outnumbered, everyone in the room more experienced than him.

"Looking for a way to escape?" Salvatore asked, slowly approaching. "Pity for you, there isn't one."

Corrado violently shoved him toward the ground, forcing him on his knees in the middle of the room. He let go of the back of his neck and withdrew his gun.

"Please don't do this!" Carmine pleaded, the words tumbling from his mouth. "I swear, just . . . fuck! This isn't necessary!"

Before he could say any more, Corrado shoved the muzzle of his gun against the back of Carmine's skull. He closed his eyes, tears burning their way to the surface as he bowed his head in desperation.

If there's a fucking God, He won't let me die today.

"How dare you tell me what's necessary!" Salvatore yelled. "This is what I was talking about! You think you know better than everyone! I gave you a simple order, and you had every opportunity to do it, but you disobeyed me! Vincent never would've hurt you, and now, because you betrayed me, my men are dead! Your father got what he deserved, and frankly so did your mother! Your entire family is a disgrace!"

Carmine fought back a sob, his body shaking violently at those words. His world was imploding and there was a gun pointed at the back of his head.

Corrado was a perfect shot. He *never* missed his target.

His uncle, his own fucking family . . .

"Please," Carmine whispered. "Please don't fucking do this."

As soon as those words passed his lips, something slammed hard into the back of Carmine's head. He fell forward onto his hands and knees, splinters of wood from the floorboards digging into his palms.

He knew he couldn't give up. He couldn't go down without a fight. He wouldn't win, but he *wasn't* a coward. He wouldn't just stand there and let them steal his life. Maybe a month ago he would have, or even yesterday, but not now. Not today.

"Good-bye."

The lone word slipping from Corrado's lips set Carmine in motion. He dropped flat against the floor and rolled as a deafening bang sounded, the gunshot echoing in the room. He braced himself for a scorching bullet to tear into his flesh, but he felt nothing. No blood. No pain.

Adrenaline or sheer fucking luck?

Carmine forced himself to his feet and turned for the door when something across the room captured his attention. The man at the window dropped with a thump to the floor, blood pouring from a wound dead center in his forehead. Salvatore turned in horror as Corrado knocked Carmine to the floor again on his hands and knees. As he scurried away, Carmine watched in shock as Corrado used the distraction to swiftly reach into Salvatore's waistband with his left hand and pull a pistol from it.

Salvatore turned back around, his eyes wide when he saw both guns now pointed at his head. "What are you doing?"

"Following orders," Corrado said calmly. "When I initiated, I took an oath. I swore to Antonio DeMarco that I would be a man of honor, a man who always put the organization first. They may just be words to some, but they have meaning to me. *La Cosa Nostra* or death. That's what I swore. I choose *La Cosa Nostra* and always have. It's a real pity you chose death, sir."

Corrado lowered his gun and fired two shots, bullets ripping through both of Salvatore's knees. He let out a blood-curdling scream as he collapsed. Corrado stood stoically as Salvatore desperately tried to pull himself away, his legs gushing blood and soaking his gray pants.

"Do you know what happens to rats, Carmine?" Corrado asked. "What we do to vermin, the disloyal and dishonorable?"

"Yes," he responded weakly, his voice shaking. It was an urban legend within the organization, a story everyone whispered about but had no proof it ever happened. "Rats for the rats."

Corrado took the few steps toward Salvatore, thrusting his foot out and kicking him square in the nose. Carmine flinched as Salvatore cried out, trying to shield himself as Corrado kicked him a few times in quick succession. The brutality in his uncle's movements terrified him, anger and passion erupting from him. He did it again and again until Salvatore's face poured blood like a leaky faucet.

"This place is infested," Corrado said, his words strained as he fought to catch his breath. The rage had taken a toll on his composure. "If you listen carefully, you can hear them in the walls, scratching and scurrying around. It won't take the rats long to catch a whiff of the blood. As soon as they realize there's fresh meat, they'll swarm. It's a brutal way to go, being eaten alive."

Carmine's stomach churned ruthlessly and he resisted the urge to gag. What kind of monster would think to do such a thing?

Corrado turned to him as if he had heard Carmine's silent question, the vacant expressionless mask enshrouding his face the only answer he needed. He seemed inhuman, the monster from the legends, the one he had heard about. The Kevlar Killer. No remorse, no emotion, and absolutely no conscience. "Sal knows this already. It's why he chose this place. He just didn't anticipate being the one to face the horror."

Corrado slipped his gun back in his coat, ignoring Salvatore's incessant yelling. He focused his attention on the pistol he had taken from the Boss, removing bullets from it one by one. He spun the chamber as he started toward the door, pausing in the doorway to lay the pistol on the floor. "I left a single bullet in your gun, Salamander. It'll take you a while to drag yourself over here to it, but I'm sure you'll manage if you want the suffering to end. The choice is yours."

"You traitor!" Salvatore spat. "You'll burn in Hell for this!"

Corrado laughed bitterly. "I'll probably burn in Hell for most of what I've done in my life, but this is one of the few things I feel is actually worth it."

He walked out without another word.

The moment Carmine heard his uncle's footsteps on the stairs, he jumped to his feet and ran after him, tripping on a loose board and nearly falling in his haste. He could still hear Salvatore screaming as they exited the house but it didn't seem to faze Corrado as he headed for the car.

Carmine opened the door to climb in the passenger seat when it all hit him. Hunching over, he dry heaved on the road.

Corrado waited patiently for Carmine to get himself together before starting the car to drive away.

"Won't people hear him screaming?" Carmine asked as he wiped his watery eyes.

"Possibly, but it doesn't matter," he replied. "Like you said, anyone who comes to this neighborhood is up to no good."

They drove in silence, the atmosphere suffocating. Carmine had reached the end of his rope, on the verge of a breakdown as he tentatively clung to the last shred of his sanity. It pressed upon Carmine, the memory of everything he had been through tearing through his system at once—the chaos, the destruction, the pain, the murder.

"Why'd you do it?" he choked out.

Corrado glanced at him. "Would you rather it had been you?"

"Not Sal." He shook his head as the tears continued to stream from his eyes. "My father."

Corrado let out an exasperated sigh and swung a sudden right, pulling the car along the curb and cutting the engine.

"Your father died a long time ago," he said, his voice low. "Just because he was walking around and breathing doesn't mean he was alive, Carmine. We die the day we lose the will to go on. We die the day we stop caring about life. The Vincent I knew, the man who made you, whose blood flows through your veins, ceased to exist when you were eight years old. He died in that hospital room as he held vigil beside your bed, mourning the loss of his wife. I watched every painful second of it as it happened and did nothing to stop his death."

Corrado avoided looking at Carmine, instead staring out at the vibrant full moon in the sky. "He had work to do, so he kept going until it was done. He'd finally finished, so it was time for him to go. To him, it was better than the alternative. He had no intention of going to prison."

"But why would he?" Carmine asked, shaking his head. "It didn't have to be this way. I mean, the Feds . . ."

"You're wrong," he said. "Your father didn't make a deal for himself. He didn't turn state's evidence against me. He accepted his fate long ago. Your father cooperated for *you*. He cooperated for Haven and everyone else you love. He gave them what they wanted so they'd leave his family alone, and in the process he did Maura's memory justice by saving a young girl."

Corrado paused briefly to collect his thoughts before he continued. "He'd made his decision, but I couldn't let him do it himself. He wouldn't find the peace he sought if he did. He wanted to be with your mother. He wanted to live again, with her. I made it so he could."

Carmine stared at him as he processed his words. "Why'd you ask him for forgiveness then?"

"What?"

"When you pulled the trigger, you said 'Forgive me.'"

Corrado shook his head. "I wasn't asking *him*."

Starting the car up again, Corrado pulled away from the curb. "We have one more thing to take care of tonight, so pull yourself together."

They drove across town to the run-down strip club, the one he had been to before when Corrado killed Remy. The crummy lot was packed, the back row filled entirely with familiar sedans. Corrado parked along the side of the building, climbing out and glancing around cautiously. "Are you registered to vote?"

"Uh, no," Carmine said as he got out of the car.

Corrado nodded, as if that answer didn't surprise him, and motioned for Carmine to follow him inside. The club was packed, the air thick with smoke. They slipped by the bouncer without saying a word, Carmine keeping his attention on his uncle as they headed to the back room.

"Voting's important," Corrado said, pausing at the cellar door. "People like to feel like they actually have a say in what happens, even if it's just an illusion."

Corrado opened the cellar door and voices filtered out instantly, but they quieted once they descended the stairs. Carmine hesitated on the bottom step, looking around the small grimy space with shock. There were at least twenty-five men present, mostly Capos from what he could tell—the highest-ranking men left within the collapsing organization. They all looked at Corrado as he entered and he nodded toward another man, who cleared his throat to gain everyone's attention. "We all know why we're here. Nominations?"

A few people said Corrado's name, while others just murmured in agreement.

"Any others?"

The basement remained completely silent.

"Any objections?" the man asked. "Speak now or take it to the grave."

Carmine looked around. The men appeared nervous, their shifty eyes everywhere except for on Corrado. The room once again remained silent, no one speaking up.

The entire scene was strange to Carmine.

"Moretti it is, then," the man said. "This meeting never happened."

Corrado turned back around, motioning for Carmine to go right back up the stairs without having spoken a single word. They headed out to the parking lot, pausing beside the car not more than five minutes after arriving. "Like I said, people like to believe they have a choice, even if they really don't."

Corrado got in the driver's side and Carmine slipped into the passenger seat, eyeing him warily. "You're the Don now?"

"Yes."

"What would've happened if someone objected? Would they have been allowed to leave?"

"They would've certainly left the room," he replied. "Just in a dozen pieces."

————————

Carmine listened for sounds as he opened the front door, noting the house was completely silent, but the glow from the television illuminated the living room. Haven lay on the couch fast asleep, her shoes kicked off and sitting on the floor in front of her.

Carmine walked over and crouched down, stealthily slipping his gun under the couch before pushing some stray hair from her face. She stirred a bit but still slept, and he remained there for a moment, just watching her breathe.

If he hadn't been sure before, it was at that moment he knew it. It was then, watching her sleep, that he *felt* it. He didn't know what would happen in the future, but somehow they would make it if they gave it a try.

He fought back tears again, still unable to get himself under control. Life overwhelmed him, tugging him in opposite directions while he stood stagnant, trying to remain whole. He was surrounded by violence and death, the ugliness eating away at him, but then, on the other side, there was her. She was peace, and hope, and pure fucking beauty. She was the good that he hoped would overpower the bad.

"Haven," he whispered, running the back of his hand along her cheek. *"La mia bella ragazza."*

She stirred again and opened her eyes, blinking rapidly with confusion. It seemed to strike her where she was, a sleepy smile curving her lips. "You're back."

"And you waited."

"Of course I did. I told you I wouldn't run from you, Carmine."

"I won't either," he said, smiling softly. "I won't leave you again."

"You swear?"

"You fucking know I do."

She laughed, eyeing Carmine curiously as she sat up. She placed her right hand on his cheek, gently stroking his skin and brushing her thumb along his mouth. "Have you been crying?"

"Maybe," he replied, leaning forward to softly press his lips to hers. She didn't pull away that time, didn't turn her head. Instead, she moved her mouth in rhythm with his. It was sweet, and innocent, but it was enough.

He ducked his head and nuzzled into her neck, inhaling deeply as he kissed the exposed skin. Her presence was overwhelming, the touch and scent and taste of her driving him wild.

"Do you still feel that?" he asked, nipping at the skin near her collarbone. "The electricity between us? *Please* tell me you feel it."

"I feel it," she whispered.

"I need you, *Haven*," he said, his voice cracking as the words caught in his throat.

"I know."

A strangled sob escaped his throat, the sound causing her to grip him tighter, and she whispered quietly as he cried in her arms. He couldn't seem to stop himself—she destroyed his walls all over again, broke Carmine down so it all came flooding out.

42

Life was a whirlwind, each day rapidly morphing into the next. Haven stayed with Carmine, things between them relaxed as she made herself at home. It was platonic, except for the occasional kiss and gentle touch.

Exhausted, Carmine grew wearier every day. Nightmares plagued his sleep and he tried his best to stay sober, but the liquor seemed to call to him. Haven never said a word about it, but he could see the concern in her eyes whenever she saw him take a drink. The looks got to Carmine, guilt chipping away at him every time he swallowed the harsh liquid.

But it wasn't enough to make him stop.

Despite that, things were going well—almost *too* well, in fact. Carmine was waiting for everything to cave in around them. It felt too good to be true, like he had missed the fine print listing an expiration date.

People left them alone, though, much to his surprise. He thought for sure his brother would be knocking the door down to see Haven, or Corrado would be calling to deal with business, but there was nothing.

No visits, no phone calls, not a goddamn thing.

It was almost a week later when there was finally a knock on the door. Carmine begrudgingly opened it, surprised to see a mailman standing on the porch. He glanced down at an envelope in his hand, squinting as he read the name. "Carmine DeMarco?"

"That's me."

"Certified mail," he replied, handing a small card to Carmine to sign. He scribbled down his name before giving it back, and he handed Carmine the letter. He thanked him before shutting the door, strolling to the living room and plopping down on the couch beside Haven. He saw it was from the lawyer and tore the envelope open, pulling out a piece of paper.

"What's that?" Haven asked.

His eyes scanned the letter. "They're reading my father's will on Monday. Apparently he left me something."

"Why do you sound surprised?" she asked. "You're his son."

"I don't know," he said, shrugging as he set the paper down. "It still doesn't feel real. I mean, I know it is—I know he's gone. I fucking *saw* it. But it's still hard to believe it really happened."

"I bet," she replied. "Do you want to talk about it?"

He shook his head. "That's the last thing I even want to *think* about right now."

"Okay," she said, leaning over and pushing Carmine backward on the couch. She wrapped her arms around him and settled her head onto his chest as he grabbed the remote, turning on the TV and flipping through channels. They stayed that way the rest of the evening, forgetting about everything except what was happening within the walls of the house.

Once again, it didn't last. The next day, at the same exact time, there was another knock on the door. Carmine grumbled as he walked over to it, pulling the door open. The same mailman was standing on the porch, holding a familiar-looking envelope in his hand. "Fucking déjà vu. Weren't you *just* here for this shit?"

He nodded and looked down at the envelope in his hand. "Haven Antonelli?"

"Oh, yeah," he responded, opening the door farther and yelling for Haven. She appeared, looking between Carmine and the mailman in confusion. He motioned toward the letter. "It's for you, *tesoro*."

"Me?" she asked with surprise, taking the card from the man. She signed her name to the bottom of it, her handwriting precise and perfect cursive. He smiled watching her, knowing how hard she fought to learn to do that. She handed the card back and he gave her the envelope, telling her to have a good day before departing. She didn't respond, just stood at the door staring at it.

"Why are you surprised?" he asked, playfully repeating her words from the day before. "You're his son's girlfriend."

She glanced up at Carmine and raised her eyebrows. "Am I?"

"Are you what?"

"Am I your girlfriend?"

He hesitated at her question. "I don't know, are you?"

She smiled. "I asked you first."

"Do you think it's too soon?"

"I don't know, do you?"

He stared at her as he tried to make sense of their conversation. "I don't know. This is fucking ridiculous, Haven."

"It is," she said, turning her attention back to the envelope in her hand. "I wonder what he left for me."

"Could be anything," he replied as she opened it and read the paper giving her the time and date to appear. "Money, property . . . who knows."

"But why?" she asked. "None of that matters to me."

He shrugged. "I guess we'll find out on Monday."

They spent the weekend together, catching movies and having dinner as he showed her around Chicago. Monday approached quickly and he dressed around noon, putting on some black slacks and a white button-down shirt, trying to look halfway decent since Corrado would be there. He slipped on a pair of black and white Nike's and headed downstairs while Haven was in the shower, opening the freezer and pulling out the bottle of Grey Goose. He took the top off the bottle and brought it to his lips, taking a big swig. It burned his throat but soothed his nerves, his anxiety lessening almost immediately.

They made it to the lawyer's office at exactly a quarter after one, right when the will reading was set to start. Haven sat in a large black office chair around the long wooden table, and Carmine pulled out the chair beside her to sit down. She smiled and reached under the table, taking his hand. The family surrounded them—Celia and Corrado, Dominic and Tess. Even Carmine's grandmother was present, although she looked less than happy to be there with them.

Mr. Borza cleared his throat to get started. "Everyone here knew Vincent well, so I think we can all agree that he wouldn't mind if we kept it informal. He left a letter with his wishes, so I'm just going to read it."

Haven fidgeted in her chair, looking at Carmine anxiously. He squeezed her hand, hoping she would relax as Mr. Borza started reading.

It's with a heavy heart that I write this. I'm sorry for any pain I've caused you all. Everything I've done has been with you in mind, and I know I've made mistakes, but I've always tried to do what I felt was best. I don't expect you all to understand, but I hope with time you'll find peace with my decision. I assure you I have.

During the next twenty minutes, property was divided and personal items were bequeathed. The house in Durante went to Dominic, while the place in Chicago was officially turned over to Carmine. Tess was given a vast savings bond—as was Dia, who couldn't be there—while he left his mother enough money to sustain her.

Celia was left a bunch of mementos, while Corrado was given the key to a storage unit. The rest of his assets, his stocks and bank accounts, were to be split equally between Carmine and Dominic.

The reading was winding down when Haven's name was finally

read. The eyes of everyone in the room darted to her. She fidgeted from the attention, the apprehension clear on her face.

"I'm leaving you an envelope," Mr. Borza read. "It seems petty in comparison to what the others have been given, but I don't think you'll mind. What's inside is selfishly as much for me as it is for you, and I wish I would have delivered it in person like I originally planned, but this will have to do."

Mr. Borza held a white envelope out to Haven and she took it carefully. Curiosity burned inside of Carmine but he knew it was none of his business, so he turned his focus back to the lawyer.

"I have one last request," Mr. Borza read, "a favor to ask of my son, Carmine."

Carmine rolled his eyes. "Why am I not surprised?"

Everyone laughed as Mr. Borza continued. "I ask that he go to Saint Mary's Catholic Church and meet with Father Alberto. I left something there, something I think he'll someday need."

Mr. Borza set the letter down on the table. "That's it."

Carmine glanced at Haven, fighting back the emotion flooding him, and tensed when he saw tears streaming from her eyes. She had torn the envelope open and it sat on the table in front of her, her hand clutching a piece of paper she had pulled from it.

"*Tesoro*, what's wrong?" he asked quietly, reaching over and wiping the tears from her cheeks. She looked at him and shook her head before hesitantly holding the paper out to him. He took it carefully, smiling as he read the words scribbled in the middle.

You were worth it.

———

"We should celebrate," Celia said. "Have a family dinner in honor of Vincent. We can go out somewhere, or I can cook."

"I'll do it," Haven chimed in, shoving the paper back in the envelope.

"You don't have to, dear."

"I know," she said. "I haven't really cooked a meal in so long, since I was on my own. It'll be nice to do it again."

Celia smiled. "Would you like to borrow my kitchen?"

"No, I can do it at home." Almost instantly her eyes widened and she started stammering. "I mean, you know, at Carmine's."

A smile tugged the corner of Carmine's lips. *Home.*

"I know what you mean, sweetheart." Celia winked. "And I'm sure I speak for everyone when I say we'd love to have your cooking again."

"Hell yeah," Dominic declared. "I've missed it."

———————

A few hours later, Carmine stood near the doorway of his kitchen, watching as Haven fluttered around, humming to herself. Groceries covered every inch of his counter, more food than had been brought into his house in over a year.

"So what do you need me to do?" He knew enough to make a sandwich, but starting from scratch was something he had never had to do. "I should do something."

He hoped Haven didn't have high expectations, because he was probably going to fuck things up . . . as usual.

"Uh, can you start the chicken?" she asked.

He eyed the whole chicken wrapped in packaging on the counter. "Start it, like, put it in the oven?"

"No, I need you to clean it."

His brow furrowed in confusion. "What do you mean, 'clean it'? I'm not plucking a fucking chicken."

She rolled her eyes. "It doesn't have feathers, but you have to wash it out."

He didn't like the sound of that. "Do I just wash it in the sink or what?"

She nodded and grabbed a cutting board, setting it on the counter beside the sink. "Pull the insides out and run cold water over it."

He grabbed the chicken and set it down on the cutting board, grabbing a knife and slicing open the packaging. Grabbing one of its legs, Carmine turned it around so the opening faced him. He stared at it for a moment with disgust before glancing at Haven. She was busy cracking raw eggs into a bowl of torn bread to make stuffing.

"I'm supposed to stick my hand up there?" he asked, cocking an eyebrow at her when she nodded. He took a deep breath and thrust his hand inside, cringing at the feel of the cold poultry against his skin. He came upon a package of some sort and grabbed it. "What is this, anyway?"

"It's the giblets," she said, shrugging. "Neck, liver, gizzard, heart."

Carmine's eyes widened as he yanked his hand out, taking a step back in disgust. "What the fuck? Why is that in there, Haven? Who wants a chicken heart?"

Haven grabbed the package and tossed it in the trash. "People make gravy and stuff with them or just eat them whole."

"People eat the chicken's heart?" he asked, repulsed. "Please tell me you've never fed me that shit."

She shook her head, laughing. "No, I haven't. I wouldn't be surprised if someone else did and you never knew it, though." She grabbed the chicken and set it in the sink. "Can you wash it out, please?"

"Sure thing."

He turned on the water and attempted to hold the chicken under the faucet, giving up after a moment and instead grabbing the spray hose. He pressed the trigger, water firing out of it like a gun, and hosed the chicken down. "Is that it?"

Haven wasn't paying attention to him, wrist deep in a bowl of stuffing, the gooey bread sticking to her fingers.

"Haven."

"What?"

He pointed the hose at her when she looked his way, on a whim pressing the trigger at close range. She gasped as a blast of water shot her neck, instinctively flicking her hands as she tried to shield herself. Raw stuffing flew in his direction, a clump of it smacking him in the face.

"You bi—" He cut himself off abruptly as her eyes widened, choosing to shoot her again instead of finishing.

Chaos erupted as she dodged toward him, trying to pry the hose from his hands. They wrestled for it, shoving and grabbing, as water from the spray soaked both of them. Haven managed to wiggle past him and got her hand on the faucet, turning the water off as laughter erupted from her chest. "I can't believe you. I'm soaked!"

"You started it." He wrapped his arms around her from behind. "You ignored me."

"I didn't hear you."

"Same difference."

Wiggling out of his grasp, she grabbed the bowl of stuffing and pushed it toward him. "Can you handle the rest?"

He considered her question. "As long as it doesn't involve any fucking voodoo shit with chicken hearts."

She laughed. "Forget about it."

"No, tell me what to do. Just gimme a job that doesn't deal with organs."

"Or water," she mumbled, looking around. "Can you, uh, chop vegetables?"

"Yeah, I can do that." He smirked. He could work a knife, at least.

Haven pulled out some carrots, celery, potatoes, and onions, and she gave Carmine instructions, but all he heard was that he needed to cut them up.

They were vegetables—how hard could it be?

Haven shoved her mixture in the chicken, instructing Carmine to throw the vegetables in the pan with it. He chopped the celery and carrots with no problem but the potatoes were trickier because she didn't tell him to peel them first.

Or did she? He hadn't been listening.

Carmine got to the onion and eyed it suspiciously. Haven

looked at him as he removed the skin, but she stopped him before he could cut into it.

"Do you want me to do that?" she asked. He shook his head and she reached past him, grabbing some vinegar and rubbing it on the cutting board. "Vinegar messes with the chemical process so it doesn't burn as much."

He raised his eyebrows curiously. "*Jeopardy*?"

"Just a trick I picked up along the way. Open flames help, too. I can get you a candle."

"I don't need a candle, Haven. I can handle an onion."

She smiled but didn't respond. Carmine took his knife, cutting the ends off of the onion before slicing it down the center. The moment it came apart, the gases hit Carmine and he blinked rapidly as his eyes started to burn.

Every cut seemed to intensify the sting. He squinted, his eyes welling with tears. It got so bad after a few minutes that his vision blurred, and he blinked to clear it, only succeeding in pushing the tears over the edge. He groaned and cut faster, turning his head to the side to brush the tears away with his arm. He lost focus, cutting blindly, and cursed as pain shot through his finger.

He dropped the knife and pulled his hand away in shock, seeing the spot of blood form. It was a small cut, barely anything at all, but the juices from the onion made it burn. He stuck his finger in his mouth as a natural reaction and cringed at the rusty onion taste.

Haven pulled his hands away from his face, frowning. "Are you okay?"

He nodded and she pulled him to the sink, placing his hands under a stream of cold water, washing his cut.

"Look at you, fixing me up," he said. "When did we change places?"

"When you decided to try to cook."

Carmine splashed some water on his face before turning off the faucet and grabbed a towel as he leaned back against the counter. He watched Haven as she finished cutting the onion, feeling inadequate when it didn't seem to affect her. She preheated the oven and worked quickly, throwing together their food with ease.

Once she had it all in the pan, she turned to Carmine with a smile. "When the oven's ready, can you put the chicken in? I need to go change."

"Sure."

He stood there for a minute after she left until a string of beeps sounded through the kitchen. Carmine grabbed the pan and stepped toward the stove, oblivious to the puddle of water on the floor. His foot skidded in it as he slipped, absentmindedly letting go of the pan as he caught himself. He managed to stay on his feet but the pan hit the floor, the chicken and vegetables scattering around the kitchen.

He scrambled, grabbing the ingredients and shoving them back in the pan, as footsteps quickly descended the stairs. Cursing under his breath, he grabbed the chicken just as Haven walked back in.

She gasped, freezing in the doorway as she surveyed the mess.

"Five-second rule?" he suggested, holding the chicken up by its leg.

"When's the last time the floor was washed?"

"Does this count?" he asked, motioning toward the puddles.

"No."

"Then, uh . . ." He paused, calculating. ". . . Eleven years ago when my mother lived here."

She just stared at him, blinking. He dropped the chicken, letting it hit the floor with a splat, and reached into his pocket for his phone. He dialed Celia's number and waited as it rang. "Yeah, uh, can we reschedule dinner for tomorrow night? Great. Thanks."

He hung up with a sigh and looked over at Haven. "How do you feel about Chinese?"

"Chinese is great," she said, sliding her eyes to the chicken on the floor. "Salmonella? Not so much."

———

The church pew felt like steel beneath Carmine, his entire bottom half numb and tingling. Restless, he tapped his foot, trying to pay attention to the service, but it all sounded like *blah, blah, blah* to him.

"Why's he fidgeting?" Gia asked, her voice a mock whisper that seemed to echo through the church. Worshipers in the surrounding rows turned to look, scowling. "He looks like he's possessed! There's a demon in that boy!"

Celia quietly scolded her mother while Corrado let out a low, bitter laugh. "It's called addiction. He hasn't had a drink today."

Gia sneered. "Don't let him take communion then. He'll steal all the wine."

Carmine rolled his eyes, relaxing back into the seat, but his leg steadily bounced as Haven grabbed his hand. What made him decide to tag along for Sunday Mass, he wasn't sure, but he certainly regretted it now. Sweat formed along his brow as anxiety crept through his veins, bubbling up under the surface of his flushed skin.

The rest of the service dragged by slowly. He sat in the pew during communion, ignoring the snide comments that slipped from his grandmother's lips as she moved past to join the procession to the altar. Haven remained right beside him, silently absorbing everything, her eyes wide with innocent fascination.

She had never been inside a church before.

After Mass ended, Carmine pulled Haven into the main aisle. He made it only a few steps before stopping, hesitating as he glanced at her. "Can you ride home with Celia and Corrado?"

Her brow furrowed with confusion, but she nodded, not questioning him. He gave her a quick kiss, making sure they would get her home safely, before he headed toward the front of the church. Father Alberto stood at the altar, talking to a few parishioners. He noticed Carmine's presence and excused himself, making his way over to him. "Ah, Mr. DeMarco, do you need to use my telephone again?"

Carmine chuckled, pulling out his cell phone. "No, I'm covered today."

"A ride?"

He pulled out his keys. "All set there, too."

"So what can I do for you?"

"I was hoping we could talk."

Father Alberto smiled. "Absolutely."

The priest led Carmine into the back office, the same one the two of them had sat in before, and motioned for him to take a seat. Carmine nervously ran his hand through his hair as he sat down, remaining quiet as the priest settled into his chair.

"It's good to see you," Father Alberto said. "I wanted to catch you at the cemetery after Vincenzo's funeral, but you were preoccupied with the young woman. I didn't want to interrupt."

"Yeah, that's Haven. She, uh . . . she's . . ."

"I know who she is," Father Alberto said. "I've heard quite a bit about her."

"From my father?"

"Oh, that I cannot say." The priest smirked, a twinkle in his eye. Definitely his father. "Confessions are confidential."

"Even after the person's dead?"

"Definitely. Your relationship with God doesn't end with death, son."

"I'm not surprised," Carmine muttered, gazing across the desk at the priest. "That's sorta why I wanted to talk to you. When they read my father's will, he asked me to do him a favor. He wanted me to come here . . . said he left something."

The priest nodded, not an ounce of surprise registering in his expression. He had been expecting him. "That he did. But before I give it to you, tell me something."

"What?"

"How do you feel?"

Sighing, Carmine shook his head. "How does it *look* like I feel?"

"You seem to be holding it together pretty well."

"Yeah, well, looks are deceiving."

"Nonsense. Maybe you're the one who can't see."

Carmine paused, hesitating for a fraction of a second, but the weight of his grief became too heavy to hold back. The dam broke, the words gushing out in a furious unyielding wave of emotion. It flooded the office, nearly drowning Carmine as he choked on the confession of his sins.

Father Alberto gazed at him, silently taking in his rant, and didn't speak until Carmine finished. There was nothing formal about it, no asking for forgiveness from God or man. It was just Carmine and his truth, and the one person who could hear it without looking at him differently.

The one person who could hear it and never tell a living soul.

"How do you feel now?" the priest asked when the office grew silent again.

"I feel like I need a drink," he muttered.

The priest laughed lightly. "I'll tell you what you can do instead."

"I don't need Catholic penitence," Carmine said. "I'm not fasting or repeating Hail Mary a dozen times. That's bullshit."

"Ah, I wasn't going to tell you to," he said. "I was merely going to suggest you make a list. Write down the names of everyone you feel you've wronged and find a way to make it right again someday."

"That would take the rest of my life."

Father Alberto shrugged. "You have something better to do? I once knew a man who tried to drink his pain away. He drank to forget his family, he drank to dull the loss of a life, and when he finally sobered up, he had to make up for it somehow. He was righting his wrongs until the day he died."

Carmine gaped at him. *His father?*

"Speaking of which, this was left here." Father Alberto reached into his desk, pulling out a long gold chain and holding it up. A simple gold band swung from it, Carmine's chest aching at the sight. He recognized it, had seen it thousands of times, on the finger of the first woman he ever loved and later around the neck of the first man he revered.

His mother's wedding band.

"I'm sure you know what to do with it," the priest said, handing it to him.

Carmine carefully put the chain around his neck and concealed it in his shirt. The metal felt cold against his bare chest. "Thanks."

"You're welcome. I also noticed you didn't take communion. Would you like to do it now?"

Carmine shook his head as he stood. "Maybe next time."

"Next time," the priest mused as Carmine headed for the door. "I'll take that. It means you might be back some day."

———————

Twenty-four hours later, the six of them met at the Moretti home—Haven and Carmine, Celia and Corrado, Tess and Dominic—for a family dinner to honor Vincent's life. It had been moved from Carmine's house, since he didn't even have a dining room table, and Haven and Celia went in together on cooking the meal.

They gathered around, plates piled high with food, and shared laughs as they ate to their hearts content. Dia was the only one missing, having returned to her life in Charlotte. That weighed heavily on Haven's mind during dinner as she thought about the life waiting for her back in New York. Kelsey had called her dozens of times, but Haven had been too conflicted to return any of those calls.

"This is nice, having us all here," Celia said. "I tried to get Mom to join us, but she wouldn't."

"Meno male," Corrado muttered.

"Hey, she's not that horrible." Celia paused as everyone cast her skeptical looks. "Okay, so she's a handful. But she's relied on Vincent a lot the past few years, so the rest of us are going to have to step up now that he's gone."

"I hardly know her," Dominic said.

"Same here," Carmine replied. "And what little I do know says she doesn't want shit to do with any of us."

"Not true," Celia interjected. "She's just stubborn."

Corrado scoffed. "I mean no disrespect, *bellissima,* but your mother's issues reach far beyond sheer tenacity. We both know she has a deliberate cruel streak."

"Maybe so, but she's family."

"True, which is why I'll do what's expected of me," Corrado replied. "Doesn't mean I'll like it, though. I have no idea how Antonio dealt with her all those years. The man was a saint."

"My father?" Celia asked. "Did we even know the same man?"

"Every man sins, Celia. Even the saints."

Dinner wore on, as did the conversation. It was well past nightfall when they separated, Tess and Dominic heading back to Indiana, while Carmine and Haven made their way down the block. All was silent between them, their fingers loosely entwined as they strolled along. Carmine seemed content, his shoulders relaxed, but something brewed in his expression. He stopped abruptly a few feet from the blue door, his hand slipping from Haven's as she continued on.

She turned to him at the loss of connection, seeing the furrow of his brow and the hard line of his lips. "What's wrong?"

"Tell me about New York."

She raised her eyebrows. "Now?"

"Yes."

"But I already told you."

"You told me what was wrong about it, what you were missing, but I wanna hear the good. You know, the dream. *Your* dream."

He didn't say it, but she saw it in his eyes: He wanted to know if leaving her had really been a mistake.

"Well, New York was busy, just like you said the city would be," she started. "There was always something going on. People everywhere."

It all spilled out of her, every detail of her life there, as the two of them stood along the street in the darkness. She held nothing back, wanting him to know she had had a good life. It may not have been perfect, but things rarely were.

Carmine listened intently, drinking in every word, and didn't speak until she was done. "You love it there," he said quietly.

"I do." She smiled. "I really love it."

They stared at each other again as that truth hung in the air between them. Haven watched his expression slowly shift, another question forming in his eyes. She didn't address it, not acknowledging its existence, instead waiting for him to be the one. She waited for him to ask, for him to gather up the courage to say the words.

Love me more, his eyes said.

"Do you, uh . . . ?" He ran his hands down his face as he let out a deep sigh. "Would you stay?"

"Stay?"

He nodded. "Stay here."

"I would."

The corner of his mouth twitched as he restrained a smile. "Will you?"

"Stay?"

"With me." He cleared his throat nervously. "You know, stay with me?"

She opened her mouth to respond, but the words didn't have time to escape her lips. Something in Carmine snapped, his anxiety getting the best of him.

"Christ, I can't believe I just asked you that. What the fuck is wrong with me? It's not right! I can't ask you to choose me!"

She grabbed his arm, stopping him as he started pacing. "You're not asking me to choose you. There's no choice about it. It's always been you. Your father once told me that we always have a choice, but I think he was wrong. I think sometimes things choose us. It's like with breathing. It's natural. It's a part of us. It just happens. We can hold our breath and try not to breathe anymore, and it'll work for a few minutes, but we'll eventually pass out and nature takes over. We can't just *not* breathe, just like I can't just *not* love you."

"But New York," he said. "Your life."

"The best parts of life have nothing to do with a place. Love, friendship, happiness . . . I don't need to be in New York to have those things. I have it all here."

"But school? Painting? What about that?"

"I can do those things anywhere, Carmine. But you . . . you're in Chicago."

The hopeful smile twisted his lips, held back no more. "Clean slate?"

"As clean as our slate can get."

"Which is still pretty fucking dirty."

She laughed, watching him for a moment before extending her hand. A nervous blush warmed her cheeks. *Clean slate.* "I'm Haven."

"Carmine." He took her hand. "You have an interesting name, Haven."

"It means a safe place," she said.

"I know," he replied, entwining their fingers again. "And something tells me it fits you perfectly."

43

The heads of the five families gathered around a long table in the back room of a swanky Italian restaurant just outside of New York City. Their unrestrained chatter overshadowed the music from the violinist in the main dining room, their laughter and exuberance palpable from the parking lot.

The hostess pointed Corrado in their direction the moment he stepped inside, no words necessary. They had been expecting him. He approached the men, personally greeting each one before slipping into the only empty chair.

"Moretti," the Don of the Calabrese family said. "We're glad you could join us."

Corrado tipped his head. "The pleasure's all mine."

Drinks flowed as the men discussed everything from politics to music, side skirting business issues for most of the night. The conversation was fluid, almost friendly, but Corrado wasn't fooled—he was being tested. They watched his every move and weighed his every word, gauging whether or not they wanted to do business with him. He had met them all before while on the job, but this was different.

This was the interview of his life.

"What brings you to New York?" Sergio Geneva, head of the Geneva faction, asked. "How long are you here for?"

"Just for the night," Corrado said. "Brought my nephew and his girlfriend."

"So personal reasons?"

"Mostly."

The Calabrese Don looked at Corrado across the table. "I'm glad you're here. There's something I wanted to talk to you about. This friend of mine, Sammy Graves . . . he opened up this new casino. You know which one I'm talking about?"

"Of course."

"He's a good guy, on the straight and narrow. Got a family and kids. I tried to help him out, get his place off the ground upstate, give him a line of credit, but he declined. Wanted to do it himself, every bit of it legal."

"That's honorable," Corrado said.

"So I'm sure you can see how this deal he made with Chicago is a bit of a thorn in his side. He never wanted that, you know, never wanted to make deals."

"Understood," Corrado said. "You tell him he has nothing to worry about with Chicago. A friend of yours is a friend of mine."

The Don raised his glass. "I'll pass the message along."

"How's the truce in Chicago?" another of New York's dons asked.

He considered the question. "Delicate."

"O'Bannon still pushing his luck?"

More like Sal pushed him over the edge first. "It's only a matter of time, I figure, before he tests us again."

"You let us know when that happens," he said. "Anything you need, you just ask. We're all friends here."

Corrado nodded, picking up his glass to take a sip as the conversation once more switched to things of no consequence. Although his expression remained stoic, his eyes hard and dark as he portrayed the cold man they knew him as, satisfaction glowed inside of him.

He glanced down the table, his eyes connecting with Johnny Amaro, boss of the Amaro family and one of the few men Corrado had considered a true personal ally over the years. His family had run that faction since the beginning, passed down from father to son for decades. Johnny raised his glass in silent celebration.

Nailed it.

———

Cardboard boxes packed the living room of the downstairs apartment in the brownstone on Eighth Avenue, stacked one on top of another and filled to the brim. They were sectioned off into two piles: some to take along, others to leave behind. Haven's life was once more being categorized and evaluated, things disposed of as she moved on with life.

A bittersweet sensation collected in her chest, happiness and sadness colliding as she finished packing her things to move to Chicago. It was getting to follow your dreams, only to have to turn your back on others. It was breaking one promise in order to keep another, a feeling she suspected Carmine could relate to.

"You know, you don't have to do this," he said, standing in the middle of the room, his hands in the pockets of his jeans. "We can work something out."

She glanced at him. "Like what?"

"I don't know." He shrugged. "We could commute."

"Commute?"

"Yeah, you stay here, I stay there. We visit when we get the chance."

"Is that what you want?"

"No."

Haven laughed to herself, placing the last of her books in a box. She picked up the journal belonging to Maura and opened it, haphazardly flipping through the pages as she considered his words. She came to a page about halfway through, reading an inscription in red marker at the top of the page.

Sometimes I lose perspective, but it helps to stop and look around.
I may not have it all, but I have more than enough. And enough,
it seems, is more than most have.

Haven set the book in the box before closing it. "We have something a lot of people don't have, you know."

"What?"

Smiling, Haven shoved the box of books to the side along with the other belongings she planned to keep. "A chance. We aren't promised tomorrow, so we shouldn't take today for granted."

Carmine helped her pack the rest of her things before excusing himself to make a call. He slipped to the bedroom as Haven stood in the living room, surveying the boxes. A commotion rang out in the foyer of the building, and Haven swung around just as the front door to her apartment thrust open, slamming into the wall.

Kelsey appeared, her wide eyes frantic like a mad woman. Haven was about to greet her friend when she bolted forward, yelling hysterically. "What the hell? Where have you been? What happened? What are you doing?" Kelsey spun in a circle, pointing at the boxes. "Are you moving? Really? Are you in some kind of trouble? Why haven't you called?"

The bedroom door yanked open then as Carmine burst in. "What's with the fucking shrieking?"

Kelsey blinked rapidly as her attention darted to him. "Who are you?"

Carmine narrowed his eyes. "Me? Who the hell are *you*?"

Haven let out a deep sigh as she waved between the two of them. "Carmine, this is my friend Kelsey. Kelsey, this is my, uh . . . Carmine."

The two stared at each other, neither one acting as if they had heard her. Kelsey's expression softened eventually, though, her eyes turning from panicked to suspicious. "I might've heard about you once or twice."

"Likewise."

Rolling her eyes at their standoff, Haven scanned the apartment, making sure everything was boxed. The white walls were barren, the place suddenly feeling much smaller than before.

"So you are?" Kelsey asked. "You're moving?"

Haven turned to her friend, guilt flaring inside of her. "I am."

"Why?" Kelsey's eyes darted from Haven to Carmine. "Let me guess . . . because of *him*."

Carmine stood there, arms folded across his chest, mouth twitching like he was fighting the urge to interject.

"No, not because of him," Haven said. "*For* him."

"Is there a difference?"

"A smart man once told me there was."

Kelsey sighed. "Look, Hayden, I—"

"Hayden?" Carmine interrupted, brow furrowed. "What the fuck?"

Haven frowned as she explained. "That's my name here."

"Why?"

"Corrado's idea," she muttered. "He picked it."

"Wait, what?" Kelsey shook her head in confusion. "Your name *here*? Jesus, is that not your real name? Who are you?"

Uh-oh. "I can explain." Haven paused. "Well, actually, no I can't."

"You can't?"

She slowly shook her head. Kelsey's attention moved to Carmine, who shrugged just as his phone rang. "I can't explain either," he replied, glancing at the screen before holding his phone up. "But maybe he can."

———

An hour later, after awkward bouts of strained conversation between the three of them, Corrado showed up at the apartment. He stood in the middle of the living room as Kelsey sat on the couch, watching him warily.

"Do you know who I am?" he prompted.

"An officer of some kind?" she asked. "Isn't that what we decided?"

Corrado smirked. "I'm Corrado Moretti. My father, Vito, died in prison while doing a life sentence for a murder commissioned by Antonio DeMarco." He pointed to Carmine. "Antonio was his grandfather. His name's Carmine DeMarco, and his father, Vincent, died in a shootout at Salvatore Capozzi's house." He pointed to Haven. "Salvatore was her great-uncle. Her name's Haven Antonelli, and her father, Michael . . . well . . . let's just say it all comes full circle."

Kelsey gaped at him, her mouth hanging open.

"We're a family," he continued. "Sometimes we fight, and sometimes we go our separate ways, but at the end of the day, we're still a family. Do you understand what I'm telling you?"

After a few seconds of hesitation, Kelsey nodded. "I grew up in New York. I know all about the, uh . . ."

"The family," Corrado said, finishing her sentence for her.

"The family," she repeated. "My dad, he . . ."

"He's a senator who was ushered into Congress based on his last name. His father—your grandfather—was the senior senator from New York who headed a special committee to investigate organized crime. It was because of his committee that my father was eventually convicted."

"I, uh," Kelsey stammered. Something flashed in her eyes. Fear? "I didn't—"

"I don't believe in punishing the son for the sins of the father," Corrado continued, cutting her off. "Your father doesn't believe in it, either. He and I have a mutual understanding of sorts about it."

"You do?"

"Yes, you see, there's no such thing as coincidence. There are no accidents in life. Everything that happens is the result of a calculated move that leads us to where we are. And where we are, Kelsey, is right here in this apartment, having this conversation that never happened. *Capisce?*"

She nodded slowly. "Yes."

"Good." Corrado started for the door. "Haven, Carmine, we'll leave in the morning. I have one more loose end to tie up tonight."

The construction site stood still at near midnight, the equipment switched off hours earlier. There was no drilling, no shouting, no sawing—not even the hum of the generator echoed through the lot. It appeared abandoned, but a sliver of light shining from a window of the small trailer indicated otherwise.

Corrado quietly slid through the lot under the cloak of darkness, avoiding going near the motion-sensor security lights that aligned the place so not to draw any unnecessary attention. He headed to the trailer, walking swiftly yet silently, and gripped the door with his glove-clad hand. It was unlocked and gave no resistance when he pulled on it, opening right away.

Gavin sat hunched over at a small desk along the side, facing away from the door. His spine straightened when Corrado stepped inside, his shoulders tense and body rigid, but he didn't turn around to look. His focus remained on the notebooks scattered in front of him, illuminated by a dim lamp on the corner of the desk. Lines and columns of names and numbers filled the notebook pages, various statistics written down as probabilities were worked out in the margins like elaborate algebra problems. To a naïve person it might have looked like he was a student studying diligently for an arithmetic exam, but Corrado wasn't naïve . . . nor was he ignorant.

"You should never sit with your back to a door," Corrado said. "Didn't your father teach you that?"

"My father taught me a lot," Gavin replied coolly. "One of the biggest things he taught me is that if Corrado Moretti shows up at your door, you're about to have a really bad day."

The corner of Corrado's lips twitched. "It's good to see you, too."

Gavin's shoulders relaxed a slight bit as he slowly turned around to look at him, his expression guarded. Corrado couldn't blame the boy for being on edge.

"Did you need something?" Gavin asked tentatively. "I'm just going through the neighborhood books, but if you need me to do something . . ."

"No, quite the opposite, actually," Corrado replied. "I stopped by to tell you your services were no longer needed."

Corrado reached into his coat swiftly and Gavin tensed once more, pushing his chair back against the desk as far as it would go. Fear shone from his eyes as he braced himself for something that never came. Corrado merely pulled out a thick envelope and held it up. "What's the matter? Did you think I was here to kill you?"

Gavin answered at once. "No."

Knowing it was a lie, Corrado let out a sharp laugh as he tossed the envelope down on the desk, on top of one of the notebooks. "You haven't done anything that warrants death . . . that I know of. But I appreciate your help and wanted to give you a little something to express my gratitude."

Hesitantly, Gavin reached for the envelope and glanced inside. In it, wrapped together, was ten thousand dollars in crisp, new one hundred dollar bills. Gavin blinked rapidly as he skimmed through the cash but said nothing. Corrado had commissioned him months ago to keep an eye on Haven. Gavin had kept her safe during his absence, even periodically sending coded messages to the jail to update him.

"That's all I came for," Corrado said. "I'll let you get back to your books."

He reached for the door to leave when Gavin jumped up from his seat, clutching the envelope. "Wait."

Corrado turned back around. "What?"

Gavin shook his head as he stepped forward. "I can't take this. I know it was supposed to be a job, that I was supposed to keep an eye on her for you, but it doesn't feel that way. It feels wrong to take your money. It feels . . . dishonest."

Corrado raised his eyebrows. "That's an awful lot of feeling, Amaro. Your father also should've taught you there's no place for emotions in this life."

"I know that," he said, "but she's not really a part of this life. I know you said she's important to your family, but she's just a girl . . . a regular girl. Being with her wasn't work. It was kind of nice. And my father . . . well . . . one thing he did teach me was you don't rob a friend. And taking this feels a hell of a lot like stealing."

Corrado took the envelope and slipped it back into his coat with a shake of his head. "How did she get to you?"

"Huh?"

"I'm just curious how she won you over," he replied. "How she got under your skin and made it worth risking offending me by refusing my money."

Gavin sighed, his eyes drifting across the room to where a small white kitten lay, fast asleep in the corner. "Honestly? I don't know how it happened."

Corrado stared at him for a moment before turning to leave. "They never do."

44

Carmine stood quietly near the doorway of the art studio, leaning against the wall with his arms crossed over his chest. The large room looked almost like a warehouse, everything painted off-white except for the dark concrete floor. Bright fluorescent lights hung from the ceiling, illuminating the dozens of colorful paintings on display around the room. The artwork shone prominently, begging for attention, but nothing stood out more than the scene in the middle of the room.

Haven sat on a small brown stool, a canvas set up in front of her. Crumpled paper littered the floor around her feet, sketches she had discarded tinged with splatters of paint she had spilled throughout the day. The messy chaos that surrounded her fascinated Carmine, considering she was the most naturally organized person he had ever met. She couldn't let laundry pile up, floors needed to be swept every day, and dishes had to be washed as soon as they were dirtied. She believed everything had a place where it belonged, but at times like these, all of that went out the window.

When Haven painted, it was just her and the canvas. A tornado could hit and take the roof off the building and she probably wouldn't flinch. The apocalypse could come and Jesus could be standing right behind her, trying to take her to Heaven, and she would keep him waiting until she finished. No one interrupted her, not even Carmine, which was why he just stood there, waiting by the door.

He didn't mind, though. He enjoyed watching her. Seeing her there, listening to her humming as she worked a mere few feet in front of him, set his soul at ease. Not long ago he had been so close to giving up, exhausted by life's sudden twists and turns, but she showed up right when he needed her the most.

It had been a few months since she had moved to Chicago. A new school year started, and she had enrolled at a small art school downtown, while Carmine continued on with his life . . . the same life he had been involved in since leaving Durante. It was the same, the shift in power not altering his circumstances at all, but yet something was different. He approached it another way. He wasn't as reckless . . . not now that he had a reason to come home at night.

He still fucking hated it, though. Hated every second of life in *La Cosa Nostra* with every fiber of his being.

Haven sighed loudly, the sound exaggerated in the empty room. She stood and pushed her stool back to pace back and forth in front of the canvas. The painting of the tree looked fine to Carmine, but he could tell she felt something was wrong with it. She added a bit more color to the trunk before blending some yellow in with a few of the leaves, setting her paintbrush down as she took a step back. She eyed the canvas intently, tilting her head to the side as if looking at it from a different angle would somehow change the image.

Carmine chuckled under his breath and strolled over to her. She stiffened when she sensed him, taking a deep breath before relaxing again. "How long have you been here?"

"A little while," he responded, placing his hands on her hips. He pulled her body back against his and leaned down, nuzzling into her neck. "How did you know it was me?"

"I smelled you," she replied casually.

His brow furrowed. "Are you saying I stink?"

She laughed and nudged Carmine playfully as she turned around. "Of course not. You smell good, you know that."

"Yeah, I do." He smirked. "Like motherfucking sunshine, right?"

She rolled her eyes. "Don't get cocky."

"Hmmm, why not?" He pulled her closer, pressing himself against her. "I always liked being *cocky* with you."

She blushed and turned back to her painting.

"So a tree, huh?" he asked. "It's nice."

"It's wrong," she said, tilting her head to the side again as she studied it. "Don't you think so?"

"Uh, it looks like a tree to me. What's wrong with it?"

"I don't know," she said. "It's missing something. It doesn't feel like the same tree, does it?"

"What tree?" he asked. "The white tree of Gondor? The fucking whomping willow? The one Eve stole the apple from?"

"The tree in Durante," Haven said impatiently. "You didn't even recognize it, so obviously it's not right."

"It's a tree, *tesoro*. It has wood and leaves and acorns and shit. I'd say it's perfect."

"It doesn't have acorns," she said. "It's a sycamore tree. Does it really look like an oak tree? They're nothing alike."

He sighed. How was he supposed to know? "Haven, baby, you could tell me it was the Joshua tree and I'd agree because I can't tell the difference."

She let out an exaggerated huff as she looked at him. "This coming from the same person who spent nearly an hour picking out a Christmas tree that time?"

"What can I say? I'm finicky. I don't deny it. But not all of us have your memory. You see something and the picture of it is burned in your brain forever, but the only greenery I can identify is the kind I can smoke."

"You mean this kind?" she asked, picking up her paintbrush. She dipped the tip into the container of green paint and quickly drew the outline of a marijuana leaf on the corner of the canvas.

He laughed. "Yes, that kind, but you probably shouldn't have done that. You fucked up your painting."

She shook her head with frustration, sticking her paintbrush in a container of murky water. "It doesn't matter, Carmine. It was already fucked up."

He gaped at her. "What did you just say?"

"I said that it was already—"

"Christ, *tesoro,* you can't say that shit!" He cut her off before she could repeat herself. "Do you know what it does to me?"

She smiled, blushing, and her eyes darted directly to his crotch. Yeah, she knew *exactly* what it did to Carmine. Closing his eyes, he let out a groan.

"I'd apologize, but I can't honestly say I'm sorry," she admitted.

"Yeah, well, you shouldn't apologize then," he muttered. "You should always mean what you say and say what you mean."

"But you never say anything mean," she added.

His brow furrowed. "That's not a part of the saying."

"It fits."

"No, it doesn't. It's bullshit. Sometimes you *have* to say something mean."

She looked at Carmine incredulously. "There's never a time when you have to say something mean."

"Yes, there is."

Her eyes narrowed. "When?"

"Plenty of times."

"Name one."

He didn't balk at a challenge, not even one that came from her. "When someone says something mean to you first."

"Then you just walk away," she said. "Two wrongs don't make a right."

"Well, what if you *can't* walk away? What if they won't let you?"

"And you think saying something mean is going to *help* you if that's the case?"

She had Carmine there. "Well, what if you got something on you, like in your teeth. Shouldn't I tell you?"

"Yes, but that's not mean. That's helpful."

"What if it's something permanent though, like your nose? What if you have a crooked, fucked-up nose?"

Her hand immediately went to her face, her fingers running down the ridge of her nose as she eyed Carmine hesitantly. He groaned, realizing it sounded like he was telling *her* that. He recalled how self-conscious she had been years before and felt like an asshole. *Way to go, DeMarco. Insult her next time . . .*

"Not you, *tesoro*," he said. "I didn't mean you. Your nose is fine. Fucking great, even. I'm just saying, you know, hypothetically . . ."

"Well, hypothetically, why would it be necessary to tell me? It wouldn't be hurting you, so why hurt me?"

She had Carmine again. "Well, what if your painting sucked? Like this tree—what if it was honestly the worst tree ever painted?"

"It probably is."

"But what if it was for a grade, and I had to tell you so you wouldn't fail?"

"It *is* for a grade."

He looked at her with disbelief before glancing back at the canvas. "You painted a marijuana leaf on *schoolwork*?"

She shrugged. "It doesn't matter."

Her nonchalance stunned him. "There's something wrong with you."

She laughed. She fucking *laughed*. If she were ever going to prove Carmine right, it was then. There was *seriously* something wrong with her.

"I can start over," she said. "Maybe I'll paint something else."

"You shouldn't do that," he said. "I like this one."

"Why?" she asked, eyeing the painting peculiarly again. "It's just a tree."

"But it's *our* tree," he said. Hadn't they just been through that? "We climbed that motherfucker together twice. Fell out of it once. That makes it special."

The smile that curved her lips warmed Carmine from the inside. He loved that smile. It meant she was happy—that he had made her happy. There was no better feeling than that. After spending so many years doing nothing but disappointing everyone who came into contact with him, it was nice to do some good for once.

"Okay, then. Maybe I'll paint over it."

"Yeah, make some happy clouds to go with your happy little magical tree," he joked.

They stood there for a moment, engulfed in a serious silence as she mused over her painting, before Carmine grabbed her and pulled her to him again. She spun around with a laugh, wrapping her arms around him in a hug, but froze after a second when her hands slid down his back, reaching his waistband.

"Oh God, please tell me that's not . . ." She trailed off, pulling out of the hug. "Is that what I think it is?"

"Depends on what you think it is."

She gripped his waistband, her eyes narrowing. "You brought a gun in here, Carmine? You can't do that!"

"Why not?"

She gaped at him. "Because there's a sign on the door that says so! You can't bring concealed weapons in this place!"

"*Tesoro*, relax. I carry it everywhere—you know that."

"Yes, but *here*?" she asked. "It's unlawful!"

Now it was *his* turn to laugh. "We live in Chicago. Me just breathing in the direction of a gun is illegal. Would you rather I get rid of it completely?"

"Yes."

Her answer was quick and firm, catching him off guard. She looked at Carmine with certainty and he shook his head. "So you'd prefer me defenseless?"

She blanched. "Of course not."

"Then what's the big deal?"

"I don't want you to get caught."

"I won't."

"You can't know that."

"But I do," he said. "I know what I'm doing."

"All right, but—"

"No buts."

She huffed at the interruption and completely ignored him. "But why do you bring it places like here? I get that you need it for work, but why when you're with me?"

He shrugged. "You never know when something might happen."

"So? You never know when it might rain, but I don't see you carrying an umbrella everywhere just in case."

He chuckled at the absurdity of the comparison, even though she was completely serious. "The weatherman usually warns me when that's gonna happen."

"And you don't get warnings? Corrado doesn't tell you when something's going to happen? What happened to intuition?"

"Well, yeah, but I can't always plan. Sometimes I only have time to react."

She thought he was paranoid. Christ, he probably *was* paranoid, but rightfully so. He knew how ruthless the streets could be and if she were thinking clearly, she would see it too. He understood, though. His life still scared her. Hell, it scared Carmine just as much, but the best way to deal was to always be prepared.

And regardless of what she insisted, sometimes you had to be mean to make it. It was how the game was played. If you aren't the predator, you end up the prey.

"Besides," he added, "last I checked, a little rain couldn't kill you."

"But lightning can if it's a storm."

"And you think an umbrella would help you in that case?" he asked, throwing one of her earlier arguments back at her.

He waited for her to respond, figuring she would have something to say, but all he got was silence—completely tense, unnerving, motherfucking silence.

"Do you trust me?" he asked after a moment, knowing they were at an impasse and getting nowhere fast.

"Yes."

"Then trust me about this, okay? We can argue about trees and phrases and any other thing you feel passionate about, but just give me this."

She sighed, frustrated, but he knew that sound meant she was giving in. "Fine, but I get to pick where we go tonight."

He frowned. "Yeah, about that . . ."

It was a Friday, which had become their day. Their schedules conflicted a lot, with her in school and Carmine out doing whatever he was told to do, but Friday nights were the exception. It was when the two of them got to be together and do the things normal couples did, like seeing movies and going to fairs. It was the one night a week when they put everything aside, when they didn't have to think about the chaos in their lives, and they could finally just *be*.

Corrado seemed to understand, so he usually left Carmine alone that day. *Usually* being the key word. Sometimes he threw a wrench in their plans.

"There's this thing tonight. Everyone's supposed to be there."

"What kind of thing?" she asked, her eyes narrowing slightly.

"Just a thing," he said, shrugging. "The new underboss's son is getting married or whatever so they're having a get together at Sicillitas."

Typically those kinds of events took place at the Boss's house, but Corrado wasn't like the guys who used to run things. He tried to keep the Mafia out of his home, so special occasions were often spent in someone's business now. Sicillitas was an upscale Italian restaurant owned by one of the Capos.

"So you have to go," she said quietly.

"*We*," he corrected her. "Corrado specifically said 'You and Haven.'"

She frowned. He didn't blame her. He didn't want to go either, but Corrado was all about showing a strong front. He had gone out on a limb and vouched for her, something that made a few of the guys question his judgment. Haven integrating smoothly into their world was important to him.

Plus, even if Corrado would never admit it, Carmine was pretty sure he actually *liked* her being around.

"We won't stay long," he assured her. "The first chance we get, we'll get the fuck out of there and do whatever you want."

"Fine," she grumbled.

He watched as she gathered her stuff, cleaning up paints and throwing away the discarded papers. He felt bad for not helping, but he knew he would do more harm than good. This was her sanctuary, and you just don't go fucking with someone else's safe place.

She put on her coat and grabbed the painting of the tree before turning back to Carmine. "You ready?" he asked. She nodded and smiled softly, but it didn't reach her eyes. No, they were filled with dread, the happiness he had given her moments earlier forgotten.

It made his chest ache. He needed a drink. Or two. Or ten. Something—anything—to dull the bitter ache of disappointing her.

Carmine led her out of the studio and she got into the passenger seat of the Mazda, clicking her seat belt in place as he climbed in beside her. The drive home was silent, awkwardness surrounding them, seeping through Carmine's skin and twisting his insides. He hated when things got like that between them, because he never knew what to say to her. *Sorry you're annoyed,* tesoro. *I can't help I'm a loser* and *Get used to it, since I'll probably keep disappointing you* just didn't seem to cut it, even though it was how it usually made Carmine feel.

She said not a single word when they arrived home, grabbing her things and getting out of the car before he could even shut off the engine. She used her key and disappeared inside without waiting for Carmine. He took his time and she was nowhere to be found when he finally made his way into the house. He went straight for the refrigerator, opening the freezer and grabbing the chilled bottle of Grey Goose. He pulled the top off, tipping the bottle back and taking a long swig.

He leaned against the counter and sipped on the vodka. His

chest still ached, the alcohol doing nothing to ease his guilt, as he listened to the shower turn on and back off again on the second floor.

He heard her footsteps in the hallway eventually and replaced the top on the bottle, slipping it back in the freezer as Haven made her way downstairs. The moment he saw her, his heart skipped a beat. Her damp hair was slightly wavy, the dark locks nearly identical in color to her plain black dress. Her bare feet slapped against the wooden floor, exposing strikingly red painted toenails, but her skin, while scarred, remained untainted by makeup.

Simple, but beautiful. That was her.

Haven eyed Carmine peculiarly when she saw him lingering in the kitchen. "What are you doing?" she asked, her eyes drifting to the freezer before settling back on him. He didn't blame her for her suspicions. She knew him well.

"Nothing." It was true. Sort of. He wasn't doing a thing but standing there.

"What *were* you doing?" she clarified.

"Nothing," he said again. Not so true that time.

"Uh, okay," she mumbled, still watching Carmine as she walked to the sink. "Are you going to change before we go?"

He glanced at his clothes. He had on a tie, at least—seemed good enough to him. "Do I need to?"

She shrugged. "I don't think Corrado would be happy about the shoes."

His gaze shifted to his Nike's. "Yeah, you're right," he said, pushing away from the counter. He started to walk away but Haven grabbed his arm to stop him. He turned around, looking at her curiously, and she yanked Carmine toward her as she stood up on her tiptocs.

He froze, dumbfounded, as she smashed her lips to his. When he finally got his wits about him, he parted his lips to kiss her back, but she abruptly pulled away, letting go completely. She took a step back. "You were drinking."

There was no anger, not an ounce of hate in her voice. She wasn't accusing Carmine—it was a simple statement. He had been drinking.

"A little," he replied. She nodded and turned away to look out of the window. He stood there for a moment, but she didn't speak again. The subject was closed, nothing else to say.

He headed upstairs to the bathroom and glanced in the mirror, surveying his reflection after splashing water on his face. He hardly recognized himself some days. Dark, heavy bags aligned his bloodshot eyes, his skin dry from the fickle Chicago weather. He had slicked his hair back that morning with pomade so it appeared a shade darker, making him seem paler than usual.

He went into the bedroom and grabbed a pair of black shoes from the closet, sitting down on the edge of the bed to put them on. Haven walked in while he was tying them and scrunched up her nose. "Your shoes are scuffed."

"It doesn't matter. It's not like the military where I need to shine the sons of bitches."

"Are you sure?"

"Yeah, I'm sure," he replied as he glanced at his watch. It was already fast approaching eight o'clock, when Corrado had told Carmine to be there. "Are you ready?"

Carmine waited as she slipped on a pair of black heels, and they both grabbed their coats before heading out again. Haven was quiet as she got in the car, not speaking as he pulled away from the house. He fiddled with the radio anxiously, needing a distraction, and Haven just stared at him with a frown.

"What now?" Carmine asked, annoyed.

"*Nothing.*" She stressed the word, her answer speaking volumes. She was sending a message with that motherfucker. It was a *You asshole, who do you take me for? I can't believe you thought you could fucking fool me* kind of *nothing*.

"I'm sorry."

"Are you?"

"Yes."

"For what?"

He looked at her, knowing what she wanted to hear. She wanted him to apologize for drinking, but he couldn't do it. "I'm sorry for disappointing you," he said. "I hate that shit."

"I know," she replied, reaching over and stroking his cheek before running her fingers through the hair near his neckline. She hit a snag and he grimaced. "What *I* hate is when you do your hair like this."

He glanced in the rearview mirror at himself. Corrado preferred them to look clean-cut, but he hated it, too. "I kinda look like my fath—"

He gripped the steering wheel tightly, unable to even get the entire thing out. It had been four months . . . about sixteen weeks . . . one hundred and twenty-something days . . . and the wound was just as raw as it had been that fateful night. He still saw it sometimes when he closed his eyes, reliving the moment his father had taken his last breath.

Sometimes it was so hard he could barely breathe, in so much pain he felt like he was the one with the bullets lodged in his chest.

Haven massaged Carmine's neck as he focused on the road, trying to get himself back under control.

"So since someone's getting married, does that mean I can have whatever I want?" she asked offhandedly, distracting him from his thoughts.

His brow furrowed. "What?"

"Isn't it true when someone gets married, you can ask a Mafia boss for something and he can't refuse?"

It took a moment for what she had said to register. He laughed. "Have you been watching *The Godfather*?"

She blushed. "No."

"Well, it's not true, anyway," he said, shaking his head. "They say the day of the Boss's daughter's wedding he won't refuse anyone a favor, but it's bullshit."

"Oh," she mumbled.

"What would you want, though?" he asked curiously. "If you could have one wish granted, what would you ask for?"

"I don't know. What about you?"

"I'm happy," he replied. "There isn't really anything anyone could give me."

She looked at Carmine incredulously. "There *is* something someone could give you. Actually, it's what I'd ask for."

"What's that?"

"Your freedom."

Carmine wasn't sure what to say. "Well, too bad it doesn't work that way."

"Yeah, too bad."

They arrived at the restaurant within a few minutes. He led Haven inside and saw his uncle right away, sitting at a table in the back with Celia. A slew of men gathered around them like a massive human shield of protection, but Celia managed to spot them through the crowd. She waved, the movement catching Corrado's attention. He looked over as they approached, his expression blank, but Carmine could see the annoyance in his eyes.

"Up," he barked at the two guys sitting across from them. They didn't hesitate before pushing their chairs back, vacating them, and Corrado motioned toward the now empty seats. "Sit."

Haven immediately took a seat in the first chair, looking at Carmine apprehensively. He gave her a smile, trying to be reassuring, but the truth was he was just as nervous.

"You're late," Corrado said, glaring at Carmine from across the table.

He glanced at his watch: five minutes after eight. "I guess I am."

"You *guess* you are?"

"Yeah," he replied. "I tried to be on time, but I—"

"But nothing." His voice was sharp and Carmine shut up right away, a few people quieting down as they looked in their direction. "There's no excuse for tardiness."

"I know, I'm just saying—"

"I know what you're saying, Carmine," he interrupted again. "And *I'm* saying there's no excuse."

"Yes, and I—"

"He's sorry," Haven blurted out.

Corrado looked at her peculiarly, his expression unreadable. "Is he?"

She nodded hesitantly. "Yes, sir."

"Well, at least there's that."

Things were tense as Corrado continued to stare them down, Haven still fidgeting and making Carmine even more anxious. After a moment Celia sighed and shook her head, turning to her husband. "If you're done throwing your weight around, I'd like to eat."

Corrado finally broke eye contact with Carmine to look at her. "I'm not throwing my weight around."

"Yes, you are," she said. "You're just a big bully. You act like he *blatantly* ignored what time to be here. It was just a few minutes, no harm done."

"This time," Corrado retorted. "It might not mean anything right now, but five minutes can be a matter of life and death in other situations."

"Yes, *other* situations. Meaning not this one, so give the boy a break."

"He's not a *boy*, Celia," Corrado said, his expression darkening a bit.

"He is," she argued. "He's my nephew."

"He's my *soldato*."

"He was my nephew first."

"It doesn't matter. He's mine *forever*."

Carmine froze when Corrado spoke those words, a sickness brewing in the pit of his stomach. He had witnessed a lot of ridiculous conversations in his life but having them argue over him was surreal.

Celia pushed her chair back and stood. "I'm going to the ladies room."

Corrado shook his head when she stormed away and the underboss, sitting to his left, clapped him on the shoulder. "Ah, *chi non ha moglie non ha padrone.*"

Carmine smirked at his words and Corrado smiled, but it was forced. He was furious that Celia had challenged him in front of his men. He reached for his glass on the table in front of him, taking a drink as Haven leaned toward Carmine.

"What did that guy say?" she whispered, trying to be quiet, but Corrado overheard her.

He set his glass back down and answered before Carmine had a chance. "He said a man without a wife is a man without a master."

She tensed. "Oh."

"I forgot you don't speak Italian," he said. "Have you ever thought to learn?"

The color drained from her face at being put on the spot, the eyes of everyone nearby going straight to her. Most people within the organization knew by now she was a *Principessa* by birth, even though few of them ever had any actual contact with her. They were intrigued, naturally. Carmine understood their curiosity, but that didn't mean it annoyed him any less.

"Uh, yes," she said. "I've learned a little bit."

"From Carmine?"

She glanced at Carmine and he immediately felt bad, seeing the panic in her eyes. She was trying her best to stay cool on the surface, but he could tell she was a mess inside. "He's taught me some, yes."

"So I assume you know the bad words, then," Corrado said.

She nodded. "I know other things, too, though."

"Like?"

She looked at Carmine again, like she expected him to rescue her, but he couldn't. Even if he tried, Corrado would stop him.

She realized after a second that he wasn't going to say anything. She turned back to Corrado, picking at her fingernails under the table. "Like *ti amo* and *sempre*."

"And?"

"And *ciao. Buongiorno. Grazie. Prego.*" Her pronunciation was spot on. It was simple, but it was better than nothing. "And uh, *Vaffanculo?*"

They all just stared at her, the silence managing to grow even more awkward.

After what felt like an hour, Corrado's expression softened and a smile tugged at his lips. He let out a laugh—a genuine fucking laugh. "That was a curse."

"Oh." She turned bright red. "Carmine uses it a lot."

"Doesn't surprise me a bit."

There was quiet chatter as everyone relaxed, the Boss's demeanor influencing the others. The tension receded from the room and Haven loosened up, her posture no longer stiff. Celia returned, she and Corrado both relaxing as they whispered to each other. Carmine watched them, their natural chemistry obvious. Despite everything, the fighting and violence and outright bullshit their lives could sometimes be, they were *happy* together. They loved each other and it was the love that got them through everything else. As long as they had that, nothing would tear them apart.

Carmine glanced at Haven, reaching under the table and taking her hand. He squeezed it and she smiled softly, gazing back at him. He saw that same type of love in her eyes, the kind of love that was damn near unbreakable.

There was food and drinks, conversation and laughter. Time passed swiftly and Carmine found he actually enjoyed himself. A smile continuously graced Haven's lips as she talked to people, not seeming at all nervous to be around his kind.

His kind. He hated saying it, but it was true. *La Cosa Nostra* was his family. And like a real dysfunctional family, he fucking hated them most of the time.

He looked around the restaurant, seeing all types of people having dinner. There were couples and families, friends and business associates. All seemed content and relaxed, completely oblivious to the danger in the room with them. It was strange to Carmine how people didn't even flinch from their presence, like they were desensitized to violence and pain. They seemed ignorant to the fact that lifelong criminals surrounded them, their children and wives breathing the same air as cold, calculating murderers.

Well, most seemed oblivious. His gaze fell upon a man in the corner by himself, his attention focused on the tables surrounding them. His eyes locked with Carmine's after a moment, and even across the room he could see the coldness. The man certainly wasn't what he would call a friendly face.

Carmine stared him down for a while before the man stood, tossing some money on the table and walking out.

The night continued on, as did the food and drinks. The crowd thinned, thoughts of that man going right out along with the others.

"Can I get you guys anything else?" a waitress asked eventually, stepping over to their table. It was nearing ten in the evening. Corrado and Celia were a few feet away, talking to the soon-to-be bride and groom.

Haven shook her head, stabbing at the tiramisu on her plate with a fork. "No, thank you."

The waitress glanced at Carmine and he nodded, picking up his glass and holding it out to her. She walked away without a word, returning with another vodka and Coke. He thanked her, taking a drink as she moved on to the next table.

Haven set her fork down and looked at Carmine, her eyes wandering past him. "Do you know how they met?" she asked, motioning toward the couple.

"It was arranged," he replied.

"An arranged marriage? They do that?"

He shrugged and nodded at the same time, a half-assed answer since he wasn't sure how to explain it. "They've known each other since they were kids. They were just . . . put together, I guess. I don't know if that makes sense, but it's how most of them do it. They just pair off with other people in the life. It's easier that way."

She looked downright perplexed for a moment before understanding crept into her features. "Like Michael and Katrina."

He nodded. "And their parents before them. Pretty much everyone in here did it. They don't like outsiders coming in, so they stay in the inner circle. My father broke protocol."

"So did you," she said.

"I don't know, *tesoro*. You're one of us."

"*But* you didn't know that, and I definitely wasn't in your inner circle."

"True."

"Would you have, though?" she asked. "Would you have come back here and eventually found someone like everyone else?"

"No."

"How do you know?"

"Because there's no one else for me," he replied. "These people care about bloodlines and rank and power and shit, but none of that matters to me. I'd never pursue a woman because of who her father is. Chances are I'd just hate her. In case you haven't noticed, most of the women in the life are spoiled, uptight bitches who feel like people owe them. And I refuse to accept the fact that I owe *anyone* a thing . . . except you, maybe. So, no thanks."

Haven shook her head. "So you'd just be alone?"

"If I'm gonna be miserable either way, I'd rather be miserable alone," he said. "Why are you asking, anyway?"

"I just wondered about it all," she said, still watching the couple. "Do you think those two love each other, at least?"

"It's possible," he replied. "Sometimes what they feel is real. I know Celia wouldn't stay with Corrado if she didn't love him, so it's possible those two will get married and be happy, too."

"And you don't think you would have ever tried?"

Her questions made his head spin. "I don't know."

"But don't you think it's important to have someone around who understands?"

Before he had a chance to even think about how to respond to that, Corrado and Celia started back in their direction. Celia took her seat while Corrado paused beside Carmine, eyeing him warily. "How many drinks have you had?"

He hesitated, looking at his half-empty glass. "Uh . . ."

"The fact that you have to think about it is answer enough," he said, holding out his hand. "Give me your keys."

Carmine's heart pounded hard as he took in his uncle's stern expression. He reached into his pocket and pulled out the keys to the Mazda. Corrado snatched them from him.

"Here," he said, tossing the keys to Haven. "Make sure he gets home safe."

"Yes, sir," she said quietly.

"There you go throwing your weight around again," Celia commented.

Corrado let out a slightly bitter laugh. "Well, he doesn't have a wife yet, so I'm the only master he's got for the time being."

Carmine fought the urge to roll his eyes as he picked up his glass when Corrado was called away from the table again. He turned to Haven after downing the rest of his drink. "You ready to go, *tesoro*? I've had my fill of *family* for the time being." He peeked at his aunt Celia. "No offense, of course."

"None taken," Celia said. "Go, have fun."

Haven stood and smiled as they walked away. They almost slipped out undetected, but Corrado spotted them as they neared the door and called Carmine's name. "Be available in case I need you, and next time wear cleaner shoes. How hard is it to shine them? It takes all of five minutes."

"Uh, yeah," he muttered. "I wasn't thinking."

Haven looked smug about it, but her expression shifted quickly when Corrado spoke once more. "Haven?"

She went rigid. "Yes, sir?"

"You did well tonight," he said. "It's been a pleasure."

Her eyes lit up. "Thank you, sir. I'm glad you invited me."

Carmine grabbed Haven's hand and tugged on it, wanting to get out the door before Corrado decided he had something else to say.

"Were you telling the truth?" Carmine asked as they strolled through the packed parking lot. "Are you glad he invited you?"

"Yeah," she replied. "They were all actually really . . . *nice*."

"Sure. The nicest motherfuckers I know, *tesoro*—like rainbows and sunshine."

She laughed, bumping against Carmine playfully. "You know what I mean. They weren't cold to me like I thought they'd be, since I am . . . or I mean, I *was* . . ."

"They aren't stupid," he interrupted, squeezing her hand. "Corrado would kill them if they disrespected you."

She seemed taken aback and stopped beside the car. "He'd really do that?"

"Of course he would," he replied. "Corrado doesn't have kids, and you're the closest thing he's got to a daughter."

Her eyes widened. "*Me?*"

"He vouched for you. In their minds, he gave you *life*. I mean, come on, Haven. He demanded your presence tonight, knowing you wouldn't want to be here. He only tortures his real family that way. You're in, whether you like it or not."

"I think I do," she said quietly. "Like it, I mean."

"Good. Now let's get out of here." He held out his hand. "Keys?"

She laughed dryly, pushing it away. "I don't think so. *I'm* driving."

She gave Carmine a playful wink as she walked around to the

driver's side. He rolled his eyes and grumbled, feigning annoyance, although he didn't mind if she drove. He trusted her. Always had and always would.

She started the car as he put on his seat belt, knowing she wouldn't leave the parking lot until he did. She adjusted the mirrors and fiddled with the seat so she could reach the pedals and he held his tongue, refusing to get upset over something so petty. Years ago he would have snapped, but losing her once gave Carmine a new outlook. The seat's position could be fixed, as could the mirrors. The entire car could be replaced, for that matter, but she was one of a kind.

Carmine glanced around as she situated herself, spotting a form trudging through the parking lot. His eyes narrowed as something clicked in his mind, recognition dawning. It was the man from the corner in the restaurant, the one that had left at least an hour before. He kept his head ducked as he weaved through the cars, but there was no doubt in Carmine's mind that it was the same man.

The guy slipped into a dark Chevy Camaro. He drove past them as Carmine quickly studied the car, getting a brief glimpse at the Illinois license plate. All he could make out were the first two letters, JK.

"Do you know that guy?" Haven asked, noticing he had been watching him.

Carmine shrugged it off. "No. He has a nice car, though."

The drive home from the restaurant was a hell of a lot different than the drive to it. Haven drove the speed limit—if that—while he lounged in the passenger seat, alcohol buzzing through his veins. Haven excused herself when they arrived home as Carmine locked up, making a point to enable the alarm for the doors and windows.

He strolled into the kitchen and took out his gun, sticking it in a top cabinet. Grabbing the bottle of Grey Goose from the freezer, he leaned against the counter and took a swig, closing his eyes and savoring the burn as it coated his throat. It was only a minute later that he heard Haven approach and he opened his eyes, seeing her in the doorway. "Whatcha wanna do, *tesoro*?"

She said nothing as she slowly strolled in his direction, having discarded her heels somewhere between the door and Carmine. He took a second drink as she paused in front of him, and she grabbed the bottle when he finished, gently taking it from his hands. Hesitating, deliberating, she brought it to her lips and tipped the bottle back. She grimaced as the liquor filled her mouth, the swallow bitterly painful by the look on her face.

Reaching behind Carmine, she tipped the bottle and slowly dumped the rest of it down the sink drain, her eyes remaining on him the entire time.

Carmine had a brief moment of panic. His insides seized up and he felt sick to his stomach, watching the liquor disappear. He pushed the feeling back, refusing to let it control him. He could stop if he wanted to . . . if he *needed* to. It wasn't the end of the world. There were more important things in life, and he didn't need the vodka to make it through his days.

He chanted that in his head, willing himself to believe it.

Haven grabbed his tie then, the knot loosening as she tugged on it. He offered no resistance, putting up no fight as she pulled him away from the kitchen counter and led him toward the stairs. She let go eventually but he didn't falter, blindly and wordlessly following her upstairs. His feet were heavy like concrete slabs, his body weary and mind just as tired, but obedience ran through his veins.

He closed the bedroom door when they made it there, the single click of the lock echoing loudly through the still silence. He glanced at Haven, watching in the light from the glow of the moon as she unzipped her dress and let it drop to the floor. The pressure in his chest, the burn and craving of the addict, lessened a bit when she turned to face him.

"Do you remember the first time we made love?" she asked quietly.

"Of course I do."

"You worshiped me that day," she said. "Actually, thinking about it, you worshiped me every time. You were so attentive and always made me feel your love, but I never really had the chance to do the same. I tell you I love you all the time, and I do . . . I love you so much, Carmine . . . but I don't show you enough."

"But you—"

She held her hand up to silence him before he could object. "Just shut up, okay? Why do you always have to talk?"

He cocked an eyebrow at her, a surprised chuckle escaping his lips as he waved for her to proceed. *Sassy.*

"I don't show you enough," she repeated. "You do so much, you go through so much in life, and you need to be shown love, too. You deserve to be worshiped."

Carmine remained right in front of the door, not daring to move. He held his breath, watching intently as Haven removed the rest of her clothes and stood in front of him completely naked. He slowly scanned her, drinking in every drop of her petite frame, his eyes tracing her soft curves. The silvery scars that coated her skin glowed under the moonlight, intricate patterns that told countless stories—some of which only he would ever know. They were secrets she had told him, secrets he would take with him to the grave, whether that be tomorrow or a century away.

She stepped forward, grabbing his tie again, but this time she undid the knot and tossed it aside. Slowly, carefully, she unbuttoned his shirt as he remained still, fighting the urge to reach out and caress her skin. She removed his shirt, her hands tracing his abs before reaching for his belt buckle, staring into his eyes as she unfastened it.

He licked his lips, his mouth suddenly dry as the nerves inside of him bubbled up. His heart hammered as his pants dropped to the floor, her hands shoving his boxers down to his ankles. A cool chill ripped up his spine and he shivered as the air hit his erection, making it jump as it throbbed harder than he could ever remember it being before.

"Christ," he muttered, falling back against the bedroom door as Haven dropped to her knees. She took him in her mouth, warmth enveloping him, goosebumps immediately springing to every centimeter of exposed skin. "Oh, fuck."

He knew he wouldn't last long. He couldn't. Within a matter of minutes, as she sucked and licked and stroked, he could feel the pressure building in his gut. He wanted to warn her, but he couldn't find the words. All he could do was curse and sputter, gripping the back of her head as he spilled down her throat.

She climbed to her feet when he finished, her hand still wrapped around him, gently stroking as he grew hard in her palm again. She kissed his chest, making her way to his neck, before he leaned down and captured her lips with his.

The rest of his clothes were discarded on the floor before she pulled him over to the bed, making him lie down. She didn't hesitate, no wavering as she climbed on top of him, sinking down into his lap. He filled her completely, deeply, her body tight and formed to his like leather against damp skin, clinging, suffocating, taking his strained breath away.

He lay with his eyes open, watching her move, savoring her passion. He could feel her devotion, her desperation, her craving; he could feel her need, her want, her love. He could feel it all each time she shifted her hips, their bodies slapping together as he filled her to the hilt. And he could hear it in her voice, her throaty groans and raspy words when she cried out his name again and again as orgasm shook her to the core.

She drove him madder with every moan, every thrust pushing him further to the brink. He wanted to flip her over and pound into her, take her hard, ravish every inch of her and claim her flushed body as his own, but he didn't. He couldn't. There would be plenty of time for that later. Now it was her time, her rules, her game.

And it was a game he was elated to play. The sensations building inside of him stirred up something, a vaguely familiar euphoria, the high of all highs . . . it infiltrated his cells, blanketing his entire body until he felt like he was floating on air.

And it didn't take a bitter bitch named Molly to do it this time.

45

They lay in bed together later that night, her head on his bare chest, her long hair a tangled mess. Carmine rubbed her back as her fingers explored the trail of fine hair leading down his stomach.

"I love you," Haven whispered. "You're the best thing that's happened to me."

The best thing. It was a far cry from the disgrace he felt like earlier. The conviction in her words made him want to believe it. Even though he still thought she deserved better, that she deserved more, he wondered if maybe, just maybe, he could be good enough.

She fell asleep before he could find the words to share the sentiment, her soft snores filling the room. Carmine lay there holding her, but despite his exhaustion, he couldn't fall asleep. His mind worked a million miles a minute, a feeling overtaking him that he couldn't push away. It invaded his body, nagging and prodding, putting Carmine on edge. He was alert, noise intensifying the paranoia. Something was off—he could feel it.

Carefully, so as not to wake Haven, he slipped from underneath her and climbed out of bed. He tiptoed across the room to the window and pulled some slats of the blinds apart to look out into the night. It was nearing three in the morning, the sky pitch black and the city quiet. Carmine surveyed the street, looking for any sign of trouble, and tensed when his eyes fell upon a car out front.

A vaguely familiar-looking dark Chevy Camaro.

He stepped back from the window and gave Haven a quick glance before heading out of the room. Instinct took over, every move calm and calculating. He found his pants and pulled them on before grabbing his gun downstairs. He made sure it was loaded as he quietly slipped out the back door. He headed around the house and came up behind the Camaro, eyeing the license plate.

The moment he saw the letters JK, his adrenaline kicked into overdrive.

Staying in the shadows, he watched the car for a bit. The man was alone with the driver's side window down, his attention focused away from Carmine's house. Every time headlights flashed nearby he would watch them like a hawk until they passed. He was waiting for something, but Carmine wasn't sure what until a set of headlights shone their way. The man ducked as a black Mercedes sped by them before swinging into a driveway about a block away.

Corrado.

Carmine wasn't sure what to do, torn between reacting and alerting Corrado, but he didn't get much time to consider his options. The driver's side door swung open and the guy climbed out, keeping his head down as he started down the block. Without even thinking Carmine followed him, dodging streetlights while trying to keep up with his pace. The man slowed when he neared Corrado's house, staring at it peculiarly like he was trying to assess how to get inside. The living room light was on and Carmine could see shadows, Celia's laughter faintly filtering out of a cracked window.

The man ducked beside Corrado's house and Carmine hesitated, taking a deep breath and clutching his gun before darting behind him. The invader had almost made it to their backyard when he heard Carmine's footsteps. He swung around, alarmed by the presence, but it was already too late.

Carmine slammed him into the side of the house, shoving his gun against his temple. "If you move, I'll blow your fucking head off."

He cursed and shook as Carmine patted him down, frantically pulling everything out of the guy's pockets. He found a gun in his coat and made sure the safety was on before sticking it in his waistband.

Grabbing the man's wallet, Carmine flipped it open and yanked out his driver's license. "Oisin Quinn. What kinda name is that?"

"Don't hurt me," he begged. "I'm not looking for trouble!"

"Bullshit," Carmine spat. "You don't lurk around this neighborhood with a gun if you aren't looking for trouble."

"I swear it's a mistake!"

"What is?"

"This!"

"What the fuck is this?" Carmine asked, pulling him away from the house and shoving him into the backyard. He stumbled but caught himself before he fell, and hesitated for a second before he took off sprinting through the yard.

For a brief moment, Carmine remained frozen in utter disbelief. He had just let go of the guy. How fucking stupid could he be?

Adrenaline kicked in again. Carmine aimed with his finger on the trigger, a hair away from pulling it, but lowered the gun and took off after him instead. Carmine managed to catch him, tackling him in the grass at the edge of the yard. Panicked, the man swung, trying to fight Carmine off, and his fist connected with the right side of his jaw. Pain ripped through his cheek, sending him over the edge.

If he wanted a fight, Carmine was going to give him one.

He pulled his arm back that clutched the gun, slamming him straight in the face with it. A lifetime worth of aggression came pounding from his fists, disappointment and anger, shame and heartbreak. Carmine didn't know the man, but that mattered not—he took his pain out on him, battering him with pent-up hostility he needed to let go of.

After he was beat down, Carmine pulled him across the yard and forced him on his knees right outside Corrado's back door.

"Stay there, motherfucker," he spat, giving him a swift kick in the side out of frustration. His jaw ached and he was out of breath, blood splattered on his hands.

"I'm certainly glad you decided not to shoot him."

The voice caught Carmine off guard. He looked up, seeing Corrado standing motionless at the back door, watching them. "Fuck, how long have you been there?"

"Long enough."

"And you couldn't help me?" he spat, annoyed that Corrado had just watched.

"You seemed to have it handled," he said. "Besides, it was quite entertaining."

Carmine glared at him. "Entertaining? There's nothing entertaining about this!"

"I disagree."

"Well, you're wrong," Carmine said, reaching into his waistband for the guy's gun. He cursed yet again when he came up empty-handed and glanced around, realizing it had fallen out during their scuffle. He found it a few feet away and picked it up, handing it to Corrado when he stepped outside. "He could've killed me."

Corrado laughed dryly. "You're exaggerating. You had him, no problem."

"You couldn't have fucking known that."

"Yes, I could. He didn't do his homework if he parked in front of your house."

"How do you . . . ?" Carmine stopped, narrowing his eyes when it struck him. "Wait, you knew he was there?"

"Of course I did," he replied. "He wasn't sly, Carmine. Even *you* noticed him."

"Son of a bitch," he grumbled, aggravated. "I did all of that for nothing?"

"I wouldn't say it was for nothing," Corrado replied, smiling with amusement. "Like I said, it was entertaining."

Carmine shook his head as the guy knelt there, crying with his head down. "Who is this Oisin Quinn asshole, anyway?"

"Is that his name?" Corrado asked as he took the guy's driver's license. "I'm assuming the Irish sent him. Is that right?"

The guy whimpered. "Please! I'm sorry, just . . . please!"

"Don't beg," Corrado said. "Tell me who sent you."

"I don't know," he cried. "They paid me."

"Who paid you?"

"A guy, he said it would be easy!"

Corrado squatted down beside the guy and grabbed him. Carmine could see signs of his anger boiling over and took a step back. One thing Corrado despised was being underestimated. "Do you know who I am?"

"Yes. Well, no. I mean, they gave me your address, told me where I could find you tonight. They said it would be in-and-out."

Carmine shook his head, stunned by the idiocy, although a part of him was undoubtedly on edge.

"I hate to break it to you, but somebody wanted you dead," Corrado told the guy. "They knew you wouldn't walk away from this . . . from *me*. You don't send a nobody after the head of *La Cosa Nostra*. I made you the moment you walked in the restaurant."

Carmine's brow furrowed as he tried to think back, looking for any sign that Corrado had been on edge. He ran through the night in his mind before their very last conversation struck Carmine. "Motherfucker, you *knew* this would happen!"

Corrado smiled slightly, almost like he was proud. *Jackass.* Instead of replying, he waved his hand dismissively. "Go home, Carmine. I'll finish this."

He grumbled to himself and walked away, hearing the guy yell as he made his way around the house. His cries were cut off damn near instantly by a small pop, almost like the sound of a little snapping firecracker. A single shot with a silencer, he guessed. He definitely wasn't hanging around to find out for sure.

Jogging home, Carmine hoped like hell no one had seen him.

The house was quiet, everything still. Heading into the kitchen, he washed his hands before tucking his gun back away for safe-keeping. The empty vodka bottle still sat on the counter beside the sink, taunting Carmine. After what he had just gone through, he could have used a drink.

You don't need it, he told himself. *You're alive. You have your girl. There's nothing more you need.*

He made his way upstairs, the bedroom door open, the bed nothing but a tangled mess of sheets and blankets—no Haven anywhere to be found. Quietly, he crept down the hall and saw a bit of light dancing on the wall from one of the spare rooms. He paused in the doorway, seeing her in front of her canvas with a small paintbrush in her hand. She wore a pair of Carmine's black boxers and a plain white t-shirt. They hung loosely on her, practically swallowing her frame.

She was working on the painting of the tree again, the mari-juana leaf magically gone and blended into a stormy looking sky. He took a few steps closer, smiling at the sight of her working. "I'm surprised you're awake."

"Yeah, well, ADT called and woke me up," Haven said. "Ap-parently *someone* went out the back door and forgot to disable to alarm. Lucky I could get to it before they alerted the police."

"Oh, fuck." That would have been a disaster. "Sorry about that."

"It's okay," she responded. "I have your back."

Carmine chuckled under his breath at her wording, her tone playful, but he knew without a doubt she meant what she said. She had his back. Anything he needed, any time he needed her, she would be right there and do whatever he asked. She wasn't just his support system—his life vest as he drifted along a tumultuous river of turmoil—she was his everything. Without her, he would sink.

Haven turned around, her brow furrowing as her eyes scanned Carmine. "What in the world were you out doing? You're filthy!"

He glanced down, seeing the dirt and grass stains covering

his jeans. He shrugged as she laughed, reaching over to pluck a leaf from his unkempt hair. He realized how crazy he must have looked—barefoot and shirtless, covered in filth.

"Just had some shit to take care of, *tesoro*."

"Looks like you've been playing football."

"I *feel* like I've been playing football," he muttered, rubbing his jaw. "Either that or I had my ass kicked."

"Is that where you go at night when you disappear? A secret underground fight club?"

"Can't say, *tesoro*. You know the rules," he replied, laughing it off. "Anyway, the painting looks good."

"Yeah, I figured out what it was missing," she said, sticking her paintbrush into a container of water before pointing out the two shadowy figures clinging to the branches. "Us."

Carmine smiled, wrapping his arms around her from behind. Leaning down, he kissed the nape of her neck. "Well, it's perfect now. I know sometimes it's hard seeing what's right in front of you. I've personally fucked up a few times missing what should've been obvious."

"Like?"

"Like what you said earlier, about needing someone around who understands you," he replied. "Because you're right—it *is* important. When I left you back in Durante, I thought I was leaving for that reason. I thought I was coming here to be with people like me, who live the same life I do, but I was wrong. These people don't understand me. They *can't*. They might know what I've been through, but they have no clue how it feels. How it feels to lose your mother to this shit and to be robbed of a childhood. How it feels to have to pay for everyone else's mistakes. They don't get it, but you . . . you *do*. You're the only one who ever has. I thought we'd be okay apart, but I was sorely mistaken. I don't need much, *Haven*, but I do need you."

"I need you, too, you know," she said. "You make me feel safe."

He smiled, kissing the top of her head. Twenty minutes earlier he had practically stared down death, tackling a man who probably wouldn't have hesitated to kill him, and yet she still felt safe with him. Despite everything, she trusted him. She believed in him. She *loved* him.

And he loved her . . . more than anything in the world. She had given herself to him again, every barrier between them broken down. All of those unanswered questions, all of the worry, every single bit of it had been resolved the moment they came back together.

"Haven," he said. "If I could have anything, I know what I'd ask for now."

She pulled back from their hug to look at him with genuine curiosity. "What?"

Carmine took a step back, reaching around his neck to pull off the gold chain. He unfastened it, removing the small ring, and eyed it in his palm momentarily before dropping to his knee. "If I could have anything in the world, it would be for you to marry me."

And just like that, all of the air was sucked from the room. She stared at Carmine with shock and his heart pounded furiously as he waited for her to say something . . . any-fucking-thing.

After a moment, tears formed in the corners of her eyes and one slid down her cheek. He brushed it away quickly as she smiled, the sight putting Carmine at ease. That smile was the only answer he needed.

"You wouldn't ask for your freedom back instead?" she asked quietly.

He shook his head. "It wouldn't be shit without you."

46

"This is completely unnecessary," Haven grumbled, gazing out the darkly tinted side window. Buildings whipped by at a steady pace as they drove through the streets of Chicago, the scenery a blur in the darkness.

"Mr. DeMarco disagrees, ma'am," a voice said politely from the front seat.

"Calling me ma'am is unnecessary, too," she said, glancing at the driver. She noticed he was watching her in the rearview mirror, nervousness written on his face. It was obvious he was new, not wanting to mess up his first chance to prove himself.

"Sorry, ma'am," he responded, his voice low as he averted his gaze.

She smiled softly as she looked back out of the window, the irony of the situation not at all lost on her. It astonished her how much had changed, their lives altered in ways they never would have imagined at the beginning. Haven often thought about everything that happened to lead them where they were, curious how things might have turned out had the circumstances been different. She knew it was senseless, because it was impossible to change anything, but she couldn't help but wonder.

No matter how many times she thought it through, it always went back to a single event that had been the start of it all—the murder of her grandparents.

Grandparents—she doubted she would ever get used to saying it. She never considered a family outside of her mother. Carmine offered to explain what he knew, promising he would be more open with her in the future, but it was actually Corrado who told Haven the whole truth. He relayed stories he had heard about the type of people they had been, a strong family full of pride. Corrado said they had been overjoyed to have a daughter. It was startling to hear about her mother's beginnings and to learn how much she had been wanted . . . how much she had been *loved*.

"Ma'am?" Haven glanced back over at the driver and saw he was watching her again. "There was an accident on Highway 41 that blocked northbound traffic. I had to take a detour, but it'll only be a few minutes longer."

She glanced at her watch, faintly making out the time in the darkness—a quarter past ten in the evening. "Okay."

"I apologize for any inconvenience."

"It's fine," she said. "And please, call me Haven."

She gazed back out the window for the rest of the trip. He didn't speak again until he pulled up in front of the large white house, parking the limo along the curb. He got out and glanced around cautiously before opening her door. She climbed out of the car. "Thank you."

"You're welcome, ma'am."

She shook her head, knowing it was pointless to correct him again, and pulled out some cash. He tried to refuse her tip, saying it was an honor to drive her, and she rolled her eyes as she stuffed the money in his coat pocket.

The house was dark and silent, nobody home. Haven kicked her shoes off right inside the door before heading into the kitchen, grabbing a glass from the cabinet and pouring some water into it from the faucet. Leaning against the counter, she took a sip as her eyes scanned the kitchen. There were used paper towels on the table with some cups sitting out, and the dishes definitely hadn't been done during the day. Part of the counter was covered in crumbs and an empty jar of peanut butter sat beside the sink, the lid halfway on with a dirty knife laying beside it. Something sticky had also been spilled, the floor in desperate need of mopping.

She sighed as she looked away from the mess, her eyes drifting toward the calendar on the wall. It was chaotic, writing scribbled all over it and days crossed out, but nothing stood out more than one date at the bottom.

June 29

The square was circled with a red marker and Haven smiled as she read the words neatly written in the box: *wedding*. It had been a year since they had found their way back together, and in a mere five days they planned to make it official.

Marriage. It was still hard to believe they had come that far. It hadn't been easy because they couldn't wrap themselves in a bubble like they had done in Durante. They had to be a part of that world, had to integrate themselves into it and discover where they fit. It was occasionally a source of conflict as they sought to find balance between them as a couple and them as individuals, but it wasn't so bad that they couldn't work through it together. They disagreed on details, like how to be safe, and while she sometimes found it overwhelming, she tolerated a lot of what Carmine wanted. She would never get used to the bodyguards or car services, but she knew it was a small price to pay for Carmine's peace of mind.

Because peace of mind was something Carmine rarely got.

Haven took another sip of water before setting the glass down on the counter. She started to walk away but hesitated, turning back around and grabbing the glass again. She put it in the dishwasher and quickly gathered the other dishes that had been left laying around. The sticky floor would have to wait but the rest she couldn't walk away from, because despite everything that was different, some core things still remained the same.

Like Corrado had said: *Cambiano i suonatori ma la musica è sempre quella*. The melody's changed, but the song remains the same.

———

Carmine took a deep breath to steady himself, inhaling the scent of greasy cheese and spicy pepperoni. His stomach rumbled, churning ruthlessly. He couldn't tell if it was actual hunger or purely his frazzled nerves.

He stepped into the busy pizzeria and spotted Corrado sitting alone at a table along the side. Carmine's gaze remained focused on the shiny, checkered linoleum as he approached his uncle, ignoring the intense look he received from the register.

"Corrado," Carmine greeted him. "I mean, uh, sir."

Corrado didn't bother looking up. He simply kicked the chair out across from him as he pulled a piece of pizza from the small box on the table. It smelled strongly like onions and peppers and sausage.

Carmine's stomach churned harder. Definitely nerves.

He took a seat, trying to avoid smelling the food by breathing through his mouth. Neither spoke as Corrado ate, casually slouched in the chair as if he had not a care in the world. After he finished, he closed the empty box and sat back, crossing his arms over his chest. "I'm listening."

"I . . . well, I mean, we . . ."

"We?"

"Haven and I," he clarified. "We wanted to know if—"

"Why isn't she here?" Corrado asked, cutting him off. "If she has a problem, she's more than capable of coming to me herself."

"She had a school thing tonight." Carmine sighed. "It's not a problem anyway. It's more like a favor."

"You call me up and say it's important—so important I take time out of my dinner for you—and it's because you want something?"

"Yes."

"This better be good."

Carmine took a deep breath, cringing as he inhaled the scent of the food, and forced the words from his lips before he lost the nerve. "You know we're getting married tomorrow . . ."

"Of course I know," he replied. "I received my invitation and made plans to come. I *am* still invited, correct?"

"Correct."

"Okay, then. There's no problem. I already made sure to clear your schedule for the weekend, so you shouldn't have any problems consummating the marriage."

Carmine cringed at his wording. "It's not that."

"Then what is it? I'm getting impatient."

"We want to know if you'll give Haven away."

Corrado stared across the table at him, unmoving, barely blinking, as if he hadn't heard Carmine speak at all. He had, though, and after a minute or so he slowly shook his head, as if trying to process the words. "Give her away."

"Yeah, you know, walk her down the aisle when we get married."

"I know what you mean, Carmine."

"Her dad, well . . . you know. And I'd ask my dad, but well . . . you know."

Corrado had killed them. Carmine didn't say it out loud, but they both thought it.

"Fine," he said. "I'll do it."

Carmine's eyes widened. He had expected a staunch denial. "No shit?"

"Language."

He blanched. "I mean, uh . . . so you'll do it?"

"Yes."

Carmine smiled, relief settling in, but it wasn't near enough to calm his frazzled nerves. Just being within a block of that building put him on edge.

"You're fidgeting," Corrado pointed out. "Were you that nervous to ask me?"

"No," he replied. "I was, but that's not my problem."

"Then what is?"

Carmine stared at his uncle, baffled how he could seem so comfortable. "It doesn't bother you to be here?"

"Why would it?" Corrado eyed him with confusion. "I eat here all the time."

"Yeah, but . . ." He leaned over the table, whispering. ". . . his kids."

Corrado had killed them, too. Both of them.

Corrado's eyes drifted past him toward the front register. Turning, Carmine eyed the owner, John Tarullo, curiously. He only vaguely recognized the man from when he was a kid, remembering eating here a few times with his parents. He knew it had been John, though, that saved him that October day. He owed him a lot—his life, to be precise—but Carmine could hardly stand to look at the aging man.

He was a walking, talking, unhappy fucking reminder of everything Carmine had been through.

Sensing the attention—or maybe it was purely coincidence—John chose that moment to look at the two of them. His expression remained stoic, strictly business, but Carmine could sense the deep sadness in his dark eyes.

"I did what I had to do," Corrado said. "Had I let them live, had I let them continue as they were, my family would've been jeopardized. So no, it doesn't bother me, but losing one of you? That might."

Corrado stood, heading for the door, and nodded politely to John Tarullo before disappearing outside.

———

After taking a shower and putting on some comfortable clothes, Haven made her way downstairs and saw the light on in the kitchen. Carmine stood in front of the refrigerator with the door wide open, glaring inside of it, home from wherever he had been while she was at school. She didn't ask, and he didn't tell.

"Can't find anything?" she asked.

"Nope." He shut the door, his eyes scanning a takeout menu stuck to the front of it with magnets.

"I can make something," she offered. "You have to be tired of eating out."

He chuckled in amusement, cocking an eyebrow suggestively. "Depends on what I'm *eating out*."

"Pervert." She could feel the heat rising into her cheeks, knowing it was useless to try to hide it.

"Yeah, but you love it," he said playfully.

"I do." There was no use denying it—he knew Haven well.

Carmine laughed as he turned away, his attention going back to the menu. "I'll just order Chinese. It's late and you shouldn't have to cook, especially considering you already cleaned the kitchen once tonight. Don't think I didn't notice that shit. I could've done it, you know. I *would've*."

"I know you would've," she said truthfully. Carmine never did certain things, like laundry or mopping, but he was good at picking up after himself. He didn't enjoy it, but he did it for her. "I didn't mind it."

"Well, thank you."

He grabbed the cordless telephone from the wall and dialed a number quickly. "Yeah, I need a delivery. The name's Carmine DeMarco," he said when they answered, pausing briefly as they looked up his name. "Yes, that's me. I need an order of the pork mu shu wraps, some Mongolian beef, the kung pao chicken, and two orders of your won ton soup. I don't know, large? Oh, and some egg rolls. How many come in an order? Two? Is that it? That's a fucking rip off."

He glanced at Haven, raising his eyebrows. "Did I miss anything?"

"Uh, no."

"Yeah, that's it. And don't forget the fortune cookies," he said into the phone, his brow furrowing. "What do you mean you don't have any fortune cookies? You're a Chinese restaurant. You *have* to have fortune cookies. What? No, I don't care if they're complimentary. Don't give me that bullshit. I don't feel fucking *complimented* right now. Find some."

He ended the call, slamming the phone down on the counter, making Haven flinch. He pulled open the freezer door and looked inside. Haven knew immediately what he was doing, having acted on impulse out of frustration. He stared at the empty spot where the vodka bottle had once been stored before slamming the door again and opening the refrigerator.

Haven grabbed the can of Coke from his hand and gently rubbed his back. "Fortune cookies aren't that serious," she said, nudging him aside to grab a glass from the cabinet. Carmine leaned against the counter and watched as she made a cherry Coke. "You don't even eat them. You think they taste like cardboard."

"Yeah, but you do," he replied. He fidgeted and appeared agitated, rubbing the palms of his hands on his pants anxiously. "You like them."

She smiled softly as she handed him his soda. "Well, thanks for thinking of me, but it was unnecessary. Just like sending that limo for me was unnecessary."

"Maybe the cookies weren't, but the limo was *definitely* necessary," he said, taking a sip of his drink. "You couldn't walk home."

"No, but I could've taken the bus," she replied. "I kind of like it, anyway. I never got to go to school and ride the bus or anything. Makes it feel authentic."

He stared at Haven doubtfully. "You weren't taking the bus home."

"Why? It's not that big of a deal."

"It *is* a big deal," he retorted, raising his voice. "The bus stop isn't close to the house so you'd still have to walk in the dark."

"It's just a few blocks over," she replied, hoping to reassure him so he would calm down. "It would've only taken a few minutes if I cut down the alley by—"

Haven stopped speaking abruptly when it struck her what she

was saying. Carmine stood frozen, his body rigid. The bus stop was near the old theater a few blocks away, down from where Carmine's piano recital had been held that October night in 1996. The alley was the one Carmine had taken with his mother, the one he hadn't gone near since.

"Okay," she conceded. The odds of something actually happening to her were slim, but once again it was more about his peace of mind. "No bus at night, but I still want to take it during the day."

"You're the only person I know that *prefers* public transportation," he grumbled, not happy with her compromise but he didn't disagree.

"I just don't see the point in driving if I don't have to," she explained. "And limos are too flashy. I like fitting in but you sending a car to pick me up from class doesn't help that. If it gets late and I can't take the bus, I'll call a taxi."

Carmine laughed dryly. "And you say *I'm* stubborn."

"You are stubborn," she said. "Maybe you're just rubbing off on me."

It was quiet for a moment before his lips curved into a smile. "Yeah, I'll rub something off on you, all right."

"Oh God," she groaned, shaking her head as she looked away from him.

He chuckled at her reaction before sighing, resigned. "No taxi, but I can make it more low profile. They have cars that aren't as conspicuous. If I feel like I need to send a car, I'll send one of them. Otherwise, whatever, I guess the bus is fine."

"Thank you," she said, smiling. "You're good to me, you know."

He rolled his eyes and started to respond but was cut off by his cell phone ringing. Without a moment's hesitation he bolted from the room.

There was a knock on the door eventually. Carmine reappeared and stepped outside. Haven's curiosity got the best of her, so she made her way to the kitchen to peek out the window. Her brow furrowed when she saw Carmine standing on the front step with two men, neither of whom she recognized. They all seemed tense, the conversation between them serious—business, she assumed. Her heart rate quickened as it usually did when she witnessed him at work, a bit of fear naturally brewing inside her.

Carmine suddenly glanced in the direction of the window, his expression hardening when they made eye contact. She stepped out of his sight, not wanting to anger him, and looked toward the street when a car pulled up to the curb. The two men briskly walked past the window and Carmine opened the front door, heading straight for the office again as the deliveryman approached the house with their food.

Before he could knock, Carmine came back out with his wallet and opened the front door. "Your total is $47.75."

"Christ, that's fucking expensive," Carmine muttered. Haven strolled toward the doorway of the kitchen and paused, watching as he thumbed through his cash. He pulled out a fifty and handed it to the guy, hesitating before grabbing another five dollar bill. She smiled as he handed it to him for a tip before grabbing the bag of food and shutting the door.

"You shouldn't be so nosy," he said when he spotted Haven standing there.

"I wasn't being nosy. I was just *curious*."

"Same damn thing," he muttered under his breath before adding, "Just be careful, okay? You know that shit makes me nervous."

Haven grabbed a soda from the fridge for herself and picked up Carmine's cherry Coke, following him into the living room. They settled onto the couch and ate dinner, chatting casually as they watched television. After they were full Carmine put the rest aside, pulling out a white paper bag and opening it. He laughed as he poured the contents out on the coffee table. Haven looked in shock at the dozen fortune cookies, reading the writing on the clear plastic covering them. They had ordered from Satay, but the cookies came from a place called Ming Choy.

"You scared them into buying fortune cookies from another restaurant."

"I probably should've tipped more for that shit, huh?" he said, unable to hide his amusement. He grabbed one of the cookies and tossed it on her lap before picking up another for himself. He took the cookie out, breaking it apart quickly to pull out his fortune.

"The important thing is to never stop questioning," he read before tossing it down and grabbing another. "That's just fucking stupid."

She laughed and pulled her fortune out. "Your dream will come true when you least expect it," she said, reading the strip of paper as she took a bite of the cookie, earning a grimace from Carmine. "My dreams already came true: family, friends, school, marriage. Couldn't ask for much more."

"You aren't married yet, *tesoro*."

"I know." She smiled as she gazed at the scrap of paper. "Tomorrow."

"Tomorrow," he agreed.

———

The next afternoon, Haven stood in front of an antique full-length mirror, taken aback by her reflection.

Her hair was curled, the top half pulled back, as a small gold tiara kept her veil in place. Her white dress was simple, one shouldered and long with a train in the back, and she had on a pair of high heels. It wasn't flashy but it was undoubtedly beautiful, the way she had always envisioned it.

Tears stung her eyes as her thoughts kept shifting to her mother. Haven missed her terribly and wished she could be there, imagining how proud she would be to see her at that moment. It was everything she wanted for her, everything she told Haven she would find in the world. Once upon a time she had doubted her, thinking it was impossible, but now it was becoming real.

The door behind Haven opened and she glanced behind her as

Corrado walked in. She quickly turned away from him, nervous, as Corrado nonchalantly paused behind her in the mirror. He was quiet for a moment, his silence doing nothing to ease her anxiety.

"*Principessa della Mafia*," he said finally, his voice calm. "When Vincent first confessed to me who you were, I told him I couldn't see it. I said you didn't look like one of us."

Haven fidgeted, her heart pounding so hard in her chest that it hurt.

"I see it now," he said, staring at her reflection in contemplation as the corner of his lips turned up into a smile. "I don't know why I couldn't see it before."

His declaration caught Haven off guard. She gaped at him and he cleared his throat, still uncomfortable with anything even remotely close to affection. "I'll give you a moment."

He walked out without another word. Tears pooled in Haven's eyes when she heard piano music start up, thoughts of her mother returning. She recalled when she saw her that final time in Blackburn, remembering the last words she ever spoke. She said she would always be with her, in her heart, and the world was a better place with Haven out there in it. She wanted her to live her life, to be happy and follow her dreams, and that day she knew exactly what her destiny was: Carmine.

"Thank you, Mama," Haven whispered into the empty room, giving one last look at her reflection before grabbing her bouquet of white roses. She joined Corrado in the hallway, taking his arm as he held it out to her.

He led Haven into the church and they paused at the beginning of the aisle, giving her a moment to take it all in. Her vision blurred from dizziness, the sight before her overwhelming. The pews were packed full of people, some of whom she didn't recognize, and they all stood up the moment they entered. She knew a lot of them weren't there for her, the members of the organization and their families, but she didn't mind. They came for Carmine, and out of respect for the man beside her.

Haven glanced toward the front, her eyes falling upon Carmine. He stood frozen in spot, a look of wonder on his face. Haven lost the battle against her tears, a few streaming down her cheeks as they started down the aisle.

Corrado let go of Haven when they reached the front, nodding at Carmine before making his way over to the front pew with Celia. The music stopped and the priest said a brief prayer, followed by a collective shuffling as everyone sat back down. Haven handed Tess her bouquet to hold as Carmine continued to stare at her, happiness radiating from him in waves. She scanned him quickly, something she always did when she saw him . . . always looking for injuries, making sure he remained intact, and she laughed when her eyes fell upon his feet.

"Nike's?" she whispered. "What happened to your shoes?"

His smirk grew. "I forgot them."

Her tears continued to fall. He quickly brushed a few of them away while the priest started addressing them. "Carmine and Haven, have you come here freely and without reservation to give yourselves to each other in marriage?"

"Yes," they said simultaneously.

"Will you honor each other as man and wife for the rest of your lives?"

"Yes," they said again, not even having to think about it.

"This isn't customary, but the bride and groom have asked to be able to speak and the church has happily agreed to grant their request."

The priest glanced between Carmine and Haven curiously and she cleared her throat, trying to get the lump that was forming to disappear. "The first time you asked me to marry you was three years ago. You told me it didn't have to be that day, or the next day, or even that year. You just wanted me to swear I would when I was ready. I said yes, of course, and I meant it with everything in me. We were young and maybe we were naïve, thinking we had it all figured out, but one thing I *never* doubted was that we were meant to be."

Haven paused to wipe her cheeks as more tears spilled from her eyes. "When I first met you I wasn't sure what to think. You were nothing like anyone I'd ever met before. The things you made me feel were scary, and I wanted nothing more than to stay away from you, but I couldn't. I was drawn to you. You gave me hope. You believed in me and helped me, and most of all, you loved me. *Me*. Out of all the people in the world, you picked me. I was used to being overlooked, used to being invisible, but you saw me. I wouldn't be the person I am today without you. I love you, Carmine Marcello DeMarco, and I want you to know I'm ready now. I'm ready to spend the rest of my life with you."

"*Sempre*," he whispered, choking on the word. He was trying to keep his composure, not wanting to crack in front of so many people.

"*Sempre*." Haven meant it with every fiber of her being. He was hers forever.

"I'm sure you remember our first encounter, the morning in the kitchen in North Carolina, and what a disaster it turned out to be," Carmine said. "I didn't expect anyone to be there. I dropped my orange juice and you started to clean it up, trying to help, and I, uh, well, you know what I did."

Haven smiled sadly at the memory. He had been so angry back then . . . so broken. Carmine still had cracks in him, scars from where he had once shattered, but he was holding himself together now and that was what mattered.

"What you don't know, though, is that as we sat like idiots in that puddle of juice, all I could think about was how beautiful you were. How beautiful you *are*. You were scared and confused, and I know I wasn't helping that, but underneath it all you were just beautiful, Haven. You had me the very first time I laid eyes on you. I remember thinking later that morning you were going to complicate my life." He paused as he laughed to himself. "And complicate it you did. Everything I knew, everything I believed . . . all of it went out the window. You turned me upside down and made me *feel* again. You saved my life, even though I didn't realize it needed to be saved. I thought I was fine, that I didn't need anyone else, but I was wrong, because I do. I need *you*. Christ, I—"

Haven's eyes widened as the priest inhaled sharply. Carmine stopped talking, realizing what he had just said. "Shit," he spat instinctively, stammering. "This is a god—"

Haven knew what he was going to say before the word slipped out and clamped her hand over his mouth before anyone else heard. He stared at her cautiously with panic in his eyes. Haven smiled softly, so he wouldn't think she was upset, and he visibly relaxed. When she removed her hand, he leaned forward, brushing his lips against hers. She kissed him back, parting her lips and softly moaning as his tongue came into contact with hers.

"Not yet, man," Dominic said, grabbing Carmine and pulling him away. "You're getting ahead of yourself."

The priest cleared his throat, and Carmine let out an exasperated sigh. "Sorry, Father."

"Would you like to finish?" hc asked.

"Uh, no." Carmine shook his head. "I think I've said enough."

"So since it is your intention to enter into marriage, join your right hands, and declare your consent before God and his Church," the priest said, obviously wanting to get the service over with. Carmine grasped Haven's hand, linking their fingers together and squeezing gently.

"Carmine, do you take Haven to be your wife? Do you promise to be true to her in good times and in bad, in sickness and in health, to love her and honor her all the days of your life?"

"I do."

"Haven, do you take Carmine to be your husband? Do you promise to be true to him in good times and in bad, in sickness and in health, to love him and honor him all the days of your life?"

"I do."

"You have declared your consent before the Church. May the Lord in his goodness strengthen your consent and fill you both with his blessings. What God has joined, men must not divide."

They exchanged rings at his word and her hand shook as Carmine slipped the simple gold band on her finger, the one she knew belonged to his mother. She gazed at it, emotion overwhelming her when the priest declared them husband and wife.

"*Now* you kiss," Dominic said, nudging Carmine. Haven glanced up again and saw Carmine glare at his brother before focusing on her, his face lighting up with love. He grasped her chin gently and leaned forward, her eyes drifting closed as their lips came together.

His kiss was sweet but there was passion behind it . . . passion she looked forward to feeling for the rest of her life.

47

Just a few more."

Carmine tried to stop squirming, but the suit was beginning to suffocate him. It felt like they had been standing there for hours as the photographer snapped picture after picture, posing them in every position imaginable in order to get a good shot. He did his best to keep his eyes focused on the camera, but his attention was drawn to the woman beside him.

"Relax," Haven said quietly, sensing his discomfort.

"I'm trying," he muttered.

"Everyone smile!" the photographer shouted. Carmine smiled on demand, ready to get it over with, and he snapped off a few pictures in quick succession. "That's a wrap."

He exhaled in relief and loosened his tie. "That shit took *forever*."

"It wasn't *that* bad." Haven laughed. "It was only like twenty minutes."

Carmine grabbed her hips and she yelped as he quickly pulled her to him. "You're wrong, Haven DeMarco. It *was* that bad, because it was twenty minutes that I couldn't do *this*."

He smashed his lips to hers, kissing her deeply, and Tess groaned. "I don't want to see that."

"Then stop fucking looking," he spat, pulling away from Haven long enough to get the words out. He went right back to kissing her.

"We're heading inside," Dominic said, patting Carmine on the back. "Don't keep everyone waiting too long."

They stood there for a while, continuing to kiss, as everyone else filtered into *Luna Rossa* for the reception. Eventually she pulled away from him, panting as she tried to catch her breath, her cheeks flushed. "Maybe we should go inside."

"Fuck that," he said, trailing kisses down her jaw line as he made his way to her neck. "Let's leave."

"We can't *leave*, Carmine," she said. "These people are here for us."

"So?" he whispered. She laughed, pushing away from him, and he sighed. "Okay, you're right. We need to go in."

"See?" she said, grabbing his hand. "It'll be fun."

"Yeah, but I think we'd have *a lot* more fun if we were alone right now."

"Maybe so," she said. "There will be plenty of time for that later, though."

"I sure as fuck hope so."

She started to walk away, tugging on his arm, and he begrudgingly moved from his spot. They were met by loud applause the moment they stepped inside. Haven blushed and ducked her head, and Carmine chuckled as they walked down the path toward the head table that had been set up. She thanked everyone as they took their seats, waiting for the staff to bring out the food. Plates were set in front of them as someone came over with a green glass bottle and filled their glasses. Carmine nodded in greeting as he poured the bubbly liquid in his glass, picking it up and bringing it to his nose. He grimaced at the smell and Dominic laughed from his seat nearby, swirling his drink around in his glass.

"Never thought I'd be at my little brother's wedding drinking sparkling white grape juice," he said, shaking his head.

"We have white jasmine sparkling tea, too," Haven chimed in. "And vignette wine country sodas. They look just like champagne but are alcohol free."

Carmine sighed and set his glass down without taking a drink, not liking the turn the conversation was taking. It was an open bar for the guests—Corrado's gift to them, he had said—but Carmine was still banned from drinking in the place.

They stopped discussing it when everyone had their plates. Carmine picked up his fork and poked at the food, his stomach queasy. His palms were sweaty and he started shaking his leg under the table, feeling uncomfortable in his own skin.

The compulsion to drink still lingered in Carmine. He craved the liquor, his body screaming for just a little taste to keep it satiated. He could practically feel the burn in his throat, needing a little of that warmth in his chest again for old times' sake . . . just enough to keep the panic attack at bay.

He knew that didn't work from experience, though, because he had given in to it before. It begged for a tiny sip but that was never enough, because once he got it, he wouldn't be able to stop. A sip turned into two, which turned into an entire bottle, which eventually led to waking up the next morning with a splitting headache, a very pissed off boss, and no recollection of what the fuck happened the night before.

Yeah, he had no desire to go *there* again.

Haven reached under the table and grabbed his thigh, forcefully stilling his leg. He glanced at her cautiously and she smiled, no signs of anger in her expression. She could usually tell when he was struggling. "Are you okay?" she asked.

"Yeah, I'll be fine," he replied. The tension started receding from his body as he gazed at her. She glowed, and his chest swelled with emotion at the twinkle of happiness in her eyes, hoping she saw the same thing shining back at her. She meant everything to Carmine. His love for her was stronger than anything else, more potent than the drugs or alcohol had *ever* been. She was his world, his fucking life, and now she was his wife.

His wife . . . who would have ever thought Carmine DeMarco would have a *wife*?

"You should eat your food," she said quietly, her smile turning mischievous as she turned her attention back to her plate. "You'll need the energy later."

He groaned at the insinuation and stabbed the meat on his plate. It seemed to be some kind of pork, but he wasn't entirely sure. Celia had handled the caterers because neither Haven nor he really cared much about the formality of receptions. He was all about ordering some pizza and letting the motherfuckers help themselves, but evidently that wouldn't fly with the company they kept. "Don't worry, Haven. I'll have *plenty* of energy for you."

"Oh, I'm not worried," she said as she took a bite. "You should be, though."

He laughed as he started eating, already feeling better. The shakiness was usually fleeting, although the thoughts were always in the back of his mind.

He was taking a drink when Dominic stood, tapping the side of his glass with his fork, calling for everyone's attention. "I think everyone here knows who I am but in case you don't, my name's Dominic. I'm Carmine's older and *wiser* brother, although he'd never admit that. He has, however, admitted that *I'm* the best man, and as the best man it's my duty to stand up here and try to embarrass his ass," he started. "There's so much I could say about Carmine, so many words out there to describe him that it's almost impossible to know where to start. He's stubborn, foolish, finicky, moody, erratic, quick to judge, and even quicker to react. I tend to think he's pretty ugly, too, but that's just my personal opinion."

"Fuck you," Carmine muttered, running his hand through his hair.

"I forgot to add he has a foul mouth, which you all got to witness today. The priest is probably blessing the church again right now," he said humorously. "Some lesser-known qualities about Carmine are that he's protective over the people he loves, and he fights for what he believes in. He comes off as being selfish, but he's probably the most selfless person I know.

"And then there's Haven, who has to be the most patient person alive to put up with him. At first she and Carmine seemed to be complete opposites, the timid, naïve girl that was experiencing everything for the first time and the jaded, reckless boy who was pretty much sick of it all. I don't think any of us could've predicted that these two people from different ends of the spectrum would meet in the middle, but they did. They balanced each other, found peace in each other, and together they managed to find love. I know that sounds cheesy, like I'm quoting a damn Julia Roberts movie or something, but it's the truth. What they have is rare."

Carmine glanced at Haven and she smiled, reaching under the table to take his hand as Dominic continued.

"I don't know if you all know this, but in high school my brother was kind of a hotshot football player," he said. "I'm not trying to be cliché or anything, but one thing my own marriage taught me is that relationships are like football in a lot of ways. It's a team sport and you have to work together to be successful. There are highs and lows, good plays and bad calls, and if you're going to step out on the field, you need to be ready to play the game. Big mistakes get you benched, and, depending on how bad you screwed up, they can cost you a fortune before you're allowed back on the playing field. There will always be rivals, people trying to knock you out of the game, but if you're lucky, you'll end up with a nice ring to show for your hard work. But it's not over there, you know. That's when it really starts, because for the rest of your life you'll be trying to prove to everyone that you, out of everyone, deserved to be given that ring."

He paused, snickering to himself. "That's not the biggest way relationships are like football, though. No matter what you do, no matter what happens, the point of both is to score as much as you can. Without scoring, the entire thing is really just a waste of time."

Carmine chuckled as Tess flung her napkin at Dominic. He

laughed and playfully blew her a kiss before diving right back into his speech. "I think I should wrap this up. My old lady's throwing penalty flags," he joked, holding his glass up. "So on behalf of my wife, Tess, and I, I want to toast the couple. To Carmine, who couldn't do better, and to Haven, who quite frankly, couldn't do worse."

They raised their glasses in toast as Carmine kissed Haven. The DJ spoke up, announcing it was time for the first dance. Panic flashed in Haven's eyes as he took his jacket off. She hesitated before letting him lead her out onto the empty dance floor. He could tell she was uncomfortable with everyone watching, but she tried her best not to let her nerves show.

He pulled her to him when "18th Floor Balcony" started playing, his hands on her hips guiding her as they started swaying to the music. She put her arms over his shoulders, her fingers playing with the hair at the nape of his neck as she stared into his eyes. He could see the tears she fought back, her eyes sparkling under the lights.

"I love you," he said quietly.

"I know you do," she replied, her smile growing. "I love you, too."

"I'm sorry for fucking up the ceremony."

"Don't be silly. You didn't mess it up."

"I cursed at Father Alberto, Haven," he said. "I broke the third commandment. Or maybe it's the second . . ."

"It's the third," she said. "And it's not that big of a deal. I mean, that's not the only commandment you've broken and I'm sure it won't be the last one, either."

"Is that supposed to make me feel *better*?" he asked, laughing when she shrugged nonchalantly. "Yeah, well, I didn't break any others standing in the middle of a church."

"True, but it could've been worse," she said. "You managed to make it through the entire thing without saying the F word."

"For only the second time in my life," he muttered.

"Exactly, so you should be proud. It's quite the accomplishment for you."

"*Funny,*" he said sarcastically. "I wanted to do the shit right, though."

"You did," she insisted. "It was very *you,* Carmine. I wouldn't have had it any other way."

The song ended, and everyone converged onto the dance floor. Dominic immediately pulled Haven away and Dia took her place without hesitation, rattling on excitedly through two songs. He stole Haven back on the third, wanting to be with his bride, and they danced until it was time to cut the cake. The incident was a disaster, turning into a full-blown food fight as they flung frosting around and tried to smash pieces in each other's faces. More of the cake ended up *on* people than in their stomachs as they laughed and wrestled.

Afterward they got cleaned up, and Carmine took his seat as Haven prepared to throw her bouquet. Dominic sat beside Carmine, still stuffing his face.

"Seriously, bro, a Catholic wedding?" Dominic asked, his words mumbled with his mouth full. "Did you take confession beforehand? I bet that took hours."

Carmine shoved him, knocking the cake off his fork. "We talked about eloping, but it didn't feel right. She dreamed about this her entire life and I couldn't let her memory of the day be of some fat jackass in an Elvis suit."

"Makes sense," Dominic replied. "I figured you guys would get married like Mom and Dad did . . . something small and intimate."

"Yeah, we thought about that, too," he said. "It was my idea to have the big wedding, though. Nothing about us is traditional and I wanted to at least do this, have this one thing, so we could say we did shit right. And quite frankly, I wanted the whole world to see it. She spent her life in hiding, thinking people were ashamed of her and that she was worthless. I wanted her to be seen."

Dominic smiled, amused by something. Carmine ran his hand

through his hair anxiously. "I know that probably sounds fucking stupid . . ."

"No, it sounds, I don't know . . . *sweet*? Almost as sweet as this cake."

A throat cleared behind Carmine then. He turned, freezing when he saw Corrado. He hadn't heard him approach, which wasn't surprising considering he had a knack for sneaking up on people. "Sir?"

"I need to see you in my office, Carmine," he said, his tone matching his expression. Stiff. Emotionless. Tense.

"Now?" he asked incredulously. "Can't it wait?"

"No."

Corrado walked off, leaving Carmine nervously sitting there beside his brother. He rocked in his chair for a few moments, purposely delaying it, before getting up and following his uncle down the hallway. When he reached the office, he saw his uncle sitting behind his desk. Carmine stepped inside and closed the door.

He waited for Corrado to tell him to have a seat, but he didn't.

"A man's word means as much as his blood," Corrado said. "It's an old Sicilian expression your grandfather used to say. Your word's your salvation. What a man says, what he swears to, carries as much weight as who he is and what he does."

Carmine stared across the office, keeping a straight face despite the anarchy going on inside of him. He watched as his uncle reached into a desk drawer, pulling out a small caliber .22 handgun and a large knife. The blade was serrated, six inches in length. Corrado placed them on the desk in front of him before closing the drawer.

"You gave your word over two years ago," he continued. "In exchange for help, you bartered your freedom. You promised allegiance, and that's something I take seriously. When I gave myself to the life decades ago, I knew it was for as long as I breathed. Some men have it handed to them, like Vincent, but I fought hard to prove myself. Antonio made me. He made me prove I was dedicated, that I wanted it, and I did. I like to think that's why I'm still alive today and your father's no longer with us."

A light laugh escaped Corrado's lips. It sounded to Carmine a lot like amusement mixed with cynicism. "It only took a few months for your grandfather to give me his blessing to marry his only daughter, but it took years before he trusted me enough to let me inside his organization. Because to men like us, it comes first—before our families, before our friends, before everything, it's *La Cosa Nostra*."

Picking up the knife, Corrado eyed it intently, running his fingers carefully along the blade. "Before we'll welcome you in, you first have to bleed for us. Nowadays it's usually a simple prick of the trigger finger, a tiny droplet of blood on a piece of paper. Painless, leaves no lasting scar, no mark identifying them as a man of honor. But back in my day, it was *real*. Did you know that?"

Carmine swallowed, trying to wet his painfully dry throat. "Yes, sir."

"So did you bleed for Salvatore?"

"No," he said. "All he wanted was my word."

Corrado continued to gaze at the knife. "Give me your hand."

For a brief second, Carmine blanched in fear, but there was no hesitation in his steps. He knew there couldn't be. He extended his right hand and Corrado grabbed it, roughly yanking him closer and pinning it against the desk.

"A man's word means as much as his blood," Corrado repeated. "Sal only wanted your word, but I require your blood."

Carmine squeezed his eyes shut when he felt the knife against his skin. Gritting his teeth, he forced himself to stay silent as the jagged blade cut into him. It slowly sliced across his palm, a searing burn igniting his hand as it tore into his flesh.

When it was over, Carmine opened his eyes again and relaxed, but he was too soon. Corrado grasped his hand tighter, violently closing it into a fist. Stabbing pain shot up his arm and he couldn't hold back the strangled grunt that forced its way from his chest. Tears of agony stung his eyes, but none fell down his cheeks.

"You asked me to give Haven away, and I agreed," Corrado said, still holding him there, "but I wasn't just talking about walking her down the aisle. You want her? You love her? You've bled for her. She's yours."

He pushed him away from the desk and pulled out a rag to wipe the blood from his knife. Carmine clutched his wounded hand to his chest, keeping it fisted. After Corrado's knife was clean, he placed it back in the drawer.

"I'll give you the girl, but you can't have the organization," Corrado continued. "You'll never prove yourself worthy of the oath, and nothing you can do will change my mind. You'll never be a man of honor. You're not cut out for this life, and I refuse to just hand it to you like Vincent had it handed to him."

Carmine stared at him as those words sunk in. He had no clue what to say, or if a response was even warranted. His words weren't cruel, no anger was in his voice. It was emotionless, spoken matter-of-factly. He would never be one of them. That was that.

"As far as I'm concerned, your personal debt to *La Cosa Nostra* has been satisfied," Corrado said. "You owe nothing more."

Carmine blinked rapidly. "That means . . ."

Corrado waved dismissively. "It means you're free to go."

Free. That word echoed through Carmine's mind so feverishly he nearly forgot about the throbbing in his bleeding hand. "Go where?"

"Wherever you want," he replied. "You should probably consult Haven first, though. Something tells me she wouldn't be so forgiving the second time around."

Dumbfounded, all Carmine could do was blink and nod in agreement.

Corrado stood up from his desk and walked around to face his nephew. Grabbing his arm, he pried his hand open and pressed the rag against the wound. The bleeding had slowed, but it still stung ferociously. After cleaning it up, Corrado wrapped it with a white bandage. "Now get out of here. Walk away."

Carmine started to turn but stopped, those words washing through him, comforting the ache inside of him. *Walk away.*

"I'm tired of running," Haven had said. *"I want to be able to walk away."*

Without even thinking about it, he flung himself at Corrado, wrapping his arms around his uncle in a hug. Corrado's body remained rigid as he just stood there, caught off guard by the display of affection. The hug was over in a matter of seconds.

"Can I ask you something, Uncle Corrado?" Carmine asked when he reached the door.

"Yes."

Carmine motioned toward the .22 still laying on the desk. "What was the gun for?"

His answer was immediate. "In case you hesitated."

Carmine's brow furrowed. "Would you really have shot me for that?" he asked, pausing for two beats before shaking his head, not giving him a chance to respond. "Actually, you know what? Don't answer that. I don't even wanna fucking know."

He opened the door and stepped out of the office, the sound of Corrado's laughter following him.

Corrado sat in his office after Carmine left, staring at the gun. It wasn't even loaded.

After a moment, he picked it up and opened his desk drawer. He dropped the gun in, staring down at it as it clanked against the unlabeled VHS tape. He had nearly forgotten it was in there, but the words he had heard as he watched it were ones he would never forget. He could still hear Frankie's voice and see his flickering face as he confessed.

"In the spring of '73, Carlo offered Ivan Volkov thirty thousand dollars to take out Salvatore's brother-in-law. He wasn't the first one hired. Seamus O'Bannon was approached first, but he wanted nothing to do with killing a man's family.

Carlo and I . . . we tailed Ivan. We didn't think he'd really do the job, and we were right. When he showed up at the house, he realized Federica and the baby were home. He left, I guess to come up with a new plan, but Carlo said we'd gone too far to walk away.

He shot them. Killed them both. Then he went into the baby's room. She was sleeping. He pointed his gun to her head, but I couldn't let him do it. I took her instead. I mean, I get it. Leave no witnesses. But what kinda witness does a baby make?

I took her to Sal, and all he had to say was, "I don't care what happens to her as long as I don't have to look at her face." But I had to look at her face, and I have to look at her daughter's face, and I can't do it anymore. Every time I see them, I feel the guilt all over again. I want to be rid of them, I want to never have to see them again, but something stops me every time.

If they disappear, no one will ever know who they are. No one will ever know what we did . . . what he did. But they're proof. And someday, somehow, I know it'll come back to haunt him, but I think he knows it, too.

I think he's going to have me killed next."

Corrado stepped out of his office a few minutes later, pausing when he reached the main floor of the club. The place was still quite packed, the guests dancing the night away and drinking heartily at the bar. Half of them didn't even notice the bride and groom had left, too wrapped up in their own lives to even take a look around them.

It was something Corrado was used to in people. *Selfishness.* They thought only of themselves and their own desires, their ego too big for them to be able to reach past it. Corrado wasn't innocent of it himself. For many years, he only saw black and white. It was his way or no way, and his way was always right.

But somewhere along the line, that changed. Maybe it was his own death that did it, or maybe it happened when he delivered death, but one day he opened his eyes and finally noticed the gray between the layers. It was subtle, but it was there, and once he saw it, he couldn't look away.

The others, though, would never see it. They would never understand. They were all built one way, put together piece by piece like droids—no conscience, no remorse, no guilt. They lost track of the things that mattered over time, and without realizing it, Corrado had, too.

He strolled through the club, grabbing a long-stemmed red rose from one of the dark glass vases on the tables. Twirling it in his hand, he strolled up to his wife and held it out to her. "For you, *bellissima*."

Her eyes widened as she took the flower from him. "Wow, what did I do to deserve this?"

"Nothing," he replied, smirking as he added, "and everything."

A smile lit up her face as he took her arm, leading her past the others into the center of the dance floor. He motioned to the DJ and the vibrating bass of a pop song abruptly cut off, Sinatra's version of "Luna Rossa" starting up seconds later.

His hands firmly grasped her hips as he pulled her close. Celia wrapped her arms around his neck, clutching the rose along his back. They swayed to the music, staring into each other's eyes.

"So Carmine and Haven ran out of here awfully fast," she mused.

"Did they?"

"Yes. Carmine looked like he was injured. I asked what happened, but he told me not to worry about it. He looked happy, though. Ecstatic, even."

"Huh."

"Do you know anything about that?"

"Maybe."

She continued to stare at him, questions clouding her confused eyes. She wouldn't ask, and he knew it. He appreciated her restraint. But this time, he felt she deserved an answer. This time, he felt she needed to know.

Leaning down, he softly kissed her mouth, a bit of her red lipstick smudging on his dry lips. She laughed, wiping it away with her free hand as he whispered, "I didn't do anything except help him."

48

Later that night, a call for a three-alarm fire went out through the emergency wire. Firefighters raced to the scene and filled the parking lot, trying to combat the vicious blaze in the darkness but to no avail. Fire ravished *Luna Rossa*, completely gutting the building and obliterating the landmark social club.

The massive pillar of smoke could still be seen across town come daybreak, but Corrado was none the wiser. He remained snuggled up in his bed at home, his strong arms wrapped around his wife as the two of them slept late for the first time in years.

It wasn't until the police knocked on the front door of the Moretti residence that Corrado learned the news: his life's work had gone up in flames, stolen from him by arsonists. They promised a full investigation, but Corrado didn't need one. He knew right away who had done the job.

Finally, after all that time, the Irish had exacted their revenge.

Had anyone else been in charge, a full-scale war would have broken out in Chicago then, demolishing the Windy City as the factions hunted one another, determined to take each other out, but Corrado was smarter than that.

After a few botched jobs and a failed assassination attempt on Corrado's life, the feud ended swiftly with a massacre at an underground gambling game run by O'Bannon. Men swarmed the place in the middle of the afternoon, disarming and slaughtering the gamblers one by one. The Irish never knew what hit them.

For good measure, and maybe a laugh or two, Corrado's men set the building on fire before they walked away.

The media called it the *Saint Valentine's Day Massacre Part II* even though it happened in the late fall. The headline on the front page of the newspaper the next day read REPUTED MAFIA BOSS TAKEN IN FOR QUESTIONING, but was followed up shortly by THE KEVLAR KILLER WALKS FREE AGAIN. Everyone knew he had ordered it, but Corrado had a solid alibi, one nobody could dispute: He and his wife had been meeting with contractors, finalizing plans to build *Luna Rossa* once again.

Those weren't the only plans in the making. While all this was happening, Haven and Carmine were across the country, safe and sound in the tiny ghost town of Blackburn. On the ground where the Antonelli ranch once stood—the ranch Corrado had purposely destroyed—the shell of a new building had already appeared. The three-story structure, designed from scratch, would someday house the first official *Safe Haven*.

"I want to build thirty-three of them in all," Haven had said. "A place for people like me to go to start their new lives. When they run, I want them to have somewhere to go. I want them to know they're not alone."

TEN YEARS LATER . . .

EPILOGUE

Leaves crunched and twigs snapped as the little girl tramped through the shadowy forest, her dirty bare feet sinking into the cool ground. The plush grass tickled as it slipped between her toes but she kept a straight face, not daring to laugh.

No, laughing wouldn't be good. Not here. Definitely not now.

Keeping her head down, eyes fixed on the ground, she followed the small trail that wove through the trees. She could hear the single set of footsteps stomping along behind her, could feel the pair of narrowed eyes burning holes into the back of her head. It made her muscles tense and she clenched her small hands into fists, wincing. Cuts and scrapes routinely adorned her body, the newest ones covering her palms. They burned, the skin rubbed away as drops of blood oozed from the filthy surface.

Ouch.

She stepped out of the trees and into the large clearing, the last remnants of bright North Carolina sunshine streaming on her as the sun started to set. Her feet suddenly moved faster then, carrying her away from the protection of the trees, but she wasn't fast enough.

A strong hand clamped down on her shoulder from behind, instantly stalling her movements. "Oh no, where do you think you're going, girl?"

Uh-oh.

She shrugged her shoulders the best she could. Where was she going? She didn't know. It wasn't as if she could escape him.

He let out a dry laugh at her lack of response. "Haven, look who I found."

The woman swung around where she stood in the yard, panic on her face as her hands clutched her swollen stomach. She looked like she was carrying a watermelon under her pink shirt, but the little girl knew it was really a baby—her daddy told her so. A little brother named Nicholas, but she secretly hoped they would be nice and give her a sister instead.

But *nice* wasn't a word she would use to describe them. No, they were anything but happy with her right now. A brother it would be. *Yuck.*

Her mama let out a deep sigh that seemed to cover the entire clearing, wrapping them all in a sense of relief. "Where was she?"

"In the woods," he replied, still keeping her locked in place. "She was climbing a big ass tree, as usual. Fell out of the motherfucker, too. She's lucky she didn't break her neck."

She shook her head exasperatedly. "Can't say I'm surprised. She is your daughter, after all."

The hand on the girl's shoulders disappeared seconds before her dad stepped around her, a pair of small pink Nike's swinging in his hand. She had discarded them in the woods as she ran along the path, preferring to go barefoot. She was like her mama that way. She couldn't stand to feel restrained. She liked to be free to run and jump and play and climb trees even though Daddy said it wasn't safe.

Her dad strolled through the yard, kissing her mama quickly before going inside the big three-story house. They had been coming there to Durante every summer since she was a baby, although the girl couldn't remember those first few years. Usually Uncle Dominic and Aunt Tess came along with her cousin Vinnie, but they took him to a football camp this year, so they wouldn't make it to visit until later.

Aunt Dia was in town, though, with her new girlfriend. They came by a few times but were staying with other family, so it was just them for now—just her and her parents in the big, old house.

She thought it would be fun, not having to share anything, but it turned out the lack of chaos only led her to get into more trouble by herself.

The little girl still didn't move from the spot in the yard, firmly rooted in the ground as her mama approached. She wiggled her toes, digging into the dirt, trying to distract herself, and couldn't stifle the giggle that escaped her lips that time.

Oops.

"What's so funny?" her mama asked, crouching down in front of her.

She shrugged her shoulders again, head still down, as she whispered, "It tickles, Mama."

Maura Miranda DeMarco could only be described as a tiny tornado, a ball of energy that couldn't be tamed. She was tiny, shorter than the average seven-year-old, but her size didn't impede her at all. She would jump any hurdle, climb any obstacle, and solve any problem in her way. A combination of both of her parents—her dad's daring personality with her mom's strong exterior—she had proven to be a force of nature since the day she was born.

Her appearance, though, contradicted her fiery personality. Long lashes framed a set of big green eyes, eyes she had gotten from her dad, while soft waves of brown hair fell into her face. Her pale complexion had a constant pink flush to her round cheeks, splashes of freckles dotting her nose. She looked like a porcelain doll, vulnerable, breakable, when she was anything but.

The girl was tough as nails. If you asked her dad, he would say she came into the world screaming and hadn't shut up since.

Usually bold and unrestrained, Maura was uncharacteristically quiet as she stood in front of her mama in the yard.

Reaching over, her mom grabbed Maura's hands and pried her fists open, surveying the bloody scrapes. Wordlessly, she led her into the house, taking her straight to the kitchen and sitting her on the counter beside the sink.

"You know better than to run off like that," she said quietly, washing out her daughter's wounds. "We have to know where you are at all times."

"I forgot," she said. "I didn't mean it."

"I know, but you have to remember." Her mama paused, sighing. "It's not safe otherwise."

Not safe seemed to be her parents' favorite thing to say.

"I'm sorry. Really, really, really sorry." Maura stared at her with wide eyes. "Really, Mama."

A smiled tugged her lips. "I believe you, sweetheart."

A throat cleared behind them. Her dad stood just inside the kitchen, leaning against the doorframe with his arms crossed over his chest. "I don't know if I believe you. You didn't throw in enough 'reallys.'"

"Really, Daddy!" Maura said, nodding so furiously she nearly knocked herself off the counter. "Really, really, times twenty-nine hundred thousand million."

"And how many is that?"

Maura opened her mouth to reply but only offered silence. She looked to her mama after a moment for an answer. "Mama?"

She laughed. "It's a lot."

"A lot," Maura agreed, turning back to her dad. "It's a lot, Daddy."

Her mama excused herself as her dad strolled over to the counter, stopping in front of Maura. She gazed at him with her big green eyes, hesitance with a tinge of fear lurking in them.

She thought she was in trouble.

"You know, you scared your mother," he said. "She hates it when she can't see you. She's afraid you'll go missing."

"Forever?" Maura asked. "Like those other people Mama talks about that no one sees?"

He nodded. "She's scared you'll disappear."

Maura stared at him, her forehead scrunched up as she processed his words. "Where would I go if I disappear?"

"Don't know," he said. "You'd just be gone."

"And I wouldn't be able to see you and Mama?"

"Nope."

"I don't wanna disappear, Daddy."

He chuckled. "We don't want you to, either."

"But why do people?" she asked. "Why does anyone disappear? Why don't we find them?"

"They're hidden," he said. "Sometimes it's forever, but sometimes, after a few years, someone finally sees them and makes it their mission to save them."

"Like Mama!" she declared, her face lighting up as she put together the pieces. "Grammy Maura saved Mama, right? That's what you say!"

"Right," he said. "And before that, your grandfather saved your grandmother."

Her bright expression dulled a bit. "But then they disappeared again."

"They died," he said. "That's different. We know where they are."

"Where?"

He sighed exasperatedly. "I don't know. Heaven, I guess? But they're still with us, too. That's what I meant. We carry them around in our hearts."

"Are they with Grammy Miranda?"

"Yes. They're all together up in Heaven, doing whatever the fuck people do there."

Maura's eyes widened as her mouth formed an 'o' in shock. "You owe money for the swear jar! Four quarters!"

His brow furrowed. "How do you figure?"

"You just said a swear! And outside you said two swears! Four quarters!"

"Bullshit," he said. "That's only three."

Maura smiled, whispering, "That was four, Daddy."

He grabbed her when he realized she had tricked him, tickling her sides. Giggles erupted from her, filling the kitchen with the sound of carefree, childish laughter. She grasped at his hands, kicking her small feet, and nearly nailed him in the crotch. He clutched her tightly, pulling her off the counter and swinging her around in a circle before setting her on her feet.

Taking her small hand in his, he led her outside and pulled her over toward the giant tree at the corner of the house. "Your mother used to climb this tree, you know."

Her eyes widened. "No way!"

"Yep," he said. "She climbed it like a champ."

He picked Maura up, pushing her toward the tree. She grasped the closest branch and pulled herself up, wiggling out of his arms. She climbed up onto it, fearlessly scaling it, and sat down against the thick trunk a few branches away. Her dad stood just below her, watching and waiting, but giving her enough space to explore on her own.

Fireflies flickered in the yard as the sky darkened. She reached out and caught one of the bugs, giggling.

"Daddy, maybe it is the same," she said, letting the bug go. "Maybe the people who disappear are just like Grammy Maura and Grammy Miranda and Papa Vincent. If I disappeared, I'd still be in your heart like them, right?"

"Yes."

"Then it's the same."

"No, it's not," he insisted. "They're gone, and I know that. I know they're never coming back. But your place is right here with your mother and me. Don't you ever forget that. If you disappeared, I'd tear the fucking world apart until I found you again."

Maura stared down at him inquisitively, pondering his words. She seemed satisfied after a moment and started to climb again, peering down at him after settling on another branch.

"Five now, Daddy," she said. "That was five swears."

ACKNOWLEDGMENTS

To my mama, who looked at me after finishing *Sempre*, a serious glint in her eyes, and said, "Corrado Moretti better not be dead." This book (especially the opening line) is dedicated to you. I only wish you were still here with us so you could read it. I miss you.

How do you adequately thank the people who have so greatly impacted your life? I'd buy you all a round of shots if I could (Grey Goose, of course. Carmine would insist on it.). This wouldn't be possible without YOU, the readers. Out of all the books in the world, I'm extremely grateful that you took a chance picking up mine.

My family is extraordinary, every single one of them. To my spawn for being so well behaved and understanding; to my father for his constant support and enthusiasm; to my brother and his family for always being there for me; to my aunts and uncles and cousins and grandparents, who I like to pretend don't read the sex scenes. I love you all.

So many people have been here from the beginning of this journey, notably Traci Blackwood, who tirelessly went through my words again and again, enduring characters wearing invisible watches and standing still as statues. I'll never be able to thank you enough. To Sarah Anderson, who spends countless hours in writing sessions with me and somehow manages to make sense of my 'wonky finger syndrome' when I wish her "Good Loki" instead of "Good Luck" (eh, it works . . . #TeamLoki).

To all of my Twitter and fandom friends, both old and new, who tolerate my incessant rambling and error-ridden postings. It would take me forever to name you all, but you know who you are. You guys see me at my rawest and still stick around. You should be sainted (or maybe committed, I'm not entirely sure). Never let anyone belittle what you love. Read books, write fan fiction, camp out at premieres, and attend cons. Do what makes YOU happy, no matter what others may say. Your passion should never be a source of embarrassment. Fly your fangirl flag with pride. Life is too short for all the negativity.

To my rock star agent, Frank Weimann, and everyone else at Literary Group International, for taking a chance on *Sempre* (and me). To Lion Shirdan, for believing in my words. And to the amazing folks at Simon & Schuster/Pocket Books (especially my lovely editor, Kiele Raymond) . . . publishing with you is a dream come true. Forever humbled to be a part of the S&S family.

Special thanks to Nicki Bullard, the most kick ass "assistant" to ever grace a book signing. You looked at me freshman year and thought, "I'm not sure about this bitch." Forever grateful you saw past the itty-bitty turquoise dress and over a decade later remain my best friend. How has it been that long?

To the book blogs out there, notably *Bookish Temptations*, *Maryse's Book Blog*, *Aestas Book Blog*, *THESUBCLUB Books*, *Forever 17 Books*, and everyone else who has been supportive of my work along the way (I know I'm forgetting some of you). You bloggers are vital and absolutely appreciated. Books may be the heart of it all, but you are arguably the blood that keeps it pumping. Never stop reading.

Lastly, I have to acknowledge the approximately 27 million people in the world today, trapped in modern-day slavery. Human trafficking is a real problem—a problem we as a society should not tolerate. Everyone should be free to live their own life and make their own choices. If my rambling and writing has even opened up one person's eyes to the issue, then I consider myself a success.